COLD
KILLING

COLD
KILLING

LUKE DELANEY

wm
WILLIAM MORROW
An Imprint of HarperCollinsPublishers

HarperCollins books may be purchased for educational, business, or sales promotional use. For information please write: Special Markets Department, HarperCollins Publishers, 10 East 53rd Street, New York, NY 10022.

FIRST EDITION

Designed by Diahann Sturge

Library of Congress Cataloging-in-Publication Data has been applied for.

ISBN 978-0-06-221946-6

13 14 15 16 17   OV/RRD   10 9 8 7 6 5 4 3 2 1

There are so many people I could dedicate this book to, without whom my writing career would have been over before it even began, but I feel a shared dedication can somehow lose much of its power and I didn't want that as this particular dedication is so personal to me and indeed others who were also close to the man.

So I dedicate this first novel to my dad, Mike. For reasons of maintaining the anonymity of my family, friends, and myself, I cannot say too much, nor would he want me to. I could talk about his brilliance in his own field and the respect and admiration he held among his peers worldwide. I could talk about his meteoric rise from very humble beginnings to the very top of his difficult trade, but that's not really what I remember most about him.

What I remember most is his gentleness, kindness, incredible generosity, and painful honesty. He was the best moral compass a young man could have ever had, especially one with ambitions to join the police. While opportunities abounded, I was never even slightly tempted to indulge, the thought of letting not just myself but my parents down keeping me well and truly on the straight and narrow.

My dad taught me one thing above all others—that no matter how much we achieve in our chosen professions, no matter how much wealth and power we obtain, what is really important is to be a good man. Just be a good man. He was a very good man.

Sadly, Mike passed away three years ago, aged a very young seventy-two. Another victim to the great taker of men—cancer. The world has felt a poorer place ever since. He is much missed and much loved.

For Mike.

COLD

KILLING

Saturday. I agreed to go to the park with the wife and children. They're over there on the grassy hill, just along from the pond. They've fed themselves, fed the ducks, and now they're feeding their own belief that we're one normal happy family. And to be fair, as far as they're concerned, we are. I won't let the sight of them spoil my day. The sun is shining and I'm getting a bit of a tan. The memory of the latest visit is still fresh and satisfying. It keeps the smile on my face.

Look at all these people. Happy and relaxed. They've no idea I'm watching them. Watching as small children wander away from mothers too distracted by idle chat to notice. Then they realize their little darling has wandered too far and up goes that shrill shriek of an overprotective parent, followed by a leg slap for the child and more shrieking.

I am satisfied for the time being. The fun I had last week will keep me contented for a while, so everyone is safe today.

CHAPTER 1

Thursday

It was 3 A.M. and Detective Inspector Sean Corrigan drove through the dreary streets of New Cross, southeast London. He had been born and raised in nearby Dulwich, and for as long as he could remember, these streets had been a dangerous place. People could quickly become victims here, regardless of age, sex, or color. Life had little value.

But these worries were for other people, not Sean. They were for the people who had nine-to-five jobs in shops and offices. Those who arrived bleary eyed to work each morning, then scuttled home nervously every evening, only feeling safe once they'd bolted themselves behind closed doors.

Sean didn't fear the streets, having dealt with the worst they could throw at him. He was a detective inspector in charge of one of South London's Murder Investigation Teams, dedicated to dealing with violent death. The killers hunted their victims and Sean hunted the killers. He drove with the window down and doors unlocked.

He'd been asleep at home when Detective Sergeant Dave Donnelly called. There'd been a murder. A bad one. A young man beaten and stabbed to death in his own flat. One minute Sean was lying by his wife's side, the next he was driving to the place where a young man's life had been torn away.

The streets around the murder scene were eerily quiet. He was pleased to see that the uniformed officers had done their job properly and taped off a large cordon around the block the flat was in. He'd been to scenes before where the cordon started and stopped at the front door. How much evidence had been carried away from scenes on the soles of shoes? He didn't want to think about it.

There were two marked patrol cars alongside Donnelly's unmarked Ford. He always laughed at the murder scenes on television, with dozens of police cars parked outside, all with blue lights swirling away. Inside, dozens of detectives and forensics guys would be falling over each other. Reality was different. Entirely different.

Real crime scenes were all the more disturbing for their quietness—the violent death of the victim would leave the atmosphere shattered and brutalized. Sean could feel the horror closing in around him as he examined a scene. It was his job to discover the details of death, and over time he had grown hardened to it, but not immune. He knew that this scene would be no different.

He parked outside the taped-off cordon and climbed from the isolation of his car into the warm loneliness of the night, the stars of the clear sky and the streetlights removing all illusion of darkness. If he had been anyone else, doing any other job, he might have noticed how beautiful it was, but such thoughts had no place here. He flashed his identification to the approaching uniformed officer and grunted his name. "DI Sean Corrigan, Serious Crime Group South. Where's this flat?"

The uniformed officer was young. He seemed afraid of Sean. He must be new if a mere detective inspector scared him. "Number sixteen Tabard House, sir. It's on the second floor, up the stairs and turn right. Or you could take the lift."

"Thanks."

Sean opened the boot of his car and cast a quick glance over the contents squeezed inside. Two large square plastic bins contained all he would need for an initial scene examination. Paper suits and slippers. Various sizes of plastic exhibit bags, paper bags for clothing, half a dozen boxes of plastic gloves, rolls of sticky labels, and of course a sledgehammer, a crowbar, and other tools. The boot of Sean's car would be mirrored by detectives' cars across the world.

He pulled on a forensic containment suit and headed toward the stairwell. The block was of a type common to this area of London. Low-rise tenements made from dark, oppressive, brown-gray brick that had been thrown up after the Second World War to house those bombed out of old slum areas. In their time they'd been a revelation—indoor toilets, running water, heating—but now only those trapped in poverty lived in them. They looked like prisons, and in a way that's what they were.

The stairwell smelled of urine. The stench of humans living on top of one another was unmistakable. This was summer and the vents of the flats pumped out the smells from within. Sean almost gagged on it, the sight, sound, and smell of the tenement block reminding him all too vividly of his own childhood, living in a three-bedroom, public housing duplex with his mother, two brothers, two sisters, and his father—his father who would lead him away from the others, taking him to the upstairs bedroom where things would happen. His mother too frightened to intervene—thoughts of reaching for a knife in the kitchen drawer swirling in her head, but fading away as her courage deserted her. But the curse of his childhood had left him with a rare and dark insightfulness—an ability to understand the motivations of those he hunted.

All too often the abused become the abusers as the darkness overtakes them, evil begetting evil—a terrible cycle of violence, virtually impossible to break—and so the demons of Sean's past were too deeply assimilated in his being to ever be rid of. But Sean *was* different in that he could control his demons and his rage, using his shattered upbringing to allow him insights into the crimes he investigated that other cops could only dream of. He understood the killers, rapists, and arsonists— understood why they had to do what they did, could interpret their motivation—see what they saw, smell what they had smelled, feel what they had felt—their excitement, power, lust, revulsion, guilt, regret, *fear*. He could make leaps in investigations others struggled to understand, filling in the blanks with his unique imagination. Crime scenes came alive in his mind's eye, playing in his head like movies. He was no psychic or clairvoyant; he was just a cop—but a cop with a broken past and a dangerous future, his skill at reading the ones he hunted born of his own dark, haunted past. Where better for a failed disciple of true evil to hide than among cops? Where better to turn his unique tools to good use than the police? He swallowed the bile rising in his throat and headed for the crime scene—the murder scene.

Sean stopped briefly to acknowledge another uniformed officer posted at the front door of the flat. The constable lifted the tape across the door and watched him duck inside. Sean looked down the corridor of the flat. It was bigger than it had seemed from the outside. DS Donnelly waited for him, his large frame filling the doorway, his mustache all but concealing the movement of his lips as he talked. Dave Donnelly, twenty-year-plus veteran of the Metropolitan Police and very much Sean's old-school right-hand man. His anchor to the logical and practical course of an investigation and part-time crutch to lean on. They'd had their run-ins and disagreements, but they understood each other—they trusted each other.

"Morning, guv'nor. Stick to the right of the hallway here. That's the route I've been taking in and out," Donnelly growled in his strange accent, a mix of Glaswegian and Cockney, his mustache twitching as he spoke.

"What've we got?" Sean asked matter-of-factly.

"No sign of forced entry. Security is good in the flat, so he probably let the killer in. All the damage to the victim seems to have been done in the living room. A real fucking mess in there. No signs of disturbance anywhere else. The living room is the last door on the right, down the corridor. Other than that we've got a kitchen, two bedrooms, a bathroom, and a separate room for the toilet. From what I've seen, the victim kept things reasonably clean and tidy. Decent taste in furniture. There's a few photies of the victim around the place—as best I can tell, anyway. His injuries make it a wee bit difficult to be absolutely sure. There's plenty of them with him, shall we say, *embracing* other men."

"Gay?" Sean asked.

"Looks that way. It's early days, but there's definitely some decent hi-fi and TV stuff around the place, and I notice several of the photies have our boy in far-flung corners of the world. Must have cost a few pennies. We're not dealing with a complete loser here. He had a decent enough job, or he was a decent enough villain, although I don't get the feel this is a villain's home." Both men craned their heads around the hallway area, as if to confirm Donnelly's assessment so far. He continued: "And I've found a few letters all addressed to a Daniel Graydon. Nothing for anyone else."

"Well, Daniel Graydon," Sean asked, "what the hell happened to you? And why?"

"Shall we?" With an outstretched hand pointing along the corridor, Donnelly invited Sean to continue.

They moved from room to room, leaving the living room to the end. They trod carefully, moving around the edges so as not to disturb any invisible footprint indentations left in the carpets or minute but vital evidence: a strand of hair, a tiny drop of blood. Occasionally Sean would take a photograph with his small digital camera. He would keep the photographs for his personal use only, to remind him of details he had seen, but also to put himself back at the scene anytime he needed to sense it again, to smell the odor of blood, to taste the sickly sweet flavor of death. To feel the killer's presence. He wished he could be alone in the flat, without the distraction of having to talk to anyone—to explain what he was seeing and feeling. It had been the same ever since he was a young cop, his ability to step into the shoes of the offender, be it a residential burglary or murder. Seeing the scene through the eyes of the offender. But only the more alarming scenes seemed to trigger this reaction. Walking around scenes of domestic murders or gangland stabbings he saw more than most other detectives, but felt no more than they did. This scene already seemed different. He wished he were alone.

Sean felt uncomfortable in the flat. Like an intruder. As if he should be constantly apologizing for being there. He shook off the feeling and mentally absorbed everything. The cleanliness of the furniture and the floors. Were the dishes washed and put away? Had any food been left out? Did anything, no matter how small, seem somehow out of place? If the victim kept his clothing neatly folded away, then a shirt on the floor would alert Sean's curiosity. If the victim had lived in squalor, a freshly cleaned glass next to a sink full of dirty dishes would attract his eye. Indeed, Sean had already noted something amiss.

Sean and Donnelly came to the living room. The door was

ajar, exactly how it had been found by the young constable. Donnelly moved inside. Sean followed.

There was a strong smell of blood—a lot of blood. It was a metallic smell. Like hot copper. Sean recalled the times he'd tasted his own blood. It always made him think that it tasted exactly like it smelled. At least this man had been killed recently. It was summer now—if the victim had been there for a few days the flat would have reeked. Flies would have filled the room, maggots infesting the body. He felt a jolt of guilt for being glad the man had just been killed.

Sean crouched next to the body, careful to avoid stepping in the pool of thick burgundy blood that had formed around the victim's head. He'd seen many murder victims. Some had almost no wounds to speak of, others had terrible injuries. This was a bad one. As bad as he'd seen.

"Jesus Christ. What the hell happened in this room?" Sean asked.

Donnelly looked around. The dining room table was overturned. Two of the chairs with it had been destroyed. The TV had been knocked from its stand. Pictures lay smashed on the floor. CDs were strewn around the room. The lights from the CD player blinked in green.

"Must have been a hell of a fight," Donnelly said.

Sean stood up, unable to look away from the victim: a white male, about twenty years old, wearing a T-shirt that was 50 percent soaked in blood, and hipster jeans, also heavily soaked in blood. One sock remained on his right foot; the other was nowhere to be seen. He was lying on his back, the left leg bent under the right, with both arms stretched out in a crucifix position. There were no restraints of any kind in evidence. The left side of his face and head had been caved in. The victim's short hair allowed Sean to see two serious head wounds indicating horrific fractures to the skull. Both eyes were swollen almost completely shut and his nose was smashed, with congealed blood crusted around it. The mouth hadn't escaped punishment, the lips showing several deep cuts, with the jaw hanging, dislocated. Sean wondered how many teeth would be missing. The right ear was nowhere to be seen. He hoped to God the man had died from the first blow to his head, but he doubted it.

The pool of blood by the victim's head was the only heavy saturation area other than his clothing. Elsewhere there were dozens of splash marks: on the walls, furniture, and carpet. Sean imagined the victim's head being whipped around by the ferocity of the blows, the blood from his wounds traveling in a fine spray through the air until it landed where it now remained. Once examined properly, these splash marks should provide a useful map of how the attack had developed.

The victim's body had not been spared. Sean wasn't about to start counting, but there must have been fifty to a hundred stab wounds. The legs, abdomen, chest, and arms had all been brutally attacked. Sean looked around for weapons, but could see none. He returned his gaze to the shattered body, trying to free his mind, to see what had happened to the young man now lying dead on his own floor. For the most fleeting of moments he saw a figure hunched over the dying man, something that resembled a screwdriver rather than a knife gripped in his hand, but the image was gone as quickly as it had arrived. Finally he managed to look away and speak.

"Who found the body?"

"That would be us," Donnelly replied.

"How so?

"Well, us via a concerned neighbor."

"Is the neighbor a suspect?"

"No, no," Donnelly dismissed the idea. "Some young bird from a few doors down, on her way home with her kebab and chips after a night of shagging and drinking."

"Did she enter the flat?"

"No. She's not the hero type, by all accounts. She saw the door slightly open and decided we ought to know about it. If she'd been sober, she probably wouldn't have bothered."

Sean nodded his agreement. Alcohol made some people conscientious citizens in the same way it made others violent temporary psychopaths.

"Uniform sent a unit around to check it out and found our victim here," Donnelly added.

"Did he trample the scene?"

"No, he's a probationer straight out of Hendon and still scared enough to remember what he's supposed to do. He kept to the edges, touched nothing."

"Good," Sean said automatically, his mind having already moved on, already growing heavy with possibilities. "Well, whoever did this is either very angry or very ill."

"No doubt about that," Donnelly agreed.

There was a pause, both men taking the chance to breathe deeply and steady themselves, clearing their minds, a necessary prelude before trying to think coldly and logically. Seeing this brutality would never be easy, would never be matter-of-fact.

"Okay. First guess is we're looking at a domestic murder."

"A lover's tiff?" Donnelly asked.

Sean nodded. "Whoever did this probably took a fair old beating themselves," he added. "A man fighting for his life can do a lot of damage."

"I'll check the local hospitals," Donnelly volunteered. "See if anyone who looks like they've been in a real ding-dong has been admitted."

"Check with the local police stations for the same and wake the rest of the team up. Let's get everyone together at the station for an eight A.M. briefing. And we might as well see if we can get a pathologist to examine the body while it's still in place."

"That won't be easy, guv."

"I know, but try. See if Dr. Canning is available. He some-times comes out if it's a good one, and he's the best."

"I'll do what I can, but no promises."

Sean surveyed the scene. Most murders didn't take long to solve. The most obvious suspect was usually the right suspect. The panicked nature of the crime provided an Aladdin's cave of forensic evidence. Enough to get a conviction. In cases like this, detectives often had to do little more than wait for the labora-tory to examine the exhibits from the scene and provide all the answers. But as Sean looked around something was already niggling away at his instincts.

Donnelly spoke again. "Seems straightforward?"

"Yeah, I'm pretty happy." He let the statement linger.

"But . . . ?"

"The victim almost certainly knew his killer. No forced en-try, so he's let him in. A boyfriend is a fair bet. This smells like a domestic murder. A few too many drinks. A heated argument. A fight kicks off and gets nastier and nastier, both end up beat-en to a pulp and one dies. A crime of passion that the killer had no time to prepare for. He's lost it for a while, killed a friend. A lover. Now all he wants to do is run. Get away from this flat and be somewhere safe to think out his next move. But there're a couple of things missing for me."

"Such as?"

"They've probably been having a drink, but there are no glasses anywhere. Can you remember dealing with a domestic murder where alcohol wasn't involved?"

"Maybe he cleaned the place up a bit?" Donnelly offered. "Washed the glasses and put them away."

"Why would he bother cleaning a glass when his blood and fingerprints must be all over the place after a struggle like this?"

"Panic?" Donnelly suggested. "Wasn't thinking straight.

He cleaned up his glass, maybe started to clean up other stuff too before he realized he was wasting his time."

"Maybe."

Sean was thinking hard. The lack of signs of alcohol was a small point, but any experienced detective would have expected to find evidence of its use at a scene like this. An empty bottle of cider. A half-empty bottle of Scotch, or a champagne bottle to fuel the rage of the rich. But it was the image he was beginning to visualize that was plaguing him with doubt—the image his mind was piecing together using evidence that was missing as much as evidence that was present. The image of a figure crouching very deliberately over the victim. No frenzy, no rage, but evil in a human form.

"There's something else," he told Donnelly. "The killing obviously took place in the living room. We know he must have gone out the front door because everything else is locked up nice and tight. But the hallway is clean. Nothing. The carpet is light beige, yet there's no sign of a bloody footprint. And the door handle? Nothing. No blood. Nothing.

"So our killer beats and stabs the victim to death in a frenzied moment of rage and yet stops to clean his hands before opening any doors. After killing a man who may have been his lover, he's suddenly calm enough to take his shoes off and tiptoe out of the place. That doesn't make a lot of sense."

Donnelly joined in. "And if our boy did stop to clean himself up before leaving, then where did he get clean? He had two choices. The sink in the bathroom or the sink in the kitchen."

Sean continued for him. "We've seen both of them. Clean as a whistle. No signs of recent use. Not even a splash of water."

"Aye," Donnelly said. "But it's probably nothing. We're assuming too much. Maybe forensics will prove us wrong and find some blood in the hallway we can't see."

Sean wasn't convinced, but before he could reply the uniformed constable at the front door called into the flat. "Excuse me, sir, your lab team is here."

Sean shouted a reply. "Coming out."

He and Donnelly walked from the flat carefully, keeping to the route they'd used on entering. They walked to the edge of the taped-off cordon where they knew Detective Sergeant Andy Roddis would be waiting with his team of specially trained detectives and scene examiners.

DS Roddis saw Sean and Donnelly approach. He observed their forensics suits but was not impressed. "I take it you two have already been trampling all over my scene." He was right to be annoyed. The book said no one into the house except the scene examination team. "Next time I'm going to seize your clothing as exhibits."

Sean needed Roddis on his side.

"Sorry, Andy," he said. "We haven't touched a thing. Promise."

"I hear you have a dead male for me in flat number sixteen. Yes?" Roddis still sounded irritated.

"I'm afraid so," said Donnelly.

Roddis turned to Sean. "Anything special you want from us?"

"No. Our money's on a domestic, so stick to the basics. You can keep the expensive toys locked away."

"Very well," Roddis replied. "Blood, fibers, prints, hair, and semen it is."

Donnelly and Sean were already walking away. Sean called over his shoulder, "I'm briefing my team at eight A.M. Try to get me a preliminary report before then."

"I might be able to phone something through to you. Will that do?"

"Fine," said Sean. Right now he would take anything offered.

* * *

It was shortly before 8 A.M. and Sean sat alone in his bleak, functional office in the Peckham police station, surrounded by the same cheap wooden furniture that adorned each and every police building across London. The office was just about big enough to house two four-foot battered oblong desks and an extra two uncomfortable chairs for the frequent visitors. Two ancient-looking computers sat, one on each desk, enabling him to view different inquiries at the same time, and the harsh fluorescent lights above painted everything a dull yellow. How he envied those TV detectives with their leather swivel chairs, banks of all-seeing, all-dancing computers, and most of all the Jasper Conran reading lamps slung low over shining glass desks. Reality was mundane and functional.

Sean thought about the victim. What sort of person had he been? Was he loved? Would he be missed? He would find out soon enough. The phone rang and made him jump.

"DI Corrigan." He rarely wasted words on the phone. Years of speaking into radios had trimmed his speech.

"Mr. Corrigan, it's DS Roddis. You wanted an update for your briefing?" Roddis didn't recognize any ranks above his own, but his powerful position meant he was never challenged by his seniors. He decided the forensic resources assigned to each case, and it was he who knew the right people at the right laboratories across the southeast who could get the job done. Everybody, regardless of rank, respected his monopoly.

"Thanks for calling. What've you got for me?"

"Well, it's early days."

Sean knew the lab team would have done little more than get organized. "I appreciate that, but I'd like whatever you've got."

"Very well. We've had a cursory look around. The entry and exit point is surprisingly clean, given the nature of the attack. And the hallway was clean too. Perhaps we'll find something when we get better lighting and some UV lamps. Other than that, nothing definite yet. The blood spray marks on the walls and furniture have me a little confused."

"Confused?" Sean asked.

"Having seen the victim's wounds, I'm pretty sure the blow to the head all but killed him, and it certainly knocked him down. I have a blood spray pattern on a wall that would be consistent with a blow to his head with a heavy object."

"So what's the problem?"

"If the victim was prostrate when the other injuries were inflicted, then I would only expect to find small, localized sprays, but I've got numerous others, over the carpet, broken furniture, up the walls. They're not consistent with his wounds."

"Then he must have other wounds we haven't seen yet," Sean suggested. "Or maybe the blood is from the attacker?"

"Possibly." Roddis sounded unconvinced. "No obvious murder weapon yet," he continued, "but it will probably turn up when we get into the search properly."

"Anything else?" Sean asked, in hope more than expectation.

"There's plenty of documentation: address books, diaries, bank books, and so on. It shouldn't be too hard to confirm the victim's identity. That's it so far."

Sean may not have particularly liked Roddis, but he valued his professionalism. "Thanks. It'll be a help in the briefing. Might keep the team awake." He hung up.

Reclining in his chair, Sean stared at the lukewarm cup of coffee on his desk. What would it mean if the splash patterns didn't match the wounds on the victim? Had the killer been badly injured himself and the blood sprays came from his wounds? He doubted it, especially if Roddis was right about the victim being all but taken out with the first blow to the head. And if he was knocked down with the first blow, then what the hell were the other injuries about? The answers would come, he reassured himself. Wait for the full forensic examination of the scene, the postmortem of the victim. The answers would come. They always did.

He stood and looked out of his window down at the station parking lot. He saw DS Sally Jones outside furiously smoking a cigarette, laughing and joking with a couple of girls from the typing pool.

He watched her, admiring her. A five-foot-three bundle of energy. He thought she had a good pair of legs, but she carried too much weight up top for his taste. He tried to remember if he had ever seen her fair hair not tied back in a ponytail.

He loved her ability to connect with people. She could talk to anyone and make them feel that she was their best friend in the world, and so Sean sometimes used her to do the things he would find impossible to do well. Speaking with grieving parents. Telling a husband his wife had been raped and murdered in their own home. Sean had watched in awe as Sally told people unthinkable things and then half an hour later she would be laughing and joking, puffing on a cigarette, chatting with whoever was close enough. She was tough. Tougher than he would ever be. He smiled as he watched her.

Sean wondered why she was still alone. He couldn't imagine doing this job and then going home to an empty house. Sally told him she was clearly too much for any man to handle. He had often tried to sense some sorrow in her. Some loneliness. He never could.

He checked the time. She was going to be late for the briefing. He could call out the window and warn her, but he decided it would be more fun to leave it.

He walked the short distance along the busy, brightly lit corridor: doors on both sides; old and new posters pinned and stuck to the walls, uniformly ignored by passersby all too single-mindedly trying to get to wherever they were going to stop and take notice of someone else's appeals for assistance. He reached the briefing room and entered. His team continued to chatter away among themselves. A couple of them, including Donnelly, mouthed a greeting. He nodded back.

The team was relatively small. Two detective sergeants— Sally and Donnelly—and ten detective constables. Sean sat in his usual chair at the head of a rectangular wooden table, the cheapest money could buy. He dropped his mobile phone and notebook in front of him and looked around, making sure everyone was there. He nodded to Donnelly, who understood the cue. They'd been working with each other long enough to be able to communicate without the need for words.

"All right, people, listen up. The guv'nor wants to speak and we've got a lot to get through, so let's park our arses and crack on." The murmuring faded as the team began to sit and concentrate on Sean.

Detective Constable Zukov spoke. "D'you want me to grab DS Jones, boss? I think she's having a smoke in the yard."

"No. Don't bother," Sean told him. "She'll be here soon enough."

The room fell silent, Sean looking at Donnelly with a slight grin on his face. They both turned to the briefing room door just as DS Sally Jones came bursting in. There was a low hum of stifled laughter.

"Shit. Sorry I'm late, guv." The hum of low laughter grew. Sally swatted Zukov across the head as she walked past. He threw his hands up in protest. "I told you to come and get me, Paulo." The constable didn't answer, but the smile on his face said everything.

Sean joined in. "Afternoon, Sally. Thanks for joining us."

"It's a pleasure, sir."

"As I'm sure you've all worked out, we've picked up another murder." Some of the team groaned.

Sally spoke up. "We're only in summer and already we've had sixteen murders on this team alone. Eight still need preparing for court. Who's going to put those court presentations together if we're constantly being dumped on?" There was a rumble of approval around the room.

"No point in moaning," Sean told them. "All the other teams are just as busy as we are, so we get this one. As you're all no doubt aware, we don't have a live investigation running, so we're the obvious choice."

Sean was prepared for the grumbling. Police officers always grumbled. They were either moaning about being too busy or they were moaning about not earning enough overtime. It was a fact of life with police.

He continued. "Okay, this is the job. What we know so far is that our victim was beaten and stabbed to death. At this time we believe the victim is Daniel Graydon, the occupier of the flat where we're pretty certain the crime took place. But his facial injuries are severe, so visual identification has yet to be confirmed. We are treating the flat as our primary crime scene. Dave and I have already had a look around and it's not pretty. The victim would appear to have been hit on the head with a heavy object, and that may well have been the critical injury, although we'll have to wait for the autopsy to confirm that. The stab wounds are numerous and spread across a wide area. This was a vicious, brutal attack.

"It is suspected the victim may be gay, and the early theory is that it was probably a domestic. If that's the case, then the killer himself could be hurt. We're already checking the hospitals and custody suites on the off chance he was picked up for something else after fleeing the scene. I don't want this to get complicated, so let's keep it simple. A nice, neat, join-the-dots investigation will do me fine."

Sean looked toward Sally.

"Sally, I want you to pick four guys and start on door-to-door immediately. That time of night, beaten to death, someone must have heard or seen something. The rest of you, hang fire. The lab team is looking at the victim's personal stuff, so we'll have a long list of people to trace and chat with soon enough. I don't expect it to be long before we have a decent idea who our prime suspect is.

"Dave. You go office manager on this one." Donnelly nodded acknowledgment. "The rest of you check with Dave at least three times a day for your assignments. And remember," Sean added, "the first few hours are the most important, so let's eat on the hoof and worry about sleep when the killer's banged up downstairs."

There were nods of approval as the group began to break up. Sean could sense their optimism, their trust in his leadership, his judgment. He hadn't failed them yet.

He prayed this case would be no different.

It was almost 1 P.M. and Sean had spent the morning on the phone. He'd told the same story a dozen times. To his superintendent, the Intelligence Unit, the gay and lesbian liaison officer, the local uniformed duty officer, the community safety inspector. He was sick of telling. Sally and Donnelly had returned for their meeting and sat in his office. Sally had brought coffee and sandwiches, which Sean ate without tasting. It was the first thing he had eaten since the phone call from Donnelly early that morning, so he was happy just to get something into his stomach.

Between bites they talked, all of them aware they hadn't a moment to waste on a proper lunch. The first days of a murder inquiry were always the same—so much to get through and so little time. Forensic evidence degraded, witnesses' memories faded, CCTV tapes would be recorded over. Time was Sean's enemy now.

"Anything from the door-to-door, Sally?" he asked. "Give me good news only."

"Nothing," she replied. "I've still got guys down there knocking on doors, but so far all we're being told is that Graydon kept himself to himself. No noisy parties. No fights. No problems. No nothing. Everybody says he was a nice kid. As for last night, nobody saw or heard a thing. Another quiet night in South London."

"That can't be right," Sean argued. "A man gets beaten to death within a few feet of what, four other flats, and no one heard it?"

"That's what we're being told."

Sean sighed and turned toward Donnelly. "Dave?"

"Aye. We've managed to make copies of his diary, address book, and what have you. I've got a couple of the lads going through that now. Expect to be informed about next of kin pretty soon. No boyfriend yet, though. No one name coming up over and over. I'll be sending the troops out to trace friends and associates as and when we have their details. Oh, and the coroner's officer has been on the blower. The body's been moved from the scene and taken to Guy's Hospital. Postmortem's at four P.M. today."

Sean's mind flashed with the images of previous postmortems he'd attended as he pushed what was left of his sandwich to one side.

"Who's doing it?"

"You've got your wish there, boss. It's Dr. Canning. Anything more from the forensics team at the scene?"

"Not yet. Roddis doesn't reckon they'll be finished until

about this time tomorrow, then as usual everything gets sent to the lab and we wait."

A young detective from Sean's team appeared at the door holding a small piece of paper pinched between his fingers. "I think I've found an address for the parents." The three detectives continued to look at him.

"I'll take that, thanks," Sally told him. The young detective handed her the note and backed away from the door.

Sean knew his responsibilities. "I'll come too. Shit, this is gonna be fun. Dave, I'll see you back here at about three thirty. You can take me to the postmortem."

"I'll be here," Donnelly assured him.

Sean tugged his jacket on and headed for the door, Sally in pursuit. "And remember," he told Donnelly, "if anyone asks, this is a straightforward domestic murder. No need to get anyone excited."

"Having doubts?" Donnelly managed to ask before Sean was gone.

"No," Sean answered, not entirely truthfully. For a second he was back in the flat, back at the scene of the slaughter, watching the killer moving around Graydon's prostrate form, but he saw no panic or fury in his actions, no jealousy or rage, only a coldness—a sense of satisfaction.

Donnelly's voice snapped him back. "You all right, guv'-nor?"

"Sorry, yes I'm fine. Just find me the boyfriend—whoever he is. Find him and you've found our prime suspect."

"I'll do my best."

"I know you will," Sean told him as he watched him stride back into the main office.

CHAPTER 2

I thoroughly enjoyed the time I spent with the little queer. I made it look like a domestic murder. I've heard fights between people like him can get nasty, so I had a bit of fun with the idea.

He was easy enough to dispatch. These people live dangerous lives. They make perfect victims. So I hunted among them, looking for someone, and I found him.

I had already decided to spend the evening stalking the patrons of a Vauxhall nightclub, Utopia. What a ridiculous name. More like Hell, if you ask me. I told my wife I was going out of town on business, packed some spare clothes, toiletries, the usual things for a night away, and booked a hotel room in Victoria. I could hardly turn up at home in the early hours. That would arouse suspicions. I couldn't have that. Everything at home needed to appear . . . normal.

I also packed a paper painter's suit that I bought at Homebase, several pairs of surgical gloves—readily available from all sorts of shops—a shower cap, and some plastic bags to cover my feet. A little noisy, but effective. And last but not least a syringe. All fitted neatly into a small knapsack.

Avoiding the CCTV cameras that swamped the area, I

watched the entrance to the club from the shadows of the railway bridge as the sound of the trains reverberated through the archways.

I had already spied my target entering the club earlier that evening. The excitement made my testicles tighten. Yes, he was truly worthy of my special attentions. This wasn't the first time I had seen him. I had watched him a couple of weeks earlier, watched him whore himself inside the club to whoever could match his price. I had been searching for the perfect victim, knowing the police would only check CCTV from the night he died or, if they were especially diligent, maybe the week before.

I had stood in the midst of the heaving throng of stinking, foul humanity, bodies brushing past my own, tainting my being with their diseased imperfection, while at the same time inflaming my already excited, heightened senses. I so wanted to reach out and take each and every one of them by the throat, crushing trachea after trachea as the dead began to pile at my feet. I fought hard to control the surging strength within, then terror gripped me, terror like I have never felt in my entire life. Terror that the real me was revealing itself, that all those around me could see me changing in front of their very eyes, my skin glowing a brilliant red, bright white light spilling from my eyes and ears, vomiting from my mouth. Heavy drops of sweat had snaked down my back, guided by my swelling, cramping back muscles. Somehow I had managed to move my legs, pushing through a crowd of squabbling worshippers until I reached the bar and stared into the giant mirror hanging behind it. Relief washed over me, slowing my heart and cooling my sweat as I could see I hadn't changed, hadn't betrayed myself.

Now the time for watching was over. It was time for my prize, my release, my relief. All was in place. All was as it needed to be. At last I saw him leaving the club. He was shouting good-byes, but seemed to be alone. He walked casually under the railway bridge, heading toward Vauxhall Bridge. I moved quickly and silently to the other side of the railway bridge and waited for him. As he neared, I stepped out. He saw me, but didn't look scared. He returned my smile as I spoke to him.

"Excuse me."

"Yes," he replied, still smiling, stepping closer to the streetlight to better see me. "Is there something I can do for . . . you," he said, recognition spreading across his face. "We really must stop meeting like this." Yes, I'd been with him before. A risk, but a calculated one. A little more than a week ago, inside the nightclub, I'd introduced myself without speaking, making sure he saw my smiling face just long enough so he'd recognize it again. Later I met him outside. I paid him what he asked, all in advance, and we went back to his flat where I defiled myself inside him and even allowed him to defile the inside of me. The sex wasn't important, or even pleasurable—that wasn't the point of being with him. I wanted to feel him while he was alive, to understand he wasn't merely an inanimate thing, but a real live person. I couldn't be with him like that the night I dispatched him in case I left the faintest trace of semen or saliva on his body. Being with him a week or so before would give any such evidence time to degrade and die. And of course we practiced safe sex: he to protect himself from the Gay Plague and I to protect myself from detection. I'd shaved away my pubic hair so none could be left at the scene and wore a full-faced rubber mask that also covered my head, stopping any head hairs from being left either, as well as rubber gloves to eliminate the risk of leaving fingerprints—all of which the little queer thought was simply part of the fun. But the fun, the real fun, was yet to come, and I had more than a week to fantasize about the events that lay ahead.

The days had passed painfully slowly, testing my patience and control to the limit, but the memories of the night I had been with him and the thought of things to come carried me through, and before I knew it he was standing in front of me, his small, straight white teeth glistening in the streetlights, his oval-shaped head too large for his scrawny neck, perched on slim, narrow shoulders. His hair was blond and straight, shoulder-length, styled to make him look like a surfer, but his skin was pale and his body weak. The most athletic thing he had ever done was drop to his knees. His T-shirt was too tight and short, revealing his flat stomach, disappearing into hipster designer jeans worn to provoke the sexual urges of his peers.

I told him I needed to be with him again. I lied that I had been inside the club and had seen him dancing, that I had been too nervous to approach him then, but now I really wanted him. We talked some more crap then he said, "You know I'm not cheap. If you want to be with me again it'll cost."

He suggested we go to my place, so I told him my boyfriend would be there, but he started rambling on about not taking people back to his flat and how last time had been an exception, until I pulled another two fifties from my wallet and thrust them into his hand. He smiled.

We went to my car, fixed with false plates, and drove to his shithole in southeast London where I was sure not to park too close to his block. Telling him I didn't want to take the risk of being seen walking to his flat with him, I suggested that he go ahead and leave the door unlocked.

I waited a couple of minutes, then, as the street was empty, no one staring from windows, I walked to the flat. The block was old, cold, and smelled of piss, but he had been a good boy and left the door unlocked. I quietly entered and flicked the lock on. He appeared around the corner at the end of the corridor, from what I knew was the living room. He spoke.

"Was that you locking the door?"

"Yes," I replied. "Can't be too careful these days."

"Afraid someone's going to burst in on us and spoil the party?"

"Something like that."

The excitement was unbearable. My stomach was so cramped with anticipation I could hardly breathe. Inside, my mind was screaming, but I was still wearing my nervous smile as I walked into the living room.

The whore knelt by his CD player. I told him I wanted to clean up a little and headed for the bathroom down the hallway.

I took my bag with me, and quickly, if somewhat awkwardly, pulled on the suit, the shower cap, rubber gloves, and finally the plastic bags over my shoes. I looked in the mirror, filling my lungs with air drawn in hard through my nose. I was ready.

Fully prepared, I returned to the living room. He turned and saw me dressed and resplendent. He started to giggle, covering his mouth as if to stop himself.

He spoke to me. "Is this how we're going to get our kicks tonight then?"

They were the last words he spoke, although he may have said "please" a little later. By then the blood bubbling up into his mouth made it just a gargle.

With a smooth, swift, practiced hand I grabbed an iron statue of a naked Indian he kept on his side table and I used it to smash his skull, not hitting him hard enough to kill him straightaway, merely to render him semiconscious and virtually paralyzed. He had been on his knees when I hit him, which was good—less distance to fall meant less noise when he hit the floor.

I watched him for a while, standing over him like the victor in a prizefight, watching his chest rise and fall with each painful, strained breath, the blood initially spurting from the wound in his head, then slowing to a steady flow as his heart grew too weak to pump it at the pressure his body required to stay alive. Every few seconds his right leg would twitch like a dying bird.

It wouldn't have been as I had dreamed if he hadn't been at least partly conscious when I went to him with an ice pick I found in his drinks cabinet. I needed him to be alive as I cut him. I needed to see him try to stop me each time I pushed the ice pick into his dying body: not stabbing frenziedly, but placing it deliberately against his pale skin. Now and then he would reach up and pitifully try to defend himself from the torture. I told him not to be a naughty boy and continued with my work. It was a shame his brain hemorrhaging had caused his eyes to turn red, as I had wanted to contrast his blue eyes against the pale bloodied skin. Next time I'd do better.

His perforated body almost began to disgust me, to make me want to flee from the scene, but I couldn't stop yet. Not until all was as close as it could be to how I had seen it in my mind the first time I knew I would be visiting him. When he finally died, a slow, quiet hiss of air escaping from his lips and the breaches in his chest wall told me that my fun had come to an end. I put on a clean pair of surgical gloves and took the three hundred pounds in cash I had given him earlier from his pants pocket. I really didn't want to leave that behind. I carefully and quietly broke apart some furniture and generally arranged the room as if a violent struggle had occurred. Next I used the syringe I'd brought to draw blood from his mouth and sprayed it about the room: on the walls, over the furniture, on the carpet, making spray patterns to suggest a violent struggle had taken place. Then I moved to the corner of the room I had left clean. I removed my protective layers and put them inside a plastic bag and put that bag inside another plastic bag and repeated this twice more. I ensured that each plastic bag was tied securely and finally put the bundle in my knapsack. I put new plastic bags on my feet, not wanting to take the chance that I might step on a spot of blood—that sort of evidence can be difficult to explain. I put on another clean pair of rubber surgical gloves and left the living room. I would burn all of it in my garden the following evening, the safest way to dispose of such incriminating items. To burn them in a public place risked attracting attention, while burial would leave them at the mercy of inquisitive animals.

I moved quietly to the front door. I took the plastic bags off my shoes and looked through the peephole. Nobody about. Just to be sure, I listened at the door, careful not to let my ear press against it and possibly leave a mark, like a fingerprint, which I hear can happen.

When I was totally happy, I slipped out of the flat, leaving the front door open so as not to make any more noise than necessary. The statue of the Indian and the ice pick I threw in the Thames as I headed north to my hotel. The thought of the police wasting hours searching for weapons that wouldn't help their investigation in the slightest pleased me.

When I reached my hotel I slipped in through the side door next to the bar, generally used only as a fire exit. I knew it could open from the outside and had no CCTV camera trained on it. I already had the key card for my room, having checked in earlier that day. I took a long shower, keeping the water as hot as I could bear, scrubbing skin, nails, and hair vigorously with a nailbrush until my entire body felt like it had been burned by flames. I had removed the plug cover to allow any items washed from my body to flow easily into London's sewage system. After the shower I took a long steaming bath and scrubbed myself again. Once dry I lay naked on the bed and drank two bottles of water, at peace now. Satisfied. Soon sleep came and I dreamed the same beautiful dream over and over.

CHAPTER 3

Thursday, late afternoon

Sean and Donnelly walked along the corridors of Guy's Hospital, heading for the mortuary. They were accompanied by Detective Constable Sam Muir, who would be acting as exhibits officer—taking responsibility for any objects the pathologist found on or in the body during the postmortem. Sean wondered if he would bump into his wife, Kate, one of the all too few doctors attending to the never-ending flow of patients through the Accident and Emergency Department—the sick and injured from the surrounding areas of Southwark, Bermondsey, and beyond. Some of London's poorest and most forgotten, living in public housing projects where violence and crime were seldom far away, all of their degradation and suffering going unnoticed and unseen by the swarms of tourists wandering around Tower Bridge and Tooley Street. If only they knew how close they were to some of London's most dangerous territory.

His mind returned to the victim's parents. He and Sally had

called at the small town house in Putney. A desirable neighborhood on the whole, but boisterous on weekend evenings. Sally
had done most of the talking.

Daniel had been their only child. The mother was devas-
tated and didn't care who saw her fall to the floor screaming.
Her despair was a physical pain. When she could speak, all she
could say was the name of her son.

The father was stunned. He didn't know whether to help his
wife or collapse himself. He ended up doing neither. Sean took
him into the living room. Sally stayed with the mother.

They knew their son was gay. It had bothered the father at
first, but he had grown to accept it. What else could he do other
than push the boy away? And he would never do that. He said
his son worked as a nightclub manager. He wasn't sure where,
but Daniel had been doing well for himself and had no money
problems, unlike other young people.

He hadn't met any of his son's friends. Daniel hadn't kept in
touch with his old school friends. He came home quite often,
almost every Sunday, for lunch. If he had a boyfriend then neither he nor his wife knew about it. Their son had said he wasn't
interested in anything like that. They hadn't pressed him.

The father had asked what they were to do now. His wife
would be finished. She lived for the boy, not him. He knew it
and didn't mind—but with the boy gone?

He wanted to know who would do this to his boy—who
would do this to them? Why? Sean had no answers.

As the three detectives entered the mortuary they could see
Dr. Simon Canning preparing for the postmortem. A body lay
covered with a green sheet on what Sean knew would be a cold,
metal operating table. Water continually ran under the body to
an exit drain as the pathologist did his work, so that the whole
thing resembled a large, shallow stainless-steel bathtub.

Some detectives could detach themselves from the ugly reality of postmortems, bury themselves in the science and art of the procedure. Unfortunately, Sean was not one of those detectives. For days to come images of his own postmortem would blend with the memories of his shattered childhood. Meanwhile Dr. Simon Canning was busy arranging his tools— bright, shiny metal instruments for torturing the dead.

"Afternoon, Detectives."

"Doctor. Good to see you again," Sean replied.

"I doubt that," said the pathologist. Canning was pleasant enough, but businesslike and succinct. "I hope you don't mind, Inspector. I've started without you. I was just having a bit of a cleanup before continuing. Right then, shall we get on with it?"

The doctor pulled back the sheet covering the body with one quick movement of his arm. Sean almost expected him to say, "*Voilà!*" like a waiter lifting the lid off a silver platter.

The hair on the back and side of the head was matted with blood—it looked sticky. Sean could clearly see the gashes in the side of the head and the small stab marks all over the naked body.

"Seventy-seven," Canning told him.

Sean realized he was being spoken to. He glanced up at the doctor. "Sorry?"

"Separate stab wounds. Seventy-seven in total. None in the back of the body. All in the front. Made by some form of stiletto knife, or an ice pick, but it's the first blow to the head that killed him. Eventually."

Dr. Canning pointed to the head wound. Sean forced himself to lean closer to the body. "One can see the ear is missing. Not cut off, but more a case of the victim being hit so hard that whatever he was hit with crushed the skull and still had enough energy to tear the ear away as the swing of the object carried through."

"Nice" was all Sean said.

"And the victim was on his knees when the first blow was

struck," the doctor continued. "We can see the cut to the scalp is angled downward, not upward. The killer swung low, not high."

"Or he was hit from behind?" Sean offered.

"No," Canning told him. "He fell backward, not forward. Look at the stains from the flow of blood. They run to the back of the head, not toward the face."

He looked at the detectives, making sure they were concentrating on what he was saying and not what they were seeing. He had their attention.

"But that's all straightforward. The interesting thing is the angle of the stab wounds. Bearing in mind of course that our friend here has wounds from his ankles to his throat, I can be almost positive the victim was already prostrate on the floor when he was stabbed. That in itself isn't unusual." The doctor paused to catch his breath before continuing his lecture. "The interesting bit is this—most of the stab wounds are at the wrong angle of entry. You see?"

"I'm not quite with you, Doctor."

"It's like this." Canning looked around for a prop. He found a pair of scissors. "First, I know the killer is probably right-handed. The angle of the stab wounds tells me that, as does the fact the victim was hit on the left side of his head. Now, imagine I'm the killer. The victim can play himself. In order to stab somebody from head to toe, the killer would have to be at the side of the body. Not on top, as you would first imagine. If he sat astride the body then it would have been difficult to reach around and stab the thighs, the shins." The doctor twisted his body back toward the victim's feet so as to give a practical demonstration. His point was well made.

"Also, the entire body has puncture wounds. There isn't a large enough unmolested area to suggest the killer was sitting astride the victim."

"So the killer was kneeling on the side of the victim when he stabbed him. That doesn't help me," Sean told him.

Canning continued. "What I'm saying is that the killer didn't crouch down next to the victim and stab away as we would expect in most frenzied crimes of passion. This killer moved around the body stabbing at different areas. There's no doubt about it. It's as if the killer didn't want to be uncomfortable. He didn't want to overstretch, almost as if he was placing ritual stab wounds, or something of that nature. It's a strange one.

"If you ask me, I'd say this was probably not a frenzied attack. These stab wounds are deliberately placed. Controlled. The killer took his time."

Sean felt a coldness grip his body and mind as he flashed back to the image he'd had of the killer's careful, machinelike actions as he stabbed the victim to death. He ran a hand slowly through his short brown hair. He could deny many things, but he couldn't deny his instincts. His gut told him things were going to become difficult. Complicated. The domestic theory was beginning to leak, and in all likelihood they weren't looking for a scared lover anymore. There would be no tearful suspect surrendering to custody because he couldn't deal with the guilt. They were now after something else. Sean was sure of it. He exhaled deeply, his mind swirling with questions.

"We need to get back to the office. Are you finished here, Doctor?"

"Almost. One last thing." He pointed to the victim's wrists. "It's very faint, but it's there. On both wrists."

Sean looked closely. He could see some discoloration of the victim's skin. Thin bands of slightly darker tissue. Canning continued his analysis.

"They're old bruises. Probably caused by ligatures. He was tied with something. I'll have a look under ultraviolet; that'll show up any other old injuries. I'll check the entire body. All my findings will be in the final report."

"Fine," Sean said, the sense of urgency clear in his voice.

"Please, Inspector. Don't let me hold you up. I'll keep you informed."

Donnelly spoke. "D'you want me to sack looking for a boy-friend, boss?"

Sean shook his head. "No. Let's check it out as a matter of course. The boyfriend could still be the killer. Young Daniel here may have hooked up with some freak and not even known it. No forced entry to the flat, remember?" Sean said it, but he didn't believe it. Besides, if there was a boyfriend around, he had a right to know about Daniel. They needed to find him any-way.

"We'd better get back and break the good news."

"You gonna tell the superintendent about this, boss?" asked Donnelly.

"I don't have much choice." He glanced at his watch. "It's getting late. I wouldn't want to spoil his night. Better to tell him tomorrow—after that it looks like the circus will be coming to town. Just don't be one of the clowns."

"And the rest of the team?"

"They've got more than enough to be getting on with for to-night. Sort out a briefing for tomorrow morning. I'll put them in the picture then."

Sean and Donnelly made for the exit. Sean needed the fresh air. They walked through the swing doors and were gone.

CHAPTER 4

If only you were capable of understanding the beauty and clarity of what I am doing. You see, my very being is testament to Nature. To her mercilessness. Her complete lack of compassion. Her violence. You have cast aside Nature's rules and chosen to live by other laws. Morality. Restraint. Tolerance. I have not.

So here we stand, packed into this mechanical coffin, trundling under the streets of London. They humorously call this one the misery line. Look at you. None of you has the faintest idea of what I am. You look at me and see a reflection of yourselves. That is my necessary disguise.

Come closer and I'll show you who I really am.

Damn, these trains can be unbearable in summer. All of us forced to breathe in each other's filth. Six thirty in the afternoon—everybody trying to get home to anesthetize their brains with alcohol, cocaine, television, whatever. Anything to black out the awfulness of their miserable, pointless lives. But before they can indulge in those little pleasures they have to suffer this final torture.

I usually distract myself by picking a passenger at random and imagining what it would be like to cut their eyes out and then slit their throat. The stench of all these potential subjects is very stimulating to my imagination. Maybe I could introduce myself to someone before going home to my dutiful wife and well-behaved children? One day, when I work out how to get away with it, I'll slit their throats too.

What about that passenger there? A nice-looking young lady. Well dressed, attractive haircut, good figure. No engagement or wedding ring. Interesting. Telltale signs like that give me all the information I need. The lack of rings could mean she lives alone or with some girlfriends. I could follow her back to her flat. Yes, I'm almost certain she lives in a flat. I'd pretend to be a neighbor who has just moved in. We would walk through the building entrance together. I would be sure to jangle some keys so she wouldn't suspect foul play. Then she might invite me in for coffee: it's happened before. A quick check to see if anyone else was in or expected soon, and, if not, well then I could have some fun with the pretty girl with the nice haircut.

Not tonight though. I must get home on time and be the good husband. Disguises as successful as mine need a lot of maintaining. But I can't wait much longer. Before the little queer it had been more than a week since I visited anyone properly. The one before that was nothing but a quickie. A mere sketch. Some lawyer type with a briefcase. I made that one look like a robbery. Stabbed him twice through the heart and remembered to take the cash from his wallet.

He looked surprised. I asked him the time and as his lips parted to speak, I stabbed him. I pulled the knife out of his chest, then stabbed him again. This time I left the blade in and held on to it as he slumped to the ground. He had the same look in his eyes as the others. More quizzical than afraid. He was trying to speak. As if he wanted to ask me, "Why?" Always people want to know why. For money? For hate? For love? For sexual pleasure? No, not for any of these petty motivations.

So I whispered the true reason why in his ear. It was the last thing he would have heard. "Because I have to."

CHAPTER 5

Friday morning

It was hot in the way only a giant metropolis can get. The heat mixed with the fumes of four million cars, taxis, and buses. It made the road warp.

Sean was late. He had a briefing to give at ten and had wanted to be at work at least an hour and a half before that to prepare his thoughts. Thanks to the traffic along the Old Kent Road and his three-year-old daughter, Mandy, who'd decided to throw a tantrum because of Sean's broken promise to take her to Legoland, he would barely have time to read through his incoming e-mails. He'd tried to read them on his iPhone as the traffic staggered forward, but after almost driving into the back of the car in front of him for the third time he'd thought better of it.

His team had been assigned initial tasks the previous day—now he hoped those tasks had moved the investigation forward. The briefing he would soon be chairing was an opportunity for the team to tell him what they had discovered so far. DS Roddis and his forensics crew had finished at the scene and Roddis would be present to detail their findings. Findings that could be critical to the investigation.

He rang Sally to let her know he was running late.

"I'll be there within half an hour if this traffic starts moving. Briefing is still at ten unless I call again."

"Do you want everyone in the briefing room?" Sally asked.

"Er . . . no," Sean answered after a second's thought. "We'll do it in our incident room, there's more space."

"No problem." Sally had more to say and knew she would have to speak quickly or Sean would already have hung up. "Guv'nor . . ."

He heard her just in time. "What?"

"I thought you should know some wit's come up with a name for our killer."

Sean knew he wasn't going to like this. "Go on."

"Some of the guys have christened him the 'Fairy Liquidator.' "

There was silence from Sean. He sat stony-faced, thinking about what the family would say if they knew the police investigating their son's death were calling the killer the Fairy Liquidator.

After five seconds he spoke. "Let them know in advance that from this second onward anyone using that name will be off the team, back in uniform, and directing traffic in Soho just as soon as they can get measured up for a new helmet. Take this as a first and final warning, Sally."

"I understand. I'll make sure it's not used again."

"Good." He hung up and continued his tortuous journey through the unbreathable air. Before the murder of Daniel Graydon he'd planned to take the day off and make it a long weekend with his family, doing normal things that a normal family would do—the sort of things he never did as a child.

More promises made to his wife and children broken. His stomach tightened with the sense of sadness that suddenly engulfed him—an almost panicked longing to be with his family. He shook the feelings away as best he could, chasing them from body and mind as if they were a weakness he couldn't afford to carry with him to his work. Besides, there was nothing he could do about it. It was the nature of the beast. It was his job.

Sean and his team were back in the open-plan office that was their incident room and second home. Desks were scattered about, mainly in groups of four, and most were adorned with old oversize computer monitors and, if the owner was lucky, a corded telephone. Murders in London were still being solved in spite of the equipment available rather than because of it. Sean stared through the Plexiglas into the room on the other side, watching the detectives, most preferring to sit on the edges of their desks talking in groups, while others moved with purpose, gathering last-minute stationery or squeezing in one final phone call ahead of Sean's arrival.

The incident room was already changing as the investigation developed. Where there had been blank whiteboards and bare walls the night before, now, pinned up in no particular order, there were photographs of the scene, the victim, and the initial postmortem results. The name of the victim had been confirmed: Daniel Graydon. It adorned a piece of white card and was stuck above the photographs of his mutilated body and violated home. Sean noted they'd been put up in one corner of a wall only. The rest of the wall had been left empty. Clearly someone on his team believed there could be more photographs. More victims.

The whiteboard listed tasks to be undertaken and which detective was allocated to each. All were numbered, and when one was complete a line would be drawn through it, so if the investigation was failing, the board would tell the tale. It never lied. No progression meant fewer and fewer tasks to be placed on the board, causing Sean's seniors to grow ever more anxious, more desperate, and more likely to interfere; but such concerns were for later. The first couple of days would be busy enough just collecting and preserving evidence. The early days were crucial. Evidence missed now could be lost forever.

Sean walked the few steps from his office into the main body of the incident room and waited for the detectives to become still and quiet—the noise level fading as surely as if he'd turned the volume down on an amplifier. He spoke: "Right, people, before we get into this, let's be clear that if anyone uses the term 'Fairy Liquidator' on this inquiry they're gone. Understood?" Silent nods of agreement all around the room. "Good. Now that that nonsense is out of the way, we can get down to business.

"First, you all need to know that in light of the autopsy, I no longer believe this is a domestic murder. Dr. Canning tells me that the victim would have been incapacitated with the first blow to the head, meaning there was no violent struggle."

"What about the broken furniture and the blood spray patterns suggesting a fight?" Sally asked.

"Staged," Sean told her. "Cleverly staged, but staged all the same. He's trying to throw us off the scent. The stab wounds have the appearance of some sort of ritual killing, not a frenzied attack.

"Most of you know DS Andy Roddis here, the forensics team leader. Andy's kindly given up his time to bring us all up to date on any findings from the scene."

"That's very fucking nice of you, Andy," Donnelly interjected, to the amusement of his audience.

"All right, all right," Sean hushed the room. "I strongly suggest you pay attention to what he's about to tell you." He turned to DS Roddis, gesturing with an open hand for him to begin. "Andy."

DS Roddis walked to the photographs of the scene pinned to the wall behind him. "Thank you, sir." He paced back and forth as he took up the story. "Most of the exhibits from the scene have been taken up to the forensics lab, so we won't know the full picture until they've been examined. That'll take another few days. Scientists don't work weekends, so we won't know much until Tuesday at the earliest." There was a small ripple of laughter in the room.

"In addition to staging the scene, we believe the suspect is forensically aware. There were no obvious signs of semen, saliva, or anything else that could have come from the suspect."

The team listened intently without interrupting. Roddis knew everything about the scene there was to know and they knew nothing. This was the time to listen and learn, not to question and disagree. That would come later, once they knew what Roddis knew, but until then, time to honor the ancient detective code: keep your mouth shut and your eyes and ears open.

"There's a lot of blood, but I'm betting it all belongs to the victim. Initial tests show it's the same blood type as the victim's. DNA confirmation will take a few more days. We found several head hairs about the place, but they also look like they came from the victim. The body was swabbed before removal from the scene, so you never know your luck—we may yet, under lab examination, find some body fluids belonging to the suspect. That's our best bet for getting the suspect's DNA.

"No murder weapons found yet, but it's possible the suspect cleaned them after use and placed them somewhere in the flat. All possible weapons have been sent to the lab to see if they match the victim's wounds.

"The fingerprint search was completed using chemical

treatment. We sealed the flat and pumped it full of gas. For the uninformed, we use a chemical that causes any fingerprints to reveal themselves. Much easier than crawling around the place with a brush and aluminum powder. We expected quite a lot of people's prints to flash up, which is usual for this kind of search, but we were surprised to find only a few different marks. I'm pretty sure the scene wasn't cleared of prints by the killer. I base that on the fact that we found a lot of prints about, but they were predominantly the victim's."

Sean intervened. "But there were prints at the scene other than the victim's?"

"Yes," replied Roddis. "Unless the victim was a total recluse, you would expect to find alien prints at the scene." He paused for a second and began again. "Could these alien prints belong to our killer? Well, yes they could, but somehow I doubt it. The killer has gone to great trouble to avoid leaving evidence at the scene, so I think it unlikely he would be so kind as to leave us a nice, clear fingerprint."

He could see Sean was about to jump in again, but he wasn't ready to surrender the floor just yet.

"However, the prints we have recovered have already been sent to Fingerprint Branch for searching. At the very least it may tell us something about who the victim associated with. Always useful."

Sean nodded his appreciation.

"And last, but not least, we are lucky the carpet in the hallway is new and of good quality. It was nice and deep and we found the scene quickly enough to recover some interesting shoe marks that hadn't yet degraded." Roddis took a series of photographs from his file and attached them to the board like a doctor preparing X-rays for viewing. The shoe marks looked like negatives.

"This set"—he pointed to two photographs—"belonged to

the victim. We matched them easily enough. They belong to a rare type of Converse running shoe and the unique marks on the soles, the scars, if you like, matched the individual cuts and marks on the victim's shoes."

Roddis took a step to his left and pointed at another footprint photograph. "This size ten Dr. Marten belongs to the PC who first entered the scene. Fortunately he remembered his training and walked along the side of the corridor the door closes on, so he didn't destroy what I'm about to show you." Again Roddis took a step to his left and pointed to the board.

"This mark," Roddis continued while tapping the next photograph, "was made by someone else entering the scene. It was made by a flat-soled leather shoe that was bought recently. We can see by the almost total lack of scars that these shoes have hardly been used at all. Even if we recovered the shoe that made this indentation, there wouldn't be enough unique marks on the sole to be of much evidential value. We would need approximately fifteen unique scars before we could prove evidentially they were one and the same."

"Are you suggesting this guy deliberately wore new shoes to avoid leaving a distinctive footprint?" Sally asked.

"I'm not here to suggest anything, DS Jones. I'm just here to tell you what we found. Suggestions are your field, I believe."

Roddis moved to the final set of images. They looked strange even in the photographs. Long scars ran across the sole in all directions and appeared too thick. Roddis touched the photographs, tracing the scars with his finger.

"We puzzled over this for quite a while," he told them. "We ran a lot of tests to try and replicate the marks. Nothing. Then, in the absence of any other bright ideas, we tried something. We put normal plastic shopping bags around the soles of a pair of shoes and bingo, exactly the same sort of marks. I'm no betting man, but I'd put my pension on the fact that this mark was made by the same shoe as here—" He pointed at the previous photograph he'd discussed. "Only now the shoe has a plastic bag over the sole. You can still see the shape of the shoe sole, and it certainly matches the other sole for size as well."

Sally spoke again. "Why put bags over his shoes? He's already walked the scene without bags, so why bother to try and hide his prints with plastic bags on the way out?" The room was silent in thought.

Think simply, Sean reminded himself, break it down. They were jumping ahead—trying to guess the killer in a game of Clue before one throw of the dice. Concentrate on the basics. It made no sense to walk into the scene without covering his feet and then cover them to leave. So if he didn't do it to hide his shoe prints, why did he? Sean's imagination came to his rescue, taking him back to the murder scene, looking through the killer's eyes, seeing his hands as he bent over and carefully pulled the plastic bags over his shoes and secured them. Seeing what he saw. Feeling what he felt. The answer leaped into his mind.

"We're trying to be too clever," Sean said. "He didn't do it to hide his shoe marks. He had the bags over his feet to make sure he wouldn't get blood on his nice new shoes."

Sally picked up the train of thought. "And if he went to the length of protecting his shoes, then it's probable he protected everything. His whole body."

She and Sean stared at each other. Everybody in the room was thinking the same thing. The killer was a careful bastard. The killer knew about forensic evidence. The killer knew what the police would be looking for. The killer could think like a cop? Sean broke the silence.

"Okay. So he's careful. Very careful. But he will have made a mistake somewhere. We haven't had the lab results yet, so it's too early to assume the killer's left a clean scene. Let's not give this man too much credit. The odds are he'll turn out to be another freak living at home with his mum, trainspotting and masturbating when he's not out stalking celebrities—probably watched too many cop shows on the Discovery Channel and now he wants to put all his newfound knowledge to the test."

The atmosphere in the room lightened. Sean was relieved. He didn't want a tense team. They mustn't already fear that the investigation could be a sticker, an investigation that dragged on and on without getting anywhere. Failed investigations felt like a contagious disease, infecting all those involved for years, limiting future career options, moves to the more glamorous Metropolitan Police units such as the Flying Squad or the Antiterrorist Teams.

He spoke again. "Sally, did your team finish off the door-to-door?"

"Pretty much, guv'nor. Nothing to add since last time. Nobody can remember much coming and going from his flat, which fits with the lack of other people's fingerprints inside the scene. He had the occasional guest, but certainly no parties." Sally shrugged. "Sorry, boss."

He moved on. If Sally hadn't turned up any eyewitnesses, there weren't any. Sean had no doubt about that.

"Dave?" Sean looked at Donnelly, who shifted in his seat.

"Aye, guv'nor. We've been working through the victim's address book and have got hold of most of his closer friends. The ones who appear frequently in his diary. We'll track down the remaining friends and associates soon enough.

"So far, they all say the same thing—victim was a nice kid. He was indeed a homosexual. One of his buddies, a guy called Robin Peak, had a relationship with him in the past. He was pretty sure Daniel was working as a male prostitute. Not hanging around public toilets in King's Cross though. Apparently he was relatively high end, hence the decent stuff in his flat, but this Robin guy said Daniel would hardly ever take clients back there. Only a select few who could afford to pay the extra hundred pounds or so he charged for the privilege. He would usually go to their places or a decent hotel, or sometimes he would take care of a punter in nearby toilets, though it cost extra if you wanted him to slum it.

"His flat was very much a secret hideaway. Only a handful of people knew where he lived, and we've spoken to most of them. None of them come across as the knife-wielding maniac type. We have all their details anyway.

"According to Mr. Peak, the victim liked the club scene. The gay club scene. It's also how he met most of his clients. He's well known at a number of gay nightspots. We'll begin checking them out as soon as." Donnelly looked around the room.

"How many?" Sean asked.

"About five or six."

"Have any of his friends been able to tell us where the victim was on Wednesday night, Thursday morning?"

"No. But the consensus is that he would probably have been at a club called Utopia, down in Vauxhall. Under the railway arches. His usual Wednesday hangout."

"Good," Sean said, before passing out instructions in his usual quick-fire way. "Andy—you keep on the lab's back. I want my results as soon as possible. Sooner." DS Roddis nodded.

"Dave—take who you want and get to work tracking down witnesses who were at Utopia on Wednesday. Start with the employees." Donnelly scribbled notes on a pad.

"Sally—take whoever's left and begin checking intelligence records for people who have assaulted homosexuals in the past. Not any old bollocks, I mean serious assaults, including sexual assaults. Start with the Met and if that's no good check our neighboring forces, and then go national if you have to."

Sally's head nodded in agreement as she too scribbled notes. "Check the names lifted from the victim's address book first— you never know your luck."

Sean threw the discussion open, causing the increasing murmurs to temporarily fade. "Can anyone think of anything? Have we missed anything? Anything obvious? Anything not so obvious? Speak now, people." No one spoke. "In that case the next get-together we have will be on Monday, same time. I need some results by then. The powers that be will want easy answers to this, so let's find them and finish this one before it turns into a saga."

The meeting broke up as noisily as a class of schoolchildren being dismissed for the weekend. Sean walked to his office alone, closing the door behind him. He picked up a large en-velope waiting on his desk and without thinking emptied out the contents. Copies of photographs of the victim spilled out in front of him. He stared at them, not touching them. He spun his stool around and looked out of the window, the sun still brilliant in the sky. The photographs had caught him off guard. If he had known they were in the envelope, he would have taken time to prepare himself before spilling hell across his desk.

Now he wanted to retreat from his world. He wanted to phone his wife, to be in touch with a softer reality for a minute or two—he wanted to hear her reassuring doctor's voice. He wanted her to tell him unimportant things about their daugh-ters, Mandy and Louise. Kate would be getting them ready for a trip to the park. He needed a snapshot of his other, better life, but he delayed a few seconds, long enough for ugly thoughts to rush his mind. He closed his eyes as the image of his father's fist slammed into his face, the face of his childhood—hot, sting-ing breath growing ever closer. He pressed his knuckles into his temples and pushed the past away. Once his mind cleared, he reached for the phone on his desk and dialed the number he knew so well, praying it would be answered by a voice that existed in the here and now and not just a mechanical-sounding recording of the person he needed to hear live. Moments later the phone was answered by a friendly but businesslike voice— the voice of his wife.

"Hello," she said, the pitch of her voice rising on the *o*.

"It's me."

"I guessed it probably would be—the number was withheld."

"Aren't the hospital numbers withheld?"

"Some are. For a second I was afraid I was about to get called into work for some emergency or another. Anyway—how are you doing?" Sean answered with a sigh she'd heard many times before. "That good, eh? Is it a bad one?"

"Is there such a thing as a good one?"

"No. I suppose not."

"Anyway—what are you doing?"

"In the park with the kids. Too nice a day to be stuck inside. What about you?"

"In my office looking at . . . looking at some reports," he lied as his eyes fell on the crime scene photographs. He knew Kate could handle it, better maybe than he could, but such things had no place in the park with his wife and children on a sunny day.

"Sorry," she sympathized, trying to read his voice for *signs*. "Sean?"

"Yeah."

"You okay?"

"I'm fine."

"You sure?"

He sighed again before continuing. "Just . . . the block the crime scene was in reminded me of . . . you know."

"Sean," she counseled, "a lot of things remind you of your childhood—that can't be helped. Your past will always be part of you—nothing can change that."

"I know," he assured her. "But the memories, the images are so much more real, vivid, when I'm in or close to a crime scene. Most of the time I can almost forget my childhood, but not when I'm in a place like that—not when I'm in a scene like that."

"I understand, but we've talked about this—many times. It becomes more vivid because you use your imagination as a tool, and when you open the door to your imagination, you're going to allow some demons out, Sean. It can't be helped, but it can be controlled—you've already shown that."

"I know," he admitted. "I'm fine."

"Why don't you come home a little early—have some *normal* time for a couple of hours—drink too much and fool around?"

"No chance of that," he told her. "Not for a few days yet, anyway."

"Any idea how long this one's going to take?"

"How long's a piece of string?"

"That's not good."

"Is it ever?"

"Yes," Kate told him. "When you're at home, with us— that's good."

"When I am there."

"Well, then be here. Remember, all work and no play makes Sean a—"

"Makes me a what?" he interrupted, thinly veiled anger suddenly in his voice.

"Nothing," she answered. "I was just . . . nothing. I have to go now—the kids have run off. I'll see you tonight. Be careful. I love you." The line went dead—dead before he had a chance to say sorry for snapping at her—before he had a chance to ask about the girls—before he had a chance to tell her he loved her too.

CHAPTER 6

Friday

Sean drove the car through heavy Central London traffic while Donnelly spoke, his notebook flipped open on his thigh. "The man we need to talk to works for some international finance company, Butler and Mason. After this morning's briefing, I popped into one of the nightclubs on the list. Place in Vauxhall. They were cleaning up last night's mess, but the head of security was still there. He also works the door at the club during opening hours." Sean listened without interrupting. Donnelly checked his notebook. "Stuart Young's the guy's name. Now, he says he knew our victim; not bosom buddies, but he knew him to speak to and he knew he worked the club for clients too."

"He was okay with that?" Sean asked.

"Apparently so. As far as he's concerned, it happens. If he tried to stop every bit of naughtiness that went on in the club they wouldn't stay in business too long." Sean raised his eyebrows. "And young Daniel was apparently subtle about it, didn't have too many clients, kept it all nice and low-key."

"If I was a cynic, I might suspect Mr. Young was turning a blind eye because Daniel was paying him to do so."

Donnelly continued. "Either way, Young confirms that Daniel was in Utopia on Wednesday night."

"Was he with anyone in particular?"

"Afraid not. According to Young, Daniel spent some time with a couple of his regulars, guys who have been going to the club for years."

"Have we spoken with them yet?"

"I spoke with them both myself. I gave Young my number and asked him to phone around to the victim's regular tricks. Among those who already got back to me are the men he was with Wednesday night." Donnelly flicked through his note-book again. "Sam Milford and a Benjamin Briggs. Both seemed pretty upset by the whole thing, both happy to provide samples. Neither great suspect material."

"Any other clients been in touch?"

"They certainly have. The grapevine has been working nicely for me, but they all seem much of a muchness—all very upset, all willing to cooperate. No great suspects yet, but maybe that'll change when I meet them face-to-face."

"But you don't think so, do you?"

Donnelly shrugged. "The victim's clients aren't looking too likely, so I did a little bit more digging."

"And?"

"Okay." Donnelly sounded like a mock game-show host. "Possible suspect number one—Steven Paramore, male, thirty-two years old, white. Sally had Paulo check local intelligence records and he found this guy, recently released from Belmarsh having just served eight years for the attempted murder of a teenage rent boy back in 2005. Apparently he almost beat the victim to death with his bare hands."

"Nice."

"After his release he went back to live with dear old mum, who I'm sure must be fucking delighted."

"What's his address?"

"Bardsley Lane, Deptford."

"Close to Graydon's flat," Sean said.

"Close enough," Donnelly agreed. "And he's a very angry man—served nearly a full sentence because of his bad behavior inside. It's also suspected he's a closet homosexual himself."

"Is that what you think our killer is?"

"What, a homosexual?"

"No. Angry."

"Don't you?"

"Maybe. Check him out anyway. In fact, have Paulo check him out—he dug him up."

"No problem. Now, moving on to suspect number two: Jonnie Dempsey, male, white, twenty-four years old, an Aussie, works as a barman in Utopia and is known to be a friend of Daniel's, although no suggestion yet he was anything more, but . . . Anyhow, he was supposed to be working the night Daniel was killed, only he didn't show. And he hasn't been seen since. The manager's been trying his mobile and home numbers relentlessly, but no joy. Jonnie Dempsey is very much missing. Daniel's secret lover?" Donnelly suggested.

"I don't know." Sean sounded unconvinced. "Like I said, this doesn't feel like a domestic."

"Maybe it's not," Donnelly half-agreed. "Maybe there's more to Jonnie Dempsey than anyone's giving him credit for?"

"Fine. Find him. Check him out. But neither Paramore nor Dempsey sound like they work at Butler and Mason International Finance, so why are we here? Whose day are we about to spoil?"

"The guy we're about to fall out with is called James Hellier." Sean noticed Donnelly didn't have to refer to his notebook to recall the name.

"And why should I be interested in James Hellier?" Sean asked, trying to clear his mind of the avalanche of admin and protocol he'd had to deal with since the investigation began. He needed a clear mind if he was going to have any chance of thinking freely and imaginatively.

"Show me a liar and a man with a lot to lose and I'll show you a pretty good suspect—Hellier's both those things."

"How so?"

"Stuart Young told me that Daniel generally liked to play it safe, keep to established, regular customers, so it's always a wee bit of a surprise when a new guy comes on the scene."

"And a new guy had come on the scene?"

"Aye," Donnelly explained. "Only appeared about a week ago. Kept himself to himself, didn't mix, didn't cause trouble either, but Young's pretty sure he had relations of the paying kind with Daniel at least once. He says he saw them outside the club, before they headed off together."

"Go on," Sean encouraged, listening more intently now, a mental picture of the man they were about to meet beginning to form in his thoughts. Not of his physical appearance, but of his state of mind, his possible motivation, his ability or not to take the life of a fellow man.

"Okay. First, Young told me he had asked Daniel about this newcomer a few nights after he'd seen them outside together— nothing heavy, just small talk. Daniel told him that the man was called David, no surname mentioned, and that he worked in the City and lived alone somewhere out west. But then things get a little more complicated. You see, Young was working the door the night the newcomer first appeared, when a regular punter came in, a"—Donnelly quickly checked his notebook again—"a Roger Bennett. Now Bennett, who's known Young for years, sees this newcomer David and makes for the exit sharpish. Young asks him if there's a problem and Bennett tells him there is, the problem being that Bennett knows our friend David."

"How?" Sean asked unnecessarily.

"Through work. Bennett works for a big men's magazine in the West End—you know the type of glossy rag, all cars and tits. Anyway, this new guy's been to his office a number of times to do their accounts."

"So?" Sean was growing impatient.

"The problem being, Bennett is gay, as you may have guessed, but he doesn't want anyone at work to find out. Apparently it wouldn't go down too well in his office. So he decamps from the club and asks Young to give him a ring if and when David disappears from the scene.

"No big deal, but I figure if this David's been with the victim, we need to speak to him anyway. So Young gives me Bennett's number and I give him a ring and ask him where I can find this David. He tells me he doesn't have the foggiest what I'm talking about, but when I remind him of the night he left the club on the hurry-up, et cetera, et cetera, it all comes back to him and he opens up. And guess what he tells me?"

Sean answered immediately. "He's not called David and he doesn't work in the City."

Donnelly froze for a second, a little deflated that Sean had made the leap without needing any more information. "Dead right, Bennett reckons that David's real name is James Hellier and he works for Butler and Mason International Finance. But you already knew that, didn't you?"

Sean didn't answer. "What you didn't know," Donnelly continued, a satisfied smile spreading across his face, "is that, according to Bennett, Hellier also has a wife and a couple of kiddies. Interested?"

"Hmm," Sean replied. He was interested. "Like you said, 'Show me a liar and a man with a lot to lose . . .' But this doorman, Young, did he ever see Hellier in the club before that night, or after?"

"No, but he doesn't work there every night."

"CCTV?"

"Their system's ancient—still runs on VHS, if you can believe it. They reuse the tapes after seven days. The tapes from last week are already recorded over, but we can check the current tapes to see if he's been there anytime during the last few days."

"Get it done," Sean told him as they pulled up outside an old Georgian mansion block converted into exclusive offices. Identical buildings ran the length of the long road, all painted white with black-trimmed windows and doors adorned with heavy, shiny brass numbers. Pointed metal railings fenced off the entrances to the basements, curling up and along the short flights of stairs leading to the front door, where visitors were met by pristine brass plates announcing the company within. Only Arabs and the aristocracy could afford to actually live here now.

The two detectives climbed from their Ford and walked across the pavement to the building's entrance. "Here we go, Butler and Mason International Finance. Shall we?" Donnelly rang the outside security buzzer. They didn't have to wait long. A female voice crackled back from the intercom. "Butler and Mason. Good morning. How can I help?"

"Detective Inspector Corrigan and Detective Sergeant Donnelly from the Metropolitan Police." Donnelly deliberately avoided stating they were from the Murder Investigation Team. "Here to see a Mr. James Hellier." He made it sound as if they had an appointment. It didn't work.

"Is he expecting you?" came the voice through the small metal box. Donnelly looked at Sean and shrugged his shoulders. Time to put a little pressure on.

"No. He's not expecting us, but I can assure you he will want to see us."

Whoever it was on the intercom wasn't easily bullied. "Can I ask what it's in connection with, please?"

"It's a private matter concerning Mr. Hellier," Donnelly told her. "We believe someone may have stolen some checks from him. We need to speak with him before someone empties his bank account." The threat of losing money usually opened doors.

"I see. Please come in."

The door buzzed. Donnelly pushed it open. They passed through a second security door and into the reception area of Butler and Mason, where they were met by a tall, attractive young woman. She wore expensive-looking spectacles and an equally expensive-looking tailored suit. Her hair was hazelnut brown and tied back in a perfect ponytail. Sean thought she looked unreal.

"The voice on the intercom, I assume?" Donnelly asked. She smiled a perfect, practiced smile that meant nothing.

"Good morning, gentlemen. If I could just see your identification, please?"

Neither Sean nor Donnelly had their identification ready. Donnelly rolled his eyes as they fished their small black leather wallets from inside jacket pockets and presented them flipped open to the secretary.

"Thank you." She looked up at them after examining the identification more closely than they were used to. "If you would like to follow me, Mr. Hellier has agreed to see you straightaway. His office is on the top floor, so I suggest we take the lift."

Clearly Hellier was doing well for himself. They followed her to the lift, where she pulled open the old-fashioned concertina grid and then the lift doors. She stepped inside and waited for them to join her before pressing the button for the top level. They moved silently up through the building until the lift juddered to a halt. She opened the doors and another grid. Sean was losing patience with the charade. They stepped out into the upper reaches of the building and walked along the opulent corridors without talking, the high ceilings providing plenty of wall space to hang portraits of people long since dead. The entire office reeked of money and was much bigger inside than they had expected. Eventually they arrived at a large mahogany door. The nameplate attached bore the inscription JAMES HELLIER. JUNIOR PARTNER. The secretary knocked twice before pushing the door open without waiting for a reply. "Some gentlemen from the police to see you, sir."

James Hellier was as elegant as the secretary. A little under six feet. About forty years old, athletic build. Light brown hair, immaculately cut. He looked healthy and fit in the way the rich do. Good food. Good holidays. Expensive gyms and skin-care products. His suit probably cost more than Sean earned in a month. Maybe two.

Hellier held out a hand. "James Hellier. Miss Collins said something about my checks being stolen, but I really don't think that's likely, you see—"

The secretary had already left the office and closed the door. Sean cut across Hellier. "That's not actually why we're here, Mr. Hellier. Your checks are fine. We need to ask you a few questions, but we thought it best to be discreet until we had a chance to speak with you."

Sean was studying him. In an inquiry like this a witness could turn into a suspect within seconds. Was he looking at the killer of Daniel Graydon?

"I hope you haven't come here to try and obtain client details. If you have, then I hope you've brought a production order with you."

"No, Mr. Hellier. It's about your visits to the Utopia club."

Hellier sat down slowly. "Excuse me. I'm not familiar with that club. The only club I belong to, other than my golf club, is Home House in Portman Square. Perhaps you know it?"

Sean was trying to judge the man. He was sure Hellier was lying, but he sounded remarkably confident. "DS Donnelly here's been making some inquiries at the club. You've been recognized."

"Who by?" Hellier asked.

"I'm not prepared to tell you that at this time."

"I see," Hellier said, smiling. "A silent accuser then."

"No. Just someone who wants to remain anonymous for now."

"Well, whoever it is, they're lying. I can assure you I've never heard of a club called Utopia."

"Mr. Hellier, I've had all the club's CCTV tapes from the last couple of weeks seized. As we speak, some of my officers are going through them. They'll be producing stills of all the people on the tapes. How sure are you that when I look through those stills I am not going to see a picture of you? Because if I do, I am going to start wondering why you're lying. Do you understand?"

There was a long pause before Hellier answered. "Who put you up to this?" he eventually asked in a calm voice. "Who paid you to follow me? Was it my wife?"

Sean and Donnelly looked at each other, confused. "Mr. Hellier," Sean explained, "this is a murder investigation. We're police officers, not private investigators. We're investigating the murder of Daniel Graydon. He was killed on Wednesday night, Thursday morning, in his flat. I believe you knew Daniel. Is that correct?"

"Murdered?" Hellier asked through gritted teeth. "I'm sorry. I had no idea. How did it . . . ?"

Sean watched every flicker in Hellier's face, every hand and finger movement, every sign that could tell him whether Hellier's shock was genuine. Did he sense any trace of compassion? "He was stabbed to death in his own flat," Sean told him and waited for the reaction.

"Do you know who did it—and why, for God's sake?"

"No," Sean answered as his mind processed Hellier's performance—and that was what he was sure it was. As polished as it was, as convincing as it was, a performance nonetheless. "Actually, we thought you might be able to help us with the who and why."

"I'm sorry, but I really don't see how. I hardly knew Daniel. I know nothing about his life. We had a brief physical relationship, nothing more."

"Did he know you were married?" Sean asked.

"No, I don't think so. How could he?"

"You're a wealthy man. Did he know anything about your financial circumstances?" Sean picked up the pace of his questioning.

"Not as far as I'm aware," Hellier answered quickly and confidently.

"Did Daniel Graydon at any time try to extort money or other favors from you, Mr. Hellier?"

"Look, I think I know where you're going with this, Inspector . . . sorry, I can't remember your name."

"Corrigan. Sean Corrigan."

"Well, Inspector Corrigan, I think my solicitor should be present before I say anything."

Donnelly leaned in toward him. "That's fine, Mr. Hellier. You can have a panel of judges present, for all I care, but you're a witness right now. Not a suspect. So why do you need a solicitor? And I don't know for sure, but I suspect your wife is un-aware of your nocturnal activities. And what about the other partners here at this lovely firm? Do they know you have a taste for young male prostitutes? I guess it's all a question of how much you trust your solicitor to show absolute discretion. And me too."

Hellier stared hard at the two intruders into his life, small intelligent eyes darting between the detectives, before suddenly standing up. "All right. All right. Please keep your voices down." He sat down again. "I went there once, about a week ago, but please, my wife mustn't find out. It would destroy her. Our children would become laughingstocks. They shouldn't be punished for my weaknesses." He paused. "It may be difficult for you to understand, but I do love my wife and children, I just have other needs. I have suppressed them for more than twenty years, but recently I . . . I couldn't seem to stop myself."

"When did you last see Daniel Graydon?" Sean asked.

"I can't remember exactly."

"Try harder."

"A week or so ago."

"We need to know exactly when and where, Mr. Hellier," Sean insisted.

"Try checking your diary, iPhone, or whatever it is you use," Donnelly suggested.

"It won't be in my diary," Hellier told them sharply. "I'm sure you understand why."

"But something will be," Sean said. "A false business meeting, a dinner with clients that never took place. You would have put something in there to cover yourself."

Hellier studied Sean, their eyes unconsciously locked together. He reached for his iPad with a sigh. His finger slid around the screen and within seconds he found what he was looking for—a false overnight meeting in Zurich. "The last time I saw Daniel was a week ago last Tuesday—what, ten days ago?"

"Where?" Sean pressed.

"In Utopia."

"Did you ever go to his flat?"

"No."

Sean felt like being cruel. "And did you pay him to have sex with you in the club or somewhere else?"

"I pay for sex because it's less complicated. Keeps things simple. I can't risk being involved in a relationship. That would make me vulnerable. You needn't look so disgusted, Inspector. I don't like the fact that I pay for sex. I don't like the fact that I abuse the trust of family and friends. I keep things simple for all our sakes."

"So where did you have sex with him?"

"I've admitted having sex with him—isn't that enough?"

"Are you absolutely sure you didn't go back to his flat, ever?" Sean asked.

"Positive."

"And Wednesday night. Where were you Wednesday night?" Sean continued.

Hellier paused before answering, his eyes narrowing. "You don't . . . you don't seriously think I had anything to do with his death, do you?" He looked both incredulous and frustrated.

"I just need to know where you were," Sean repeated with an almost friendly smile.

"Well, if you must know, I was at home all night. I had a pile of paperwork to catch up on, so I left here at about six and went straight home, where I spent most of the night working in my study."

"Can anyone verify that?"

"My wife. We had dinner together, but, like I said, I spent most of the night working, alone."

"Then we need to speak to your wife," Sean insisted.

"Look," Hellier snapped. "Am I a suspect or not?"

"No, Mr. Hellier," Sean answered. "You're a witness, until I say otherwise. But we'll still need to speak with your wife."

"Don't worry," Donnelly reassured Hellier. "We won't tell her what we're investigating."

"Then what will you tell her?"

"Oh, I don't know. That we're looking into an identity fraud, a case of mistaken identity," Donnelly offered. "The sooner she can confirm you were at home Wednesday night, the sooner we can clear the whole mess up. Fair enough?"

"You do want to help us, don't you, Mr. Hellier?" Sean asked.

Hellier sat silently for a time before leaning forward and snatching a pen and paper. He quickly scribbled something down and pushed the paper toward Donnelly. "My wife's name and my home address," he said. "I assume a phone call wouldn't satisfy you gentlemen."

"Much obliged," Donnelly said, slipping the note into his jacket pocket.

"Will she be at home now?" Sean asked.

"Possibly," Hellier answered.

"Good" was all Sean replied.

"And when my wife verifies that I was at home, I'm assuming that will be the end of it."

Sean almost laughed. "No, Mr. Hellier, it's a little more complicated than that. We need you to come to the station within the next two days. Whenever is convenient for you will be fine. Bring that solicitor too, if you want."

"But I've told you all I know," Hellier argued. "I'm sorry, but I really can't help you."

"You had sex with a young man who's now dead," Sean told him. "Murdered. We've taken samples from the victim's body. Forensic samples. If you had sex with him within the last couple of weeks, part of you could still be on the victim. We need to eliminate any foreign samples found on the body that may have been left by you."

"That really won't be necessary. I always used a condom. I may be foolish, but I'm not mad. You won't find any . . ." Hellier stalled, trying to think of suitable words. " . . . thing belonging to me on his body. You don't need to examine me."

Sean stood up and leaned in close to Hellier. "Oh yes I do, Mr. Hellier. And you will give me what I need. If you don't, then I'll arrest you on suspicion of murder and take the samples anyway. I'll get a warrant and search your home. I'll search this office—and we won't be as discreet about our business as we've been so far."

He wasn't bluffing; the more serious the offense, the more he could stretch his powers to the limit. He opened his wallet, took out one of his business cards, and threw it on the desk. "That's my office and mobile numbers. You have a day to call me. And I'll require a full written statement from you at the same time. You'll have to tell us about your relationship with Daniel Graydon. Absolutely everything. One day to call, Mr. Hellier, and then—"

The door to Hellier's office unexpectedly swung open. Another well-dressed man entered the office without asking. Sean assumed the rich-looking man in his late thirties or early forties had to be Hellier's boss. He gave the man the once-over, taking in details only a cop would see. He did it to everybody nearly all the time, an occupational hazard he was almost unaware of. The man had purpose and poise, and not just because of his physical presence: he was at least six feet tall, strong and fit, his tailored suit not disguising his deep chest and slim waist. But he also had an aura about him, a sense of power and control. Sean knew the man would be the sort of boss his underlings would both fear and love.

"James." The well-dressed man spoke into the room. "I heard about the theft. I trust you got hold of your bank before the bastards had a chance to cash any checks?" The man's voice matched everything else about him: authoritative and dominating, but soothing and reassuring at the same time. Sean felt it was almost gravitational, drawing whoever he was talking to toward him, like a brilliant actor performing on the stage.

"Yes. Yes, I did. Panic over," Hellier told him.

The well-dressed man thrust out a hand toward Sean and Donnelly. "Sebastian Gibran. Senior partner here. Always a pleasure to help the police in any way we can. Any idea who you're looking for?"

"No. Not yet," said Sean, shaking his hand, feeling a little thrown off center by Gibran's very presence. The handshake was firm, but not overpowering, although Sean believed Gibran could have crushed his hand if he'd wanted to.

"Well, anything we can do to help, just let me know." Gibran's smile was perfect—straight white teeth that shone almost as brightly as his eyes—and radiated warmth and charm, all wrapped in a protective sheath of power.

"Thank you. I will," Sean replied. "Don't get up, Mr. Hellier. We'll let ourselves out. And thanks for your time." Both detectives stood to leave the office.

"Allow me to show you out," Gibran offered.

"We'll be fine," Sean said, keen to be away so that he and Donnelly could begin to speak freely. "I'm sure you're very busy."

"I insist," Gibran argued, once again flashing his mouthful of brilliant white teeth. "Please, follow me."

Sean and Donnelly followed Gibran, who smiled and nodded his acknowledgment to staff members they passed, using Christian names to greet each and every one. Sean had worked in the same office for over two years and still struggled to remember everyone's name. Gibran's smoothness only made

Sean dislike him all the more. When they were alone, Gibran spoke again. "Where did you say you were from?"

"We informed Mr. Hellier of where we are from," Sean responded.

"I'm sure you did," Gibran replied. "But you didn't tell me."

"Our dealings with Mr. Hellier are confidential," Sean said firmly. "If he wants to tell you more, that's up to him."

"If James is involved in anything that could damage the reputation of this institution, then I should be informed, Inspector," Gibran argued. "Look," he said, taking a conciliatory tone, the smile back in place, "a lot of people rely on me for their welfare and security in these uncertain times. It is my responsibility to protect their interests. The need of the many is greater than the need of the individual."

"Meaning if Hellier looks like he's going to be bad for business, you'll throw him to the wolves," Donnelly accused.

Gibran stared hard at Donnelly before speaking again. "James is very privileged to have both a detective inspector and a detective sergeant investigating what appears to be a minor theft." He watched Sean and Donnelly look at each other; it was only a glance, but he noticed it. "Really, you didn't think I was that stupid, did you?"

Sean had no answer and felt he needed to counter, to try and knock Gibran out of his stride. "What did you say you do here?" Sean asked. "International finance—what exactly does that mean?"

"Nothing the police need to be concerned about," Gibran answered. "We help people and organizations raise capital for various business projects, no more. You know, oil people wanting to move into the building and property markets, property people wanting to move into the tech markets, and now and then someone literally walks in off the street with a brilliant idea but no funds. We'll help them obtain those funds."

"Well, that all sounds very noble," Donnelly chipped in.

"We're not part of the banking system," Gibran assured them. "There's no need for animosity here."

Sean looked him up and down. He had no more he wanted to say. "Good-bye, Mr. Gibran. It was a pleasure meeting you."

He could feel Gibran's eyes watching them as they finally escaped into the lift, the streets below beckoning them. Sean needed to drag Hellier out of his natural comfort zone and into his world, away from protectors like Sebastian Gibran. Then and only then would they see the real James Hellier.

James Hellier stood by his office window looking down on the detectives in the street below. He was careful not to be seen. He paid special attention to Sean. He disliked him, sensed the danger in him, but he felt no anger toward him. In his own way he appreciated him—appreciated a worthy adversary who would make the game all the more fun to play. They thought they were clever, but they weren't going to ruin things for him. He would make sure of it.

He cursed under his breath—somehow he'd been recognized at the damn nightclub and he wondered who by. He should have been more careful. It was unfortunate, but not entirely unexpected. He needed to stay calm. They had nothing on him. Police talk and threats meant nothing. He would wait and see if anything developed. He wouldn't panic and run. There was no need. Not yet.

But he would have to be careful of Gibran too. Trust him to come and stick his nose in where it wasn't wanted. He thought he was so fucking clever, senior partner at Butler and Mason, the self-appointed sheriff of the company. If it came to it, he would be long gone before Gibran found out. Gibran should remember who gave him a job at Butler and Mason in the first place. It was Gibran who personally checked his references, glowing reports from previous employers in the United States and Far East. Only thing was, not a single one of them was real. If Gibran had actually gotten on a plane to check Hellier's background properly, he would have eventually discovered that Hellier's previous employment history was a myth. But he knew Gibran would rely on telephone calls and e-mails, all of which were easily arranged, especially for someone like Hellier: he had friends in low places and dirt on some in high places. Gibran had been no more difficult to fool than any of the others. And while Hellier might never have been to university to study accounting or high finance, what he'd learned on the streets, what he'd learned in order to survive, had left him more than qualified to work anywhere he liked.

Hellier moved away from the window and sat back in his desk chair, his hands pyramided in front of his face. He liked his life, he liked all the privileges being James Hellier brought and the cover it provided for his other activities, past, present, and future. He wasn't going to let Inspector Corrigan or, for that matter, Sebastian Gibran, spoil it for him now, not after all these years. He loved to play the game. He enjoyed the money, but it was the game he loved, and this one wasn't lost yet.

Sean and Donnelly sat in their car outside Hellier's office building. "Well?" Donnelly asked. "What d'you think about Mr. James Hellier? Did you get a feel for him?"

"He's a smooth bastard," Sean replied. "And so was his boss, for that matter. Like a couple of fucking clones. But Hellier, he's trying to be something he's not, whereas Gibran's persona seemed genuine, effortless. We'll have to watch out for him. He looks like the sort who'll be wanting to stick his nose into our investigation. As for Hellier, behind the suit and haircut there's an angry man." He didn't tell Donnelly about the animalistic odor he'd smelled leaking through Hellier's skin. A musky smell, almost chokingly strong. The same odor he'd smelled on others in the past. Other killers. "But why is he so pissed off with the world?"

"Pissed off with the world?" Donnelly questioned. "I thought he was just pissed off with us."

Sean realized he was moving too fast for Donnelly. "You're probably right." He needed to give Donnelly something more tangible, more logical. "But there are already two possible motives for him. First, he was having an intimate relationship with Graydon, and somewhere along the line it went wrong."

"So we're back to a lovers' tiff?"

"Or," Sean continued, "Graydon was blackmailing him and Hellier thought, probably correctly, the only way to make it stop would be to get rid of him. He's a walking blackmail victim and Graydon liked nice things—remember his flat?"

"And the seventy-seven stab wounds?" Donnelly asked. Those needed explaining. "If he just wanted him out of the way, why not do it nice and neat—one shot, one well-placed knife wound, strangulation? Makes me favor a domestic bust-up."

"No," Sean reminded him. "Remember what Dr. Canning told us—the wounds were placed around the body, almost ritually, as if the killer wanted us to think it was a rage attack to get us chasing our tails looking for a jealous ex-boyfriend. Or even a motiveless stranger's attack. That and the lack of forensics at the scene leave me thinking it was premeditated, which means blackmail was his most likely motivation. Or something else we haven't thought of yet. Everything else was staged."

Donnelly looked less than completely convinced. "Well, in the absence of anything better than a missing barman and a recently released homophobic homosexual, it's worth running with, so long as you're convinced Hellier has it in him to kill."

"Let's just say I get a very bad feeling about him," Sean replied. "His attempted show of compassion made me feel sick.

Everything about him seemed off, as if he was hiding behind the facade of being a happy family man."

"Why are you so sure he was faking it? I thought he registered some real surprise that Daniel had been killed."

"False sincerity. I've seen that too many times."

Donnelly had worked with Sean long enough to know that sometimes it was best to simply accept his word and move on. "You're a scary individual," he said. "Now all we need is the evidence to prove your theory."

"That's the hard part, as always."

"Arrest him. Search his house, office, car. Get a look at his bank accounts. Compare his prints and samples to anything and everything from the scene."

"No," Sean insisted. "I sensed no panic when we asked him about being in the flat. He knows he's left it clean. Or maybe I'm wrong and he's never been there. Anyway, we're getting ahead of ourselves. I need to know more before I draw any lasting conclusions. Let's have him followed for a while."

"Round-the-clock surveillance?" Donnelly asked.

"Starting as soon as possible," Sean confirmed. "He may have missed something. Something that could betray him. If we're lucky he'll lead us to something that'll hang him or at least give us grounds to dig further."

"If we're very lucky," Donnelly pointed out.

"Right now we don't have much else, so let's start digging into his past. A man like Hellier doesn't just appear. Have criminal and intelligence records checked, see if Mr. Hellier here hasn't got some skeletons in his closet."

"What about Inland Revenue, employment records, general background information?"

"Not yet. We haven't got enough for production orders. Let's stick to our own records first—see what we can turn up."

"It'll be done," Donnelly told him. "Anything else?"

"Yeah," Sean answered. "You take the car and get back to the office. Concentrate on tracking down the rest of the victim's clients and let me know as soon as you turn up someone or something interesting."

"Fine. And yourself?"

"I'm going to have a little chat with his wife."

Sean took the tube from Knightsbridge to King's Cross, noting all possible CCTV points that Hellier could have passed, including those covering the taxi rank outside the station, where Hellier probably hopped into a cab for the last leg of his journey home, although from here their journeys differed—Sean traveling the rest of the way by bus. Black cabs were an expensive luxury for him, not a realistic mode of transport. Not so for Hellier. Even so, it hadn't taken him long to get to Hellier's place: 10 Devonia Road, Islington, close to Upper Street and the Angel underground station.

Hellier's house was another beautiful Georgian town house and looked like a much smaller version of the Butler and Mason office building. Sean was beginning to feel undervalued and underpaid, but at least the time alone had settled his racing mind and allowed him space to clear his thoughts. He bounced up the steps and gently tapped the chrome knocker twice. After an acceptable wait a woman opened the door. "Hello" was all she said. Sean had expected her to say more. He showed her his identification and tried to look as unofficial as he could.

"Sorry to bother you. I'm Detective Inspector Corrigan, Metropolitan Police."

"Oh," she replied, attempting to feign surprise. So Hellier had called and warned her. No matter. Sean had assumed he would—that wasn't why he was here. He was here for a chance at a snapshot into Hellier's life.

"Mrs. Hellier?" Sean asked, smiling.

"Yes. Elizabeth. Is there a problem?"

Sean was struck by how much she looked and sounded like a female version of James Hellier: tall, slim, attractive, well spoken, the product of finishing school and two skiing holidays a year, the best of everything her whole life, but unlike with Hellier he could sense her naiveté. Was that why Hellier had married her?

"Nothing to worry about," Sean lied. "I'm just looking into an identity fraud case. We think someone may be trying to pass himself off as your husband, James."

"Really?" she asked.

"I'm afraid so. They tried to make a substantial purchase in Harrods on Wednesday evening. I've already spoken to your husband and he says he was home all night with you. If you could confirm that, then I'll know for sure the person we have in custody is lying to us."

"But if you've already spoken to my husband, why do you need me to confirm he was at home?"

Naive, but not stupid, Sean thought. "I like to be thorough. Maybe we should discuss this inside," he suggested, hoping to see Hellier's things, to walk in the skin of James Hellier, even for a few minutes.

"That's not really convenient right now. My children will be home from their tennis lesson any second. I wouldn't want them to start worrying. I'm sure you understand. But I can tell you that James was here on Wednesday, although I hardly saw him. He was working in his office most of the night."

Sean couldn't stop himself from looking past her into the house and sensed her trying to grow large to prevent him. She wanted him to stay out of her family's life.

"Of course," he said. "I understand—and thank you. You've been very helpful. Well, I'll leave you in peace." He turned to leave, then quickly turned back, speaking before the door

closed on the opportunity. "One more thing . . ." He registered
the annoyance on her face, the slight flushing of the facial capil-
laries, only minutely visible beneath her tanned skin. He waved
his finger vaguely at the front of the house and spoke casually.
"I was wondering, which room is your husband's office?"

She stumbled. Clearly her husband hadn't warned her to expect this type of question. "Does it matter?"

"No," Sean replied, smiling. "Not really." He waited, not
moving, knowing she would give in to the silence.

"This one here," she said, surrendering, pointing to one of
the front ground-floor windows, eager to be rid of him.

"Ah," he said. "If I had a house like this, that's where I'd have
my office too." Satisfied, he knew it was time to leave. He had
sown the seeds of doubt in her and she would sow the seeds of
fear into Hellier. He imagined the panicked conversation she
would have with her husband later that day, both questioning
each other, doubting each other. "Well, I've taken up enough of
your time. Good-bye, Mrs. Hellier. Tell James I said hello." She
didn't respond. He heard the door slam before he reached the
last step.

Sean made the long journey on public transportation from Islington back to Peckham, jealously watching the vast majority
of his fellow commuters wearily heading off for the weekend
while he was heading back to work, all thoughts of home and
rest still just a distant hope. He'd had little more than six hours'
sleep in the last two nights and knew the next few days would
be no better. Reminding himself to buy some caffeine pills, he
used the public entrance to the police station and climbed the
stairs to the incident room without acknowledging anyone.
As he crossed the room toward his office he casually observed
who was there and who was missing. He assumed those not
there would be running down whatever inquiries Donnelly

had assigned them. He entered his office and sat heavily in his chair. Within seconds Donnelly was at his open door, a heavy bundle of witness statements and completed actions cradled in his arms. He didn't seem to feel the weight.

"How'd you get on with Hellier's trouble and strife?"

"She's lying for him," Sean answered. "Said he was home all night. I got the feeling it wasn't the first time she's covered for him."

"Aye, but does she know what we're investigating?"

"Not unless Hellier's told her, which I doubt."

"So technically he has an alibi."

"Yeah, but you could drive a bus through it. She said he was in his office all night, alone. It's on the ground floor next to the front door. He could have slipped out and back easy."

"But you don't think he went home, do you?"

"No, I don't," Sean confirmed. "What have you turned up?"

"Well, from a criminal records point of view, Hellier's as clean as a whistle. Not even a parking ticket, as far as I can tell. He's been working at Butler and Mason for a few years now; before that he was working for some American company in New York, and prior to that he worked in Hong Kong and Singapore."

"Where d'you get all that from?" Sean asked, impressed.

"I Googled him," Donnelly answered with a wry smile. "Technology. Our greatest friend and our greatest enemy. Oh, and I called a pal of mine at Revenue and Customs—asked for a cheeky favor. As far as they're concerned, he's legit. Since being back in the UK he's paid his taxes on time and up front, no problems."

Sean looked disappointed, although he hadn't really expected anything else. "With his taste in after-work pleasures you'd think he'd be a little bit shy about plastering his face all over the Internet," Sean suggested.

"No photographs," Donnelly told him. "Lots of info, but no photographs."

"He's a careful one," Sean said. "Just like whoever killed Graydon. Very careful."

"Plenty of people working in the financial sector have taken their mug shots off the Internet since the banking crisis."

"Yeah, but Hellier's a financier, not a banker."

"Guv'nor," Donnelly reminded him, "we live in a country where seventy percent of the population don't know the difference between a pedophile and a pediatrician."

Sean sighed. "A good point well made." He rubbed his eyes hard enough to make them water before rummaging in his desk drawers for painkillers. "What about the others who were with him on the night he was killed?" he asked without looking at Donnelly.

"Most have come forward now or been traced," Donnelly answered, "but nothing interesting. One or two are known to police, but all for minor stuff. We've gathered a small mountain of forensics and fingerprints for comparisons, so you never know."

"Maybe, but I'm not feeling particularly lucky right now," Sean sighed. "What about our two missing persons?" he asked. "What were their names again?"

"Steven Paramore and the barman, Jonnie Dempsey. We've checked at the home addresses of both. Paramore's mum says he hasn't been home for a few days now and James's flatmates are saying the same about him."

"Untraceable suspects," Sean complained. "That's all I need."

"Maybe this'll cheer you up." Donnelly grinned as he dumped the heavy pile of papers he'd been holding on Sean's desk.

Sean spread his arms in protest. "What's this?"

"Witness statements so far, completed actions, and other

assorted shit that you ought to read. Superintendent Feather-stone wants a full briefing in the morning."

Sean sank deep into his chair, all thoughts of home comforts slipping farther and farther away. It was going to be another long evening alone, with only the image of Daniel Graydon's defiled body for company.

Hours later Sean arrived home exhausted but wide awake, the worst possible combination. He was in need of a strong drink, something that would instantly slow his mind and body without filling his bladder. If sleep came he didn't want it chased away by having to get up to urinate.

Kate had waited up for him. He wished she hadn't. He didn't want to talk. He wanted a drink, a sandwich, and to watch some trash on TV. He passed the living room where his wife sat, speaking into the room as he headed for the kitchen. "It's only me."

After a few seconds Kate followed him into the kitchen. "You're back late," she said, her tone neutral.

"I'm sorry," Sean replied, conscious that he seemed to be saying that more and more. "You know what it's like when I get a new case—first few days are always a nightmare."

"A nightmare for who?" Kate asked, her words more provocative than she had intended.

"I don't know," Sean answered. "For me? For you? For the guy who's just had his skull smashed in, dead before his life's even started? For his parents, who have to come to terms with the fact that their only child is gone and never coming back?"

An oppressive silence gripped the room. Kate took a breath. "Are you okay?"

Sean accepted the truce. "Yeah. Of course. I'm tired and grumpy, that's all. Sorry. Are the kids asleep?"

"It's after eleven. What sort of mother would I be if they

weren't?" She moved toward him. He had his back to her while he looked around for a glass. She put her arms around his waist. He was in good shape for a man in his late thirties. He had the physique of a middleweight boxer, a legacy from his teenage years. The sport had been one of the things that had kept him out of trouble while too many of his childhood friends turned to a life of crime. "I'm glad you're home," she said. He leaned back into her.

"I'm glad too. Sorry. I should have called. Must have lost track of time. How's Mandy? Will she forgive me?"

"Well, she's only three. You've plenty of time to make it up. But never mind little Miss Mandy. What about me? How are you going to make it up to me?"

Sean was smiling slightly. "I'll buy you a bunch of flowers."

"Not good enough, Detective Inspector. I was thinking of something a bit more immediate and a lot more fun."

Kate led him to the stairs and made for their bedroom. As Sean's foot reached the top step he heard a voice coming from Mandy's room.

"Daddy."

He looked apologetically at his wife. "I'd better stick my head in," he whispered.

Kate slipped her shirt off, her brown skin shining in the semidarkness. "Don't be long," she said. "I might fall asleep."

Sean quietly entered Mandy's room, the night-light illuminating a small pajama-clad figure. She grinned uncontrollably when she saw him. "Daddy."

"Hey, hey, sweetie. You're supposed to be asleep," Sean reminded her.

"I was waiting for you to come home, Daddy."

"No, you mustn't do that, because sometimes Daddy doesn't get home until very late."

"Why don't you get home till late, Daddy?"

"Now is not the time to talk about it, honey. We'll talk about it tomorrow."

"Mummy says you're catching bad men."

"Does she?" Sean said, not meaning it to be a question.

"What have the bad men done, Daddy?"

"Nothing that you should be worried about," he lied. "Go to sleep now. Daddy is here. Daddy is always here."

Sean found himself stroking her hair. He watched her eyes flicker shut, but even when he knew she was asleep he couldn't leave her. Kate would understand. He needed this—needed something to balance the horror of what he dealt with day in, day out. Needed something to suppress the darkness that always lurked just beneath the surface.

CHAPTER 7

There were three others before the little queer. I've already told you about the solicitor type I stabbed in the heart. That means there are two I've not mentioned.

The first was a young girl. Seventeen or eighteen. I'd parked forty meters from the entrance to an abortion clinic. I didn't have to wait long. These places do a good trade.

This clinic was in Battersea. Quite far from where I live. It was a low-rise, modern sandstone building. Very discreet. It was not far from Battersea Rise. Close to Clapham Common. Nice in the summer. Lots of traffic though, and too many mahogany-skinned immigrants fleeing poverty, war, and starvation.

I knew exactly what I was waiting for, and then, there she was. It was a few weeks ago and wasn't as warm as it is now. She hurried along the pavement. Collar turned up against the mild chill as well as to hide her face. She entered the clinic with her head bowed.

I waited for her. A couple of hours and there she came. Hurrying back along the pavement. I could smell her shame. Probably a Catholic. I hope so.

I caught up with her soon enough, keeping pace, about five

meters back. She was too trapped in her own private hell to feel my presence.

I was close enough to see her properly now. She was slightly built. Good. And she was clearly crying. Good. She was also alone. What type of young girl would come here alone? Simple. One who hasn't told anybody about her little problem. So Mummy and Daddy didn't know yet. She was perfect. All she needed to do was keep walking in the direction we were heading. I'd already checked out several routes away from the clinic and most had possibilities. But there was a nice concealed railway line on this one, running under a bridge, hidden from the road above. Close to the scene of the Clapham railway disaster.

I was wearing a raincoat I'd bought, with cash, from Marks & Spencer on Oxford Street a few months ago and hadn't worn until then. It was a common enough coat. Nothing special. Deliberately so. I also wore brand-new plain leather-soled men's shoes and had a pair of leather gloves nestled in one coat pocket. A large bin liner was stuffed into the other pocket.

I had to get the next bit exactly right, or this would be over before it began. We approached the break in the roadside wall that led down to the railway. I put the gloves on. I had to move fast now. Anyone around and this was off.

I ran the short distance between us and punched her as hard as I could in the center of her back. I felt her spine give way to my fist. I heard the air rush from her lungs. She couldn't make a sound. She dropped to her knees.

I grabbed her from behind and pulled her through the break in the wall. She was no match for me, but I couldn't risk being caught by a flailing arm. If she had scratched me, I would have cut her fingers off and taken them with me rather than make a present of my skin, my DNA, for the police.

The way down to the railway lines was exactly what I'd been looking for. I discovered it a while ago when I was out scouting for good spots. The bank fell away steeply, but not so steeply as to stop you walking down. But the best bit was that up against the arch of the bridge there was a concrete ledge, a meter wide, on the ground. Past that there was only soil and dust. It meant I could make the girl walk on the soil, hence leaving her footprints, while I walked on the concrete in my plain shoes, leaving none. It would appear as if she'd walked the last walk of her pitiful life alone.

I dragged her to the bottom of the bridge arch and pushed her against the side of it. I stared into her eyes, hard. They were green and beautiful. She was terrified. The art I imagined was becoming reality. I decided she wouldn't give me any trouble. I spoke gently.

"If you make a sound or fight or try and run, I will hurt you. Do you understand?" I was calm.

She frantically nodded her head. Then she squeaked out a few pathetic words. "Please. Don't rape me. Please. I've just had an operation. Please. I won't tell anyone. Please."

"I won't hurt you," I promised. "I need you to stand there quietly for a few seconds." I could hear the train lines begin to whistle and knew a fast train was approaching. I peeked around the corner and saw the train flying toward me. I'd timed this already. Once it passed the hut on the siding, I had five seconds before it hurtled past me.

I gripped the girl by her right arm with both my hands. Five. Four. Three. Two—and I swung her out from behind the bridge arch.

It was as if she jogged out onto the line. She even managed to avoid tripping over the first rail. She made it all the way between the tracks.

The train that hit her must have looked huge. I saw her stiffen just before it wiped her from the face of the planet. I wonder what she thought, if anything.

I didn't wait to see where her body landed. I quickly turned and ran up the railway bank. I was well protected from anyone looking out of the train window. I'd had my fun, but ultimately the poetry was lacking. The violence was too mechanical. I hadn't been able to see her eyes or hear her last breath as the train ripped the life from her. The work lacked feeling. No texture. No color. I would do better next time.

I wonder where the train was going.

As I drove away, I could hear the first sirens approaching. A few days later there was a sad little article in the *Evening Standard* about a girl who'd had an abortion then killed herself by jumping in front of a train. Apparently all parties had decided she couldn't live with the guilt. The shame. She still had a receipt for the abortion in her pocket. The last line of the article read, "Police are not looking for anyone else in connection with her death."

CHAPTER 8

Saturday

S ean was in his car, on his way to the station, when his phone rang. The display showed no number. It made him cautious. He answered without giving his name. "Hello?"

"I need to speak with Detective Inspector Sean Corrigan." He recognized the voice. It was Hellier.

"This is DI Corrigan."

"We'll do it your way, Inspector. I'll meet you today. I'll be at the Belgravia police station at two P.M. I expect absolute discretion." Hellier hung up.

Fine, Sean thought. Pick any station you like, but come tomorrow I'll have a set of your fingerprints, your DNA, and your statement. Once I have them, it's only a matter of time before the web of lies begins to disintegrate.

Sean and Donnelly sat in their Mondeo in Ebury Bridge Road, Belgravia. They had a good view of the front of the police station, but were far enough away not to be seen. Sean wanted to watch Hellier as he approached, wanted to see how he looked ahead of their meeting.

At 1:40 Sean and Donnelly saw Hellier striding along Buckingham Palace Road. He fit the affluent area perfectly. Sean focused the lens of the camera on Hellier's face and pressed the button. "A little present for the surveillance boys," he told Donnelly.

"When's that starting, by the way?"

"As soon as Featherstone authorizes it. I put in a request first thing this morning."

"Rather him than me," Donnelly said, thinking of the reams of paperwork Detective Superintendent Featherstone would have to complete before surveillance could begin.

Hellier looked confident. He was with another man who carried a briefcase.

"I fucking knew he'd bring his lawyer," said Sean.

"That'll be one expensive mouthpiece," Donnelly replied as they watched Hellier and his solicitor enter the station.

"We'll give it a few minutes," Sean said. "Let them get a bit pissed off. Then we'll go see them. See if we can't rattle his cage."

"Aye," Donnelly agreed.

"Any luck with criminal records?"

"No. Nothing on criminal records or the intelligence system. He appears clean."

"I find that hard to believe."

"Maybe he's had an identity change," Donnelly suggested.

"Wouldn't surprise me. A set of his prints will soon answer that."

"Shall we dance?"

"Why not?" They climbed from their car and headed after Hellier.

* * *

Sean and Donnelly sat across the table from Hellier and his solicitor, Jonathon Templeman, in the witness interview room.

Templeman spoke first. "Inspector, my client has a right to know why he has been asked to come here today."

Sean smiled. "You make it sound as if Mr. Hellier is a suspect."

"It feels as if he's being treated like one. Asked to come to a police station. Of course my client wishes to cooperate, but his rights must be respected. If he is a suspect, then he needs to be informed."

"Mr. Hellier is not a suspect," Sean told him. "That's why we're in the witness room, not an interview room. If Mr. Hellier was a suspect, he'd have been arrested by now."

Sean knew the solicitor didn't believe a word he was saying. He would have realized the police suspected his client was involved in the murder of Daniel Graydon and he would do all he could to protect Hellier, but he wouldn't want to force Sean's hand. Wouldn't want to precipitate Hellier's arrest.

"I don't know how much your client has told you, Mr. . . . ," Sean said, looking at the business card the solicitor had handed him, " . . . Mr. Templeman, but from my initial conversation with Mr. Hellier I know he had sexual relations with a young man who was found murdered some days later."

"My client's sexual orientation is not an issue here," Templeman intervened. "It's no longer illegal to be gay, Inspector." He was being deliberately provocative. He knew the best way to defend a client, whether they were guilty or not, was to be aggressive toward the investigating officers. Show no signs of cooperation. Never be civil. Always attack.

"Mr. Templeman," Sean said, "I have no interest in Mr.

Hellier's sexuality. What I do care about is that a young man has been murdered. Mr. Hellier is an important witness. Possibly the best I have. I need a full witness statement and full forensic samples for elimination purposes. And his fingerprints."

"A witness statement is out of the question," Templeman said, still speaking for Hellier. "The body samples we agree to. We understand the need to eliminate my client from the investigation as quickly as possible."

Donnelly joined in. "This isn't a shoplifting we're investigating. This is a murder inquiry. Mr. Hellier will give a full written statement and he'll do it today." His voice was calm.

"My client has not witnessed any offenses in relation to the death of Mr. Graydon. He can provide no useful information, therefore he will not be providing a witness statement. Such a statement would be of no use to the police, yet it could be both embarrassing and damaging to my client."

"Embarrassing?" Donnelly said. "I don't care how embarrassing it could be. Maybe you would like to meet the boy's parents. You could explain to them how your client is more concerned about being embarrassed than he is about helping to find their son's killer."

"No statement."

Sean knew Templeman meant it. "I'll have Mr. Hellier summonsed to court to give evidence if necessary."

"Then that's what you'll have to do, Inspector."

"Fine," Sean said. There was more than one way to skin a cat, but why wouldn't Hellier make a statement? Sean didn't believe the bullshit about public embarrassment. Hellier didn't want to say anything the police could prove was a lie. Best to keep his mouth shut. Hide behind his expensive solicitor.

"So, no statement," Sean said. "Samples, you agree to?" He was looking directly at Hellier, who remained dumb.

"I've already said we agree to body samples," Templeman informed him.

"And fingerprints. For elimination purposes." Sean waited for the answer, hoping he sounded casual enough.

"Why do you need my client's fingerprints?" Templeman asked. "I thought Mr. Hellier had made it quite clear that he'd never been in the victim's flat. Unless you found prints on the body, which is most unlikely, I don't see why you would want my client's fingerprints for elimination."

Sean spoke quickly. A delay would have alerted Templeman and probably, maybe more so, Hellier. "Not on his body. On some cash we found in his pocket," he lied. "Your client paid for sex. So unless he used a credit card, the cash could be Mr. Hellier's. It's already been chemically treated and we've been able to recover a number of prints. If the prints aren't your client's, then they could be the killer's."

"Very well," Templeman said. "My client is prepared to provide a set of elimination prints."

Hellier nodded his agreement to provide his fingerprints.

"Good." Sean called a young detective constable into the room. "This is DC Zukov. He'll take you to the surgeon's room where a doctor will take your body samples, then he'll take your prints. Understand?"

Hellier didn't reply.

"I need a full set, Paulo," Sean told DC Zukov. "Palms and fingertips too. And the side of his hands."

Zukov nodded and looked at Hellier. "If you'd like to come this way, sir."

Templeman and Hellier followed DC Zukov from the room. Donnelly made sure they were out of earshot.

"That was a bit of a porky-pie, boss. We don't have any fingerprints on any cash that I know of. Could cause us problems if anyone discovers we tricked our suspect into giving his prints—like the Crown Prosecution Service, for example."

Sean wasn't concerned. "Fuck 'em. I'll cross that bridge when and if I come to it. Right now, I want his prints in case we get lucky at the scene."

"He seems pretty confident he's never been inside Graydon's flat," Donnelly reminded him.

"Yeah, but we only need him to have made one mistake, just one mistake, and we'll be able to put him in the flat, and then I'll have him."

"You're sure it's him, aren't you?"

"I don't know. The more I see him, the more I'm next to him, the more sure I am he's hiding something. But it's almost as if this is a game to him—as if he's somehow enjoying it. I don't know, but there's something . . ." Sean didn't finish his thought.

"Maybe you just really want it to be him?" Donnelly argued. "Maybe you just don't like the smug bastard with his expensive attorney?"

"No," Sean answered quietly, without looking at Donnelly. "I can feel his guilt."

"Guilt, aye," Donnelly agreed. "But guilt for the death of Daniel Graydon?"

"I don't know," Sean admitted, "but I've got a very strong feeling James Hellier and I are going to cross swords again, and soon."

CHAPTER 9

James Hellier left the Belgravia police station two hours later, only slightly annoyed at being kept longer than necessary. Feeling pleased with himself, he indulged in a little smile. He hoped his attorney hadn't noticed.

They walked along the road a short way. Hellier felt certain he was being followed by the police. No matter. No need to tell Templeman. No need to tell anyone.

So the police had samples from his body. The detective constable had made sure the doctor was thorough: blood, saliva, semen, hair of various types. All for elimination purposes. All given voluntarily. The detective had had a strange name. Paulo Zukov. Hellier had been tempted to ask him if he was more wop than Slav, or the other way around. He had managed not to.

Hellier and Templeman shook hands and went their separate ways. Templeman clearly had no notion that Hellier might be anything other than an innocent man dragged into somebody else's mess. God bless lawyers. They pump them full of some serious self-importance bullshit in law school. They all think they're in a John Grisham novel, protecting the innocent from their oppressors.

They'd taken his fingerprints too. He'd known Corrigan

was lying about finding prints on the victim's money, even if his lawyer had not. It was unfortunate he had to give them, but he had foreseen it. It wouldn't be a problem. It mustn't be a problem. It wasn't.

Sean and Donnelly watched Hellier leave the same way they'd watched him arrive. They watched him shake hands with Templeman and move off. Hellier looked over his shoulder, back toward them, and walked on.

Donnelly broke the silence. "He thinks we're following him."

"Not yet, we're not," Sean replied. "I just got a message from Featherstone—surveillance starts tomorrow. What about the other men the victim had sex with? Have we spoken to all of them now?"

"We have. They came forward of their own accord. They're not happy about admitting to paying for sex, but not exactly ashamed either."

"Not like Hellier," Sean stated rather than asked.

"No. The others seem straightforward. They've provided statements, prints, and samples, no problem. None of the lads who interviewed them gets any sort of feeling. We'll run them all through the system anyway, but no one looks interesting."

"Any sign of a boyfriend?" Sean asked. "No matter what I think of Hellier, I still have to consider that possibility."

"According to his friends, there was no boyfriend, now or in the recent past, other than the possibility he was seeing our missing barman, Jonnie Dempsey."

"And further back? No jilted john with an ax to grind?"

"Apparently not. It appears Daniel was more careful with his private life than he was with his business one."

"Anything else?" Sean asked.

"I took the liberty of sending out a national circular, asking if other forces have come across any murders similar to ours."

"And?"

"And nothing. Our little shop of horrors appears to be unique."

"So," Sean said, "Hellier's still our main man. Until I say different." Donnelly opened the car door unexpectedly. "Going somewhere nice?"

"I just want to check on Paulo. Make sure everything went okay."

"Don't worry about Paulo. He knows what he's doing." Sean trusted Paulo. He trusted all his team.

"All the same. I'll not sleep tonight if I don't check."

Sean wasn't used to seeing Donnelly so concerned. "Okay, check. I'll wait here. And ask him if he needs a lift."

Donnelly was gone. Sean watched him running across the road, dodging the traffic. He moved pretty well for a big man.

DC Zukov waited for Donnelly in the basement toilet of the Belgravia police station. He was relieved to finally see Donnelly's considerable frame enter, shrinking the room. Donnelly stopped in front of the large mirror and began to comb his scruffy salt-and-pepper hair with his hands.

"There's no one else in here. We're fine," Zukov assured him.

"Then why are you fucking whispering?"

Zukov spoke normally. "I don't know. It's just that I'm not used to talking to strange men in public toilets."

"I hope not, young man." In an instant Donnelly's tone became more serious. "Did you get what I asked for?"

Zukov smiled. He put his hand in his inside jacket pocket and pulled out a small plastic evidence bag containing two hairs that only minutes earlier had been plucked from Hellier's scalp. He handed it to Donnelly, who snatched it away. "I take it the official samples have been sealed accordingly?" he asked.

"As you requested," Zukov told him. "Everything's been

bagged and tagged properly. These are the little extras you wanted kept off the books."

"Good." Donnelly opened an empty metal cigarette case and folded the bag carefully, making sure he didn't bend the contents. He put the bag in the case and snapped it shut. He tucked it into his blazer pocket and patted it. "Just to be on the safe side. You never know when you're gonna need a helping hand."

"You gonna leave them in Graydon's place to be found by the forensics boys or you got some other idea how to use them?" Zukov asked.

"I'm not going to do anything with them," said Donnelly. "Not yet anyway."

"Why? What are you waiting for?"

Donnelly puffed out his chest and raised himself to his full height. "Listen up, son. These are the three rules of life according to Dave Donnelly: Number one—never accept a bribe, no matter how skint you are. Number two—never fit up an innocent member of the public. Villains, fine, but never Joe Public. Number three—never, absolutely never, fit anyone up for murder unless you're absolutely positive they did it and it's absolutely necessary to get them off the streets. Understand?"

"So you're not positive Hellier's our man?"

"No. Not yet. He's not our only suspect either, remember? Now drop this lot off at the lab before it closes, then run his fingerprints up to the Yard. The guv'nor wants them compared to marks from the scene *tout suite,* so don't take no for an answer. Understand?"

"Not a problem," Zukov replied. "And what will you be up to?"

Donnelly looked him up and down before answering. "Not that it's any of your fucking business, but I thought I'd head back to the nick with the guv'nor, see if I can't find out what's going on in that head of his."

"Problems?" Zukov asked.

"I'm not sure yet. Let's just say I get the feeling the man's not telling me everything he knows."

At about 5 P.M. Sean was back at his desk plowing through e-mails and paperwork, oblivious to the chatter and ringing phones in the incident room. A detective constable whom everyone called Bruce knocked on his door frame, somewhat startling him.

"Fingerprints returning your call, guv'nor," he said without enthusiasm, but Sean felt his heart jump and his stomach sink. He crossed the office and took the phone.

"DI Corrigan speaking. You can give the results to me."

"I don't have the results yet," the anonymous voice replied. "The marks from the scene are still being worked up. Identification Officer Collins is working that case. He'll run comparisons to your scene as soon as he can, starting with the various elimination prints you've sent us. If you're lucky, they'll be ready by Monday or Tuesday."

"This is a murder investigation," Sean reminded him. "I need them yesterday."

"Sorry," said the voice. "Monday or Tuesday is the absolute earliest they'll be ready. Listen, we're snowed under here. Antiterrorist Unit just landed a rush job on us. We've been told to make it a priority, no exceptions. Sorry."

Sean understood. It was an unavoidable sign of the times "Okay. Thanks. You can get him to call me direct with the results. One more thing," Sean quickly added before the line went dead. "Can you check for a set of conviction fingerprints for someone for me?"

"Sure," came the answer. "What's the name?"

Sean was unaware that Donnelly had moved within earshot. "James Hellier. Do you need a date of birth?"

"No. The name's probably unusual enough. Give me a minute." Sean waited, the two or three minutes that passed feeling so much longer, before the voice finally spoke. "No. No prints for that name here."

Sean felt the emptiness of disappointment. "No problem," he managed to say, and hung up.

Donnelly cut through his state of melancholy. "Interesting line of inquiry."

"Meaning?"

"Asking Fingerprints if Hellier had a set of conviction prints on file, given that we already know he doesn't have any convictions. Remember, I checked."

"I thought I'd double-check," Sean said. "I thought maybe his conviction never got sent from the court, or someone forgot to put it on the Police National Computer. Worth a try."

"I see, belt and braces, eh. Any luck?"

"No," Sean answered. "Hellier's clean."

Hellier sat in his study watching for movements in the American money markets on his computer. His wife popped her head around the door without warning, but she wouldn't enter fully before asking. Elizabeth knew when to leave him alone; it was part of her role as the perfect wife, and she was paid well. She liked her life.

"Are you okay in here, darling?" she asked.

"I'm fine, sweetheart. Just catching up on a bit of work. I won't be long. Promise." He threw her a charming smile.

"You work too hard. It's almost ten o'clock."

"Go to bed. I'm fine."

"Don't stay up too late, darling."

"I won't."

His wife blew him a kiss and left. Time to make a phone call. Hellier slid his hand under the desk and peeled a piece of tape from the underside. He examined the two keys stuck to the tape, then pulled one free and carried it across the office to the built-in walnut cabinets. He listened for sounds outside the office before opening the cabinet door and kneeling on the floor. He pulled the carpet back to reveal a floor safe sealed into the concrete foundation of the house. He unlocked the safe with one of the keys and took out a small address book. He locked the safe, closed the cabinet, and went back to his desk. He found the number he was looking for and dialed. After a few ringing tones the phone was answered by a sleepy voice. "Hello? Hello? Christ."

Hellier spoke. "It's me. Don't you recognize my voice?"

Hellier was met by silence. Then the voice spoke with urgency. "Please tell me you're calling from a public phone."

Hellier could hear the fear. "Don't worry about that. We've more important things to discuss."

"Like what?"

"Like are you sure you took care of things? You wouldn't have been lying to me, would you?"

"Jesus Christ. Why are you asking me this? I took care of it. I told you. Why the panic? Have you fucked up?" The voice sounded calmer.

"No, but your flat-footed friends are making trouble for me. It's important I know you did what you were paid to do."

The voice was silent. Hellier gave the person time to think. After a few seconds the voice returned, almost whispering now, nervous. "Christ! They haven't connected you to Korsakov, have they?" The mention of that name made Hellier lean back into his comfortable chair and smile, as if he was recalling a happy childhood memory. Stefan Korsakov. A name he hadn't heard in ages. "Have the police connected you to Korsakov?" the voice demanded impatiently.

"No," Hellier answered, still calm and smiling, "and they

never will. Korsakov's never coming back. I made sure of that a long time ago. Don't you remember? You should. After all, you helped me bury him."

The voice snapped back. "If you've fucked up, you're on your own. I won't help you again."

Hellier needed to remind him. "If they take me down, I'll make sure you come with me. Keep that in mind." He hung up before the voice could answer.

The voice had sounded genuine enough. Time would tell if he was speaking the truth. For both their sakes, Hellier hoped he was.

CHAPTER 10

Sunday

Shortly before 8 A.M. Sean arrived at work and Sally pounced on him immediately. "Guv'nor."

"What is it, Sally?"

She spoke in a whisper. "Superintendent Featherstone's been floating around asking for you."

Sean rolled his eyes. "Thanks for the warning." No sooner had he entered his office than he heard a knock on the side of the open door. He walked to his chair and sat down before looking around. "Morning, boss. Aren't you supposed to be at church?" He pointed to a chair.

Featherstone accepted the invitation, sinking into the visitor's chair with a slight groan. He was a tall man, over six feet two, heavily built, with red hair. "I haven't been to church since my second wife left me." He spoke with no more than a trace of London in his accent. "How's the Graydon investigation going? Any progress for me?"

Featherstone had hardly any detective experience, rising

instead through the ranks as an accelerated-promotion candidate, but he had hit a ceiling at superintendent after failing or refusing to become one of the new generic breed of senior officers in the Met. He was a little too rough around the edges; a little too outspoken, and far too prepared to get his hands dirty. Realizing he could go no higher, he transferred into the Criminal Investigation Department.

Sean could do business with the man. He knew that Featherstone was shrewd enough not to interfere too much with the way Sean conducted his investigations and that he would watch Sean's back more than most.

"We're still waiting on forensics and fingerprints."

"How about other lines of inquiry? Any witnesses?"

"We've spoken with a number of witnesses from the club. Some have supplied statements and elimination samples. Nothing of interest so far. The killer went to a lot of trouble to avoid leaving forensic evidence at the scene. It looks premeditated. Our best chance for now seems to be James Hellier, the potential blackmail target."

"Any solid proof yet that the victim was blackmailing him?"

"No. Hellier's clever. He's covered his tracks well. That's why I requested authorization for round-the-clock surveillance—it could be our only hope of catching him out."

"What about the victim?" Featherstone asked. "If you can turn up some blackmail letters, prove he was trying to screw Hellier, then you'd be halfway there."

"Nothing on paper from the victim's flat. The techs have his computer, but it'll take time to recover his e-mails."

"Any other credible suspects?"

"Well, one of the barmen from the club's gone missing. Apparently he knew the victim and possibly could have been romantically linked to him. Other than that we're trying to find a recently released nutter who did eight years for the attempted murder of a young gay man. He lives close enough to the scene to be a cause for concern. He also appears to have gone missing."

"At the very least they need to be found and eliminated."

"They will be."

"We need to be careful with this one, Sean. You can bet, with a gay victim, someone, somewhere will be watching the investigation's progress, waiting for a chance to accuse us of being homophobic. Let's not hand the media a stick to beat us with."

"I'll bear that in mind," said Sean.

"Speaking of the media," Featherstone asked, "what about an appeal? *Crimewatch*? Save some shoe leather and let the television do the donkey work."

"It's a bit too soon for that. I'd rather no one knew what we're up to just yet."

"You still camera shy?" Featherstone smiled. "If it comes to it, I can take care of that side of things. I know you're not exactly a fan, but I've got some people in the media I can trust. We can do a piece for the papers and try to get a slot on *Crimewatch*. I'll have my secretary make a few calls."

"No need. I'll get it arranged and let you know when the telly people want you. Should be able to sort it out in a day or so." Sean hoped he'd bought some time.

Featherstone got to his feet. "Fine. Let my secretary know the time and place and I'll be there. You can give me a full briefing beforehand."

"Not a problem."

"I'd better get myself up to the Yard. Commissioner's called an emergency meeting. On a Sunday—can you believe that?"

"Sounds like trouble."

"Bloody Territorial Support Group, kicked the shit out of some student on the last anticapitalist march. Turns out the kid's parents are connected, so now we're all going to be issued with foam truncheons. Wankers." Featherstone looked to the heavens and walked from the office heading for the exit.

Sally appeared at Sean's door. "Problems?"

"No," Sean told her. "Not yet."

Donnelly ate his sausage sandwich. It was the best Sunday-morning breakfast he could hope for under the circumstances. He stood close to the small wooden hut in the middle of Black-heath where he'd bought the sandwich. It was a well-known spot, used mainly by hungry taxi drivers and police looking for a place to talk without being overheard.

He enjoyed the gentle cooling breeze that whipped off the flat, wide heath. In winter, it was the coldest place in London. He spotted the dark blue Mondeo pull up opposite. Detective Sergeants Jimmy Dawson and Raj Samra stepped from the car. They could only have been police.

The detective sergeants worked on the other two murder teams in South London. They carried out the same roles on their teams as Donnelly did on his. Meeting regularly helped maintain the strong bond between detective sergeants and en-gendered a feeling that they were the ones really running the police.

Donnelly smiled to himself and stuffed the remains of the sandwich into his mouth. He waited for the men to cross the road. "For Christ's sake, Raj. You're the only Indian in the Met who looks more like a copper than Jimmy here."

"I like looking like a copper. You should try it sometime. In-stead of looking like a bag of shit," Raj replied.

The trading of insults was routine. Jimmy joined the con-versation. "What're you doing in the middle of Blackheath on a Sunday morning, Dave? Exposing yourself to students again? If it isn't that, then I'll assume you want a favor."

"Jimmy, Jimmy." Donnelly sounded insulted. "Are the best sausage sandwiches in London not a good enough reason for you?" Dawson didn't reply. "And you, Raj. Thinking I would ask for favors. Me. Dave Donnelly."

"Well, I don't eat pork, so it better be something other than the sandwich."

"I didn't know you were a Muslim," Donnelly said.

"I'm not. I'm a Sikh."

"You should wear a turban—you'd be a commander by now."

"I'm not interested in playing that game," said Samra.

Donnelly gave a short stunted laugh before his face turned serious. "Okay, gentlemen, I'll assume you know what sort of case my team's working on. I want to know if anything similar comes up. If one of your teams gets it first, I want to be called to the scene immediately. Understand?"

"If it looks linked, it'll be passed to your team anyway. What's the rush?" Dawson asked.

"No," Donnelly snapped. "I didn't say I want my *team* informed immediately. I said *I* wanted to be informed immediately, before anyone else. Including DI Corrigan."

Donnelly watched them exchange glances. He knew they would be happy to help, but not if it meant being dragged into a dangerous situation. Dangerous for their careers. He understood their concerns.

"Don't look so worried, boys." He tried to sound less serious. "I just want first crack at any new scenes. I'm getting a taste for this case. I need a wee peek at an uncorrupted scene. You know, before the circus arrives and takes the feel out of the place. That's all." His fellow detective sergeants stared at him blankly, their way of letting him know they didn't believe a word he was saying. "Okay, for fuck's sake. You boys drive a hard bargain. Listen, our prime suspect is a clever, slippery bastard. Any forensic evidence we find at the next scene may require a little helping hand, if you catch my drift. But it has to appear genuine. The forensics boys have to find it, not one of my team, so I'll need to be in and out of there before anyone's the wiser. Clear?"

"Well, why didn't you just say so?" Samra mocked. "We'd be happy to help," he added, and meant it, knowing that one day he or Dawson might require a similar favor from Donnelly.

"I thought your job was shaping up to be a blackmail?" Dawson asked.

"I know Corrigan better than he thinks," Donnelly told them. "He thinks there's more to our prime suspect than he's saying. Forget the blackmail element. You get anything a bit nastier than usual, I want to know."

"Okay," Samra said with a shrug. "I'll make sure you're called straight off."

"Good, but keep it quiet. Tell your teams to call you, then you call me. Keep it nicely between the three of us."

"If you want to take jobs off my hands, that's fine and dandy with me," Dawson said. "But if anyone asks, we never had this conversation."

Donnelly spread his arms to show his good intentions. "Boys, please," he pleaded. "I promise. Nothing dodgy. Trying to solve a murder here, that's all."

The two detectives were already crossing the road. Samra called back to Donnelly: "Drag me into anything naughty and you'll be solving your own fucking murder."

You just do as you're told, Raj my boy, Donnelly thought to himself. Just do as you're told.

It was midmorning by the time Sean walked from his office into the briefing room where his team was assembled. He wasn't in the mood to let the room settle naturally. Time to push along. "All right, all right. Listen up. I haven't got all day. The quicker you listen, the quicker we can get on with it." The room settled into silence. "So far we have three possible suspects: Steven Paramore; Jonnie Dempsey, the missing barman; and James Hellier. The reasons why Paramore and Dempsey are suspects are obvious, so they need to be found and spoken to. Hellier's more complicated," Sean told them. "My best guess is still that our victim was attempting to blackmail him. No other motives have come to light and we've spoken to pretty much all his friends and family. Any last lingering possibility that this could be a domestic hangs on whether the victim was having a relationship with Jonnie Dempsey, and so far no one's been able to confirm whether he was or wasn't. Dempsey is only a suspect insofar as he worked at Utopia, knew the victim, and now he's missing and can't be found, so all other suggestions are welcome."

"Maybe we should consider a stranger attack," Donnelly spoke up. "A random killer."

"No forced entry, remember?" Sean reminded him.

"Maybe the killer posed as a client?" Donnelly suggested. "Talked his way into the flat."

Sean was beginning to suspect Donnelly knew his blackmail theory was little more than a smoke screen. A screen that allowed Sean time to think. Time to walk in the killer's shoes—to feel him. To understand him. "From what we're being told of our victim, he was too careful for that." Sean tried to steer Donnelly away from the possibility for a while longer, until he had things straight in his own mind.

"But it has to be a possibility?" Donnelly insisted.

He had to give Donnelly something. "Possibly," Sean answered. There was a ripple of noise around the room.

"If it's a possibility, then what are we doing about it?" Sally asked.

"We've released a national memorandum, police eyes only, checking for recent similar cases," Sean reminded them.

"Maybe we should go farther back?" Sally suggested.

"As it happens, I've already asked General Registry to send me a number of old files." He sensed Donnelly's discontent. "I've asked them for anything involving vulnerable victims where an excessive use of violence was involved, going back over the last five years. But don't get too excited, we're doing these checks as a matter of protocol, not because I think we have a madman on our hands."

"That'll be a lot of files," said Donnelly. "You'll need some help going over them."

"No," Sean snapped. "I'll read them myself."

"What about Method Index?" Sally asked "They may have data the General Registry doesn't. Something older or something that never made it to court."

"Good," Sean said. "Look into it, Sally. Take some help if you think you'll need it."

"And Hellier?" Donnelly asked. "What about Hellier?"

"Surveillance started on him this morning," Sean told them. "Link up with them as soon as you can and keep them on the right track." Donnelly nodded without speaking. He didn't seem too happy. Sean raised his voice slightly. "Don't lose focus, people. Hellier is still our prime suspect and blackmail our prime motive. We'll look into other possibilities because we have to, but I don't want anyone going off on a wild-goose chase when we have an obvious suspect right in front of us. As for Paramore and Dempsey, let's get hold of Customs and Immigration—see if either have left or tried to leave the country. Paulo." DC Zukov raised his head. "You take care of it, okay?" Zukov nodded once. "We've all got work to do, so let's get on with it." The meeting broke up.

Sean reached his office just as Donnelly caught up with him. He knew Donnelly would want an explanation.

"Are you going to tell me what's really going through your mind?" Donnelly asked.

"Let's not make a drama out of it, Dave."

"How long have you known this wasn't about Hellier being blackmailed?"

Sean closed the door to his office. "I don't."

"Come on, guv'nor. Protocol, my arse. If you've requested old files from General Registry, then you're looking for something else."

Sean sighed. He could see no sense in keeping anything from Donnelly anymore. "All right. Hellier wasn't being blackmailed, but I still think he could be our man. The second time I met him I really began to believe it could be him."

"Can I ask why?"

"Graydon wouldn't have tried to blackmail him. From what we've learned about him, he was too passive to attempt blackmail. Especially someone like Hellier. He's too intimidating. Too threatening."

"Then why have you got the team chasing the blackmail theory, not to mention Paramore and Dempsey?"

"I need to make things appear straightforward, just for a while longer. It'll buy me time to think the way I need to think. Once I show my hand, things will get a lot more complicated around here. I can't see clearly when I'm crowded, and besides, Paramore and Dempsey must be found and spoken to. I could turn out to be wrong about Hellier."

"So you don't think Hellier was being blackmailed, but you do think he could have killed Graydon."

"I do."

"Care to share why?"

"Because I don't believe in coincidences. Hellier's bad to the core. It's simply in his nature. You know the type of animal I'm talking about. We've both dealt with them before. And now someone Hellier was connected to is dead.

"If I'm right about him, then his motive for killing is the killing itself. He's a very rare breed; the chances that Graydon came across two such people are extremely remote, although not impossible."

Donnelly slumped in a chair, exasperated. "Bloody hell, guv, this is all a bit loose. You wouldn't want to take it to court."

"Agreed, but there's another way to go after Hellier. He has no anxiety about this case. When I speak to him about it, I can't feel anything. No panic, concerns, doubt, nothing. He's absolutely sure he's gotten away with it."

"If he did it," Donnelly reminded him. Sean ignored the warning.

"He was at his most confident when we were talking about the Graydon case. So long as we stuck to that, he was totally in his comfort zone. That tells me he's left us very little, if anything."

"But?"

"But at other times I've sensed his anxiousness."

"About what?"

"About something else. Something that could betray him." Sean sat and faced Donnelly. "Something in his past. Maybe he's—"

"You think he's killed before?" Donnelly interrupted.

"If he's the type of animal I think he is, then there is a very real possibility he has. When I read the old case files from General Registry, hopefully some detail will stand out."

"You are aware of what you're saying?"

"Of course I am." Sean looked him in the eye. "That's why this has to stay between the two of us for now. I'll fill Sally in when I get a chance."

"God forbid the powers that be find out you reckon you're onto a serial killer. This place will go fucking crazy with senior officers trying to get their faces on the telly."

"Then they'd better not find out."

"Indeed," Donnelly agreed as he stood up. "But there's one thing that still doesn't make sense to me."

"Go on."

"Why would Hellier kill Graydon if he knew we could connect them? Why would he pull us on top of him like that? Is he trying to play games with us? Is he one of those sick fuckers who wants to get caught?"

"No," Sean answered. "Hellier absolutely doesn't want to get caught. Trust me. There is nothing self-destructive about Hellier."

"Then why?"

"For one of two reasons. Because he wanted to or because he had to."

"Well?" Donnelly asked, his hands held apart. "Which one is it?"

"I don't know," Sean confessed. "I just don't know. I keep going over it and over it, but every time I think I'm close to understanding why, it all melts away. There's something not quite right, something I'm missing. Christ, it's so close I could fucking touch it, but I can't see it yet."

"We'll find out why soon enough," said Donnelly.

"To be honest, with Hellier I'm not so sure." The doubt was unusual for Sean. "That's why we go after his past. Identify his earlier offenses. That's where he's vulnerable. I'm certain of it."

"If indeed he has offended before."

"He has," Sean insisted. "There's no doubt. All I need to know is who, where, and when. And why the hell his prints aren't on file."

"I don't know, boss," Donnelly admitted. "This all feels like a bit of a stretch to me. Maybe we shouldn't be homing in on Hellier so much? Stretch our horizons a little. See if we can't rake up a few more viable suspects."

"You think I'm fixating on Hellier?" Sean snapped. "You think I'm putting the investigation at risk?"

"That's not what I said."

"But it's what you're thinking." Sean regretted the words as soon as they'd left his mouth. He wished he could explain to Donnelly how he could be so certain of something long before the evidence justified it. How he'd seen the killer strutting around Daniel Graydon's flat, calm and content, the dead man lying in an ever-increasing pool of blood, of no concern to him now—an empty shell that had served its purpose. But he knew he couldn't tell Donnelly what he had seen. He couldn't tell Donnelly that when he looked into Hellier's face he saw more than just skin, bone, and flesh—he saw into the man's soul and could see only darkness.

Sally walked into New Scotland Yard, a huge glass building just around the corner from Parliament Square. Standard searches of criminal intelligence and conviction databases had yielded nothing. It was time to try something a little different, which was why she'd come to check the Method Index. They kept records of serious and violent crimes, as well as unusual crimes. If an offender used the same peculiar method more than once, it was possible he or she could be identified here. Sally walked into the Method Index office and glanced around the small beige room. Wooden desks were squeezed together. Ancient, worn-out computers filled every corner. Large posters adorned the walls advertising what the department could do for you. Everything seemed old. The two people in the room looked surprised to have a visitor. One, a thin, bespectacled, middle-aged man nervously closed the filing cabinet he'd been tending and hesitantly moved toward Sally. He spoke shyly.

"Are you looking for somebody?" He had a Yorkshire accent, unblunted by years in London.

Sally realized they didn't get many visitors. "Well, if this is Method Index, I guess I've found the right place." She tried to sound enthusiastic. "DS Sally Jones, from Serious Crime Group South." She held out her hand and hoped the mention of her unit might stir some interest. The nervous man seemed confused. "The Murder Squad," Sally added. "SCG is the Murder Squad."

"Oh," the man said. "That's what you're called now. They keep changing the names of things so much I can never keep up." He accepted the offer of Sally's outstretched hand and shook it with a smile. "I'm DC Harvey Williams. Everyone calls me Harve. They put me in charge of this little team a few years ago and I think they've forgotten about me, to be honest." He pointed at a young man with long hair who was sifting through an ocean of paper files. "That's Doug. He's a civilian. The rest of the team are off today. In fact, the only reason anyone's here is because we're moving all our old paper files onto the computers. We don't get much of a chance for overtime here, so when they offered . . ."

So this was the Met's answer to the world-famous FBI Behavioral Science Unit. An aging detective constable the world had forgotten about and a handful of unqualified civilian employees. She may have made a mistake coming here, but on the other hand, what did she have to lose apart from an afternoon?

DC Williams continued. "How can we help you, DS Jones?"

"I'm interested in any profiles of murderers that fit our case."

Williams pursed his lips. "We don't do profiles here, I'm

afraid. We have methods of crime used by people. Not profiles of them."

Sally understood the difference. A profile referred to a psychological profile of an offender. It was rarely used by the Metropolitan Police. Despite being highly publicized in the media and films, the truth was that psychological profiles were of very limited value. Matching methods of crime to offenders was far more useful.

"I apologize. Slip of the tongue."

"No need to apologize," he said cheerfully. "Grab a seat. Anywhere you like. No small-time imperialists in this office. Now, tell me what you're after. Spare me no details. The devil's always in the details. Absolutely always in the details."

London steamed. Sean couldn't remember another summer like it. No rain. No wind. No relief. The devil's own weather. His mobile was ringing. He kept driving and answered, "DI Corrigan."

"Hello, guv'nor." It was Donnelly. "Just to let you know, I'm with the surveillance team. Making sure they don't spend a week following the wrong man."

"Good. Any movement from Hellier?"

"Nah. He's still at home. He hasn't been out anywhere yet. He's only looked out the window once. Didn't seem to be checking for us, though."

"I'm coming to join you," Sean announced. "I'll call your mobile when I'm in the area. If he moves, ring me." He hung up.

Donnelly turned to DC Paulo Zukov, sitting next to him. Zukov spoke. "Problem?"

"Nah, but be aware. The guv'nor's on his way."

"So what makes you think Method Index can help with your murder?" DC Williams asked. "Unusual, is it?"

"A little unusual," Sally replied. "The victim was stabbed an excessively large number of times, having already been half killed with a couple of blows to the head. The weapon used was an ice pick or stiletto knife of some sort. More important, the victim was a homosexual. Almost certainly a male prostitute.

"I'm not interested in someone with a history of homophobic behavior per se. I'm looking for something heavier. Really violent attacks. Possibly sexual attacks or attacks that could have some sexual overtones. Anything like that. Can you help?"

"We can work with that. As for the drunken queer-bashing stuff, we wouldn't have that sort of attack on our records anyway. Not distinct enough."

DC Williams walked over to a large gray cabinet in a corner of the office. He talked as he thumbed through the files within. "Some of our records go back fifty years or so. The really sensitive ones. Preferred methods of terrorists, professional hit men, that sort of thing. But mostly our records refer to sex offenders, pedophiles. People most likely to reoffend. We don't have too many murderers. Most are such dull affairs, one-off acts of stupidity. But you would already know that."

Sally was relieved. She didn't fancy spending the entire day reading through ancient files in the cramped office.

"We've got only a few hundred on record," Williams added, grinning. Sally slumped. "Shouldn't take too long if we both look through them."

He pulled out as many files as he could manage and carried them to Sally's desk. "That's the last decade of interesting murders of homosexuals. Unfortunately, most of our records haven't been transferred onto the computer system yet, so if you have a look at this little lot, I'll see what we have on our computerized records." He began to whistle as he tapped away on the terminal's keyboard.

Sally took off her jacket and pushed all the files to one side of the desk. She picked the first one at random and began to read.

Hellier knew they were there. He could sense their presence. He couldn't see them from his study, but it made no difference. They were there. They were good. Not clumsy. Not impatient. He wondered how many would be on the surveillance team. They called the officers on motorbikes "solos." Pathetic police jargon. Still, he had a problem. Things would get difficult if he was followed everywhere by these flat-footed fools. DI Corrigan was responsible, no doubt. Christ, he was an irritating fucker. How best to deal with DI Corrigan?

Time to make another phone call. Maybe he would go for a run a little later, weaving through the Sunday crowds in Upper Street's antiques market before jumping on and off a few buses and underground trains, laughing at the police as they struggled and ultimately failed to keep up with him.

He spoke to the police he couldn't see.

"I hope you're prepared for a long day, fuckers. You'll have to improve your play if you want to win the prize."

Sally carefully read the first dozen files. It was clear why these particular murders had been deemed unique enough for Method Index's files of infamy. Some were almost funny they were so bizarre, but most were just horrific.

Her thoughts began to drift to the victims. Had they had any idea of what was going to happen to them? Had they been scared, confused, or even angry once they realized death was upon them? And why had they been selected? What had drawn their killers to them? The way they looked, moved, or spoke? Or was it pure bad luck? The wrong place at the wrong time? Probably a little of each.

She'd been reading for over three hours. A couple of times something pricked her attention, but each time her interest faded away as she uncovered details inconsistent with what she was looking for. DC Williams's voice broke her concentration.

"DS Jones . . ."

"What is it?" Sally asked.

"I think you should take a look at this. I may have found something."

Sean had joined up with Donnelly and Zukov. The three men sat quietly in the unmarked Mondeo. Sean sat in the back staring out of the window, constantly reevaluating the evidence, searching for anything he could have overlooked. The radio crackled into life with the voices of the surveillance team. "Target one still stationary in blue."

"Lima Two breaking for a natural."

"Received, Lima Two."

"Lima Three will cover."

"Received, Lima Three."

Donnelly spoke for them all. "If Hellier moves off, I hope they stop chattering in that language of theirs, because I for one can't understand a bloody word they're saying."

Sean's mobile rang. He answered it quickly. "DI Corrigan."

"Guv'nor? Sally here."

Sean sensed an increased degree of excitement in her voice. "You sound like you have something for me."

"I think I might have."

Sean checked his watch. It was almost lunchtime. He was hoping to spend most of the day following Hellier. He felt as if the longer he was close to the man, the more he could think like him. "Can it wait till morning?"

"I suppose so," Sally answered.

It was no good though and he knew it. If he didn't find out what Sally had, he would never rest. "Can you give it to me on the phone?"

"Sorry, sir. I'm driving and I need to show you this file. You'll want to see it."

"Okay," he conceded. "Dave and I will meet you back at Peckham as soon as we can. Traveling time from Islington."

"I'll be there."

"Developments?" Donnelly asked over his shoulder.

"Possibly. We need to get back to the office and meet Sally. The surveillance boys can handle this on their own."

Their car pulled into the heavy North London traffic and slipped away seemingly unnoticed.

Sean leaned against the window frame. Sally sat on a standard-issue police station chair, wooden and rickety. Donnelly also chose to stand.

Sally rested a cardboard folder in her lap. She reminded Sean of a schoolteacher about to read a story. "I dug this out of Method Index's files earlier today," she told them. "We entered the details of our murder into the system, looking for any similar crimes or methods. Eventually it threw up this character."

Sally opened the folder and pulled out a criminal records file. "This is for a guy called Stefan Korsakov." She passed the printout to Sean, who quickly scanned the list of convictions. It didn't take long.

"Why? The man's only got one conviction. For fraud. And that was almost ten years ago." Sean was puzzled. He shook his head and passed the printout to Donnelly.

Sally continued: "Conviction, yes, but Method Index doesn't only go on convictions. Here—" Sally pulled a thick bunch of papers from the folder. Sean recognized the old-style forms. "Stefan Korsakov was accused of raping a seventeen-year-old boy back in 1996. The victim had a slight learning difficulty. Nothing serious apparently, but it made him a little naive.

"Korsakov approached the boy while he was riding his bike around Richmond Park. He befriended him, gave him a can of beer laced with a stronger alcohol, then dragged him into a secluded area of the park, tied him up, gagged him, and sexually abused him in just about every way possible, climaxing with the actual rape.

"But the fact that this was a violent assault by a predatory older male wasn't the only similarity. He used a stiletto knife to threaten the boy."

"Similar to the weapon used on our victim," Sean said.

"Well, well," Donnelly added.

Sally wasn't finished. "But Korsakov's luck ran out. He spent too long with the boy. A constable from the Parks Police was sneaking through the woods looking for flashers. Apparently they'd had a rash of them in the park. He came across more than he bargained for. The file says the constable initially thought it was a bit of al fresco gross indecency between consenting males. Then he saw the bindings around the boy's wrists.

"Korsakov sees the constable and makes a break for it, but the game is over and he gets nicked before he's gone fifty feet. The arrest was made by Parks Police. CID at Richmond inherited the job. According to the investigating officer's notes on the case, he came to the conclusion it was a planned attack: Korsakov had the laced beer with him. CID suspected he had previously targeted the boy, specifically because he had learning difficulties.

"This is the bit you'll like. The investigating detective noted how Korsakov had a heightened state of awareness of forensic evidence."

"Well, our boy certainly has that," Donnelly said.

"He wore a condom throughout the assault. He also wore a

pair of leather gloves that were brand-new and he was wearing a waterproof jacket and trousers. He had an empty bin liner in his pocket."

Sean understood waterproofs were usually made of tightly woven nylon and could be as effective as a forensics suit in preventing forensic evidence transferring from the suspect to the victim and vice versa.

Sally went on: "I've saved the best till last. When Korsakov was stripped and examined back at the nick, they discovered he'd shaved all his pubic hair off. He later claimed he'd had a dose of pubic crabs and had had to shave it all off."

"Shaved his pubes off," Donnelly said. "Now that's dedication."

"But he wasn't convicted?" Sean asked.

"No," Sally answered. "He wasn't convicted of the rape. He was, however, convicted of serious fraud. His home was searched as part of the investigation and they found a shitload of papers relating to a pensions company he'd established. The investigating detectives took a dislike to him . . ."

"I can't think why," Donnelly chipped in.

" . . . so they decided to stir up as much trouble as they could. Phoned around to people who'd signed up with his pension company. Made some inquiries as to where he'd invested their money. Turned out the whole thing was a con. There was no pension company—or at least, not a real one. The money was going toward keeping Korsakov in the lifestyle he'd become accustomed to. Nice house, BMW and a Range Rover, villa in Umbria . . .

"He's a con man. A good one. An excellent forger of documents too. He forged clients' signatures and increased their payments without them even knowing. He'd also forged himself numerous official documents. Passports. Driving licenses.

All for different countries. There appears to be no end to his talents.

"He'd stolen more than two million pounds. Mainly from the elderly. He was finally convicted after a three-month trial and sentenced to four years' custody. The money was never recovered. Released from Wandsworth prison on twenty-third December 1999.

"Since his release he's not been heard of. No arrests or convictions. Nothing."

"Why wasn't he convicted of raping the boy?" Sean asked. "Seemed straightforward."

"The boy withdrew the allegation. His parents thought it would be best for him not to go through the courts. They were worried about the press finding out. Making the boy's life a public freak show. So he walks on the rape, but the investigating officers do their best to screw him anyway and he goes down on the fraud charges."

Sean spoke again. "Offenders who commit this sort of crime don't strike once then never again. No matter what the risks, he would have reoffended. He couldn't have remained dormant for so long."

"Agreed," Sally said. "Which means he's either dead, left the country, found God and changed his ways, or . . ." She stopped short.

"Or?" Sean encouraged.

"Or he's become someone else. Used his forgery and fraud skills to create a new identity for himself. A new life."

"What's Korsakov look like?" Sean asked, a seed of an idea germinating in his mind.

"I don't know," Sally replied. "There's no photograph on file. Only a description."

"Which is?" Sean asked.

Sally checked the file. "Male, white. Back in ninety-six he was twenty-five years old, slim, athletic build; short light brown hair; and no identifiable marks, scars, or tattoos."

Sean and Donnelly exchanged glances. "Sound like anyone we know?" Donnelly asked.

Sean shook his head. "I know what you're thinking, but they can't be the same person. This guy's got a conviction, so his prints are on file. Hellier has no prints on file, so he can't have been convicted of anything; otherwise his prints would be too, no matter what name he'd been convicted under."

Donnelly knew Sean was right. "Shame."

"However," Sean added, "it won't hurt our case to look into it. Sally, you stay with it. First thing in the morning, start finding out all you can about Korsakov. See what Richmond has on him and track down the original investigating officer."

Sean turned to Donnelly. "Have you still got that snapshot of Hellier that I took?"

"Aye," Donnelly answered and pulled the photograph from his jacket pocket, handing it to Sean, who in turn handed it to Sally.

"If you do track the investigating officer down, show him this," Sean told her. "See if he recognizes him."

"I thought you said it couldn't possibly be Hellier?" Donnelly argued.

"No harm in double-checking. Kill the possibility off once and for all." Sean turned to Sally. "Once you've done that, concentrate on this Korsakov character until you're happy you've got enough to eliminate him as a viable suspect."

"And if I can't eliminate him?"

"You will," Sean assured her. "You will."

Hellier only ventured out twice all day—once to the local shop for the Sunday papers and then later for an afternoon stroll with his family around the leafy suburban streets. Both his children held on to their mother's hands as Hellier walked a few paces behind.

He couldn't have made it easier for the surveillance team to follow him. He thought he had spotted some of them. Hard to tell, best to stay paranoid for the time being. Always assume the worst. That way he would never be caught cold.

Now he sat in his cream-and-steel kitchen watching his wife clear up after the evening meal. He pushed his half-eaten food away and sipped on a glass of Pauillac de Latour.

"No appetite?" Elizabeth asked, smiling. Hellier didn't hear. "Not hungry tonight, darling?" She raised her voice slightly.

"Sorry, no," Hellier answered. "That was delicious, but just not feeling too hungry." He was with her only in body. His mind was outside with the surveillance team in the streets around his house, circling him as a pack of hyenas would an isolated lion.

"Worried about something?" Elizabeth asked.

"No. Why would I be?" Hellier didn't like being questioned by anybody.

"What about this identity fraud thing the police were looking into?"

"That was nothing," Hellier insisted. "Like I told you, it was all a mistake. The police made a mistake, surprise, surprise."

"Of course," she said, backing down.

"You did tell them I was at home all night, didn't you?" Hellier asked without apparent concern.

"I said exactly what you told me to."

"Good." But Hellier could tell she needed more. "Look, I was at a very sensitive meeting that night. The company wanted me to meet some potential clients, very important clients, but they were a little worried about their backgrounds. Beware Africans bearing large amounts of cash, as we say these days. They wanted me to check them out, that's all, see if their wealth could be obviously identified as ill-gotten gains. If so, we wouldn't touch them. All the same, we can't afford to have the police sniffing around our affairs—it would be very bad for business. Our clients expect complete confidentiality and privacy. I couldn't tell the police the truth. I'm sorry I dragged you into it, darling, but I really had no choice."

Elizabeth seemed happy with that. Even if she didn't entirely believe him, the explanation itself was at least believable. "You should have told me that straightaway, dear. I would have understood. But I'd watch out for that DI Corrigan," she warned him. "He didn't come across as the usual PC Plod. There was something unnerving about him. Some sort of animal cunning."

Hellier felt rage suddenly swelling in his chest, his temples throbbing, his body trembling involuntarily, but the expression on his face never changed from calm and content. He couldn't stand to hear his adversary being complimented. Even if his wife had meant it as an insult, it gave Corrigan more credibility in his eyes, even suggested he should somehow fear him. His fists clenched under the table as he imagined Elizabeth's smashed and bleeding face, his own knuckles bleeding, shredded on her teeth.

He waited until the rage had swept over him and died, like a passing hurricane, before rising from the table. He kissed her softly on the cheek. "I'm afraid you'll have to excuse me, darling," he said. "I need to do a little work. The price we have to pay."

Hellier headed for his study. He went through the ritual of recovering the key to his safe and then opening it. He flicked through the small address book he'd pulled from inside and found what he was looking for. He called the number.

"Hello?" the voice answered.

"You'd better call off your fucking dogs," Hellier hissed.

"That's not possible. I haven't got that sort of influence." The voice sounded matter-of-fact. Hellier didn't like that.

"Listen to me, you fucking moron. As much as it amuses me having these incompetents trying to follow me, they might just stumble across something we'd both rather they didn't. So you'd better think of something, and soon."

"I've already done more than I should," the voice protested. "I've stuck my neck out. I can't do anything else. I won't."

"Wrong again. I hope you're not going to make a habit of slipping up. I think you know how costly your mistake could be."

Hellier didn't wait for a reply. He hung up. He heard his wife call out. She wanted to know if he wanted coffee.

CHAPTER 11

I was late for work today. No matter. I went to my corner office, in an old building in Central London. I have a lovely view of the street below. I like to watch people walking past. The office is all mine. I'm wealthy, but I hate this job. I shouldn't have to work. Everybody else works, and I'm far from being like everybody else. I shouldn't have to work, but it is necessary for my illusion.

I sit in my leather chair and absorb a couple of tabloid papers while slurping on a skinny caffè latte. Two sugars. The papers are full of the usual garbage. Famine threatens millions in some African country. Flooding threatens millions in some Asian country. The usual appeals for money and clothes. Some rock star on the television, suddenly remorseful about his wealth and fame, screaming about how guilty we should all feel.

Why can't everyone understand? These people have been selected by Nature to die. Stop interfering. Nature knows best. You keep them alive now, so in a year's time they die of a disease instead, or you cure the disease and they die of starvation. So you rid the world of starvation and they kill each other by the tens of thousands in tribal wars. These do-gooders are ignorant fools trying to buy a ticket into heaven. Let us leave these millions to Nature—let them fucking die.

I am Nature itself. I do what I was born to do and I don't feel guilty. I have freed myself from the shackles of compassion and mercy. Some of you are simply meant to die by my hand and so you will. Who am I to argue with Nature? Who are you to? Nothing can stand in the way of Nature's design.

But I'm no sick case locked in a bed, sitting alone every night slashing my chest with razor blades while masturbating to violent pornography. Not me. I'm no self-destructive psychiatric case just waiting or hoping to be caught. Neither am I seeking fame or notoriety. I don't even want to be infamous. You'll not see me sending the police clues, playing a game, phoning them up with tasty morsels of information. None of that interests me. I'll give them nothing.

And even if they do catch up with me, they'll never prove a thing.

My third visit was the most satisfying experience of my life. A development. A further sign of my growing strength and power.

In a way it is merciful. A newborn killer can make a terrible mess of things. Prolong the victim's agony. An efficient killer is exactly that. Efficient. I grow more efficient with each kill. That's not to say I don't like to have a little fun every now and then.

Besides, I have to make a mess sometimes, to keep the police guessing. Can't stick to the same method of dispatching the chosen few. That would make it all too easy. They're already sniffing around very close to home, not that that concerns me.

I rented a car. A big fat Vauxhall, with a big fat boot to match. I parked the car in a parking lot overnight, this time in the shopping center at Brent Cross in North London. I bought a new raincoat from the same shopping center, along with new plastic-soled shoes. I bought a nylon T-shirt and a new pair of black Nike training pants, all of which I stored in the hired car until I needed them.

I was all set. I returned to the lot early the following evening. The shops were still open. I took the clothes from the boot of the car and changed into them in a public toilet. I returned to the car and quickly covered the real number plates with false ones. I had been careful to park in a CCTV blind spot.

All went smoothly and I drove south toward King's Cross railway station, a modern monstrosity of a building. I drove against the flow of traffic and arrived there around 8 P.M. It wasn't quite dark yet, so I parked the car in a side street. It was free to park at this time of night. That was important. I couldn't risk a parking ticket or the unwanted attention of a bored policeman.

I left the car and walked toward the West End, along Euston Road. From my research I knew there was a Burger King close to St. Pancras station. Despite the excited tightness in my belly I felt a little hungry, so decided to grab a bite to eat. It was as good a way as any to kill an hour and let the night grow dark. Wait until winter comes, I thought. Sixteen hours of darkness a day. What fun we'll have then.

I ate my Whopper with cheese, chewed a few fries, and slurped a diet 7UP. I amused myself watching the people milling around me, unaware that they were dancing so close to death. Young foreign students mainly, being served by life's losers.

My attention became focused on three young Spanish girls. They picked at their food and giggled. They were attracting the attention of a group of dark-skinned youths. I didn't think the youths were Spanish—probably Italian or, worse, Albanian.

Probably more interested in stealing the girls' handbags than their virginity.

I would have liked to tie up the giggling girls. Spend plenty of time with them. Watch their tears of pain and fear flow, hear their stifled squeals of agony and humiliation as I had my fun with them one by one. Then I'd make them watch and see my power as I slit their throats. A twisted, bloody tribute to the beauty of violent death.

I had to calm myself. My imagination was overexciting me and the tightness in my belly was becoming painful. I had my subject for the night. It had been arranged. Carefully planned. I had to guard against acting on impulse. The Spanish girls would live. Someone else would not.

When the time came, I left the restaurant. On the way out I walked close to the Spanish girls. I breathed them in deeply. They smelled sweet. Like bubble gum. One of them glanced at me and smiled. I smiled back. Her friends noticed and all three returned to a giggling scrum. Some other time, perhaps.

I'd been agitated by the girls. My heart beat faster than normal. I was on the point of being desperate. I'd prayed my chosen subject would be where she should be. I walked faster than I should have. Had anyone noticed me? Thought me a little out of place? On reflection, I didn't think so.

I reached my chosen vantage point, at the far west tip of King's Cross station. I was so excited I almost wandered into the range of some CCTV cameras attached to the side of the station wall. I managed to stop myself. I looked across the five lanes of Euston Road traffic and focused on the small, brightly lit café. I could see straight inside. It was typical of the cafés around the station. A real shithole. The owner sold poisonous food and child prostitutes.

The game machines by the front door were a sign. A beacon

to the young homeless. Runaways from the north and Midlands often made it no farther from the railway station than this café. From here, they would be farmed out to various pimps across London. That would then be their life. Prostitution, crime, drugs, and early death.

Other hunters visited this place. It was like an African watering hole. Most hunting illicit underage sex. Some, very occasionally, hunting to kill, but none quite like me.

She was right where she should be. Pumping money into a fruit machine. A lost cause chasing a lost cause. She must have been between fourteen and sixteen, about five foot three; long dirty-blond hair; white skin, beautiful like marble. Slim. Half my size.

I'd been watching the place off and on for a couple of weeks. Nothing took my fancy, but I persevered. After a few days she appeared, knapsack in hand. From the first moment I saw her, she was mine.

I hadn't been any closer to her yet than this. I hadn't heard her speak, so I didn't know where she was from. I didn't know the color of her eyes yet either. I hoped they were brown. Brown eyes set against that marble skin would be stunning. I needed to see her blood on that skin. I started getting an erection. I took some deep breaths and calmed myself down.

During the times I'd watched her, she hadn't been taken away by anyone. I didn't think she'd succumbed to the inevitable life of prostitution yet. Good. The more innocent they are, the greater my pleasure is. Is there anything sweeter than violated innocence?

I kept watch. Waiting for her to make a deadly mistake. No one noticed me. There were thousands of people around the station. For once the weather forecast had been accurate and it was drizzling, hence my raincoat seemed perfectly normal, even at this time of year.

She did it several times a night. Walked out of the café and around into a side street, close to where I'd parked the car. At first I wondered what she was doing. Urinating? Giving clients fumbling oral sex? Then I saw her. She was going for a cigarette. She didn't want to share it with the other runaway fuckers. And why should she? They say smoking is bad for your health. If only she knew.

I patiently watched her. Still excited, but less agitated now. I had more control over myself. I could wait. It was only a matter of time.

My patience was rewarded. I saw her speaking to the other youths huddled around the machine. She was making her excuse to leave. The others didn't seem interested. She stepped out of the café, looking up and down the street. She knew she was mere prey. She was nervous about moving away from the safety of the herd. She disappeared into the side street. I crossed the road by the crosswalk. The light rain made the yellow, red, and green lights of the street dance on the shiny road and the vehicles that passed.

The girl was out of view now, but I could smell her. Feel her. I moved in closer. Drawn to her. I had the police identification in my coat pocket. My hand rested on it. Ready. In the other pocket I had a small carving knife in case she tried to run or squeal. I'd bought the knife months ago and hidden it in my study at home. It was a common brand. Very good for slicing tomatoes, or so the sales assistant had told me.

I saw her clearly enough. Standing in the doorway of a derelict shop, smoking her cigarette. She watched me walking in her direction. I sensed her caution, but no real fear yet. Nothing that would make her take flight. I was careful not to look at her as I approached. I used my peripheral vision to watch her. I got to about five meters away from her. If she'd run then, she might have lived. Any longer and she couldn't have gotten away. I am strong. I am fast. Much stronger and faster than I look. I exercise a lot. Secretly.

I drew level and turned to face her. She was trapped by railings on either side of the doorway. With the survival instincts of a wild animal, she spoke immediately: "Come near me and I'll fucking scream. I'll scream rape and I'll tell the coppers you touched us up." She had a Newcastle accent.

I smiled at her. I thought about pulling out the knife and slaughtering her right there. There was no one around. I stuck to the plan instead. I pulled out the police badge and showed it to her. Casually.

"Oh fuck," she whispered.

"Name and age?" I asked. She huffed, like a spoiled teenager being asked to make her bed by weak-willed parents. "Name and age? I haven't got all night to waste fucking around with you," I lied.

"Heather Freeman." She finally looked me in the eyes. Hers were blue. Never mind. "And I'm seventeen."

I laughed. "I don't think so, Heather. Your parents reported you missing over a week ago. You're underage, and that means you're coming with me," I lied again.

"Where to?" she asked. She sounded slightly panicked, but not scared. She certainly wasn't scared of me.

"The police station. And then we'll call your parents. See if they can come and pick you up."

She argued a little more and I told her she had no choice for now but to come with me. I needed to get her moving while the road was still quiet. I took hold of her upper arm and gripped firmly. She winced.

"You're hurting me arm," she complained in her northeastern accent.

"Can't have you running off again, can we?" I explained.

She huffed; her skin was as soft as warm water under my fingers. She would bruise easily. I relaxed my grip somewhat. I didn't want to leave an impression of my hand in her soft skin. "Come on. My car's around the corner."

"Haven't you got anything better to do than hassle me?" she asked, her accent increasingly annoying.

"Saving you from yourself, young lady," I answered. "These streets are no place for someone like you. There's a lot of bad people out there."

She huffed again.

We reached my rented car without incident. No one had seen us. I'd checked the route several times before. It wasn't overlooked by any residential buildings. No matter how busy King's Cross and the Euston Road were, the side streets were more often than not deserted of life. Just the occasional vermin looking for a whore.

I stood her by the boot of the car, so she was slightly side on to me. I opened the boot, which was already lined with plastic sheets. I'd bought them a few weeks ago from Homebase. You use them for decorating.

Fear flashed into her body. It electrified her every muscle, her every nerve. Her eyes widened and her pupils dilated. "What's this for?" She was almost pleading.

I smashed my right fist into her jaw, careful to avoid her mouth. I didn't want to leave my skin on her teeth. She spun around on the spot and began to fall. I caught her as she did. She was limp. Moaning quietly.

With almost no effort I threw her into the boot of the big sedan. I picked up the roll of gaffer's tape, another purchase from Homebase, and neatly bound her wrists behind her back. I also bound her ankles and knees, and gagged her pretty mouth. I looked around calmly. Still no one in sight. I stroked the pale skin around her neck. God, I wanted to slice it open right there. I slammed the boot shut before I lost control. All in good time, I told myself. All in good time.

I drove east along the Pentonville Road. Through wealthy Islington, immigrant-swamped Shoreditch, decaying Mile End, and immediately forgettable Plaistow. Finally I reached my chosen destination. A large piece of wasteland in South Hornchurch, not far from the Dagenham Ford factory. A suitably grim and dark place for little Heather Freeman to meet her end.

I drove along the clean tarmac road to a small brick building in the middle of the waste ground and parked close. I put on a pair of rubber gloves and made sure my coat was fully buttoned. When I opened the boot, she was lying on her side. Tears ran down her face and across the tape over her mouth. Her wet eyes shone like the purest diamonds. I wondered if she had ever looked more beautiful. She was too terrified to manage much more than a whimper.

I pushed her face into the plastic sheets and turned her onto her stomach. Her crying became more desperate. I grabbed her by the scruff of the neck and by the tape around her knees and lifted her easily out of the boot. She was even slighter than I'd imagined. I carried her like an old suitcase into the building and threw her on the hard, cold ground. If she hadn't been gagged, she would have called out in pain.

I grabbed her hair and pulled her face close. Those beautiful eyes stared into mine. "I'm going to cut you free now. Do as I say and you'll live. Fuck up or scream and you die. You die slowly. Understand?" She closed her eyes and nodded frantically.

I pulled the knife out and made sure she saw it. She was squealing again behind the tape. She pulled away from me. I yanked her back painfully. She got the message.

First I cut the tape around her ankles. Then I pulled it away from her mouth. She gasped for air. I sensed she was about to speak. I pulled her face closer. "Speak—you die."

I cut the tape from around her wrists and she rubbed at her skin. I let go of her hair and stepped back five paces. I wanted to see all of her. It was how I had foreseen it. How I had imagined it would be.

"Stand up," I demanded, giving her a few seconds to struggle to her feet.

"Take your top off," I ordered her.

Her face was twisted in fear and shame. She began to unbutton her dirty shirt. She moved slowly and that suited me fine. When she had finished unbuttoning it, I ordered her again to take it off. Slowly she pulled it off her shoulders and let it fall to the floor. She wasn't wearing a bra. Her young breasts didn't need one.

"Take your trousers off."

Again I could tell she was about to speak. I put my finger to my lips. "Shhh." She understood and struggled out of her sneakers before removing her trousers. They lay at her feet.

"The rest," I demanded quietly.

Her sobbing intensified. She pulled her knickers off with one hand. The other covered her inadequate breasts. She turned sideways to me. The headlights from my car illuminated the inside of the building perfectly. She was perfect. I would ensure she never became anything less than perfect.

I moved close to her again. "Get on your knees."

She mouthed a please. I pointed toward my groin with the knife. Her face was becoming even more twisted with fear and disgust.

I put my hands on her shoulders and pushed her onto her knees. I grabbed her hair and bent her head back as far as it would go. Her slender neck stretched out below me. In one motion I stepped away and swept the blade across her throat.

I kept moving backward as she held her throat in both hands. The blood seeped quickly through her fingers and dropped onto her naked chest. It ran across her small breasts and onto her stomach. She fell sideways to the floor before the blood reached lower. That was a shame.

I watched the last few seconds of her worthless life. At least now she would be remembered for something. Her death had more meaning than her life could ever have. She had become the purest work of art. I resisted the temptation to masturbate over her warm body.

She died still clutching her throat. Thin lines of the reddest blood streaked her face. Her eyes stared lifelessly. Diamonds. Perfection.

I stood just watching her for over two hours. I was lost. Totally captivated. The killing had been so much more satisfying than the previous ones. The knife. The intimacy. To watch the life ebb away. The colors. The textures.

Yes, I had taken more risks than before, but it was worth it. It had been necessary and the risks were manageable. Since she was left naked, the police would assume it was a sexual attack. It was not. I won't pretend I didn't enjoy seeing her naked. I did, but it wasn't her sex I was interested in. That was irrelevant.

I left the girl where she was. Let the police have the body. I wanted them to find it. I wanted them to think they were looking for a manic killer. A spontaneous killer. A reckless killer. Not one like me.

I returned to the car and changed clothes. The used ones I tied in a plastic bag. I would take them to the city dump back at Brent Cross tomorrow, along with some old rubbish my wife had been nagging me to get rid of. After that I'd take the rented car back, having removed the false plates, of course. No doubt they would give the car a good cleaning for me too.

I drove back toward North London. Totally at ease by then.

I was beginning to realize my potential. My power and control were unrivaled. It had been the most beautiful experience of my life—to take a life in this way—not in revenge or in a fit of temper, not when my blood was boiling with hatred and anger after being insulted and wronged, but a glorious execution of my right to do as I please and take whoever I want to take—my power. No hot blood coursed through my veins. My blood ran cold and she—she was a cold killing.

There was no going back now.

CHAPTER 12

Monday

Sean hauled himself from his uncomfortable chair, stretching and yawning as he looked out of his office window at the flat roofs of the surrounding buildings, their surfaces littered with the detritus of man and nature. He hadn't slept well the previous night, too many unanswered questions swimming around in his mind. His body ached miserably. A hopping bird caught his eye, its blue-black feathers shining in the sunlight, making its white patches barely visible, drawing his attention to the nearest of the rooftops. The magpie took oversize steps toward what had brought it to this desolate place, its head constantly jerking into new positions as it checked for danger and opportunity. Sean saw what it was moving toward—the half-concealed body of another bird—and assumed it had come to feast on a dead pigeon, but as it grew closer he realized it held something in its beak, something shiny, like a polished stone. He watched, fascinated, as the bird placed the object next to the body, then squawked loudly and sorrowfully before flying away.

He squinted against the sun and focused as hard as he could on the small corpse below, the black and white feathers confirming what he'd already suspected. As he continued to watch the sad little drama more magpies came to see their fallen kinsman, each bringing gifts of twigs and shiny objects, food and things precious to their kind, always chasing away any pigeons that dared to approach the lifeless body, pecking violently at their eyes, prepared to kill to protect their dead. No matter how hard he tried, he couldn't look away, until Donnelly burst into his office holding a set of car keys, shattering his temporary escape. "Going somewhere?" Sean asked.

"Drop your linen and stop your grinnin'. Fingerprints finally got back to us. They've matched a single print from the victim's flat to Hellier. He was in the flat. There's no mistake."

"A single print?" Sean asked, confused. "Is it a partial?"

"No," Donnelly reassured him. "It's a full match."

"Just one print." Sean could tell he was alone in his skepticism. "Where did they find it?"

"On the underside of the door handle for the bathroom. The outside handle," Donnelly informed him. "You don't look overly excited," he added.

Sean chased the doubts from his mind and tried to concentrate on the fact that finally he had usable, tangible evidence. His aches and pains faded as his excitement grew. "No wonder he didn't want to give his fingerprints. Get hold of the surveillance team and find out where Hellier is now, and get Sally to sort out a couple of search teams. Once he's nicked I want his office and home searched. No shit once-over. Full searches. With forensics too. You take one team and do his house. I'll do his office with the other."

Donnelly spun on his heels and left Sean's office.

They always make a mistake, Sean thought. They always make a mistake.

***

The three unmarked police cars drove fast toward Knights-bridge. The surveillance had confirmed that Hellier was at his office. The blue lights attached to the roofs of the cars whirled while the sirens screamed at the midmorning traffic to clear the way.

Sean sat in the trailing car. He felt exuberant. He remembered that this was why he had joined the force. Driving fast through traffic. Lights flashing, sirens wailing. Envious looks from other drivers. Children pointing. It just didn't happen enough.

They would arrest Hellier at his office and then search the entire place. Inch by inch. It didn't matter to Sean who knew Hellier had been arrested. He wasn't about to be subtle.

Maybe Hellier would confess when faced with the finger-print evidence. If not, how was he going to talk his way out of it? With luck, Hellier would be charged with murder before dark.

Other officers, led by Donnelly, were on their way to Hel-lier's house in Islington. They would wait until Sean sent word that Hellier had been arrested. As soon as he was, they would have the legal power to search his home for evidence relating to the murder of Daniel Graydon. Sean thought they had a better chance of finding something incriminating in Hellier's office. Surely he wouldn't risk leaving anything for his wife and kids to stumble across at home.

The three cars braked hard outside Hellier's Knightsbridge office. They didn't bother to look for parking spaces, just left the cars to block the road. A driver remained with each. The car doors seemed to open simultaneously. Nine police officers including Sean and Sally stepped out onto the tarmac. The heat had made it sticky.

They moved menacingly across the pavement to the front

door of the building housing Hellier's office. Sally pressed the buzzer for the ground floor, which housed a different company. No need to forewarn Hellier.

The intercom spoke. "Good morning. Albert Bray and Partners. Do you have an appointment with one of our consultants?"

"I'm a police officer and I need immediate access to this building." There was a silence. Sally continued: "This doesn't concern your company or any of your employees."

The door buzzed and Sally pushed it open. The detectives moved quickly and quietly into the entrance hallway. Two remained close to the front door. The other seven walked fast up the stairs.

They reached Butler and Mason and another locked door. Sean pounded on it. Time to ruffle some well-groomed feathers. Within a few seconds the door was opened by the perfect-looking secretary. He swerved past her into the office itself. Her mouth dropped opened. Sean thought she was about to protest.

"Is Mr. Hellier in his office?" She was struck dumb. "I said, is Mr. Hellier in his office?" Nothing. "I'll assume he is. Jim. Stan." Two detectives looked at him. "You boys stay here and cover the front door. The rest with me and Sally."

They strode along the corridor toward Hellier's office. Finally the secretary found her voice. She chased after them. "You can't go in there. Mr. Hellier is in a very important meeting."

"Wrong" was all Sean said.

"You need a search warrant," she argued.

"Wrong again," Sean told her without looking.

He threw open Hellier's door and walked straight in. The other detectives waited outside. Hellier sat at his desk, and Sebastian Gibran, who'd disturbed their last meeting, sat next to him, watching them as closely as Sean watched Hellier. Two other men Sean didn't recognize sat opposite; they seemed terrified. Hellier never flinched. Sean kept moving. He was almost at Hellier's side. He showed Hellier his identification.

"James Hellier, I'm Detective Inspector Sean Corrigan. This is Detective Sergeant Jones and Detective Constable Zukov. I'm arresting you for the murder of Daniel Graydon.

"You do not have to say anything unless you wish to do so. However, it may harm your defense if you fail to mention something when questioned that you later rely on in court. Anything you do say may be given in evidence against you.

"Do you understand the caution, Mr. Hellier?"

By the book, Sean thought. Best way with a slippery bastard like Hellier, especially with three witnesses sitting there with stunned expressions on their faces.

Hellier stared hard at him. Sean saw a flash of pure hatred. Hellier smiled and addressed the three men sitting opposite. "If you'll please excuse me, gentlemen. It appears the police need me to help them with their inquiries." He stood slowly, as if bored, and dramatically held out his wrists. "Aren't you going to handcuff me, Inspector?"

"I would," Sean said, "but you'd probably enjoy it." He took hold of Hellier's upper arm. Hellier felt strong. Solid. Sean was a little surprised. "Let's go."

Gibran tried to intervene, stepping in front of them. "Is this necessary?" he asked, his voice calm and matter-of-fact. Forever Butler and Mason's chief negotiator and protector. "Surely this heavy-handedness is unwarranted?"

"Sorry, I don't remember your name," Sean said, leaning uncomfortably close to the man.

"Really?" Gibran said. "That's odd. You don't strike me as the sort of man who forgets very much about anything."

"Keep your nose out of our business, Mr. Gibran," Sean warned. "And let us decide what is and isn't necessary."

Gibran slowly stepped aside, holding out an upturned palm, indicating they could pass, as if they somehow needed his permission.

Sean and Zukov marched Hellier out of the office and along the corridor. When Hellier was certain no one else could hear or see him, his expression changed to a snarl, showing Sean a glimpse of the monster he knew lived beneath the mask. "Just get me my fucking solicitor." He spat the words into Sean's face.

Donnelly and the other officers were already inside Hellier's house. Donnelly was rifling through the drawers in the lounge, well-practiced eyes scanning papers, letters, everything. DC Fiona Cahill was at his side, handing him more papers she had found elsewhere in the room.

Elizabeth Hellier had recovered from mild shock and was now running around talking incessantly. Complaining and threatening. Her threats were idle. They could take the house apart and there would be little she could do about it.

Donnelly could bear her twittering no longer. "Mrs. Hellier, this is gonna happen with or without your objections. The quicker and easier this is, the sooner we'll be out of here. Why don't you take a seat in the kitchen? Have a cup of tea and stay out of the way."

He steered Mrs. Hellier into the kitchen, guiding her onto a stool. Another detective peered around the kitchen door.

"Dave," he said, "we've got a locked door."

"My husband's study," Mrs. Hellier said. "He always keeps it locked during the day. I don't know where the key is. I think he takes it to work."

"Fine," Donnelly said. He turned to the detective. "Break it open."

"What?" Mrs. Hellier almost squealed. "Please, contact my husband. He'll open it for you, I'm sure."

"I think he's probably got other things on his mind right now, Mrs. Hellier." As Donnelly spoke, he could hear the unmistakable sound of splintering wood.

Sean left the others to complete the search of Hellier's office. It would take hours. He'd traveled back to the Peckham police station with Hellier, who had stared out of the window all the way. Hellier hadn't responded to any approaches Sean had tried, and he'd tried plenty. Disgust. Aggression. Threats. Compassion. Understanding. It had been Sean's only chance to go one-on-one with Hellier before the rules took over. Nothing had moved him. Yet.

Even when he was booked into the custody area, Hellier never spoke except to give his name and the details of the solicitor he demanded to speak with immediately. The custody officer assured him the solicitor would be called. He was about to have Hellier taken to his cell when Sean spoke. "One other thing . . ."

"Yes?" the sergeant asked.

"We want the clothes he's wearing. All of them."

"Okay. Take him to his cell—number four's free. Forensic suits are in the cupboard at the end of the cell passage."

Sean knew where the white paper suits were. Replacement clothing for suspects whose own clothes had been seized. They marked suspects who'd been arrested for serious crimes. Rapists. Murderers. Armed robbers. Police and other prisoners alike always paid more attention to men in white paper suits.

"Is there anyone I can call to have some replacement clothes brought for you, Mr. Hellier?" the sergeant asked. Hellier didn't reply. The sergeant shrugged his shoulders. "He's all yours, guv'nor."

Sean nodded his appreciation and led Hellier to his cell.

DC Alan Jesson followed Sean and Hellier into the miserably dreary cell. He carried the brown paper bags all clothing exhibits were sealed in. Plastic bags caused too much moisture. Mold could grow quickly and destroy vital evidence. Paper let the clothes breathe. Kept evidence intact.

"Strip. Take everything off and then put this on." Sean threw the white paper suit on the stone bench.

Hellier smiled and began to undress. The detective constable carefully folded Hellier's Boss suit, Thomas Pink shirt, and the rest of his clothing, then slid them into the brown paper bags. The detective wasn't concerned about creasing the clothes, he was taking care not to lose any forensic evidence that might be entwined in the fibers of the clothing.

Sean glanced at Hellier's naked body. He had the physique of an Olympic gymnast, only slimmer, denser, and more defined. Physically he would be more than a match for Sean, and that rarely happened.

Hellier looked at him. He spoke silently in his mind. *Enjoy your moment, bastard, because you will pay for this. I swear I will destroy you, Detective Inspector Corrigan. I will end you.*

Donnelly and his team had been searching Hellier's home for over three hours. They had bagged and tagged most of Hellier's clothing and shoes, but had found nothing startling.

Donnelly was searching through Hellier's desk drawers. They'd had to break them all open, one by one. Elizabeth Hellier had sworn she didn't have keys.

All their search had turned up was further evidence that Hellier was as wealthy as he looked. He had a number of bank accounts: Barclays, HSBC, Bank of America, ASB Bank in New Zealand. Each containing in excess of a hundred thousand pounds or the foreign equivalent. Donnelly let out soft whistles as he added up the sums, but other than that he found nothing.

He needed to stand and stretch. As he pushed the chair back

from the desk he felt a stinging pain in his thigh. He looked down and saw a rip in his trouser leg.

"Oh, you bastard," he declared. "What the bloody hell was that?" He put his hand under the desk and felt around. He touched something. It was small and cold. Something metal.

He pushed the chair away and ducked under the table. He saw them immediately. Not one, but two shiny keys taped underneath the desk. He didn't touch them.

"Peter—get the photographer in here. I need a picture taken."

Only when the keys had been photographed and fingerprinted did Donnelly remove them from under the desk. The tape used to hold them in place had been carefully removed and sealed in a plastic evidence bag. Who knew how many microscopic pieces of evidence clung to its sticky back?

He held the keys up and asked the room a question. "Now. What do we use keys for?" Slowly he looked down at the drawers they'd broken open. The locks remained intact. He winced as he put one of the keys into the drawer lock. It didn't fit. He tried the other. It fit. He grimaced before turning the key. The lock clicked open. "Oops," he said. "I think we might be getting a bill for some broken antique furniture."

He tried the other drawers. The key fit them all. He dropped it into an evidence bag and sealed it straightaway. He tossed the other key around in the palm of his hand and called out across the office. "Anyone finds a locked anything, let me know."

A detective searching the walnut cabinets attracted Donnelly's attention. "Hold on, there could be something under here."

Donnelly moved closer and watched over his shoulder. He pulled back the carpet at the base of the cabinet. They stared at the floor safe. They looked at each other, then at the key in Donnelly's hand.

He pushed the key into the lock. He could feel it was precision made. It slid into place as if it had been oiled. The heavy door opened upward.

The first thing he saw were bundles of cash, neatly rolled and held in place with rubber bands. He touched nothing. He could see they were mainly U.S. dollars. Hundred-dollar bills. Some sterling too—fifty-pound notes—and Singapore dollars, again in fifties. How much in total, he could only guess. He saw the unmistakable red cover of a British passport. He flicked it open—it was in Hellier's name. This man could leave the country in a hurry if he had to.

There was something else, lying under the passport. A small black book. An address book? Donnelly was still on his knees. He looked up at the detective who'd discovered the floor safe.

"You'd better get that photographer back in here. And the fingerprint lady too. I don't know what all this is about, but it's got to mean something."

Sally's search team had arrived back at the station at about 2 P.M. She sat with Sean in his office briefing him on what they had found and seized, the main thing being Hellier's computer, which would be sent to the electronics lab where the boffins would interrogate the system's innards. Maybe they could find something, but it would take time.

Sean's phone rang. "Hello, this is DI Corrigan."

"Front office here, sir. There's a Mr. Templeman wants to see you."

"Tell him I'll be down in a minute." Sean hung up. "Hellier's lawyer's here," he informed Sally as he set off for the front office. He walked quickly along the busy corridors and skipped down the stairs, nodding to the stressed-looking civilian station officer before waving Templeman past the waiting queue of customers. Templeman wasted no time with pleasantries. "I demand immediate access to my client."

"Of course," Sean agreed, and guided him through a side door into the station. "I'll take you to the custody suite. Follow me."

"And when do you plan on interviewing my client? Soon, I hope."

"When the Section Eighteen searches are complete and I've had time to assess the evidence."

"How long, Inspector?"

"Two or three hours."

"That's totally unacceptable," Templeman argued. "Clearly you're in no position to interview my client, therefore I suggest you release him on bail until such time as you are ready. Later this week, perhaps."

"I'm investigating a murder," Sean reminded him, "not some Mickey Mouse fraud. Hellier stays in custody until I'm ready."

Sean typed in the code on the security pad attached to the outside of the custody suite. When the pad gave out a high-pitched beep, he pushed the door open, immediately looking for a jailer to take Templeman off his hands.

"Murder or fraud, Inspector, everyone is entitled to a fair and vigorous defense," Templeman continued. "And that's what I'll ensure my client gets."

"Everyone except the dead," Sean replied coldly. "Everyone except Daniel Graydon." He grabbed a passing jailer before Templeman could reply. "This is Hellier's attorney," he said. "He would like to see his client as soon as possible."

"No problem," the jailer responded. "If you follow me, sir, I'll sort that out for you."

Sean was already walking away, Templeman calling after him: "I need to see any relevant statements you have. I'm entitled to primary disclosure, Inspector. I'm entitled to know what evidence you have against my client."

"And you will," Sean answered, already looking forward to the moment when he would reveal that Hellier's fingerprint had been found in Daniel Graydon's flat, but undecided as to who he was most looking forward to seeing squirm: Hellier or Templeman.

Sean bounced up the stairs and back along the corridors to the incident room, tired legs suddenly alive again. He reached the room in time to hear the volume within rising. It could mean only one thing: Donnelly's search team was back. Sean headed for his office, passing Donnelly en route. "My office, when you've got a minute, Dave."

Donnelly dumped several evidence bags on his own desk and headed straight for Sean's office.

"What have you got?" Sean said.

"We've seized every bit of clothing he owns and his shoes. We'll get that lot up to the lab tomorrow."

"I need something now. Something for the interview. I want to charge Hellier tonight. Tomorrow at the latest."

"Sorry, boss. No smoking gun in the house. But it's all wrong there—he keeps his office locked all day when he's not in there, even when he's at home. His wife says she doesn't know where he keeps the keys. She also says she knew nothing about the floor safe."

"Floor safe?" Sean asked.

"The jewel in the crown. Guy's got a floor safe in his study."

"Plenty of rich people have got floor safes. Doesn't mean much."

"True, but how many keep rolls of U.S. dollars in them, with their passports? There was an address book too."

"So he's prepared to leave in a hurry. Who knows why? If it was a crime not to trust banks, we'd all be in jail."

"For someone who doesn't trust banks, he's sure got plenty of money in them. Close to half a million, from what I could tell. God knows how much the final total will be."

"What about the address book?" Sean asked. Often it was

the smaller, less dramatic items that held the vital clues. A scrap of paper with a number written on it among pristine bank statements. An old person's collectible in a young man's flat. If it seemed out of place, no matter how slight, it could be the biggest lead of all.

"I just had a cursory glance. Nothing more than initials and numbers. If they're phone numbers, then they're definitely not local. Probably overseas. It's not arranged alphabetically. I've already checked for the victim's initials, DG. Not in there."

"Hellier could be using codes," Sean said. "Get every number in there up to Special Operations 11 and have them run subscribers' checks on the lot anyway. Tell them we need names and addresses by tomorrow lunchtime at the latest."

"I'll ask, boss, but that'll be tight."

"Do it anyway. In the absence of anything else, I'll press on and interview Hellier. Let's see what he's got to say about his fingerprint being in the victim's flat."

Donnelly sat in on the interview, but it would be Sean who'd ask most of the questions. The interview room was barren. A wooden table, four uncomfortable chairs. The walls were dirty beige. No pictures. The room smelled of rubber flooring and stale cigarettes. A double-deck tape recorder lay on the table. Microphones were pinned to the wall.

Sean, Hellier, and Templeman sat quietly, watching Donnelly break the cellophane tape around two new audiocassettes. He put both into the recorder and slapped the machine shut.

Sean broke the silence. "When we press start, you'll hear a buzzing sound. That'll last about five seconds. When that noise stops, we're recording. Do you understand?"

Templeman spoke for Hellier. "We understand, Inspector."

Sean could feel a "No comment" interview coming his way.

He nodded to Donnelly, who pressed the record button. The two tape reels began to turn together, the buzzing noise louder than anyone had expected. Even Sean felt his heart skip a beat. After a few seconds the noise stopped. There was a second of silence before he found his voice.

"This interview is being recorded. I'm Detective Inspector Sean Corrigan. The other officer present is . . ." He let Donnelly answer for himself.

"DS Dave Donnelly."

Sean continued: "I am interviewing—could you please state your name for the tape?" Sean spoke to Hellier. Hellier looked at Templeman, who nodded that he should speak. Hellier leaned forward a little.

"James Hellier." He leaned away.

"And the other person present is?"

Templeman knew his cue. "Jonathon Templeman. Solicitor. And I'd like to say at this point that I am here to represent James Hellier. I will advise him regarding the law and his rights. I am also here to ensure the interview is conducted fairly and to challenge any questions or behavior by the police that I deem to be inappropriate, unfair, irrelevant, or hypothetical.

"I would also like to say that against my advice"—Sean saw Templeman cast a quick glance at Hellier—"Mr. Hellier has decided he would like to answer any questions you ask."

Sean wondered if they'd staged this little performance. Templeman's idea, probably. Cast Hellier in the role of the victim of circumstance. The innocent man out to prove it. Whatever it was, Sean hadn't seen it coming. He continued with the preinterview procedure.

"You have the right to consult with a legal representative or solicitor. You can consult on the phone or have one attend the police station, and this right is free. As we know, you have your solicitor, Mr. Templeman, present here anyway. Have you had sufficient time to consult with your legal representative in private?"

Templeman continued to speak for Hellier. "Yes, we have."

"I must remind you that you're still under caution. That means you do not have to say anything unless you wish to do so. However, it may harm your defense if you fail to mention when questioned something that you later rely on in court. Anything you do say may be used in evidence. Do you understand?"

"He understands," Templeman said.

Sean decided to break this routine. "I would like Mr. Hellier to answer for himself. I need to hear that he understands from his own mouth."

Templeman was on the verge of protesting, but Hellier spoke. There was no feeling in his voice. "I understand, Inspector. The time has come for explanations."

Sean's stomach tensed. Was Hellier about to spill? Had the burden of guilt caught up with him? Few had the strength to carry their darkest secrets all the way to the grave.

Hellier and Sean locked stares. Sean spoke. "Mr. Hellier. James. Did you kill Daniel Graydon?"

Sally entered the Intelligence Office at the Richmond police station where she was met by a uniformed constable. "Are you the DS from the SCG?" he asked unceremoniously.

"Yes. I'm DS—"

"So what is it you're after?" the constable interrupted, apparently not interested.

"Information from your records," Sally told him. "Back in 1996 a man called Stefan Korsakov was charged here with a serious sexual assault and fraud."

"An unusual mix," offered the constable.

"Yeah," Sally answered. "Later the assault charges were

dropped, but he went down for the fraud. You should have a charging photograph of him. I need to see it."

"Back in ninety-six? You'll be lucky if we still have a card on him. Unless he reoffended within the last five years, his old card wouldn't have been transferred on to the new Intelligence System. It may have been shredded. We kept the more interesting ones, though. People most likely to come back and haunt us. What was the sexual assault?"

"He raped a seventeen-year-old boy in Richmond Park. Tied him up and threatened him with a knife."

The constable scratched the side of his face. "Hmm. That's definitely the sort of person we should have kept. I'll have to check in the archives. What did you say this bloke's name was?"

"Korsakov. Stefan Korsakov."

The constable began to move alongside the metal filing cabinets, which were just big enough to hold the old intelligence cards. As he did, he spoke to himself: "K, K, K, K . . . here we are." He stopped and opened the cabinet containing records of people whose surname began with K. He fingered through the files.

"Korsakov. Korsakov. Stefan Korsakov." He pulled a thin card from the cabinet. "You're in luck. We kept his card." His smile soon turned to a frown. "Bloody typical."

"Problem?" Sally asked.

"The photographs. They're not here. Some bastard's taken the lot."

"Did I kill Daniel Graydon? No, Inspector, I didn't. No matter how hard you find that to believe, it's the truth." Hellier's eyes were giving nothing away. Damn, he was difficult to read.

"Why did you lie to us?" Sean asked. "You told us you were never in Daniel Graydon's flat, which leaves me very confused as to how your fingerprint ended up on the underside of his bathroom door handle."

Hellier sighed. "I lied to you, and that was wrong. I was fool-ish to do so and I can only apologize for wasting your time. I pray to God I haven't distracted you from catching the person responsible."

Sean didn't believe a word.

"I have been to Daniel's flat. I was a client of his. I've been so for the past four or five months."

"And on the night he died?" Sean asked.

"No. I didn't see him the night he was killed. I didn't go to his flat that night. I hadn't been to his flat for over a week."

"You see," Sean said, "whoever killed Daniel got into his flat without breaking in. We believe Daniel let them in. Now what sort of person would Daniel let into his flat at three in the morning? A friend, perhaps? Or maybe . . ." Sean paused a sec-ond to make sure he still held Hellier's gaze. " . . . a client? One who made regular visits. One he thought he could trust."

Templeman could stay silent no longer. "These questions are totally hypothetical. If you have evidence—"

Hellier put a hand on Templeman's forearm. Templeman fell silent. "I want to answer their questions. Any questions. I didn't go to his flat that night."

"So why did you lie about never having been to Daniel's flat? You knew this was a murder investigation. You must have known the serious consequences of lying to us. You're not a stu-pid man."

Hellier looked at the floor and spoke. "Shame, Inspector. I don't expect you to understand. I only wish you could."

Sean had had about all he could stomach. Most of his child-hood he'd felt nothing but shame. Shame and fear. Listening to Hellier's false pleadings made him feel physically sick.

"You live a lie. You lie to your wife, kids, family, friends. You pay young men to have sex with you and then curl up in bed with your wife. You lie to the police, even though you know that may delay our investigation. And now you want me to believe you lied because you were ashamed of your sexual preferences. I doubt you've ever been ashamed of anything in your entire life."

Hellier looked up from the floor. His eyes were glassy. "You're wrong, Inspector. I am ashamed. Ashamed of it all. I'm ashamed of my life."

Sean studied him for a few seconds, looking deep into the darkness that he knew seethed behind Hellier's eyes. "So what was so special about Daniel?" He wanted to keep it personal. "Why keep going back to the same boy?" He used the word "boy" deliberately.

"I have needs. Daniel helped me with those needs."

"Enlighten me."

"I practice sadomasochistic sex. So did Daniel. I went to him for that. I generally saw him once every two to three weeks. That's what I was trying to hide. I was a fool, I know."

"What did this practice involve?" Sean asked.

"That's hardly relevant," Templeman interjected.

"There are unexplained marks on the victim's body. Mr. Hellier's sexual behavior may explain those marks. It's relevant."

"Nothing too shocking," Hellier answered. "I would tie him up, by the wrists usually. With rope. We used blindfolds, sometimes whips. Mainly it was role playing. Harmless, but not something I wanted the world to know about."

"I can understand that," Donnelly said.

"Did he ever tie you up?" Sean asked.

"No. Never."

"So when you say sadomasochistic, you filled the sadist's role, yes?"

"Not always. Daniel would beat me sometimes, but I never felt comfortable being in bondage. Daniel said I lacked confidence. He was probably right."

Hellier had an answer for everything. Sean dropped the address book on the table. It was still in the plastic evidence bag. "What's this?" he asked.

"An address book," Hellier answered. "Obviously."

"It was pretty well hidden for an address book. No names either, just initials and numbers."

"It contains certain contacts of mine I would rather my wife and family didn't know about." It was an answer that made sense. Like all his answers.

"Is Daniel's number in here?" Sean asked.

Hellier hesitated. Sean noticed it. "No."

Why would that be? Sean wondered. Here was his secret book, yet one of his biggest secrets wasn't in it. That made no sense. "You sure his number's not in here?"

"Yes," Hellier said. "His number's not in there."

Sean decided to let it go for now, until he understood more. "And the cash: I believe it was about fifty thousand in mixed currency, mainly U.S. dollars?"

"I like to keep a decent amount of cash about. These are uncertain times we live in, Inspector."

"And the money spread across the world in various bank accounts belonging to you? Hundreds of thousands, from what we can see." Sean knew these questions would get him no further, but they had to be asked.

"One thing I won't do, Inspector, is apologize for my wealth. I work hard and I'm well rewarded. Everything I have, I earned. My accounts are in order. I can show you where the money came from and the Inland Revenue can unfortunately vouch for the fact that I'm telling the truth."

Sean was getting nowhere and he knew it. He needed to knock Hellier off his stride—get personal and see how Hellier reacted. "Inland Revenue, your account, your job at Butler and Mason—it's all very top end, isn't it?" He noticed a small, involuntary contraction of Hellier's pupils that disappeared as quickly as it had come. "And you, in your thousand-pound suits and three-hundred-pound shoes—you're a polished act, James, I'll give you that."

"I don't know where you're going with this," Templeman interrupted. "It hardly seems relevant or proper."

Sean ignored him. "But underneath that veneer of yours, there's an angry man, isn't there, James? So what is it that's really pissing you off? Come on, James, what is it? What are you trying to hide? A working-class background? Maybe an illegitimate child somewhere? Or did you disgrace yourself in some previous job—got caught with your hand in the cookie jar—everything was smoothed over, but still you were shown the door? Come on, James—what is it you're hiding from me— from everyone?"

Hellier just stared straight into him, his eyes never blinking, lips sealed tightly shut, possibly the faintest trace of a smirk on his face as his muscles tensed, controlling his facial reactions, making him impossible to read.

"You know, James," Sean continued, "you can have it all— the job, the money, the wife and kids, the Georgian house in Islington—but you'll never really be like them. You'll never be accepted as one of them, not really. You'll never be like . . . like Sebastian Gibran, and you know it." Another contraction of Hellier's pupils told Sean he'd hit a raw nerve. "You can try and look like him, even sound like him, but you'll never be like him. He was born into that role. He's the genuine article, while you're a fake—a cheap imitation—and you can't stand it, can you?"

He leaned back, but still Hellier wouldn't break, sitting silently, his hands resting on the table, one on top of the other, seemingly unmoved.

Sean tapped a pen on the table. He had one other question he was burning to ask, something that just didn't make sense about the fingerprint they'd found, but some instinct warned him that it wasn't the right time yet. Like a champion poker player knowing when to slap his ace down and when to hold back, a voice screamed in his head to save the question until he himself understood its significance.

"We'll have to check on what you've said, so unless you've anything to add, then this interview is concluded."

"No. I have nothing to add."

"In that case, the time is seven fifty-eight and this interview is concluded." Donnelly clicked the tape recorder off.

"Now what?" Templeman asked.

"No doubt you'd like another private consultation with your client, and then he'll be returned to his cell while we decide what's going to happen to him."

"There's no reason to keep Mr. Hellier in custody any longer. He's answered all of your questions and should be released immediately. Without charge, I should add."

"I don't think so," Sean said, dismissing him.

Templeman was still protesting vigorously as Sean and Donnelly left the interview room. A uniformed police constable guarded the door. Sean and Donnelly headed back to their murder inquiry office.

Sean felt deflated. The interview hadn't gone well. Except for one thing. Why wasn't Daniel's name in Hellier's secret book? That made no sense. Somehow and in some way it was another piece of the puzzle.

CHAPTER 13

Sally quickly studied the man who opened the front door of the detached Surbiton house. He looked about fifty years old, five-nine. His slim arms and legs, combined with a beer belly, reminded her of a spider. His hair was thick and sandy colored, his eyes green and sharp. Sally saw an intelligence and a confidence behind them. She reckoned that Paul Jarratt had been a good detective during his years as a Metropolitan Police officer.

"Mr. Jarratt?" Sally held out a hand. Jarratt accepted it. "DS Sally Jones. Sorry to call unannounced like this, but I was in the neighborhood and wondered if you wouldn't mind helping me out with a case I'm working on."

"A case?" Jarratt was surprised.

"A murder, actually," Sally told him. "A few years ago you dealt with a case involving a man who could be a suspect for our murder."

"You'd better come in then," said Jarratt.

She entered the tidy house and followed Jarratt to a large, comfortable kitchen. "Tea? Coffee? Or something cold?" he offered.

"Tea would be good. Milk and one please."

"I'll make a pot," Jarratt said, smiling, flicking the kettle on and gathering the things he needed to make the tea.

"So how long've you been out for?" she asked. Half the force dreamed of being out. The other half dreaded it. Which was Jarratt?

"About four years now. Ill health. An old back injury finally caught up with me five years short of my thirty. I qualified for a full pension and some medical benefits, so I'm not complaining. I get a bit bored at times, but you know . . . Anyway, what can I help you with?"

Sally recognized the cue to get down to business. "I'm investigating a murder. A bad one. Young gay man, Daniel Graydon, stabbed and beaten to death."

"A homophobic attack?" Jarratt asked.

"No, we don't think so. Something else, although we're not quite certain what. Which is where you may be able to help."

"Well, I'm not sure about that," Jarratt answered. "I spent most of my time on the Fraud Squad. Number crunching was my game. Not murders."

"I appreciate that, but other than working on the Fraud Squad you also did a spell in the CID office at Richmond." It sounded like a question, but it wasn't.

"Yes. That's right. From about ninety-five till about ninety-eight, as best as I can remember. Then I got back on the Fraud Squad."

"It was a case you dealt with at Richmond that interests me—a man called Stefan Korsakov, back in ninety-six. He'd been arrested by Parks Police for—"

"Raping a young boy," Jarratt interrupted. "He bound and gagged him in Richmond Park. Threatened him with a stiletto knife, then raped him. I shouldn't think I'll ever forget Stefan Korsakov. And if you'd met him, you wouldn't either."

There was silence in the kitchen. The comment was unusual.

Police officers never exaggerated the impact criminals had on them. Sally wondered what it could have been about Korsakov that had Jarratt so spooked. She tried hard to think when a suspect had ever affected her in that way. Nothing came to mind. She sensed that Jarratt's fear of Korsakov was personal.

"What made him so memorable?" she asked.

Jarratt poured two cups of tea, adding the milk and sugar to the one that he placed in front of Sally before answering her question. "No remorse. Absolutely none. His only regret was that he got caught. And that only bothered him because it meant he was off the street and wouldn't be able to do the same thing again to someone else.

"He never said so during the interview—in fact, he never said anything during the interview—but I knew he would have killed that young lad if he hadn't been disturbed. There's no doubt. It was a hell of a blow when the boy's family wouldn't let us prosecute him for the rape. I can still remember the smirk on Korsakov's face when I told him the charge had been dropped. Talk about the devil looking after his own. It would have been better for everyone if he'd taken a long fall from a high window. Know what I mean?"

Sally smiled uncomfortably, but didn't answer. Jarratt sensed her reaction. He stood and moved to the sink, pouring his tea away as Sally watched him and tried to sense his emotions. Jarratt's nausea looked real enough.

"I'm sure I don't have to tell you what it feels like to watch an animal like Korsakov walk away, knowing it's only a matter of time before he rapes again, or graduates to murder."

"But he didn't walk," Sally reminded him, "he went down for the fraud. I hear you made certain of it." It was a compliment.

"Yes, I made certain he went down for something. I got a sniff of Korsakov's little fraud operation and dug in. He went down, all right, but it was a hollow victory. He got four years.

That was all. All those people he screwed. And we never recovered the money. No matter what we tried, we couldn't find it.

"I even had a couple of old friends from the Serious Fraud Squad in the city who owed me a favor help me look for it, but nothing. He was a clever bastard. I'll give him that."

Sally was interested in the fraud. It helped build the picture of Korsakov. But she was more interested in his violent nature. That was the road that could lead to his capture.

"Did he show an awareness of forensic evidence or police procedures?" Sally asked.

"Definitely," came the unhesitating reply. "The clothes he wore, the use of a condom, the victim he picked, and even the venue was pretty good. He just got unlucky, and thank God he did.

"And he would have learned. He would have gotten better and better. He was clever enough to learn from his own mistakes. Very organized too. His frauds were brilliantly simple. And as I've already mentioned, clever enough to hide the cash where no one could find it.

"That's not easy to do these days," Jarratt continued. "Billionaire drug dealers, bent City accountants, corrupt governments—they all spend fortunes trying to hide the money in the legitimate banking system. You can't keep millions of pounds under the mattress and, even if you could, no one accepts cash anymore, not for major purchases. Cash makes people nervous. You've got to get it into the banking system. That's where we so often catch them out and recover the money, but not with Korsakov. He was too cunning.

"So tell me, DS Jones. He's committed another rape or murder, hasn't he?"

Sally hesitated before answering. She was unsure why. "We don't know if it's Korsakov. There are similarities between your case and one we're investigating. So we're doing a little background digging. One thing's bothering me though."

Jarratt looked at her, expressionless. "Go on."

"Everything points to Korsakov being a repeat offender. You said it yourself, that he'd offend again."

"Yes."

"Yet he hasn't come to police notice at all. No convictions, no arrests, no information reports. Nothing."

"Then he's either out of the country or he's dead," Jarratt answered. "Only pray it's the latter."

"Or maybe we just haven't caught him."

Jarratt gave a low laugh. "I know we're not perfect, but there's never been a repeat offender who hasn't been caught within a couple of years. Even in the dark ages, before computer cross-referencing, DNA, *Crimewatch,* we still caught the people eventually. They would always make a mistake.

"No. If he was in the country, he would be offending. He wouldn't be able to stop himself any more than we could stop treating everybody with suspicion. It's in his nature. Or he may have become a ghost, never keeping one identity too long, never staying in one place longer than a couple of months. He's capable."

"I'll check with public records," said Sally. "See if they have anything on him. And thanks to you, we'll have a set of fingerprints for him. I'll have them compared to any marks recovered from our scene."

Jarratt's eyes narrowed. "If it's a death certificate or fingerprints you find, then please call me. If he's sunning himself in Thailand, I'd rather not know."

Sally thought Jarratt suddenly looked old. She wouldn't push him any further. "Well, thanks for your time," she said, and stood to leave. "Oh, one more thing."

"Yes?"

"You did take photographs of Korsakov, when you charged him?"

"Of course."

"It's just, when I checked his intelligence records at Richmond, there were no photographs attached."

"Unfortunate, but not unusual," Jarratt replied.

"Can you think of anyone else who may have wanted or needed photographs of Korsakov?" Sally asked. "Maybe I can still track them down."

"Not really," Jarratt answered. "No one's ever approached me about him."

Sally sighed. "Oh well, never mind."

Jarratt led her to the front door. His hand rested on the handle, but he didn't turn it. "Can I ask what put you on to Korsakov?" he asked. "What put you on to me?"

"Method Index," Sally told him. "You were down as the officer in the case." Jarratt said nothing. "Oh shit," Sally suddenly said, fumbling in her handbag. "I almost forgot. Could you do me a favor and have a look at this photo?" She pulled the surveillance photograph of Hellier out and handed it to Jarratt. "Do you recognize him?"

Jarratt held the photograph and looked at it without interest. Sally saw nothing in his face. "No," he said. "Is it someone I should know?"

"Just a loose end I wanted to tie up, and now I have. Anyway, thanks for your time."

"Anytime," Jarratt said. "It's nice to feel useful again." They shook hands before Sally left and headed to her car.

"He's a sly one, all right," Donnelly said, "thinking on his feet. Covering our evidence as we find it."

"Then we'll have to find more," said Sean.

"How about DNA? Body samples?"

"Irrelevant," Sean reminded him. "He admits to having sex with the victim, and now he admits to being in his flat—any samples we find prove nothing. That wouldn't matter if we were to find the victim's blood on Hellier or his clothing, but it's going to take the lab days to process the things we seized today."

"So what are we going to do—just let him walk out of here?"

"That's exactly what we're going to do," Sean answered. "We charge him now, we're saying we've got enough evidence to convict him. We both know that's the rule. Once he's charged, we lose the right to question him further or to take more samples. We charge him now and we couldn't even make him take part in a fucking identification parade. I've made that mistake before. I'm not going to make it again. We have to come at him from another angle. One he won't be expecting."

"You're talking about identifying another crime he's committed?" Donnelly asked, without enthusiasm.

"I am," Sean confirmed, noting Donnelly's skepticism. "Something occurred to me during the interview. What if he's making it up—the whole story about having an ongoing client-customer relationship?"

"I don't follow."

"What if he wasn't having any sort of relationship with Graydon? What would that mean?"

Donnelly shrugged in confusion.

"It could mean he'd selected Graydon. Simply picked him from the crowd and killed him. All this bollocks about seeing him every few weeks, Graydon taking care of his physical needs, it's all a smoke screen, trying to confuse us—throw us off the scent. He's trying to lead us by the nose in the wrong direction. Maybe it's so much simpler than we were thinking: he went looking for a victim and found one, then he killed him. But he made mistakes—he was recognized in the club and he left a single print at the scene. Now he's covering his tracks, try-ing to make up for those mistakes. He knows that if he admits he's only ever seen Graydon once, then he's flagging himself up as a predator. He'll bring us right down on top of him. Much better this way. He thinks he's smart enough to get away with it, and that will be his downfall."

"But we know he did see the victim at least once before," Donnelly reminded him. "The doorman, Young, saw them together outside the club, remember? He was a distance away, but he was sure it was them and he was sure they headed off together, so he couldn't have just picked him up the night he killed him."

Sean had already considered everything Donnelly had said. "Of course he'd seen him before. Been with him before. That was important to him."

"Why?" Donnelly asked.

"Because that made the victim real. He needed to taste him and feel him. Fantasize about him. So he picks him up inside or outside the club, it doesn't really matter, and they probably go back to Graydon's. They have sex. Hellier drinks it all in—absorbs everything—and once he's sure Graydon is worthy of his special attentions he leaves, but watches him. He watches him for days, his excitement building, the fantasy in his mind growing increasingly violent and depraved until he can stand it no more, so he waits for him, outside the club. When Graydon eventually appears, alone, he follows him. Stalks him. Maybe he followed him all the way home or maybe he stopped him in the street—the victim wouldn't be too afraid; after all, they'd already had paying sex together. But whatever happened once they were back at the flat, Hellier made his fantasy come true. Only, as we know, he made two mistakes: the fingerprint and being seen with the victim. So he spins us this story about some sort of relationship he was having with the victim and has us chasing our tails, desperately trying to establish some logical reason for why he would want to kill Graydon, knowing we'll never find one, because there isn't one. And while we're looking for it we'll miss the real reason he killed Daniel Graydon—because he wanted to. Because he had to."

"Christ," Donnelly cursed. "So what now?"

"Take someone with you and bail Hellier out. Tell him to come back in two weeks. His attorney will ask why he needs to come back. Tell him we'll be checking his story. That Hellier hasn't been eliminated yet.

"And scramble the surveillance team again. I want Hellier picked up the second he steps out of the station. We run twenty-four-hour coverage. We keep the pressure on and wait for him to drop the ball. Sooner or later he's going to hang himself. Who knows, maybe he already has."

Hellier stood in the corridor of the police station, waiting to exit the building. First Templeman went outside to ensure no one was about. When he returned, the news wasn't good.

"I'm sorry, James. Looks like the media's gotten hold of this."

"What?" Hellier snapped. "You sure they're here for me?"

"I'm afraid so. They've already asked me for a statement. They know you've been arrested on suspicion of murder."

"That bastard Corrigan. He told them. He's trying to destroy me." Hellier's words were venomous.

"Listen," said Templeman, "you need to stay calm. I'll speak to them, deny you've been arrested, tell them you're helping the police with their inquiries. You stay in here until I'm finished, then I'll bring the car around. And I also recommend you cover your face when we leave."

"What?" Hellier's voice was raised.

"Just in case there's a photographer sneaking about. You can use my raincoat."

"You want me to crawl out of here with that over my head, like some pedophile? You might as well tell them I'm guilty."

"Please, James, try and stay calm." Templeman almost had his hands on Hellier's chest. "A name's nothing if they don't have a face to go with it."

Hellier sounded cold. "Fine, but hear this. No one humiliates me without paying the price."

"I wouldn't be talking about revenge if I were you, James," Templeman advised.

A look of disgust spread across Hellier's face. He put his face close to Templeman's. Templeman could smell a virile, animal stench on Hellier's breath. "You do as I fucking tell you and get me out of here. I'm expected at the damn industry awards dinner tonight. There'll be hell to pay if I'm not there. Sebastian's already on my back." Hellier stretched the stiffness out of his neck, the cracking noise making the lawyer shudder. He snatched Templeman's coat from him and gave him a final order. "Get me a damn taxi."

By the time Sally arrived back at the murder inquiry office, it was already early evening and she was keen to catch up on developments. The place was all but deserted, except for Sean, who sat alone in his office. Sally knocked on the door frame, making him look up. "Everything all right?" she asked.

"Wonderful," Sean answered sarcastically.

"I take it Hellier didn't confess then."

"Correct."

"And his fingerprint in the victim's flat?"

"Said he'd lied earlier. He now admits to having been there on several occasions in the past."

"That's exactly what I'd say if I was in his position."

"Me too," Sean agreed. "We bailed him, pending further inquiries. Anyway, how did you get on with what's-his-name?"

"Korsakov," she reminded him. "I managed to track down one of the original investigating officers, which was interesting enough, but he couldn't tell me much more than Method Index had. The intelligence record at Richmond was a bit thin, no photographs either.

"If you have no objections, I thought I'd have Korsakov's prints compared to any recovered from the scene. You never know your luck."

"Be my guest," Sean told her. "The identification officer dealing with this is IDO Collins. Now, if you'll excuse me, I need to go home before my kids forget what I look like. You should go home too. Get some sleep."

"I will," she said, then hesitated. "If he's guilty, we'll get him sooner or later. It'll only be a matter of time before we can prove it."

"Of course we will," Sean assured her. "We always do, in the end. By the way, speaking of Hellier, did you show your man the photograph?"

"I did."

"And?"

"Meant nothing to him. Sorry."

"Don't worry about it," Sean said. "It was a long shot anyway."

Jarratt sat at home with his wife and daughters. An article on the local evening news program caught his eye. Somebody had been arrested for the murder of Daniel Graydon. That was the name DS Jones had mentioned. The name of the murder victim.

The reporter standing outside the Peckham police station had used the term "helping police with their inquiries." Jarratt knew that meant he'd been arrested.

It was only a small item on the news. The death of a prostitute caused little stir in London these days. He listened to the reporter's closing statement.

"Although the police have so far refused to comment, it is believed that the man helping with their inquiries is one James Hellier, a renowned accountant and partner with the respected firm of Butler and Mason, whose offices are in the exclusive Knightsbridge area of Central London.

"The solicitor representing the man believed to be Mr. Hellier claimed his client had nothing to hide and was happy to assist the police in every way possible, although he declined to confirm the man was indeed James Hellier."

This was disastrous. Everything he feared most was becoming reality. Jarratt's chest was close to exploding. He excused himself and went to the kitchen. He poured too much whiskey into the first glass he saw. His hands shook as he took large sips. He needed to calm down, get control of himself and the situation. He thought he might be about to have a heart attack. He knew what was coming next.

Sean sat quietly staring at the television without really watching it. He'd chosen to sit on a chair instead of next to Kate on the sofa. She could feel his tension.

"Sean," she called across to him. Nothing. She called again. "Sean." He rolled his head to face her. "Do you want to talk about it?" she asked.

Sean puffed out his lips and exhaled. "Not really."

"It might help to talk," she persevered.

"It's nothing," he lied. "I thought I had our prime suspect today, but he wormed off the hook."

"You'll get him. Remember what you always tell me: it's only a matter of time, no matter how difficult it may look at first."

"Yeah, but this one bothers me. Every time I think I've got him cornered, he worms his way out. At first I thought he was just thinking on his feet, coming up with answers to fit the evidence against him as and when he had to, but now I'm not so sure. I think he has a strategy. The moment he knew we were onto him, he invented a story to lead us into a blind alley—and it's my fault. I showed my hand too soon. I should never have let him know he was a suspect. I should never have gone to his office in the first place. I should have watched him. Watched and waited for him to lead us to the evidence. Now I have to play the game with him, and from what I've seen so far he's a bloody good player. If I didn't know better, I'd say he was even enjoying it."

Sean sprang from his chair and made for the kitchen. He grabbed a glass and filled it with water. Kate followed him. She'd seen him like this before, usually during difficult cases, but not always. It was better to get him to talk than allow him to dwell on matters. She wouldn't let him slip away into the dark places his past could take him. "Don't let it get on top of you," she warned. To anyone else it would have been an innocent enough comment, but not to Sean.

"What's that supposed to mean?" he asked.

Kate realized her mistake. "Nothing. I only meant don't let this case get too personal."

"It's always personal," Sean told her. "For me, it's always personal. It's how I stop them."

"I know, but you need to be careful. Don't try and do everything alone."

"Why?" Sean asked. "Afraid I'll lose it?"

"That's not what I meant."

"Isn't it?" he said, his voice calm.

She knew his past, about his childhood, his father. The beatings and abuse. Everything. Sean had always been honest with her about that. She understood that the rage and hate from his childhood were still inside him somewhere. How could they not be? But she knew he was nothing like his father, like the people he hunted. If she'd had any doubts, no matter how small, she would never have married him, let alone had his children. This was just Sean venting his frustrations. She'd dealt with it before and she knew she'd have to deal with it again.

"Don't do this, Sean," she pleaded. "I don't deserve this."

It was enough to make Sean pause. "I'm sorry," he said. He sipped his water. "Do you ever think about it though? Aren't you ever a little afraid I may become like him?"

Kate knew he was talking about his father. "No. Never. You realized you had this thing inside you, and you wanted to stop it, stop it before anyone got hurt, and you did."

"With a lot of help," he reminded her.

"None of it would have worked if you hadn't wanted it to."

"Christ," Sean said, before taking another swig of water, "sometimes I feel like such a fucking stereotype: boy is abused by his father, the boy grows into a man only to become an abuser himself. From victim to offender. It's all too fucking predictable."

"But you didn't," she reminded him. "You grew up to be a cop. You use your past to help people, not to hurt them." A silence fell between them. Kate moved toward him and held his face in her hands. "Your past is a curse, but it has left you with a gift. You can think like these people. You can recognize them when others see nothing. You can predict them."

"Not this one," Sean told her. "I can't see through his eyes yet. I don't know why, but I can't. Whenever I try, it's like someone pulling a screen across, blocking me."

"It'll come," she assured him. "Give it time and it will come."

There was a silence, then Sean spoke again. "Do you know what it's like, being able to think like them?"

"No," Kate answered. "I look at you when you're like this and I thank God I can't. Who would want that burden?"

"I can feel what they feel," he said. "I can sense their excitement, their relief. Pain. Confusion."

Kate stroked his hair, the way a mother would a child. "And you use it to stop them. To stop them hurting people."

"Sometimes I feel like I'm too close. So close that I could slip into darkness any second."

"Then perhaps you should see Dr. Richardson? It has been a while since you spoke to her."

"No," Sean said, snapping a little. "I'll be fine. I'll sort it out myself. I just need you to remind me now and then. To remind me who I really am."

"You know who you are," Kate reminded him. "Ever since you decided you were going to be a policeman. Ever since that moment, you've known exactly who you are."

"I suppose so," he answered unconvincingly.

"There's something else though, isn't there? You've got that look on your face you always get when something's drilling a hole in your head. So what is it?"

"I saw something strange today," he confessed.

"The jobs we do, we see strange things every day."

He ignored her interruption. "Outside my office window, on the flat roof below, in amongst the ventilation outlets. It was a dead bird. At first I thought it was just another dead pigeon, but then I realized it was a magpie. I knew it was a magpie because other magpies kept landing next to it. I assumed they'd come to feed on its body, but I was wrong—they were bringing it gifts: twigs, small shiny stones, things to eat. I watched them for a while and then I realized, I realized what they were doing. They were mourning its death. Magpies mourn their dead. I never knew that."

"And that upset you?" Kate asked.

"No. Not upset me, made me wonder, that's all."

"Wonder what?"

"We don't judge them, do we? Magpies. When they're feeding on roadkill or killing the chicks of other birds as they try to hide in their nests, we don't judge them. We don't judge them because, as far as we're concerned, they're only doing what's in their nature to do. They're just animals, after all. But that's what I thought separated us from animals, the fact that we mourn our dead. Only now I know magpies do too. A murderous, heartless killer that mourns its dead."

"Meaning?" Kate asked.

"Meaning maybe we're not as different from the animals killing each other to survive as we'd like to think. Meaning maybe that's what the men I hunt are doing. Killing because it's in their nature to. They were born to do it, yet we pass judgment on them as if they were normal like you and . . ." He stopped before including himself.

"Whether it's in their nature to do it or not, someone has to stop them, and right now that someone is you."

"I know."

Kate sighed. "I'm proud of what you do. I'm proud it's you who goes after them. It scares me sometimes, but I wouldn't want it any other way."

Sean pushed his glass away. "Thank you," he told her softly. "Thank you for putting up with me. Promise me one thing though."

"What?" Kate asked.

"Don't ever let me go. Don't give up on me."

Kate slipped her hands around the back of his neck and pulled him closer. "That'll never happen," she promised. "I love you. Just don't push me away. Don't ever push me away."

Sebastian Gibran sat at his table in the middle of the Criterion Restaurant in Piccadilly Circus, an exclusive, expensive, and cavernous former ballroom in the heart of the West End. Usually the reserve of the rich, the famous, and wannabes, tonight it was for the exclusive use of London's financiers. The lights were dimmer than usual, but Gibran could still make out pretty much everyone in the place. As he absentmindedly joined in with small talk he searched the room for Hellier. He couldn't see him and checked his watch again. Hellier was already late, appetizers had been served and eaten. Soon the various speeches would begin. He knew he wouldn't be the only one who had noticed Hellier's absence. His searching was disturbed by the restaurant manager appearing at his shoulder, leaning in to speak quietly in his ear.

"Excuse me, sir, but some gentlemen would like to see you in the private bar." Gibran knew who the gentlemen were and he had a good idea why they wanted to see him. He nodded once to show the manager he understood while pushing his chair away to stand, throwing the napkin from his lap onto the table.

Gibran moved inconspicuously across the restaurant and up a short flight of stairs to the private bar, various security and waiting staff casually moving out of his way, as if they'd all been warned of his coming. Two gorillas in thousand-pound suits held the doors open for him as he entered the bar and was immediately ushered past the most senior people in the world of finance he'd ever seen assembled in one place to a corner where two aging men sat in large comfortable chairs, at a table made up for their exclusive use. The men had brown skin and silver hair; crystal-clear, sharp, intelligent eyes; and wore platinum watches vulgarly encrusted with diamonds. Gibran could imagine the cars they drove, the houses they lived in, and the call girls they would sleep with later that night. One had a glass of blood red wine on the table in front of him and the other a martini; the latter was smoking a fat Cuban cigar and nobody told him he couldn't. Gibran recognized them as two of the owners of Butler and Mason. He'd seen them twice before and spoken with them only once.

Neither of them stood to greet him. The one sucking the

cigar spoke first. "Sebastian." He had an Austrian accent. "Sorry to drag you away from dinner, but it's been such a long time since we've had a chance to speak."

Gibran resisted the temptation to remind them that they had never really spoken. "It certainly has," he managed to reply, but instantly noticed the old men's displeasure at his answer, as if he was somehow disrespecting them. "But I understand how busy you must be and I'm kept well informed of everything I need to know."

"Of course," the wine drinker reassured him in an Eastern European accent, "and we hope you understand how valued you are to our organization."

"I've always felt I belonged at Butler and Mason." Gibran told them what he knew they wanted to hear. "I believe in what we do, and that's the most important thing for me."

"Excellent," the smoker declared. "But now we hear that one of our employees has drawn unwanted attention to our business. Unwanted attention from the police."

Gibran found he needed to clear his throat before speaking. "Bad news travels fast," he said, but it prompted no response. The smoker puffed on his cigar and stared at Gibran through the thick clouds that floated from his mouth. "It won't be a problem," he tried to reassure the old men. "I believe it's a simple case of mistaken identity. I expect the police to clear things up very soon." Gibran could feel their eyes dissecting him and knew that if he made one wrong move now, by morning his desk would have been cleared for him and his name wiped from the company records. But the pressure didn't disturb him: he was used to it. He enjoyed it and the old men knew it, that's why they paid him as well as they did.

"Should we suspend him while we wait for this . . . this misunderstanding to be cleared up?" the wine drinker asked.

"Best not to," Gibran explained. "We don't have enough evidence of any wrongdoing and neither do the police, or so his legal representatives tell me. They're keeping me fully informed of any developments. For now, I'd rather keep him where I can see him."

"Does this employee know you're talking to his legal people?" the smoker asked.

"No. He believes he has client confidentiality."

"Good," the wine drinker eventually said. "We know you're aware of your responsibilities."

Another veiled warning, Gibran thought: clear up the Hellier problem or don't expect to be around too long at Butler and Mason. "I'm always aware of my responsibilities, gentlemen," he replied calmly. "Believe me, there's nothing I take more seriously."

"Of course you are," the smoker agreed. "You have a great deal to offer. Which is why we were wondering if you have ever considered becoming involved in politics?"

Gibran found it difficult to hide his surprise. "Politics?" he asked. "I'm sorry, gentlemen. I'm not a political animal."

The man with the cigar laughed, smoke spilling from his gaping mouth. "Trust me, to be successful in politics, it's better not to be too political."

The wine drinker laughed in agreement, but Gibran didn't see the joke, just their self-assured arrogance and condescending belief that somehow they understood how everything worked. No, it went beyond that; they believed they *controlled* how everything worked.

"We're not asking you to consider becoming an MP, merely whether you'd be interested in a role as a special government adviser. It could be arranged. You'll find all governments are desperate for the advice someone like you could offer them, otherwise all they have are civil servants whispering in their ears about things they know nothing about."

"Which political party did you have in mind?" he asked them.

Again the mocking laughter of wisdom from old men. "Whichever one you want," the wine drinker answered. "Our organization makes very generous donations to both the main players. We feel a man like you could almost immediately be placed in a position of real influence at the government level. Adviser to the minister for trade, perhaps?"

"Or perhaps the foreign secretary would interest you?" the smoker offered. "We have to plan for the future to remain competitive. To have someone of influence in the heart of government would be very useful for our organization."

"Well, I'll certainly take it under consideration," Gibran promised, "but I've always enjoyed working away from the limelight. I like to make things happen without being seen. It seems to suit my personal ambitions better."

"Fine," the smoker replied. "But don't take too long to make up your mind. What we're offering you is something very special. Remember, Sebastian, religion is dead. These days it's not down to priests and popes to tell us who to worship. Heavenly gods are dead to mankind. It's the gods made of flesh and blood that people worship. Urban gods. Would you like to be an urban god, Sebastian?"

Was that what these old men thought they were? Gibran asked himself. Gods? And did they really believe he would ever want to be like them, old and weak? Their power was an illusion, built on markets that could disappear overnight.

The smoker didn't wait for him to reply. "And don't forget to take care of that little problem we discussed, before it gets . . . embarrassing."

"Of course," Gibran said. "But we should bear in mind that

this particular employee knows a great deal about our, shall we say, business practices. If it was felt we needed to move him on, then I think it would be best to move him to one of our lower-profile offices, in say Vancouver or Kuala Lumpur. Somewhere we could still keep an eye on him. I would be uncomfortable having someone with that amount of knowledge potentially working for a rival."

"Agreed" was all the wine drinker said.

Once again the restaurant manager appeared at his shoulder, speaking softly into his ear. Gibran nodded once that he understood.

"Well, if you'll excuse me, gentlemen," he addressed the old men while getting to his feet, "it appears to be speech time." They said nothing as they disappeared behind a cloud of heavy white smoke.

Hellier entered the Criterion shortly after 9 P.M., late but unconcerned. He took his seat at the table and was relieved to see Gibran wasn't there: at least now he could order himself a proper drink. He nodded at the other people around his table, some of whom he knew and others he didn't. He didn't care either way, and neither did he care what they thought of him. He grabbed a passing waiter.

"Large scotch with ice," he demanded. "And make sure it's single malt." He released the waiter and searched the room for Gibran, who was nowhere to be seen. He was probably hiding in a toilet somewhere, preparing his annual speech. Hellier wished they'd let him make a speech. He'd like nothing more than to tell a room full of sanctimonious shits a few home truths.

As he waited for his drink and the next speaker, his mind kept wandering to Corrigan. Hellier knew cops, he understood how they worked, but there was definitely something about Corrigan that disturbed him, warned him to be more careful than usual. He must beware of hubris, stay focused, and stick to the script. There was to be no ad-libbing on this one. Corrigan was dangerous to him; he sensed it. His thoughts were disturbed by someone in a dinner jacket and bow tie tapping a microphone on the small stage.

"Ladies and gentlemen, please welcome our next speaker tonight, Sebastian Gibran, from Butler and Mason International Finance." The room applauded generously, if politely, while Hellier groaned inside. Thankfully his drink arrived at the same time. He swallowed half of it in one go.

Gibran raised his hand to bring an end to the applause. "As most of you know," he began, "I'm not one for making public speeches. But it is always a special privilege to be invited to address so many influential people from our industry."

Modest applause rippled through the room, drowning out the obscenities Hellier was muttering under his breath.

"Thank you," said Gibran, feigning modesty. "Thank you." He waited for the applause to cease. "I've worked in finance all my adult life, but never in more trying times—times where the creation and ownership of wealth are seen as morally corrupt, not just by those consumed with the politics of envy, but by power-hungry politicians who are all too keen to appease the noncontributing majority. They assume so much and know so little.

"A long time ago, one of the richest men in the world, when he was close to death, gave away everything he had, absolutely everything. When asked why, he said, 'There is no greater sin than to be the richest man in the graveyard.'" Laughter floated around the room. Gibran continued before it had stopped. "The thing is, he was right. There is no point in wealth for wealth's sake. This is not merely my personal ideology, this is the ideology of my organization.

"Since the banking sector abandoned all caution and reason in the pursuit of quick individual profits, people have lost faith in anyone even remotely connected to the financial markets, and that includes us. We have become fair game for anyone looking to ascribe the blame for their own failings to the mistakes of others, and we need to be aware that this is the brave new world in which we all now live. Only the other day I was having dinner with my wife and friends when a woman boldly informed me that the trouble with people like me is that we have no product, that all we do is make money for our masters who reward us with money. That essentially we produce nothing. We're never going to make a beautiful piece of furniture or educate a child. We don't build houses or save the lives of the sick. We create nothing and therefore have no value ourselves."

Hellier watched Gibran as his words silenced the audience who sat waiting for him to continue, waiting for him to assure them that they did have value, did have a place in the greater society. Hellier realized how different he was from everyone else in the room, how the mere thought of exclusion from anything terrified them, whereas he was able to embrace it when necessary, to make it his greatest ally. But even he was drawn into the speech and found himself eagerly awaiting Gibran's next words. Study him, Hellier told himself. Watch Gibran perform and learn from it. Study his speech patterns and changes in tone. Study his pauses and body movements, the way he looks around the room, searching for eye contact. If he ever had to make a speech, he would imitate Gibran, imitate him exactly. His mind flashed back to the interview with Corrigan—the accusation that he was no more than a cheap imitation, a generic copy of Gibran. Corrigan had an insightfulness almost as acute as his own. He must never forget that if he wanted to win the game.

"So," Gibran continued, "I explained to that person that our very essence was about creating product. I explained to her that without people like us there would be no Microsoft Corporation. Bill Gates's brilliant idea would have remained just that: an idea. It took finance raised by companies like ours to make it reality. And what about pharmaceutical companies and the drugs they make that save millions of lives: would any of them exist without finance to make their birth possible? No, they would not, and nor would any other non-state-owned business, be that a company making millions of cars or a family business making postcards. They all needed finance to exist in the first place. So, I told this woman, don't ever tell me that I have no product." He took half a step back from the microphone, triggering enthusiastic applause.

"But we must do more than this," Gibran continued. "There is no point in having a small, separate class of the superwealthy if the rest of society is reduced to a disillusioned underclass of the jealous, living their lives without hope or aspiration. In my heart I'm a socialist, but I believe all men and women should be equally wealthy, not equally poor. However, no government can ever achieve this. Their hands are tied by four-yearly elections and the need for short-term success. To build a society of the future worth living in takes time. It takes decades, not four years, which is why we must accept responsibility for things that have been too long left for the government to control. We should be financing the building of private but affordable schools. And in those schools we should be educating children who want to learn in environments free of disorder and dysfunction."

Gibran paused to allow applause as Hellier looked around at the audience, who were warming to Gibran's rhetoric.

"And we should finance the building of affordable private

community hospitals, where those who are sick and injured through no fault of their own can receive immediate and expert care, unhindered by the need to treat smokers, drinkers, and the obese. And we should finance the building of private housing estates with their own private police, paid to protect the families and homes of those who live on them. Areas that will be safe from rioters and looters. And eventually everyone will want this better way of life. They will no longer be prepared to send their children to failing schools or their elderly relatives to failing hospitals. And through the ethical use of profits, insurance, and payment protection, the public sector and the billions it sucks up and wastes will become obsolete. Through finance, the private sector will succeed where every government to date has failed."

Applause erupted in the room, making Hellier laugh inwardly at how expertly Gibran had played them. But his mood soon began to darken as he realized he was witnessing the birth of Gibran as a worthy adversary, a dangerous adversary. So now he had two: Corrigan and Gibran. But which one should he be more cautious of? At least Corrigan was obvious and predictable, the raging bull who would keep coming straight at him until he was defeated or victorious. But Gibran was the snake in the grass, waiting to strike. He was the shark that swam below a calm sea, waiting until he smelled blood in the water. Hellier would respect the threats both men represented, but he would never fear them. He watched as Gibran's speech drew to a close.

"However," Gibran warned his audience, "such ambitions can only be achieved in a new climate of competitive cooperation. Clearly, we cannot be seen to be forming cartels, but true progress cannot be achieved by individual businesses working toward individual goals. Cooperation is the key. But remember, we can only ever be as strong as our weakest link."

Gibran's eyes suddenly looked through the crowd and came

to rest on Hellier, who felt them burning into his skin, as if Gibran were publically branding him a liability. Hellier resisted the temptation to smile: Gibran might think he was smart, but he'd just showed Hellier his hand. No matter what happened next, Hellier would be ready for him. When the time came, he would be ready.

CHAPTER 14

I had to wait so very long before finding him. I searched and searched for years, then finally, it was he who found me. He simply walked into my life one day. Surely he had been sent to me, a gift from Nature herself.

His eyes betrayed him. Immediately I knew he and I were alike. We were the same animal. There was no mistake. He had hidden his nature well; his facade of normality would deceive anybody. Anybody but me, that is. But when he looked at me he saw nothing. I could see the contempt he had for me, the same as he had for everybody else. My disguise hid me even from my own kind. Now all I had to do was wait a little while longer. A year or two. Then I could begin.

My favorite film is *West Side Story*. Why? Because of the violence. It's pure and total violence. The dancing is violent. The music is violent. The scenery is violent, so is the red sun that washes over the city in every scene. The film's a statement about the dominance of violence over every other aspect of life. Romeo and Juliet. Violence defeats love. Violence is the only truth.

I understand this. You do not. You hide from violence. Cower in its presence. You damn it as the scourge of modern life. Punish your youth for being violent. Try to ban it from your television. Try to stop it at your football matches. Your government spends billions of pounds every year trying to remove violence from society.

But violence is life. Without violence there would be no life. Violence is the driving force that is life. It represents the ultimate beauty of life.

Evolution is violent. Species evolve through violent competition. The strong kill the weak and so the species develops. Without violence we would still be living in trees. No. Less than that. We would still be single-celled organisms. And yet you treat violence as your enemy, when it is your greatest ally.

I understand violence. I embrace it. I harness it. Through violence I am evolving into something beyond imagination.

CHAPTER 15

Tuesday

Early morning and Sean was already at his desk. The office was growing increasingly active as the detectives drifted into work. A knock at his open door made him glance up. Superintendent Featherstone waited to be invited in.

"Boss," Sean acknowledged. "How's it going?"

Featherstone held two coffees in to-go cups. He placed one in front of Sean then sat down. "Never known a DI turn down a free coffee."

"Thanks," said Sean. As he lifted the drink, he realized why Featherstone was there. Sean hadn't consulted with him prior to arresting Hellier. Technically, he should have. "While you're here, there are a few things I need to update you on."

"You don't say," Featherstone said. "Such as the arrest of a suspect, maybe?"

"Among other things . . ."

"An arrest I learned about from the television."

"I'm sorry," said Sean. "That shouldn't have happened, and it won't happen again."

"I know things can get a bit manic at times," Featherstone said, "but I'm here to keep those that would otherwise interfere off your back so you can do what you have to do. I can't do that if I don't know what's going on. In future, make a quick call. Okay?"

"Of course," Sean agreed. Featherstone was as good a senior officer as Sean could hope for and he knew it. He needed to keep him on his side.

"This James Hellier character," Featherstone asked. "You sure he's our man?"

"As sure as I can be, but that means nothing without some usable evidence."

"If there's evidence to find, then you'll find it. Whatever course of action you decide to take will get my backing."

"Appreciated."

Featherstone stood to leave. "By the way, this Hellier—he sounds like the sort of man who may have connections, if you understand my meaning."

"I'll bear that in mind, guv. Before you go, are you still able to front a media appeal for me?"

"You should do it yourself," Featherstone answered. "It would do you no harm to increase your public profile. If you ever want to be a chief inspector it's the sort of bollocks they love to see on your CV."

"Not really my thing," Sean demurred.

"Your call. So, what do you have in mind?"

"I think it's time we did a press conference. I'll arrange it and let you know where and when."

"I'll be there," Featherstone replied without enthusiasm. "We'll speak soon."

Hellier listened to Sebastian Gibran drone on from the other side of an obscenely wide oak desk, flanked by two old men

rarely seen in the office. He assumed they were two of the owners of Butler and Mason, about whom little was known, even
among the employees. They had olive skin and spoke only pass-
able English. Hellier thought they looked old and weak.

"It's important for you to understand, James," Gibran urged,
"that we fully support you in what must be a very difficult time
for you and your family, and I speak for the entire firm when I
say none of us believes these ridiculous allegations."

Hellier was almost caught daydreaming. He realized just in
time he was expected to answer. "Yes, of course, and thank you
for your support. It really means a lot to my family and me." He
sounded suitably genuine.

"James," Gibran insisted, "you have been one of our most
valuable employees since you joined us. You needn't thank us
for supporting you now."

*Sanctimonious bastard. One of their most valuable
employees—I've made these fuckers millions. And they never
cared how the money was earned either, so long as it kept rolling
in. Support me during these difficult times. What fucking choice
do you fools have? You need me a hell of a lot more than I need you.*

"Well, all the same, I'm very much indebted to you. To you
all," Hellier lied. "I feel very much a part of the family here and
would hate for that to change."

"So would I," said Gibran, although his tone and expression
were less than reassuring. "But incidents such as your late arrival at what is possibly the most important annual event in our
diary will not go unnoticed. I'm sure you understand."

"I understand," Hellier lied. "And I apologize for being late,
unreservedly. Once this whole mess with the police is cleared
up, I'll be able once again to give a hundred percent to this firm."

"Good," said Gibran. "Because not only are you important
to the company, you're important to me personally, James, as a
valued friend."

* * *

Sally had been at the Public Records Office all morning. She was bored and frustrated. The clerk helping her search for records relating to Stefan Korsakov seemed bored too. He was no more than twenty-five and still had traces of acne. He wasn't impressed with Sally's credentials. Sally didn't know his name. He hadn't told her.

These days the bulk of the records were on computer, with only the clerk having access to the system. That was fine with Sally, so long as she didn't have to wait much longer among the millions of old paper records stacked from floor to ceiling in the dark, cavernous building.

She heard footsteps approaching along the corridors of shelving and she was relieved to see the clerk return holding a piece of paper, but he wasn't smiling.

"I've found the person you're interested in. Stefan Korsakov, born in Twickenham, Middlesex, on the twelfth of November 1971." He put the paper on a desk and smoothed it out for Sally to see. "Stefan Korsakov's birth certificate," he announced. "This is the person you're interested in?"

"Yes," Sally answered. "I was beginning to think I'd imagined him."

"Excuse me?" the clerk asked.

"Never mind. Don't worry about me."

"Really." The clerk sounded bored again.

"Is he still alive?" She looked up at the clerk. "If he's dead, I need to see his death certificate."

"Do you know where he might have died?"

"Not a clue," Sally answered honestly. "Does that help?"

"I take it you want me to do a national search?"

"Sorry. Yes." Sally sensed the clerk's annoyance rising.

"That'll take days. Maybe weeks. I'll have to send out a circular to the other offices around the country. All I can do is wait for them to get back to me."

"Fine." Sally pulled a business card from her handbag and gave it to him. "Here's my card. My mobile number is on there. Call me as soon as you know. Anytime. Day or night."

"Will there be anything else?"

"No." The word was barely out before Sally changed her mind. "Actually, you know what, while I'm here there is one more thing I'd like you to check for."

"Such as?"

"I'd like you to find birth and death certificates, if they exist, for this man." She wrote a name and date of birth on some paper and handed it to the clerk.

He read the name. "James Hellier. It'll be done," he said. "But—"

Sally finished for him. "It'll take time. Yes, I know."

Hellier made his excuses and left the office shortly after his meeting with Gibran. No one had questioned why or where he was going. He knew no one would.

The police still had his address book. They hadn't let him take a photocopy of it either. His solicitor was working on recovering it, or at least getting a copy. No matter. If DI Corrigan wanted to be a tough fucker, then that was fine. He had contingency plans.

He had no sense of being watched this morning. Strange. Maybe his instincts were jaded. He was tired. Yesterday had been a long day, even for him. Maybe Corrigan had accepted what he said in the interview as the truth, but he doubted it. So where were they, dug in deep or simply not there?

He walked along Knightsbridge, past Harvey Nichols toward Harrods, turning left into Sloane Street, walking fast toward the south. Suddenly he ran across the road dodging cars driven by irate drivers. A black-cab driver blasted his horn and shouted an obscenity in a thick East End accent.

He ran at a fast jog along Pont Street, like a businessman late for a meeting, hardly noticed by the people he ran past. He turned right into Hans Place and jogged around the square.

On the corner with Lennox Gardens was a small delicatessen. Hellier went in and asked for a quarter kilo of Tuscan salami; while being served, he examined the other two customers in the shop. He could tell instantly they weren't police. As the shopkeeper wrapped the meat, he suddenly ran from the shop at full speed. The shopkeeper shouted after him, but Hellier didn't stop. After about a hundred and fifty meters he slowed and walked into the middle of the street, standing on the white lines, the traffic sweeping on either side of him. He studied the entire area around him, each pedestrian, every car and motorbike, but nobody caught his eye uncomfortably. Nobody checked themselves as they walked. No car swerved away into a side street.

He wasn't being followed, he was convinced of it. And even if they had been following him, he'd lost them. They'd underestimated him, assumed he wasn't aware of surveillance and countersurveillance, and now they'd paid the price. But he knew next time they would be more aware. More difficult to shake off.

Sean studied Dr. Canning's postmortem report. Some detectives found it easier to look at photographs rather than spend time at the scene. He realized the value of having everything logged photographically, but preferred to be confronted with the real thing rather than these cold, cruel pictures. At the scenes he felt something for the victims: sorrow and regret—sadness. But when he studied the photographs they felt almost

more real than the scenes themselves—the stark coldness of
what they depicted and the harshness of the colors somehow
even more unnerving than the actual scenes.

The report was excellent, as usual. Dr. Canning had missed
nothing. Every injury, old and new, had been observed, examined, and described. Sean was totally engrossed. Finally he noticed DC Zukov loitering at his door.

"What is it, Paulo?" he asked.

"This little lot just arrived in dispatch for you, guv." He held
up several dozen paper files.

"Stick them down here." DC Zukov dropped them onto
Sean's desk and retreated. They were the files from General
Registry he'd asked for. Each held details of a violent death.
These weren't like the files Sally had studied at Method Index
that concentrated on unique and uncommon crimes. These
were case files of daily horrors. Young men stabbed to death
outside pubs. Children tortured to death by their own parents.
Prostitutes beaten to death by their pimps. The cases in front of
him all involved excessive use of violence, but would they contain some detail that would leap out at him? Would one reek of
the killer he hunted? Of Hellier?

He was about to begin studying the first of many when
Donnelly burst in. "Bad news, guv'nor. Hellier's lost the surveillance."

"What?" Sean couldn't believe what he was being told.

"Sorry, boss."

"Tell them to get back and cover his office and home. He'll
turn up eventually, and they can pick him up again."

"Not that simple, I'm afraid," Donnelly said wearily. "All the
surveillance teams have been pulled away on an antiterrorist
op. Sign of the times, eh?"

"Give me some good news, Dave. What about the lab? Any
news?"

"All samples taken from the victim and his flat have been matched to people who admit to having sexual relations with him, but the lab found no blood on any of those individuals or their clothes. Only Hellier is anything like a genuine suspect. In short, the lab can't help us. They still haven't processed Hellier's clothes, but I won't be holding my breath."

"Fingerprints?" Sean asked.

"Spoke with them this morning. There're three sets of prints they can't match to anyone. All the others came back to the same people who'd left body samples there."

"What about these three unmatched sets? Do they come back to anyone with convictions?"

"No. They're no good to us unless we come up with other suspects we can match them to."

"Bollocks. Okay, we cover Hellier ourselves. Who have we got that's surveillance trained?"

"I am," Donnelly said. "And I think a couple of the DCs are, Jim, and maybe Frank."

"Good," Sean said, in spite of the fact it was anything but. "We'll split into two teams and do a twelve-hour shift each. Dave, you lead Team One and get Jim and Frank to run the other."

"Hold on a minute, guv'nor," Donnelly argued. "We're talking about two teams of what, maybe five people. Almost none of whom are surveillance trained. We'd be wasting our fucking time—and I haven't even mentioned the fact he's seen more than half the team when he got arrested."

"That's why I won't be with you," Sean said. "I'm gambling that he was concentrating on me when he was arrested. You need to exercise special care too. I doubt he's forgotten what you look like. No offense."

"None taken," Donnelly replied. "But this is still little better than hopeless."

"We've got no choice." Sean sounded desperate. He was. "So let's get on with it. Take whatever cars and radios you need. Apologize to the troops for me. I'll speak to them myself later."

"Fine," Donnelly said.

Sean could hear the dissatisfaction in the DS's voice. He understood it, even if there was nothing he could do to quell it. They had to try something. What else could he do?

Hellier arrived at the antiques shop in the Cromwell Road at about 1 P.M. The shopkeeper recognized him immediately.

"Mr. Saunders. It's been a while," he greeted Hellier. "And how has life been treating you lately, sir?"

"Fine," Hellier said without smiling. "I need to make a collection. I trust it's safe."

"Of course, sir."

The shopkeeper disappeared into the back.

Hellier wandered slowly around the empty shop. He ran his trailing hand across the fine wooden furniture. He stopped to lift and examine several china pieces. Their value alone would have stopped most people from touching them. Hellier handled them as if they were Tupperware. He breathed in the scent of the shop. Leather, wood, riches, and age. He deserved it all.

The shopkeeper reappeared carrying a metal safety-deposit box. "Do you confirm that your property is kept in box number twelve, Mr. Saunders?"

"I do."

"Excellent." Pulling a key from his waistcoat pocket, he unlocked the padlock then stood back for Hellier to open the box's lid.

Hellier removed a small white envelope and another larger one. He quickly checked the contents, which included a passport for the Republic of Ireland. Satisfied, he slipped both envelopes into his pocket and closed the lid.

"Do I owe you anything?" he asked.

"No. Your account is still very much in credit, Mr. Saunders."

Regardless, Hellier pulled five hundred pounds in new fifty-pound notes from his wallet. He placed them on the desk next to the till. "That's to make sure it stays that way."

The shopkeeper licked his lips. It was all he could do to not grab the cash. "Will you be returning the property today, sir?"

Hellier was already heading for the door. He answered without looking back. "Maybe. Who knows?"

With that he was gone.

The shopkeeper liked the money, but he hoped it would be the last time he saw Mr. Saunders. He was scared of Mr. Saunders—in fact, he was scared of lots of the people he kept illicit safety-deposit boxes for. But Mr. Saunders scared him the most.

Sally drove back toward Peckham alone. It had been a long and uninteresting morning at the Records Office. Truthfully, she was beginning to feel a little left out of the main investigation and now she also had to put up with the frustration of waiting days for the results of her searches—all of which meant she had yet to eliminate Korsakov. She knew Sean wouldn't be pleased.

Her mobile began to ring and jump around on the passenger seat. In defiance of the law, she answered it while driving. "Sally Jones speaking."

"DS Jones, this is IDO Collins from Fingerprints. You sent a request up yesterday, asking for a set of conviction prints for Stefan Korsakov to be compared with prints found at the Graydon murder scene."

"That's correct," she confirmed, excitement growing in her stomach.

"I'm afraid that's not going to be possible," Collins told her.

"What? Why not?"

"Because we don't have a set of fingerprints for anyone by that name."

"You must have," Sally insisted. "He has a criminal conviction—his prints were taken and submitted."

"I don't know what to tell you," Collins replied. "I've searched the system and they're not here."

The possibilities spun around in Sally's mind. Korsakov was rapidly becoming the invisible man. First his charging photographs and now his fingerprints. Sally didn't like what she was finding. She didn't like it at all. She remembered what Jarratt had said: maybe Korsakov was a ghost.

IDO Collins broke into her thoughts. "Are you still there, DS Jones."

"Yes," she answered. "I'm still here. In fact, you know what? I think I'd better come see you."

Hellier hailed a black cab and directed the driver to take him to the Barclays Bank in Great Portland Street, around the corner from Oxford Circus. Tourists and shoppers jammed the pavements. Red buses and cabs jammed the roads. It was an unholy mess. Diesel fumes mixed with the smell of frying onions and cheap meat. The heat of the day kept the air heavy.

The cab drew up directly outside the bank. Hellier was out and paying before the driver knew it. He dropped a twenty-pound note through the driver's window and walked away without speaking.

He went to an eager-looking female cashier in her early twenties. She would want to do everything by the book. So did he. He handed her the larger envelope he'd taken from the antiques shop. It was documentation of his ownership of a safety-deposit box held in the bank's vault. "I would like access to my deposit box, please," he told her.

"Of course," she agreed. "Can I ask if you have any identification with you, sir?" She sounded like every other bank clerk in the world.

He smiled and pulled out a passport for the Republic of Ireland. "Will this be okay?"

She checked the name and photograph in the passport, smiled, and handed it back to him. "That'll be fine, Mr. McGrath. If you'd like to take a seat in consultation room number two, I'll fetch the deposit box."

Within a few minutes the clerk came to Hellier's room and placed the stainless-steel box on the table. "I'll leave you alone now, sir. Just let me know when you've finished." She turned on her heel and left the room, shutting the door with a reassuring thud.

Hellier pulled the smaller envelope from his jacket pocket, opened the flap, and shook the contents out onto the table—a silver key. He couldn't help but look around him as he put the key into the lock. It was stiff, causing him to feel a stab of panic as he jiggled it, eventually turning the lock and opening the box. Slowly he lifted the lid and peered inside. The box was as he had left it. He ignored the rolls of U.S. dollars and pushed the loose diamonds out of the way, flicking a five-carat solitaire to one side as if it were a dead insect, until he found what he was looking for—a scrap of aging paper. He lifted it closer to the light and examined it, relieved to see the number was still visible after all this time. He smiled, and spent the next ten minutes committing the number to memory. He ignored the first three digits—the dialing code—but he repeated the remainder of the number over and over until he was sure he would never forget it: "9913, 2074, 9913, 2074."

Sean read through the files from General Registry. He'd found it difficult to concentrate at first, the logistical problems of the investigation severely hindering his free thinking, but as the office grew quieter he was able to lose himself in the files.

He'd already rejected several. They were all extremely violent crimes that remained unsolved, but they just didn't feel right. Too many missing elements.

He picked up the next file and flipped open the cover. The first thing he saw was a crime scene photograph. He winced at the sight of a young girl, no more than sixteen, lying on a cold stone floor, her dead hands clutching her throat. He could see she was lying in a huge pool of her own blood and guessed her throat had been cut.

He leaned into the file. The photographs spoke to him. The victim spoke to him. His nostrils flared. This one, he thought to himself. This one. He flicked past the photographs and began to read.

The victim was a young runaway. Came to London from Newcastle. Parents reported her missing several days before her body was found. Neither parent considered as a suspect. No boyfriend involved. No pimp under suspicion. Her name, Heather Freeman. Body recovered from an unused building on waste ground in Dagenham. No witnesses traced.

Sean rifled through the papers to the forensics report. It was ominously short. No fingerprints, no DNA, no blood other than the victim's. The suspect had left no trace of himself other than one thing: footprints in the dust inside the scene. They were striking only because of their lack of uniqueness. A plain-soled man's shoe, size nine or ten, apparently very new, with minimal scarring.

"Jesus Christ," he whispered.

Sean checked the date of the murder. It predated Daniel Graydon's death by more than a week. "You have killed before, you had to have, but how many times?" His head began to thump. He searched for the name of the investigating officer and found it: DI Ross Brown, based on the Murder Investigation Team at Old Ilford police station. He bundled together his belongings and, taking the file with him, headed for the exit. He'd phone DI Brown once he was on his way.

Hellier walked along Great Titchfield Street, still in the heart of London's West End shopping area, although it was a lot quieter. He soon found a phone booth and pumped three pound coins into the slot. He heard the dial tone and punched the number keypad: 020-9913-2074.

The dial tone changed to a ringing one. He waited only two cycles before it was answered. The person on the other end had clearly been expecting a call. Hellier spoke.

"Hello, old friend," he said mockingly. "We have much to discuss."

"I've been waiting for you to call," the voice answered. "I expected it sooner."

"Your friends took my contacts book," Hellier told him, "and you're not listed in the phone book or with directory inquiries. Makes you a difficult person to find."

"The police have taken a book off you with my number in it?" The voice sounded strained. "How the hell did you let that happen?"

"Calm down." Hellier was in control. "All the numbers in the book were coded. No one will know it's yours."

"They'd better not," the voice said. "So if they've got the book, how did you find my number again?"

"You gave it to me, don't you remember? When you first came begging to me. Cap in hand. You wrote it on a piece of paper. I kept it. Thought it might come in useful one day."

"You need to get rid of it. Now," the voice demanded.

Hellier wished he and the voice were face-to-face. He'd make him suffer for his insolence. "Listen, fucker," he shouted into the phone. A passerby glanced at him, but quickly looked away when he saw Hellier's eyes. "You don't tell me what to do. You never fucking tell me what to do. *Do you understand me?*"

There was silence. Neither man spoke. It gave Hellier a few seconds to regain his composure. He pulled a handkerchief from his trouser pocket and dabbed his shining brow. The voice broke the silence.

"What do you want me to do?"

"Get Corrigan to call his dogs off," Hellier replied.

"I don't think I can do that. If I could think of any way . . . But I swear I don't have that sort of pull." The voice was almost pleading.

"You're a damn fool," Hellier snapped. "Just wait for me to call you. I'll think of something." He hung up.

Feeling better now, he rolled his head and massaged the back of his neck. He glanced at his watch. Time was passing. He needed to get back to work.

Sally sat in a side office at the Fingerprint Branch at New Scotland Yard. A tall slim man in his midfifties entered the room nervously. Sally stood and offered her hand. "Thanks for seeing me so quickly."

"No problem at all," said IDO Collins. "How can I help?"

Sally sucked in a lungful of air and began to explain herself. "This is a sensitive matter, you understand?"

"Of course," Collins reassured her.

"On the phone you said you couldn't find Korsakov's fingerprints. So what I need to find out is how the fingerprints of a convicted criminal could go missing."

Collins smiled and shook his head. "Not possible. You can't remove files from the computer database."

"Before that," Sally said. "Assume they went missing from the old filing system. Possible?"

"Well, I suppose so." Collins began to chew the side of his thumb. "But they could only go missing for a period of time."

"Meaning?"

"Well, in the old system, officers and other agencies would sometimes ask to look at sets of prints. Mostly they would view them here at the Yard, but occasionally they would have to take them away. For example, to compare them with a person the Immigration Service had doubts about, or to compare them with a prison inmate if the Prison Service suspected funny business. Somebody trying to serve a sentence on behalf of somebody else. It does happen, you know. Usually for money, sometimes out of fear."

"Or to get away from the wife and kids?" Sally half-joked.

"Yes. Probably. I wouldn't know." Collins laughed a little. He still sounded nervous. "Anyway. Prints might be taken away, but if they weren't returned quickly, within a few days, we'd chase after them. We'd always get them back. Always. We simply wouldn't stop pestering until they were returned. They're too important to allow them to disappear."

"Then perhaps you can explain how this set vanished?" Sally slid a file across the desk. "Stefan Korsakov. Convicted of fraud in 1996. He definitely had prints taken when he was charged. No mistake. Prints that you're telling me have since disappeared."

Collins looked shocked, but recovered quickly and smiled. "A clerical mistake. Give me a minute and I'll search for them myself."

She knew it made sense to double-check. "If it'll make you feel better, then it'll make me feel better. I'll be in the canteen. Give me a shout when you're finished."

CHAPTER 16

DI Ross Brown waited at the old murder scene for Sean to arrive, the police cordon tape flapping loosely in the mild breeze, tatty and spoiled now.

It was getting late, but he didn't mind waiting. His investigation had not been going well—stranger attacks of this type were extremely difficult to solve quickly. Unless you were out to make a name for yourself, they were every detective's worst nightmare. And with only three years' service remaining, DI Ross Brown wasn't out to make a name for himself. If he thought Sean could help his case, he'd wait all night.

Sean found his way to Hornchurch Marshes and drove through the unmanned entrance to the waste ground. A single road wound its way over the desolate and oppressive land to a small outbuilding. Sean could see a tall, well-built man standing outside. He parked next to DI Brown's car and climbed out. Brown was already moving toward him, his hand outstretched.

"Sean Corrigan. We spoke on the phone."

Ross Brown wrapped a big hand around Sean's. His grip was surprisingly gentle. "Good of you to come all this way out east," he said.

"I just hope I'm not wasting your time," Sean answered.

DI Brown pointed to the outbuilding. "She died in there. She was fifteen years old." He looked sad. "She'd run away from home. The usual story. Mum and Dad split up, Mum gets a new man, kid won't accept him and ends up running away to London—straight into the hands of some sick bastard.

"It's not easy to get the homeless to talk," he continued, "to get their trust. But a couple of her friends have provided us with details of her last movements.

"We're pretty certain she was abducted in the King's Cross area on the same night she was killed, about two weeks ago, give or take. We canvassed the area, but no one witnessed the abduction—our man is apparently extremely cautious and fast.

"We tried to get the media interested, but we only got minimal coverage. It's difficult to compete with suicide bombers, and they like victims to be the nice, top-of-the-class type, not teenage runaways.

"The killer drove her to this waste ground. He took her into this abandoned building, stripped her, and then he cut her throat. One large laceration that almost cut the poor little cow's head off."

Sean could see Brown was disturbed. No doubt the man had teenage daughters of his own. The nearby giant car plant dominated the horizon. It all added to the feeling of dread in this place. "Poor little cow," Brown repeated. "What the hell must she have been thinking? All alone. Made to strip. There were no signs of sexual abuse, but we can't be sure what he did or didn't make her do. Fucking animal."

"The murder of Daniel Graydon occurred six days ago," Sean said without prompting. "His head was caved in with a heavy blunt instrument, not recovered. He was also stabbed repeatedly with an ice pick or something similar, not recovered either. He was killed in his own flat in the early hours. No sign of forced entry. He was a homosexual and a prostitute."

Brown frowned. He couldn't see much of a connection to his investigation, if any. "Doesn't sound like my man. Different type of victim, murder location, weapon used. I'm sorry, Sean. I don't see any similarities here."

"No," Sean said, holding up a hand. "That's not where the similarity lies." He began to walk to the outbuilding. DI Brown followed him.

"What then?" Brown asked.

"The only usable evidence from our scene was some footprints in the hallway carpet. They were made by a man wearing a pair of plain-soled shoes with plastic bags over them. The forensics report said you recovered footprints."

"Yes," Brown said. "Inside the outbuilding."

"And no other forensic evidence?" Sean asked.

"Is that why you're here?" DI Brown asked. "Because neither of us has any forensics evidence, other than a useless shoe print?" Sean's silence answered the question. "Then I guess we're both in the shit," Brown continued, "because if you're right and these murders are connected, then this is a really bad bastard we're after here and he's absolutely not going to stop until someone stops him."

Sean's phone interrupted him before he could reply. It was Donnelly. "Dave?"

"Guv'nor, surveillance is in place at Butler and Mason, and guess who's back?"

"He's at work?"

"No mistake. I've seen him myself through the window. He's not hiding."

"Okay. Stay on him. I'll call you later." He hung up.

What the hell are you up to now? And where have you been that you didn't want us to see?

"Problem?" Brown asked.

"No," Sean answered. "Nothing that can't wait."

Sally saw Collins enter the canteen and gave a little wave to attract his attention. He sat opposite her, carefully placing an old index book on the table.

"From a time before computers," he told her. "I've double-checked both the computer system and searched manually, as well as checking the old records on microfiche. We have nothing under the name of Korsakov."

"Which means?" Sally asked.

"Well, normally I would have said that you were mistaken. That Korsakov's prints could never have been submitted."

"But . . . ?"

"But I have this." He patted the index book. "This is a record of all fingerprints that are removed from Fingerprint Branch. We still use it as a backup for our new computer records, and this way we actually get the signature of the removing party, which helps ensure their safe return. This volume goes back to ninety-nine."

Collins went to the page showing all the fingerprints of people whose surnames began with the letter *K* that were removed that year. It was a comparatively short list. Fingerprints were rarely removed.

"Here," he pointed. "On the fourteenth of December 1999, fingerprints belonging to one Stefan Korsakov were removed by a DC Graham Wright, from the CID at Richmond."

"So they were here?" Sally asked.

"They must have been."

"But this DC Wright never returned them?"

"That's the bit I don't understand," said Collins, frowning. "They *were* returned. Two days later by the same detective, along with the microfiche of the prints, which he'd also booked out."

"Then where are they?"

"I have no idea," Collins admitted.

Sally paused for a few seconds. "Could someone have simply walked in here and taken the prints and microfiche?"

"I seriously doubt it. The office is always manned and all prints and fiches are locked away. Only someone who worked in the Fingerprint Branch would have that level of access."

Why the hell would someone from Fingerprints want to make Korsakov's records disappear? Had he corrupted someone there? Paid them for a little dirty work? But in 1999 he was still in prison, so how could he possibly have known whom to approach? No, Sally decided. Something else.

"When fingerprints are returned, are they checked?" she asked. "Before being accepted."

"A quick visual check, no more," Collins told her.

"And the microfiche?"

"No. That wouldn't have been standard practice. So long as the fingerprints were in good order, that would have been that."

Sean and Brown moved into the outbuilding. There was still light outside, but inside it was dim and damp. Sean could clearly see the last remains of that horrific night: a large circular bloodstain in the middle of the floor. It was rusty brown now. The inexperienced eye would have thought it nothing. He sometimes wished his eyes could be so innocent.

The arterial spray marks went from Sean's left to right across the room. They'd almost hit the wall over twelve feet away. The detectives moved around slowly in the gloom. The scene had long since been examined and any evidence taken away, but Sean studied it closely nonetheless. He knew nothing would have been missed, but that wasn't why he was there. He was seeing that night through the victim's eyes. Through the killer's eyes.

Brown broke the silence. "We know she was on her knees when he cut her," he said solemnly, "from the distance her blood traveled and the body's final resting position. He pulled her head back and then slit her throat." Brown obviously didn't enjoy recounting their findings. "You really think these murders could be linked?"

Sean didn't answer. He knelt down. This was how Heather last saw the world. "We have a suspect," he announced suddenly.

"A suspect?" Brown asked.

"Yeah," Sean said. He could feel the clouds lifting from his mind. Could see things he'd never considered before. Standing on the spot where Heather Freeman had died fired his mind, his imagination, the dark side he buried so deep. "James Hellier," Sean continued. "Up until this point he's been hiding from us. Hiding behind a mask of respectability. A wife and children. A career. But he's out now. He's showing himself to us.

"The gender of the victims doesn't matter to him. Male, female—makes no difference. It's not a matter of sex with Hellier. It's about power. About victimization. The gender is coincidental. Two young and vulnerable victims. Easy targets."

"Why's he not bothered about leaving his footprints," Brown asked, "if he's so damn careful where everything else is concerned?"

"No." Sean spoke softly. "He's extremely concerned about footprints. He's probably experimented with dozens of methods, maybe even hundreds, but each time he comes up with the same conclusion. No matter what he tries, no matter what shoes he wears, what surface he walks on, he nearly always leaves some type of print. Even if it's the slightest impression in a carpet, like in Daniel Graydon's flat.

"He knows he'll almost certainly leave prints at his scenes, so he gives up trying not to. Instead he masks them as best he can. He wears bland shoes, probably brand-new. He changes the size of the shoes he wears. He can't change it too much, but he tries."

"Why doesn't he just commit his crimes on solid surfaces?" Brown asked. "That way he wouldn't leave an impression."

Sean fired the answer back: "Too restrictive. He would have considered it, but discounted it. He needs to spend time with them. In their own homes or somewhere like this. Spending time with them is more important to him than leaving a shoe print. For him, the risk is worth it. And what's he leaving us? Virtually unidentifiable, totally un-unique shoe marks. He'll take that chance.

"He knows how we link murder scenes," Sean continued. "We look for exact matches. Unique items. Same weapon. Same method. Same type of victim. Not 'almosts.' So he picks victims of different genders. Kills them in different ways and in different types of locations. Your victim he abducts, ours he already knew. He keeps it mixed up."

Sean kept talking. "Most repeat killers work to a pattern. To leave their calling card. When they settle on a method that works for them, they stick with it. Many only kill in their own neighborhood, where everything is familiar, where they feel safe. When they attempt to disguise their work, then you know you're dealing with a killer whose primary instinct is not to get caught."

"And your suspect fits this profile?" Brown asked.

"He paid for violent sex—been doing so for years, no doubt. That probably kept his urges, his impulses suppressed for a while, but ultimately it wasn't enough. He would have seen your victim. Fantasized about her. It's more than he can bear. He plans it thoroughly. He's extremely careful. He finds the planning thrilling, so he takes his time. Finally he grabs her. He uses a big car, or better still, a van. He probably steals one or maybe rents one.

"He brings her out here. He'd have been here, no more than

a day or so previously. He wants his intelligence to be up to date. He brings her inside . . ." Sean broke off and turned to Brown. "How much did she weigh?"

Brown stuttered, taken aback by the unexpected question. "I don't know," he said with a shrug.

"Was she big? Small?" Sean pressed him.

"She was small," Brown answered. "I went to the autopsy. She was tiny."

"Then he carried her in," Sean said. "It was quicker and quieter than dragging her." He snapped another question at Brown: "Was she tied or taped in any way?"

"We believe she was taped," Brown replied. "There were traces of adhesive across her mouth, ankles, wrists, and around her knees. The adhesive matches a common brand of masking tape. Nothing rare."

"Once inside, he dumps her on the ground," Sean continued. "He wants her untied, but he's worried she'll fight or scream. So how does he stop that happening?" He looked at Brown.

"He would have threatened her," Brown answered.

"Absolutely. He would have threatened her," Sean repeated. "He would have almost certainly shown her the knife that he eventually used to kill her. Any defensive marks on the girl?"

"No."

"Then he told her he wasn't going to hurt her and she believed him. She did as she was told. If she'd thought he intended to kill her, she would have fought him or tried to run. She agrees to do what he tells her, so he removes the tape from her mouth and limbs . . . But why is that important to him? She wasn't raped, so he could have left the tape around her ankles and knees. Why risk taking the tape away?"

Sean's vivid narration stalled, as if someone had drawn a curtain across the window he'd been looking through. He moved around the room, staring at the floor. He moved like an animal locked in a cage. It was minutes before he spoke again.

"He had to remove the tape because it was spoiling it for him. It was necessary when she was first abducted, but now it was spoiling his imagery. He'd imagined her in a certain way for so long, imagined her dying in a certain way, that he couldn't settle for less. He needed to make life imitate his fantasy. So he makes her take her clothes off. All of them. He doesn't even let her keep her underwear or a T-shirt on. He's totally without mercy. Totally without compassion for her—but this is all for our benefit. He wants us to think there's a sexual motivation for the killing, but there isn't. He enjoyed the power he held over her, of course—and making her undress was a strong show of his power. But it was purely for us. To stop us linking him to other murders." He paused for a few seconds, allowing his imagination to again become the killer's memory. "He makes her kneel down and tells her to perform oral sex on him, but he was never going to allow that to happen, never going to let her get that near him. He was never going to risk leaving forensic evidence. So he grabs her by the scruff of the neck and cuts her once across the throat. He's strong and fast. The knife is very sharp; again, probably brand-new. One hit is all it takes. What time was she killed?"

"Between eleven P.M. and three A.M. is the best we can say."

"It would have been dark then," Sean pointed out. He looked around the building for lighting. There was none. The room would have been pitch-black. "He had to have light to see."

"Maybe he used a torch?" Brown said.

"No," Sean replied. "He needed both hands free, and the light from a torch wouldn't be right for what he wanted."

"What did he want?" Brown asked.

"He wanted to see her. He needed to see her die." Sean

looked out of the window and saw his own car pointing toward the building. The headlight mountings glinted in the low evening sunlight.

"He used his car headlights," Sean said. "He would have checked that ahead of time too. He went there on the night of the murder already knowing car headlights would give him all the light he needed.

"And when she was dead, he stayed with her. He'd been dreaming about this for too long to just walk away from her now she was dead. He stood here and watched her bleed to death. Watched until her blood stopped running.

"You didn't find any signs that the body was moved or mutilated after she'd died, did you?" Sean told rather than asked Brown.

"No," he answered. "She died where she fell and wasn't touched."

"He didn't want to spoil the perfect picture he'd created. All he wanted was to stand and watch her." Sean was silent for a while, troubled by the question forming in his mind. "Did you search this wasteland for used condoms?"

"Not specifically for condoms, as far as I know, and I don't recall seeing any listed on the lab submissions form. Why d'you ask?"

"Because I think he would have masturbated while he watched her die, but he wouldn't risk leaving his DNA, so he would have used a condom. Maybe he threw it away beyond where he thought we would search." Sean looked Brown square in the eyes.

"Jesus! Where did you get that from?" Brown asked.

Sean moved on without answering. "Then he left her. He didn't cover her, not even partially. It would have been a sign of guilt. Remorse. He has no psychological need to try and make amends for his crimes. He felt nothing. He walked away feeling nothing more than a sense of relief, maybe even what for him amounts to happiness."

"But what's his motivation?" Brown asked. "Is it sexual? Is this the only way he can get a hard-on?"

"Not sexual," Sean answered. "Power. With this one, motivation is all about power."

"But there're so many sexual overtones to his crimes. Making her strip, making her go on her knees in front of him. You said it yourself: he probably masturbated at the scene."

"Because the power excites him, makes him feel alive. The sexual acts are merely a symptom, a way he can release the power he feels building up inside him."

Brown seemed both impressed and unnerved by Sean's analysis. "Done a few of these types before?" he asked.

"Some," Sean replied, managing a slight smile. "I do a lot of research."

"If I can make an observation of my own . . . ," Brown asked.

"Go on."

"If my killer, our killer, is as clever as you say, as good at disguising his methods as you believe he is, then how do we know he hasn't killed other people? How will we ever know?"

"Truth is," Sean admitted, "unless he decides to tell us about them, we probably never will."

They were back. Hellier could feel them before he saw them. Only these were clumsier than the last. Why would Corrigan put amateurs on him? Was the DI so arrogant that he thought second-raters would be good enough to follow him?

My enemy's mistakes are my greatest gains.

Hellier wasn't in his own office. He had been earlier, long enough to let the surveillance see him, but now, unseen, he used the office of another junior partner. He'd let it be known he would be working late, to make up for his earlier absence. Truth was, he needed to access certain bank accounts held across the globe. He didn't want to use the computer in his own office. The police had been in there. They could have somehow bugged his computer. They could be monitoring his online activities. He doubted they were smart enough, but why take the risk?

He was the only person left in the offices. Tonight it was essential to be alone and to move fast. The police had seized many of his bank details and they knew where most of his money was, but not all of it.

They would be moving to block his accounts, but that would require court orders and the banks would take time to comply with the orders' instructions. That would burn up a few days, and by then it would all be a wasted exercise.

Hellier was skilled on the computer. Able to cover his electronic tracks extremely well. He called up a website on the Internet. It was one he'd set up himself two years ago, but it was no more than an illusion, a front, just like a restaurant or bar could be, and as in those establishments, there was a back door. But you had to know how to find it. Hellier knew. Of course he did. The illusion was his design.

The site was entitled *Banks and the Small Investor*. There was a hidden command icon on the screen. Hellier carefully placed the cursor on the tail of the site's symbol, a prancing horse similar to the Ferrari emblem. Pin the tail on the donkey and win a prize. He smiled again, pleased with his private joke.

He clicked the cursor twice and waited a second. A type box suddenly appeared in the bottom-right-hand corner of the screen, flashing, demanding a password.

Hellier typed the password: FUCK THEM ALL.

* * *

When Sean arrived back at his Peckham office, he found it deserted except for Sally. Ignoring the NO SMOKING signs, she was puffing heavily on a cigarette. She looked up from her paperwork and was relieved to see it was Sean. She held the cigarette up. "Do you mind?"

"No," Sean answered. "What are you doing here this late?"

"Trying to work a few things out."

"Such as?"

"Such as how did Korsakov's fingerprints manage to get up and walk out of Scotland Yard all on their own?"

Sean didn't understand and he wasn't of a mind to ask for explanations. His thoughts were still with Heather Freeman.

"And why are you back here so late?" Sally asked.

"I've been out east."

"Why?" Sally sounded almost suspicious.

Sean hesitated before answering. "I believe I've identified another murder committed by our man."

"What?" The surprise made Sally stand involuntarily. "Are you sure?"

"As sure as I can be."

"Another gay man?"

"No. A girl. A teenage runaway. He abducted her from King's Cross and took her out to some waste ground in Dagenham. He made her strip before cutting her throat."

"I don't see a connection," Sally confessed. "Did Hellier also know her?"

"I doubt it. But he watched her before killing her. Once he'd selected her, he watched her. Learned her movements. Planned everything very carefully. Then he took her."

"So she was a stranger, yet Daniel Graydon was someone he knew."

"I'm not so sure anymore."

"Not so sure of what?"

"That he knew Graydon—or at least, not as well as he'd have us believe."

"I really don't understand," Sally admitted.

"I think he picked Graydon at random. A week or so before he killed him, he went to the nightclub and he selected him. He paid to have sex with him so that on the night he killed him he could approach Graydon without spooking him. Then they went back to the flat and he killed him, just like he was always going to do."

"Why didn't he kill him the same night he first met him?"

"Because he needed to kill him in his own flat. It was how he'd seen it—fantasized about it. But for that to happen he needed Graydon's trust, he needed him to feel comfortable, so he approached him inside the club, surrounded by witnesses and people who knew the victim. If he'd killed him the same night, it would have been too easy for us to work out what must have happened: stranger arrives in gay nightclub and leaves with known prostitute, next morning prostitute is found murdered. Too easy—too simple. Hellier likes things complicated, layer upon layer of possibilities and misdirection, endless opportunities to bend the evidence away from proving he's the killer. But above all, there was no way he was going to miss out on a week of fantasizing about how it would feel—killing Daniel Graydon. For him, that would have been every bit as important as the killing itself. Once he'd killed the girl in Dagenham he'd opened Pandora's box—there's no going back for him now, even though he knows we're watching him. He won't stop, he can't. Knowing we're watching him merely heightens his excitement—makes him even more dangerous."

"Did he leave any evidence at the Dagenham scene?" Sally asked.

"No. Just a useless footprint."

"Then how are we going to convict him?"

Sean thought silently before answering. "If Hellier has a weakness, if he has one chink in his armor, it's his desire for perfection."

"I don't understand," said Sally, frowning.

"He can't leave things half done, untidy, incomplete. Look at his clothes, his hair, his office, his home. Everything immaculate. Not a thing out of place. He couldn't have that. It's the same when he kills. Everything has to be perfect. Exactly how he imagines it."

Sally puffed on her cigarette. "How do you know all this?" she asked. "I've watched you study crime scene photographs in the past, and suddenly it's like you're there. Like you're the . . ." A look from Sean stopped her before she'd finished.

"I see things differently, that's all," he explained. "Most people investigate crimes two dimensionally. They forget it's a three-dimensional thing. They seek the motive, but not the reason for the motivation.

"You have to question the killer's every move, no matter how trivial. Why choose that victim? Why that weapon? That location? That time of day? Most people are happy just to recover a weapon, to identify the scene, but they're missing the point. If you want to catch these poor bastards quickly, then you have to try and think like them. No matter how uncomfortable that may make you feel."

"You feel sorry for them?" asked Sally.

Sean hadn't realized he'd shown sympathy. "Sorry?"

"You called them 'poor bastards.' Like you felt sorry for them."

"Not sorry for what they are now," he told her. "Sorry for what made them that way. Sorry for the hell that was their childhood. Alone. Scared to death most of the time. Terrified of the very people they should have loved. Fearful of those they should have been able to turn to for protection. Sometimes, when I'm interviewing them, I don't see a monster in front of me. I see a child. A scared little child."

"Is that what you see when you look at Hellier?"

"No," he answered without hesitation. "Not yet. It's too soon. I haven't broken him down to make him face what he really is. When I do, I'll know if he's a product of his past or something else."

"Something else?" Sally asked.

"Born that way. Whether he was born bad. It's rare, but it happens."

"And you already suspect that's the case with Hellier." It wasn't really a question.

"Go home, Sally," he said quietly. "Get some rest. I'll call Dave and set up an office meeting for the morning. We'll talk then, but right now you need to go home, and so do I."

Hellier typed the password and the false screen began to break away, replaced by a screen filled with twenty-four different bank insignias. Many of the major banks of the developed world were shown, as well as several more specialized ones. They all held accounts belonging to Hellier, some in that name, others in aliases he'd invented. He had excellent forged documents hidden across Europe, North America, the Caribbean, the Middle East, and Southeast Asia.

He'd created this website, which appeared to offer advice to private individuals considering purchasing stocks and shares, particularly shares in financial institutions; its main purpose, however, was to hide his complex network of bank accounts and the locations of the false identities that would allow him to gain access to them. There were so many he could never have hoped to remember them all. But with this hidden guide, no matter where he was in the world, provided he could access the Internet, he could access his funds.

The priority was to empty his UK and U.S. accounts. The others couldn't be touched by UK authorities. Fucking Americans, he thought, always happy to slam shut accounts on the flimsiest of suspicions. Always so keen to help Scotland fucking Yard. Sycophants.

He worked fast. He would be at the terminal for hours, but by the time he was finished the vast majority of his considerable wealth would have been transferred to Southeast Asia and the Caribbean. Out of the reach of the police. Now, if he had to run, he wouldn't have to be poor too. There were many places in this world where a man's tastes were restricted only by the depth of his wealth.

Donnelly and DC Zukov were hidden in the office building almost directly opposite Hellier's. Donnelly was half asleep on the sofa when he felt the phone clipped to his waistband vibrate. The display told him it was Sean. "Guv'nor."

"Where's Hellier now?"

"Still at work, like us."

"He's up to something."

"I'm sure he probably is."

"I've found another murder Hellier may have committed."

"What?" Donnelly sat bolt upright.

"About two weeks ago. A teenage runaway found dead out by the Ford factory."

Donnelly's eyes darted left and right as he thought hard. "I remember. It was on the news, right?"

"Yeah, but it's still unsolved. No suspects. I met the DI running the inquiry. They've got nothing."

"How, though . . ." Donnelly was a little confused. "How did you connect it to ours?"

"Long story, bad time," Sean said. "Phone around and organize an office meeting for the morning. I'll update you then." Sean hung up before Donnelly could ask any more questions.

"Fuck it," Donnelly said out loud.

DC Zukov lowered his binoculars and turned to Donnelly. "Problem?" he asked.

"Aye, son," Donnelly replied. "But nothing we can't handle."

Hellier sat in the deep leather chair. It creaked satisfyingly. He'd completed the transfers. It had taken him less than three hours to move over two million pounds out of his UK and American accounts. He'd left a nominal few thousand in each, to keep them fluid.

He buried the account details in the concealed web page and exited the Internet. He was happy with his night's work. Extremely happy. He couldn't help laughing. God, if they could see him, sitting here in the dark laughing to himself, they really would think him mad. He was anything but.

It was time to get home. He cleaned up the desk and took one last look around the room to make sure nothing had been overlooked, then returned to his own office. Leaving the lights on, he went to the window and peeked out through the corner of the venetian blinds. They made a plastic tinkling sound.

He had an excellent view of the road below. It was always busy, no matter what time of day or night. He could still feel the police close by. It was of no matter tonight; there were others of more concern to him than the police. The press. The vile media. They had the power to ruin him with mere rumor. They wouldn't be interested in proof. They wanted a story to titillate the masses. Something for people to drool over at breakfast. They wanted him. He couldn't afford to let them take a single photograph. He couldn't afford to be recognized.

* * *

Sally parked close to the entrance of the building where she lived in Fulham, West London. She let herself in and moved quickly through the communal areas. Dim hallway lights helped her. She tried to keep the noise down. She was a good neighbor. She entered her flat and locked the door.

Following her usual routine, she turned on the lamp in the far corner first. She preferred its gentle light to the overheads. Next she flicked the TV on, for company, then moved into the kitchen, opened the fridge, and scanned the contents before closing it again. Maybe she'd have more luck in the freezer. She did. A frosty bottle of raspberry vodka rested on its side. Grabbing it by the neck, she looked around for a clean glass. There was one by the sink. She poured a good measure of the thick vodka and threw the bottle back into the freezer.

Sally sat at her kitchen table and rocked back on her chair, kicking her shoes off, the drink in front of her. She pulled the cigarettes from her handbag and lit one. It must have been the thirtieth of the day. She thought about stubbing it out, but hey, cigarettes cost a fortune these days. Covering a mortgage on a flat in this part of London didn't leave much in the kitty for luxuries.

Staring at the walls suddenly brought on pangs of loneliness. Being thirty-something and single hadn't been part of her life plan. The partner thing had just never happened. There had been lovers, two of whom had been close to measuring up to her standards, only to fall away as the stakes were increased.

The fact of the matter was, most men were simply intimidated by her. Being a female police officer was bad enough, but a detective sergeant—that scared the crap out of them. The only ones who weren't scared off were policemen, but the idea of never being able to escape the job was unbearable. No, they had to be completely unconnected with the police or it would be better to stay single. Besides, these last couple of years hadn't left a lot of time for relationships.

Naturally, her parents were disappointed. They saw their chances of becoming grandparents slipping away. Didn't they understand modern women were choosing to have a career first and then children later in life? There was still hope on that front. After all, she didn't need a permanent partner to have children. Catching herself fantasizing about potential sperm donors, she shook the faces from her thoughts.

"Fuck it," she declared out loud. "I'm getting a cat."

Hellier could see two of them at the front of the building. One had a camera, the other didn't. One photographer and one journalist, but there would be more. The victim was of no interest to the media, no story there. Rent boy dies, who gives a fuck? *He* was the story. Wealthy, respected businessman investigated for murder. A sordid murder at that. This story would grow and grow. It was only a matter of time before the national media started to run with it. Once his face hit the papers and TV sets, life would be intolerable. He needed his anonymity. Daniel Graydon had been a mistake, but it was a mistake he would survive.

There would be more journalists covering the rear exit to the building, through the basement car park. There was only one way out. He'd found it within days of starting work at Butler and Mason. He always liked to know alternative ways of leaving a building. Just in case.

He took his house keys and wallet from his briefcase, then slid them under his desk. They would be too cumbersome for what he had in mind. Making his way to the emergency stairwell, he climbed to the top floor. He looked up at the hatch that led to the roof. It was secured with a bolt.

The next bit was the most difficult. He had to climb on the stair rail and keep his balance until he could stretch his hands to the ceiling and hold himself in place. He managed that much. His feet twisted a little on the thin metal banister as he fought to keep his balance. He reached out to the bolt with his right arm. His left hand was still pressed to the ceiling.

The bolt came out after a series of solid jerks. Each jerk almost threw off Hellier's balance. If he lost it now, he would either fall three feet forward to safety, or tumble backward down the stairwell, six flights.

He pushed on the roof exit cover. It gave way easily. He used his fingers to caterpillar the wooden cover away from the exit. Every sinew of his body was already stretched to the breaking point.

The cover removed, he sprang off the banister and hooked both hands over the outside edge of the square hole in the roof. His body dangled below as he pulled himself up and through the roof exit. Hellier was in excellent physical condition. He'd worked hard to build his strength and develop the physique of an acrobat.

He replaced the cover, making a mental note to push back the bolt in the morning before anyone noticed. He took a few seconds to straighten his clothes and admire the view from the rooftop. He felt alone, but strong. Safe. He sucked in the warm night air, heavy and moist. Time to go. He moved quickly and silently across the roofs.

CHAPTER 17

Last night I had an almost overwhelming desire to be the real me. To release the animal that hides inside and allow it full and free expression. But I resisted the temptation. Too many things to arrange first. If I'm to take advantage of the police's lapses, then I must be patient. Must take time to prepare. Their heads will be spinning soon enough.

I'm at work again; boring, but necessary. I read the papers and watch the news endlessly. I have to be sure they haven't linked any of my so-called crimes.

I've been considering looking outside of London for my next subject. Can't say the idea appeals much, though. London lends itself so well to my imagination. It truly is a magnificent backdrop, so I think I'll stay for now. But it's almost inevitable I'll have to leave before too much longer. Sooner or later some bright spark will make a connection. They'll never connect them all. Impossible. But they'll connect two, maybe more, and then they'll start to take things seriously and that won't be good for me.

CHAPTER 18

Wednesday

By 7:30 A.M. Sean was back at work. A few hours' sleep, a shower, and clean clothes had partially revived him. He would be briefing half the team soon. The other half was still across London, watching Hellier's office. Apparently Hellier hadn't gone home all night. He'd stayed in his office. He was definitely up to something.

Sean's office phone rang. "DI Corrigan speaking." He tried to disguise his tiredness.

"Morning, sir," a voice on the other end replied. "I'm DC Kelsey, calling from SO11." The name meant nothing to Sean. "You sent some numbers to us. Telephone numbers in an address book taken from a James Hellier. You wanted subscribers' checks on them?"

Sean remembered. "Yes, of course. How can I help?"

"Just a courtesy call, really. To let you know we did the checks and none of them came back as a trace. Basically, they're not telephone numbers as such."

"'As such'?" Sean asked.

"Yeah. I think they could be telephone numbers ultimately, but they're probably coded."

Sean stood up. He'd expected as much. So that was why Hellier denied having Daniel Graydon's number in the book. If he'd admitted to that, he would have had to declare his code and then they could have deciphered every number in the book. They could have traced all his secret contacts. It would have told them a great many things. Hellier was careful. The killer was careful.

"Could you decipher the code?" Sean asked.

"We don't do deciphering at SO11," DC Kelsey replied.

"Any idea who does?"

"There isn't anywhere specific that I know of. You need to find your own expert. MI5, a university lecturer, something like that."

"Tell me you're joking?" Sean said, without knowing why he was so surprised.

"Afraid not. But I get some quiet spells, sometimes. I could have a play with them for you, if you like."

"You're a good man," Sean replied. "Call me as soon as you get anything." He hung the phone up only for it to immediately ring again. At the same time Sally appeared at the door. He held his index finger up to stall her and grabbed the phone.

"DI Corrigan." Still early morning and already his telephone-answering manner was degenerating.

"Guv'nor, it's Stan." It was DC Stan McGowan, the detective in charge of the second makeshift surveillance team. "I don't know what happened here last night," he went on, "but someone on the other surveillance crew fucked up."

"What's going on?"

"I was told Target One didn't leave the office last night." Stan used surveillance language to describe Hellier.

"That's what I heard."

"Then why did we just see Target One enter it?"

Sean sat slowly. "Impossible."

"Impossible or not, I've seen him with my own eyes. It's been confirmed by observation posts one and three. And he's wearing fresh clothes too. Sorry, boss. Someone fucked up."

Sean knew what it meant. Hellier had been running free again. All night. Would there be a price to pay for their mistake? Had it cost someone their life?

Donnelly appeared in his doorway as he was slamming the phone down. "Problem?" he asked.

Sean gave a long sigh before answering. "Whoever was covering Hellier last night lost him." He sprang to his feet and began moving toward the briefing room. Donnelly and Sally followed.

"No way," Donnelly insisted. "Not while I was covering him, no fucking way. He made it easy for us and stayed at work all night, too scared of the press to show his face."

"Sorry, Dave." Sean spoke without looking at him. "It's been confirmed. No mistake. Hellier slipped past you. I need you to work out how that could have happened and when it could have happened."

"I don't fucking believe this," Donnelly protested.

"It's done, Dave." Sean still didn't look at him. "Let it go."

Sally tried to help. "There were no murders last night. I've already checked."

"You mean there were no murders discovered last night," Sean pointed out. "There's a difference," he added unnecessarily. "Let's hope there'll be no more cock-ups today."

"Wait a minute, guv'nor," Donnelly protested. "I said this half-baked surveillance was a waste of time. I had five tired detectives to cover a target. It was never going to be enough."

Sean realized his mistake. "Okay. Okay. I know you and the

team would have done your best. Maybe there's another way out of the building?"

"There is," Donnelly snapped. "Through a basement car park, but we had that covered."

"Something else then." Sean wanted to leave the subject.

"Maybe," Donnelly conceded.

They swept into the briefing room. There were only five detectives waiting for them. Sean was running out of people. The surveillance effort was putting pressure on his resources.

What chatter there had been died down quickly. Everybody automatically took a seat. Sean decided not to mention that Hellier had slipped through their surveillance. He'd let Donnelly tell them later. He knew where Hellier was now, so there was no point in making more of it. He could ill afford divisions in his team.

Conscious of time closing in on him, he got straight to business: "We may well have linked our boy to another murder," he informed the small audience of detectives. There was a murmur around the room, but no looks of surprise. Sean had told Donnelly the night before. He must have spread the news already.

"On what grounds?" Donnelly asked.

"Three things," Sean replied. "The lack of usable forensic evidence. The fact that a shoe print belonging to a plain-soled shoe approximately the same size as those found at our scene was recovered. And the type of victim."

"Hold on there, guv'nor," Donnelly said. "I thought the victim out east was a teenage girl."

Sean felt the eyes of the room watching him, waiting for a response. "I don't think the sex of the victims is relevant." He knew he had to convince his team that he was right. It was vital that he took them with him. If he lost their confidence now, he would be alone. Isolated.

"Okay," Donnelly said. "How we going to move this thing forward?"

"Publicity," Sean answered. "It's the one tool left in the box that we haven't used. It'll spread the inquiry wider than we can without it. I'm hopeful it'll turn up a key witness. Someone placing Hellier at or near the victim's home on the night of the murder. Maybe he used a cab. Maybe we'll get lucky.

"You sort out a press conference, Dave," Sean continued. "But make sure you keep our Press Bureau informed. I don't want to piss on anybody's chips. Sally, you'll take care of *Crime-watch*."

"Gonna be a TV star, eh, Sally?" Donnelly teased. Sally flicked him a middle-finger salute.

"The Murder Investigation Team investigating the East London killing will do their own press stuff," Sean announced. "At this time we're not going to mention there could be a link between the two."

"Why?" Donnelly asked.

"We don't want to panic the public," Sean told him. "We want to use the press in a controlled fashion. We're not out to make headlines here.

"Second, and more important, we don't want the killer knowing we've made a link. If it is Hellier, then let's leave him thinking we're only looking at him for the one. Keep the pressure on him for our murder and maybe he'll be distracted and make a mistake with the other. No point in showing him our hand. The next time I interview Hellier, I want to be able to take him to pieces, bit by bit. If we can get the evidence, then I'll be able to break through to him and get him talking—and if I can get him talking, I can bury him. If I can get him talking, he'll bury himself."

"What about the other two suspects?" Zukov asked before the detectives scattered. "Paramore and Jonnie Dempsey?"

"Anything, anybody?" Sean asked.

"Paramore's still missing," said Donnelly, "but Fiona's dug something up on Dempsey. Fiona..."

DC Fiona Cahill, a tall, slim detective in her midthirties with short, neatly cut hazelnut hair, got to her feet, her slightly deep voice and cultured accent further setting her apart. "I've been working my way through Daniel's friends one by one. I spoke to a guy called Ferdie Edwards who tells me that Dempsey did indeed know Daniel and that they were friends, but he also told me they were more than just that."

"Lovers?" Sean jumped in, a flicker of excitement in his heart.

"No," said Cahill. "Business partners."

"What?" Sean asked disbelievingly.

"Apparently, Dempsey worked as a kind of middleman. If he heard of a customer in the club who might be willing to pay for sex, he'd steer them toward Daniel—for a cut of the money, of course. He'd also look out for Daniel, watch his back, so to speak."

"This is all very interesting," Sean said impatiently, "but where are we going with it?"

"Well, Edwards reckons that Daniel was getting a bit fed up with the arrangement."

"You mean he was getting fed up handing over a share of his hard-earned cash to Dempsey," Donnelly guessed.

"Exactly," Cahill confirmed. "Edwards said they'd had at least one heated argument over it—Dempsey telling our victim he'd have him banned from the club if he didn't keep paying up, and Daniel telling Dempsey he already had someone else in the club watching his back who would make sure he was never barred from entering."

"Do we know who?" Sean asked.

"No. Not yet."

"Probably one of the bouncers," Donnelly said.

"Probably," Sean agreed. "What a bloody mess."

"'Oh, what a tangled web we weave when we endeavor to deceive,'" Donnelly added.

Sean took over: "Jonnie the barman has just taken a significant step forward as a viable suspect, so let's find him. And let's find out who else had Daniel's back at the nightclub. And while we're at it, let's find Paramore too. We need to speak to all of them—and soon."

"All right, everybody," said Donnelly, stepping on as soon as he judged Sean had finished. "You've all got plenty to be getting on with, so let's hustle. And make sure you return all completed actions back to me as soon as they're ready. You get the jigsaw pieces and I solve the puzzle, remember?"

The meeting broke up, the few detectives who had been there swiftly exiting the briefing room. Other than Sean, Donnelly was the last to leave. He nodded to Sean on his way out, moving a little faster than normal, but not so anyone would have noticed. Instead of returning to the incident room with everyone else, he headed for the fire exit and walked down two flights of stairs to the main part of the station. Still moving fast, he made his way to a small room that housed two old photocopying machines. It also had a phone. The room was empty. Donnelly picked up the phone and dialed.

DS Samra answered. "Hello."

"Raj. It's Dave."

"David." Samra sounded cautious. "What you after?"

"That little matter I discussed with Jimmy Dawson and yourself . . ." He let it hang, waiting for Samra to respond.

"I remember," Samra confirmed.

"Change of plan."

"I'm listening."

"I'm not just interested in homosexual murders now. I need to know about *anything* nasty, and I need to know first."

"How nasty we talking?"

"Stranger attacks. Lack of motive, lots of mess. Anything sexual too. I'm not interested in domestics, gang related, drugs, or drunks."

"I'll do my best," Raj said.

"Same as before," Donnelly continued. "Spread the word, but keep it quiet. Remember, I need to know first." He hung up.

Raj looked at his phone for a moment, then he began to make some calls. He called DS Jimmy Dawson first. If Jimmy was happy to do as Donnelly said, then so was he.

Hellier stood by the window in the office of one of the other junior partners. They drank coffee and shared a few sexist jokes. Their perfect secretary was the subject of much of their posturing and sexual boasting. It was as well she couldn't hear them.

Hellier meant little of what he said. It was important to engage in this sort of social discourse with his colleagues once in a while. Especially now, following his arrest. The innuendo that he was gay could be more damaging than being suspected of murder. Ridiculous people.

His mood was excellent this morning. He would have paid a considerable sum to have been a fly on the wall when Corrigan found out he'd slipped past them. They'd look like fools a few more times before he was finished.

And then, when the time was perfect, he'd disappear. Leave this God-cursed place and start again. But first Corrigan needed breaking. He'd sworn it. Corrigan had humiliated him and now he would pay a heavy price. The Italians say revenge is a dish best served cold. He didn't agree. His would be served scalding hot.

The perfect secretary knocked on the open door. He shook the daydreaming from his head.

"What is it, Samantha?" Hellier's colleague asked.

She looked at Hellier. "It's actually Mr. Hellier I need to see."

Hellier stood away from the windowsill. He smiled pleasantly. "Fire away."

"I have someone on the phone for you, sir, but they won't give me a name or tell me what it's about."

Fucking journalists. Fucking Corrigan. "Well, get rid of them then."

Strangely, Samantha hesitated at the door, her obedience faltering.

Hellier saw the hesitation. "Well?" he asked.

"They sound quite desperate, sir. They claim to have very important information for you. They'll only speak to you personally and in private."

Hellier's eyes narrowed. "Put the call through to my office."

Sally walked to the headquarters of the National Criminal Intelligence Service, known as NCIS, situated in Spring Gardens, Lambeth, close to both the forensics laboratory and the nightclub where Daniel Graydon had spent his last night. NCIS remained low profile. You wouldn't know they were there unless you were looking hard.

She had abandoned her car to the mercy of traffic wardens and small-time thieves. Life still functioned at the base level in Lambeth. Survival of the fittest was the nature of the game here. Any respect or fear the local population had for the police had long since disappeared. They lived by their own laws now.

Security was expectedly tight at the NCIS building. Sally buzzed the video intercom and waited. A soulless male voice eventually answered.

"State your business, please."

"DS Jones, Serious Crime Group. Here to see DS Graham Wright. I believe he works in Counterfeit Currency." She held her identification up to the camera. The door was opened after a slight delay. She walked to the reception desk. The security guard was already waiting for her. He gave her a visitor's name tag and directions to the Counterfeit Currency section. She nodded thanks and moved toward the lift.

When she reached the office, she found DS Wright sitting at his desk. He was a fit-looking man in his early forties. His dark hair was matched by clear olive skin. She found him attractive. "DS Graham Wright?" she asked.

He glanced up from his desk. "Yes. That's me."

"I'm DS Sally Jones, from SCG." She felt Wright's eyes scan her from head to toes and back.

"And what can I do for you, DS Jones?"

"Please," she told him. "Call me Sally."

"Well, Sally?"

"Fingerprints," she said. "Missing fingerprints." She studied him for a reaction. Maybe a hint of confusion, but nothing more. "Back in ninety-nine, you took a set of fingerprints out of the Yard."

"Ninety-nine?" Wright protested. "I don't think I'll be able to remember back that far. Whose prints were they?"

"Stefan Korsakov's," she answered. Wright flushed a little. She noticed it. "You remember?"

"Sure," he replied. "I remember."

"How come? It was a long time ago."

"Because I helped put the bastard away. If you're here to tell me he's dead, then you'll make me a happy man."

"Maybe he is," said Sally. "We're trying to find that out. But for now, you remember taking the prints out of the Yard?"

"Yeah. And I remember taking them back just as clearly."

Sally picked up the speed of the questions. "Why did you pull them out in the first place?"

"I was doing someone a favor. The prints weren't for me."

"Who were they for?"

"Paul Jarratt. He was a DS at Richmond at the time. I was still a DC. We worked the Korsakov case together. He asked me to pull the prints, so I did."

"Did he say why he wanted them?"

"I can't remember. Maybe he said the Prison Service had asked for them, but I'm not sure. All I know is that if someone has lost his prints, it wasn't me. If you want to know why DS Jarratt needed the prints, then perhaps you should ask him."

"You know what?" Sally told him. "I think I'll do exactly that."

The phone was ringing on Hellier's desk as he entered his office. He closed the door before answering.

"Hello. James Hellier speaking."

"Mr. Hellier," the voice on the other end began. "I hope you don't mind me calling you at work. It was the only way I could think of contacting you."

The voice belonged to a man. He sounded mature, in his forties perhaps. He spoke quite well. Hellier could hear no trace of an accent. He didn't recognize the voice, but suspected it was being artificially disguised. It sounded concerned. He could sense no harmful intent, but was as cautious as ever.

"You're not a journalist, are you?" Hellier barked the question. "Because if you are, I'll find out whom you work for and by this evening you'll be looking for a new job that you won't find."

"No. No." The man's voice was slightly pleading. Hellier still sensed no threat.

"Then who are you?"

"A friend," the man answered. "A friend who knew Daniel Graydon. And now . . . now I'd like to become your friend. A friend who can help you."

Hellier said nothing.

"Listen to these instructions. Follow them exactly if you want to meet me, but be careful. Your enemies are everywhere."

Hellier listened hard to the instructions, memorizing every detail. When the voice had finished, the phone line went dead. Hellier sat in silence with the phone pressed to his ear. His new *friend* had to be a journalist. He wouldn't put it past Corrigan to have put the vermin on to him in the first place, trying to panic him into making a mistake, but it wouldn't work. He knew how to deal with journalists and he knew how to deal with Corrigan. After a minute or two he was brought back to the world by a knock at his door.

"Come in," he said, his voice a little hoarse. The door opened as Sebastian Gibran let himself in and pulled a chair close to Hellier's desk. Hellier found himself leaning back, as far away from Gibran as he could get.

"Thought I'd see how you were. See how things were going with the police. Make sure you were okay. Nothing getting on top of you too much?"

"I'm fine, thank you, Sebastian. Despite everything, I seem to be bearing up." Hellier found it harder than usual to play the corporate game. The voice on the telephone had been an unwelcome complication.

"Good. I knew it would take more than jealous allegations to upset a man like you."

"Jealous allegations?"

"Of course. People will always be jealous of people like us. They want what we have, but they're never going to have it. It's not just wealth, it's everything. They can win their millions in the lottery as much as they like, but they'll never be like us.

Never walk among other men as we can, safe in the comfort of our own superiority. It's our right. You do understand, don't you, James?"

"A king will always be a king. A peasant will always be a peasant."

"Exactly." Gibran beamed. "That's why I brought you to this firm in the first place, James, because I knew you had what it takes. When I first spoke to you at that conference all those years ago, I knew. I'd met hundreds of financial superstars that week, but I knew you were different. I knew you belonged here at Butler and Mason—and I made damn certain I got you."

"I'm forever grateful," Hellier managed, but he was a little disturbed by this side of Gibran he'd never seen before—the perfect corporate manager and visionary seemingly replaced by a more arrogant, self-serving elitist. Was he finally meeting the real Sebastian Gibran—or was Gibran trying to trick him into lowering his guard, looking for a reason to move him on to pastures far less green?

"Any gratitude owed has already been repaid," Gibran told him. You know, James, none of us are immune from making mistakes. The very nature of our business is risk oriented. We accept that people will make bad decisions from time to time. Those decisions will sometimes cost us a great deal of money, but we accept it."

Hellier listened, trying to predict the moment when the conversation would become specific to him.

"But other mistakes, errors of judgment not related to work, are less tolerated. The people who own Butler and Mason like to portray a very particular image: they like their employees to be married, settled, and they encourage people to have children by creating a pay structure that rewards a family life. The image of this company has emerged by design, not accident, and they guard it jealously. If an employee has elements in their life that do not fit easily with our company ethos, then they would be expected to bury those"—Gibran searched for an appropriate word—"those habits, where they would never be seen. If they failed to do so, then their position here might not be tenable. If someone was to draw unwanted attention to our business, even if it was by accident, even if it was later shown not to be that person's fault, the company would nevertheless expect that person to bring that situation to a swift conclusion. We're all clear on that philosophy, aren't we, James?"

"I understand perfectly," Hellier answered.

"Listen," Gibran said, his voice and tone suddenly sounding more like the man Hellier recognized. "That was the corporate line—make of it what you will. This is from me: watch your back. I can protect you only so much. I like you, James. You're a good man. Tread carefully, my friend."

Hellier watched him for a while before answering. "I will. Thank you."

"As Nietzsche said, 'Not mankind, but Superman is the goal . . . My desire is to bring forth creatures which stand sublimely above the whole species.' That is what we are expected to be, James. The failings of normal men are not a luxury we're allowed."

"'To live beyond good and evil,'" Hellier said, continuing the quote from Nietzsche.

Gibran leaned slowly forward. "I knew we understood each other. You see, James, it's our imaginations that truly set us apart. Without them, we'd be just like all those other sad fools wandering around soulless, aimless, pointless. Only fit to be ruled over by those fit to rule. That may sound arrogant, but it's not. It's reality. It's the truth."

Sean entered the press conference room at New Scotland Yard. He walked behind Superintendent Featherstone, who would head the conference. Sean was only there to deal with specifics, not the general presentation.

Other than the TV people there were about a dozen journalists there. A lot less than there would be for a celebrity or child murder, but more than there would have been for a run-of-the-mill killing. Most of them had been following the case since Hellier's initial arrest, when Donnelly had leaked it to a contact in the media.

Featherstone introduced them and outlined the details of Daniel Graydon's murder. He began to tell the journalists what the police wanted from the public. Sally would repeat it later that night on *Crimewatch*.

"We're appealing to anyone who may have seen Daniel meet someone outside the Utopia nightclub that night. Perhaps a cabdriver who took Daniel home. A friend or acquaintance who maybe gave him a lift," Featherstone explained.

"We are also interested in anyone who may have heard or seen something later that night, close to Daniel's flat in New Cross. Did anyone see a man acting strangely in the area? Again, maybe the man responsible for this terrible crime used a cab to leave the area. Can anyone remember picking up a passenger in the early hours? Someone who aroused their suspicions?"

Sean listened absentmindedly. Featherstone was doing a professional job, sticking to the script, but there was one thing the two of them hadn't discussed ahead of the conference. A question from a journalist almost made Sean jump. "Do you have a description of the suspect?"

Featherstone was about to answer no when Sean jumped in.

"Yes," he said. It was the first time he'd spoken. Featherstone was surprised. His mouth hung open a little.

"What's the description?" the journalist asked.

"We believe we're looking for a white male, in his forties.

He's slim, fair haired, and smart in appearance." Sean was describing Hellier.

"Where has this description come from?" asked another
journalist.

"I can't tell you that at this stage," Sean answered.

The journalists' excitement grew. "Detective Inspector . . ."
The female journalist raised her voice above the increasing noise
and competition for answers. "Inspector." She caught Sean's eye.
"Have you just described James Hellier, Inspector?"

"No comment," Sean answered.

Another journalist pursued the question. "Is Mr. Hellier no
longer a suspect in this murder, Inspector?"

"For legal reasons, I can't answer that."

"Why was Mr. Hellier not charged?" another asked.

"This is an ongoing investigation, which means I can't answer that at this time."

"Is Mr. Hellier a witness in this case?"

The journalists had revealed why they were there. Hellier
was the story. Sean had known it from the beginning. He could
feel that Featherstone wanted to get the conference back on
track, which was fine by Sean. It had served its purpose. Hellier
would hear about it and read between the lines. The pressure
would be back on. It was revenge for Hellier embarrassing the
surveillance operation. For trying to cause a split in the team.
A piece on the chessboard had been moved and Hellier would
have to respond. Another question came from the floor.

"Was Mr. Hellier having sexual relations with the victim?"

"I think Detective Superintendent Featherstone will be best
placed to answer your questions." He leaned back into his chair,
signifying that his involvement in the conference was over.

"Superintendent," a journalist asked, "is James Hellier a suspect in this murder inquiry or not?"

Featherstone answered without hesitation, the media training paying off. "At this point Mr. Hellier is helping us with our inquiries. I can't reveal any more details than that until sometime in the future, but I can assure you that it is my intention to conduct as open an investigation into the death of Daniel Graydon as possible, and of course the media will be kept informed. As I was about to say, we would also like the public's help in tracing two other men that we need to speak to."

Sean wasn't listening anymore and didn't hear Featherstone giving the media the names of Steven Paramore and Jonnie Dempsey. The journalists were once again directing their questions to Featherstone, who dealt with them as beautifully as a conductor would his orchestra. Featherstone presented the user-friendly face of the police service. The clean shirt over an unwashed body. Sean sat quietly chewing the inside of his mouth, waiting for the show to come to a natural end, thinking of Hellier. Seeing him kneeling next to Daniel Graydon, pushing the ice pick through his skin. Standing over Heather Freeman as he swept the knife across her stretched throat.

Hellier had followed the instructions given on the phone exactly. He'd left work at 6 P.M. and walked out the front door in full view of the surveillance team. He hailed the first cab he saw and told the driver to take him to Victoria train station. Once there, he descended into the underground system, moving through the labyrinth of tunnels on foot, boarding trains traveling in one direction, then unexpectedly disembarking and doubling back, making it almost impossible to follow him.

An hour later he stood in Hyde Park looking up at the statue of Achilles. Large trees provided good cover. He could see the bandstand in the park, about thirty meters away. The man on the phone had said he would be there at seven thirty. He would be carrying a small blue Reebok knapsack and wearing a yellow shirt.

Hellier kept his distance. He wanted time to observe the man before he approached him. A friend of Daniel Graydon. What did he know? What had Daniel told him? What did he know about Hellier? It had to be a journalist looking for a story to titillate the masses, but had he found out more than he'd bargained for? Something that could be dangerous to Hellier? Had his phone been hacked? He doubted it. When it came to hacking a phone, he could teach any half-cocked journalist or private detective a thing or two; he was pretty certain his hadn't been. He needed to find out what they knew about him and deal with it—deal with it with extreme prejudice.

His mobile rang. The display showed PRIVATE NUMBER CALLING. He answered: "James Hellier."

"I'm so sorry. I'm afraid I'm going to be late. I won't be able to get to you until about eight. You must wait for me. It's vital that you wait for me."

Hellier checked his watch. It meant waiting for almost an hour. "This had better be worth it."

"It will be," the man said. "Please believe me. It's more important than you can possibly imagine."

"Who are you?" Hellier asked.

"Someone who has an interest in your current predicament. Someone who wants to help. Just be sure to wait for me."

"I'll be here." Hellier didn't attempt to disguise his annoyance. He snapped his mobile shut. It appeared he would have plenty of time to study his favorite London statue.

For the first time in a long while, Sean went home at a reasonable hour. Kate found it a little strange at first. She'd become accustomed to him not being there.

Sally was doing the *Crimewatch* presentation that night. Several of the team would stay on at Peckham until midnight, answering any calls from the public the appeal might bring.

Sean wasn't hopeful. He only hoped Hellier was watching. He'd briefed Sally to use Hellier's description as that of the possible killer, just as he'd done at the press conference.

He also wanted to see the presentation on the Heather Freeman murder. DI Brown would be on the show that night, but no mention would be made of the connection. How would that affect Hellier's behavior? He pictured Hellier laughing at their incompetence. Fine. Let him laugh.

His mobile began to ring. He groaned. Kate stared across the living room at him. "Hello. Sean Corrigan speaking."

"Bad news, guv'nor." It was DC Stan McGowan. "He left work at about six, but we lost him on the underground. He was definitely trying to shake us. We had no chance. Sorry."

"Why didn't you call earlier?" Sean asked. It was almost eight thirty now.

"We've been running around trying to find him. I sent a couple of boys to his home address, but he either beat them there or he hasn't gone home yet."

"Okay, Stan," Sean said. "You've done your best. Stay with it tonight. Concentrate on the home address. Tomorrow I'll see if I can't get a dedicated surveillance team back."

"Sorry," Stan said again. Sean hung up. He wondered if he could stay awake long enough to watch *Crimewatch*.

Hellier checked his watch. It was three minutes since he'd last checked. Ten past eight. The man had sworn he'd be there by eight. He was late. He hadn't called. Dammit. Where was the fool? Hellier looked at his watch again.

What did the caller really want? He'd said he could help. Who could help him? Why would they want to? Were they going to try and blackmail him? That would at least be amusing. He checked his phone. No missed calls.

He wasn't going to stand here all night. He had better things to do. He'd lost the police surveillance, but he needed to be careful. Journalists could still be a problem, even if the police weren't. He felt excitement rising in him like an old friend. Time for a treat. He deserved one.

Kate watched Sean struggling to stay awake in his chair. A bottle of Stella Artois rested on his chest. She watched it rise and fall gently. If he fell asleep properly, he would spill the beer. The cold liquid would wake him up quickly enough. She hoped it would happen. It would make her laugh, and Sean hadn't made her laugh much lately.

He was losing the battle to keep his eyes open. Hearing the presenter mention a murder in South London, Kate shook Sean by the shoulder. "I think you're on."

"Uh?"

"You're on," she repeated. "It's your case next."

Sean sat upright. He rubbed his face hard and shook his head. "Thanks."

He watched the presenter outline the case. It was supposed to be informative only, the media helping the police to catch a killer, but the presenter's background gave him away. He couldn't help using gutter-press terminology. He tried to look shocked when describing the murder as "gruesome." He paused dramatically as he informed the nation of how Daniel had been stabbed "seventy-seven times." The tabloid words flowed from his mouth: "Bloody . . ." "Horrific . . ." "Mutilated . . ." He had them all. In truth, there was only one reason the program existed. Ratings. The British public liked nothing better than watching other people's suffering from a safe distance.

The camera switched to Sally. She looked a little nervous, but you couldn't tell unless you knew her like Sean did. She was as professional as he knew she'd be. Informative, accurate, businesslike, but compassionate too.

She gave the description of Hellier as Sean had asked. He felt satisfaction at the thought of Hellier watching and listening to himself being described on national TV, but he had to remember that Hellier was like a poisonous snake. He was dangerous. It was important to keep a firm grip of his neck or risk being bitten.

The presenter tried to ambush Sally. He asked her if someone had already been arrested. If the police already had a "prime suspect." Sally had been expecting it. Her answer sounded prepared. She told him a number of people had been helping police with the inquiry, but that they were still trying to trace the whereabouts of Steven Paramore and Jonnie Dempsey. The presenter backed off, closing the piece with the usual attempt at a heartfelt appeal for assistance. He read out the two telephone numbers that also appeared at the bottom of the screen. One for the studio and one for the incident room back in Peckham. Then he moved on to the next tragedy of the night.

CHAPTER 19

I've seen her before. A couple of times. On both occasions I followed her home. She lives in Shepherd's Bush, in a flat on the first floor of an old mansion block. The building has seen better days, by the look of it, but I suppose it's not too bad for the area.

She works in a small advertising company in Holborn. She must be thirty or thereabouts. Reasonably attractive, but nothing special. Five foot five and strong, from the look of it, although not very fit. She does have very nice short brown hair though. The cut is unusually short for a woman.

But what really attracted me to her, what really caught my eye, was her skin. She has the most beautiful skin. Very lightly tanned. Faultless. It shone.

Did she know it set her apart? Was that why she kept her hair short, so nothing would distract from her skin? Probably.

But it wouldn't stay that way for much longer. She worked too hard. Always last out of the office. Trying to impress her boss or maybe just trying to impress herself.

I read an article in the *Evening Standard* the other day. Apparently young London workers are judging success by the lack of free time a person has. The most successful are judged to be those who have no time for themselves.

Pitiful. How could anyone really question my right to do as I please with you? You have no value anymore. You know that yourselves. Pointless little animals, living pointless little lives. Only I can make you worth something.

When I've watched her in the past, she hasn't left her office until after eight. Tonight was no different.

I thought about visiting her in the office. Leave a nasty surprise for her boss in the morning. Perhaps cut her breasts off, Jack the Ripper style, and leave them on his desk with a resignation note I'd make her write, just for the fun of it.

No. I couldn't guarantee the level of control I'd need. I couldn't risk being interrupted. A cleaner might walk in on me, or a fucking security guard. I would be able to deal with them easily, but the visit would be spoiled. So I decided to follow her home. Again.

She has an easy journey. Nine bearable stops along the Central line to Shepherd's Bush. The simple route makes it easier to follow her. I could wait for her to come home—I know where she lives from my previous follows—but I enjoy the thrill of the chase. It helps me build toward my climax. Allows the excitement to grow. It courses through my veins and arteries.

My blood carries the excitement around my body like oxygen. My heart beats so hard and fast I'm sure people can see my chest pounding, hear my heart thumping like a Zulu drum. But at the same time, I know they can't. It seeps into my muscles. Makes them contract and tense. Makes me feel strong. Invincible. I'm becoming alive again. I can see more. Hear more. Smell more.

I feel the twitching in my groin. I have to calm down and control it. It's difficult, especially with her sitting so close. In the same carriage, only a few seats away. I think she notices my presence, but she seems unconcerned. You wouldn't be concerned by my presence either. I read my paper, the *Guardian*.

Our stop is next. She stands first and moves to the exit door. I move to a spot a meter or so behind her. I can smell her clearly now. The scent is almost overpoweringly beautiful.

The train stops and we both step onto the platform. This is an underground station, so there's CCTV everywhere. I make a point of stopping on the platform. I lift my foot onto one of the wooden benches screwed to the wall and make a show of tying my shoelace. If the police check the tapes at all, they'll be looking for someone following her closely, not a businessman worrying about his shoes. Eventually I follow her, but I'm a long way back, exactly where I want to be.

She's out of my sight as I go through the automatic barrier and into the street. I know the route she should take and pray there are no variables to contend with. If she goes into a shop or meets a friend, I may lose her. I'll pick her up back at her flat, but the follow is important to me tonight. It is how I've seen it happening. It's the beginning of making my desires reality. If any part of the sequence is changed from the way I need it to be, then there would be no point in continuing.

It's about eight forty-five. There's still some daylight. I move fast along Bush Green, the traffic heavy even at this hour. The green resembles some kind of stock-car racing circuit and drivers are treating it accordingly.

I walk past a group of black youths loitering menacingly outside a betting shop. I feel their eyes fall upon my expensive wristwatch. I give them a hard stare and they look away. Respect.

Unexpectedly she walks out of a small newsagent's. I almost trip over her, swerving to avoid her. She's seen me. Definitely. And now I'm in front of her. I want to be behind her. Following her. This is not good. I can't stop and wait for her to pass me. I need to do something and do it right away.

I do the best thing I can think of. I walk to the first bus stop I see and pretend to be waiting for a bus. There are other people at the stop. I only hope the bus doesn't come. She walks past me. I feel her quickly look in my direction, but she doesn't seem panicked. She walks on. I wait a few seconds and follow her again.

I have to be a lot more careful now. She saw me outside the shop, saw me go to the bus stop. If she turns around and sees me again, she may run. She may go into the nearest shop or café. It won't cause me a long-term problem, but it'll destroy tonight's plans.

I keep a reasonable distance. Ten meters or so. I'd like to be closer, but can't risk it. I'm sure she can feel my presence, even at this distance. It's important to me that she can. The Chinese swear that dog meat tastes all the sweeter if the dog is terrified before being butchered. I would have to agree.

I try and anticipate when she'll look behind her and if so, which shoulder she'll look over. It gives me the best chance of avoiding her field of vision. But she doesn't turn her head. We're still walking along Bush Green and there are lots of people about, which makes her feel safe.

She turns left into a side road. Rockley Road. On either side the road is lined with four- and five-story town houses, Georgian or maybe Victorian. London's demand for housing and cheap hotels has turned the street into a mess of dirty-looking flats and run-down boardinghouses.

She turns left into a side street. Minford Gardens. This is where she lives. It's an altogether more pleasant street. Smaller houses with trees lining the pavement, but the houses are still scruffy and split into flats. It's much, much quieter.

I begin to walk faster. The excitement is rising to a point of explosion. I want to rage over this woman. I want to tear her to pieces. Rip her open with my nails and teeth. But I won't. I will show my strength. My control. I'm not like others. I've learned to control the power I have.

I close the distance between us. Walking ever faster, but so silently the sound of the breeze drowns out any noise. There's no sun in the road anymore. The houses have blocked its fading light. I'm so close. The streetlamps begin to flicker.

I'm close enough to touch her now. I see the hairs on the nape of her neck stand on end. She feels me. She spins on her heels and looks into the eyes of my mask. Soon she will meet the real me.

Linda Kotler was thirty-two years old and single. She'd been in a relationship for eight years, but when she pushed for marriage he, unbelievably, got cold feet and ran away. Christ, they'd been living together for six and a half years, but apparently the mere mention of the word "marriage" suddenly made him feel "trapped." Perhaps it was just the excuse he'd been waiting for.

She was rapidly learning what it was to be single when all your friends are couples. Eight years is a long time with someone. Her friends were his and his were hers. They thought of them as a single entity. One personality. When he left her they had been so nice, to the point of being irritating. Her married girlfriends didn't look compassionate anymore, they looked smug. And suddenly she was single. That made her a threat to their own fragile relationships. True, she'd been guilty of a little flirting with her friends' men, but she needed to feel desired. Now more than ever. Rejection hurts.

She'd been working late again tonight. Maybe she'd secretly been hoping someone at the office would invite her for a drink. It was a lovely evening for it, but no invitation came. Time to go home to her much-loved prison.

She checked herself in the mirror of her compact. Her hair was short enough not to have to worry about it. Her skin was as excellent as ever. Years of living with him hadn't changed that. She was proud of her skin. She dabbed moisturizer on her fingertips and massaged it into her face. A little lipstick was all she needed. You never know who you might meet on the tube.

Holborn Station wasn't too busy. She'd long missed the main rush hour. The platform was only sparsely populated compared to the scene two or three hours before. Rush-hour platforms scared her. She'd been brought up in a small town in Devon and the size and speed of London still intimidated her. How could those people stand so close to the edge as the trains flashed past? Was getting home a few minutes earlier really so important? They must have more to go home to than she did.

She saw him almost as soon as she slid the heavy briefcase off her shoulder. He was standing a couple of meters to her right and slightly behind her. She noticed him because she'd seen him before, about a week ago, maybe less. It happened more than people think. When you travel the same route day in, day out, eventually you start seeing the same people.

She had thought he was rather attractive. A little older than she usually went for, probably the wrong side of forty, although only just, but he clearly took care of himself. He dressed well too. She tried to catch a whiff of his cologne, but she didn't think he was wearing any.

He didn't look at her, but she somehow could feel he had noticed her. She couldn't see properly, but she was pretty certain he wasn't wearing a wedding ring, just a nice wristwatch. An Omega, she thought. So he had money too. That always helped.

The train came and they ended up in the same carriage. She read the ads adorning the carriage and sneaked glances at him. She couldn't be sure, but she thought he sneaked the odd look back. Most of the time he read his paper. The *Guardian*. So he had liberal views on the world, like her.

She wondered where he would get off the train. She guessed Notting Hill—no, Holland Park suited him better. But he didn't.

The train approached Shepherd's Bush. She sneaked one last glance at the man and moved to the exit. She wasn't one of those confident types who would sit and wait for the train to stop before staking their claim at the exit. She was always afraid the doors would close too quickly and she'd miss her stop. Worse, she'd be left on the train feeling foolish. Uncomfortable stares would rest on her.

He'd stepped off the train right behind her, but she couldn't feel him close anymore; it was as if he'd somehow faded away. He must have gone down another corridor, heading for another exit.

She wanted to be subtle. If he was somehow still behind her, she didn't want him to see her looking for him. She took the chance to glance back as she traveled up the escalator. She couldn't see him. If he had been heading her way, he should have been within view. He must have gone another way. The butterflies in her stomach left her. They were replaced with an empty, disappointed feeling. She preferred the fluttering wings.

By the time she'd exited the station, she'd forgotten he had ever existed. Ground level brought its own reality and he wasn't part of it. She hurried along Bush Green. The heavy bag slowed her, the straps cutting into her shoulder, drawing attention to her. She must learn to travel lighter. She saw a group of young black men standing outside the betting shop and pulled her briefcase closer, tightening the grip on her handbag, head down and walking past them as quickly as she could. She felt their stares as surely as if they were beating her. She felt like a racist and it made her feel guilty.

She entered the small shop. It smelled like most newsagents or liquor stores in London, spicy and sweet. She liked the smell. She liked the different cultures of London. Mostly, anyway.

It took her less than a minute to buy the pack of Silk Cut Mild. She'd tried to smoke Marlboro Lights or Camel Lights, like everyone else in London. They tasted funny to her. They didn't smell like the cigarettes adults had smoked around her when she was growing up in Devon.

As she left the shop she wasn't looking where she was going. She almost bumped straight into him, the man from the tube. It made her stop in her tracks. He swerved around her and kept going. If he'd wanted to talk to her, he'd had the perfect opportunity. He hadn't taken it. Maybe she had just imagined that he'd noticed her earlier? Being alone in London was beginning to get to her. She was craving the attention of strangers.

He walked in front of her now. Still along Bush Green. He stopped at a bus stop. He didn't seem the type to be getting a bus in Shepherd's Bush. She tried to imagine where he could possibly be going. Putney, or perhaps Barnes. If so, it was a strange route.

She passed the bus stop and kept heading west. She turned left into Rockley Road. The noise of Shepherd's Bush Green seemed to die away instantly. Immediately she felt more relaxed. Her pace slowed, almost as if she was enjoying an evening stroll. The pain of the bag strap cutting into her shoulder reminded her she wasn't. She considered stopping to light a cigarette, but decided to wait until she got home. Maybe she would have a glass of wine too. She was pretty sure she had an unspoiled bottle in the fridge.

The street was empty. Quiet. She could see and hear people in their homes, but the road itself was lifeless. It made it easier to sense a disturbance. She did. She was being followed, she was certain of it. Was it one of the men from outside the betting shop? If it came to it, they could have her briefcase and her hand-bag. Just so long as they left her alone.

She started walking faster. She was aware that she was breathing heavily under the strain. She tried to listen for foot-steps, but she could hear only her own. The streetlamps flick-ered into life. They cast faint shadows across the pavement. The noise of the leaves rustling in the trees all around her sud-denly became deafening.

She felt someone coming closer. She wanted to stop, turn, and confront them, be brave, but fear was taking hold. It licked at her skin like a fire surrounding its victim. Every hair on her back stood erect, reverberating. She felt so cold. Panic was close now.

Too late, she heard the footsteps. He had been right behind her. At the last second she spun around, ready to scream. It was him. The man from the underground. He looked as scared as she felt. He jumped back a step.

"Sorry. I didn't mean to scare you," he said. He had a nice voice. Well spoken.

"Christ," she managed to say. She held a hand dramatically over her chest. "You almost scared me to death." They both laughed.

She moved away a little from him. Her expression became serious. "Are you following me?"

He put his hand in his inside jacket pocket and pulled out a small black leather wallet. He flicked it open and showed it to her. She could see the Metropolitan Police logo on the metal badge. She sighed in relief. Her entire body seemed to relax.

"I couldn't help but notice a couple of lads having a good look at that briefcase back there." He pointed over his shoulder.

"The ones outside the betting office?"

"Yeah. I hate to stereotype people, but thought I'd watch them for a bit. Keep an eye on them."

"Is that why you stopped at the bus stop?"

"Oh," he said. "You noticed? Surveillance never was my thing." They both laughed again. "Two of them looked as if they could be following you, so I thought I'd better do the same, just in case. But I seem to have lost them back at that junction somehow.

"Do you have far to go?" he asked.

"No," she answered. "I live down here. A few houses along."

"Nice," he said. She couldn't tell if he meant it. "You'll be okay from here," he said. "I think you got away with it today." He winked at her. She could tell he was about to leave. She didn't want him to.

"You don't sound like a policeman." It was all she could think of.

"Really," he replied, smiling. "Well, we don't all sound like they do on the television. Some of us can even read and write."

' She liked him.

"Look," he said. "I've got to get on. Somewhere there's a crime being committed and all that."

She felt her embarrassment rising, but it was worth it to flirt a little. "Sorry," she said. "I didn't get your name."

"Sean," he replied. "It's Sean Corrigan." He was already walking away though.

"If he turns around he's interested," Linda whispered to herself. "Anytime now." He turned and gave her a casual wave and a slight smile. "Yes," she said to herself. "Yes."

Donnelly arrived home via his favorite local watering hole in time to catch the start of *Crimewatch*. He felt sorry for Sally being stitched up by Sean like that, but at least it meant he didn't have to do it. Although there were always ways to get out of unpleasant tasks like telly work, especially for those with a little imagination and a lot of experience. He walked up the driveway of the family home, a large semidetached in Swanley, Kent. The

five kids were all growing up fast. He had to live out here to be able to put a roof over their heads. London prices were out of the question. Still, the train ride was just about bearable and there was no need to worry about getting caught driving half drunk. He gave the decaying Range Rover, the only family car, a pat of appreciation as he passed it. It hadn't cost him a penny in years.

His wife, Karen, confronted him as soon as he opened the front door. "You're late again," she accused in her East End accent. They'd been married for more than twenty years.

"Overtime, my sweetness," he answered. "May I remind you we need every penny I can lay my hands on?" His wife answered with a roll of her eyes. "Speaking of financial burdens, where are the kids?"

Karen thrust her hands on her hips. "Jenny is out with her boyfriend, Adrian is out with his girlfriend, Nikki and Raymond are upstairs on the PlayStation, and Josh is in his bed."

"Jenny lives at home?" Donnelly asked with mock surprise.

"She's only seventeen, remember? Still at school, doing her A-levels?"

"Bloody further education," he moaned. "We'll be broke before any of our lot get themselves a job and leave home. By the time I was seventeen I was working in the shipyards in Dumbarton, earning a decent wage and learning a proper trade."

"Until you decided it was too bloody hard and ran off to join the police in London."

"Aye, well," he stalled. "All the same, I was paying my own way in the world."

"Spare me."

"Give us a kiss and I'll think about it," he teased.

"I don't bloody think so. When it comes to you, my mother was right: kissing does lead to children. And seeing how we've

got four more than we can afford, you're going to have to park your lips somewhere else. Besides, I hate it when your mustache tastes of beer."

"I've not touched a drop," he lied.

"A likely story."

"Very well, I shall retire to the living room," he sulked in a put-on accent. "I need to watch *Crimewatch* tonight anyway."

"Jesus. Haven't you had enough of the job for one day?"

"Our case is on tonight. It would be bad form to miss it. It'll be the talk of the canteen tomorrow."

"I wanted to watch that program about Princess Diana tonight."

"You can watch the repeat," he told her unsympathetically.

The television was already on in the living room. Some cheap production with a shaky set and worse acting. He pointed the remote at the offending program and surfed the channels until he found what he was looking for.

"When is your case on?" Karen asked.

"I don't know. I'll have to watch the whole bloody thing, no doubt. Bloody *Crimewatch*. Waste of bloody space, if you ask me."

"Oi. Stop your swearing, the kids might hear."

"Saying 'bloody' isn't swearing." He flopped his heavy frame into the old armchair reserved for his sole use. "Media appeals, waste of time. Expecting the public to solve crimes for us. It's not how we used to get the job done."

"We all know how you used to get the job done," Karen said.

"Bloody right. We did what we had to do to keep the baddies off the streets. We may have sent the wrong man down for the wrong crime, but they were all criminals anyway. It's our job to put them away. Didn't matter how we did it, so long as we got the job done. The people we put away never complained either. They knew the score. For them it was just an occupational hazard. It's my job to keep the scum off the streets. How I do it is my business. Everyone else can stay in their nice, fluffy little worlds."

"The old days are gone," Karen reminded him. "So you had better be careful."

"Aye," he grumbled. "Don't worry about me, love. I can look after myself."

"I don't doubt it, but who's going to look after me and the kids if you get the sack for fitting someone up?"

"Murders are different. You don't fit people up with murder. Maybe you can give the evidence a bit of help here and there, once you're absolutely certain you've got the right man, but you never fit someone up."

"Your DI Corrigan doesn't sound like the sort of man who would want you giving the evidence a bit of help."

"Don't underestimate the man," he told her. "Corrigan knows the score. He's no accelerated-promotion, graduate-entry brownnoser. He's come up the hard way. If push comes to shove, he'll do what it takes."

"Sure of that, are you?"

"Absolutely sure."

Linda Kotler half watched *Crimewatch*. She listened to the item about the murder of Daniel Graydon and then the next item too. A sixty-year-old post office attendant killed in Humberside for a hundred and twenty pounds. It was not improving her mood. She changed the station to watch something less oppressive, but found herself thinking of the policeman from earlier. Sean Corrigan.

The telephone interrupted her reminiscing. Despite her loneliness, she decided to leave it until the answering machine betrayed the caller. It was her sister. Perhaps she was in the mood to speak after all. She had a secret to share.

"It's me. It's me," she said into the phone. "Ignore the answering machine. I'm here, I'm here. Damn thing's going to record us now."

"Screening your calls again?" her sister asked. "That's a nasty habit you Londoners have."

"We have to," Linda replied. "Otherwise the only people we'd ever speak to would be telesales people and unwanted relatives. How are you?"

"We're all good, thanks." Her sister was married to a man she'd been at school with. They had three children. She was younger than Linda. Once, her sister had been a little jealous of her. Now Linda was a little jealous of her sister.

"What about you?" her sister asked. "Met a nice, good-looking man yet? Preferably rich?" It was the same question she'd been asking for the past few months. Since he had left for pastures new and green.

"No," Linda said. Then added, "Not really."

"Not really?" Her sister's tone was inquisitive. "What does 'not really' mean, exactly?"

"Well, I met this guy on the way home today and one way or the other we ended up talking. He seemed really nice, and good-looking too. It's not like we swapped numbers or anything, although if he wanted to find me, he could."

"What makes you say that?"

"Because he's a policeman. A detective, I think."

"Ooh" was her sister's reply. "And does he have a name?"

"Sean," Linda answered. "Sean Corrigan."

Having introduced myself, I let her go. For a while anyway. It's the way I've seen it happening. Now I need to lose myself for a few hours. Wait for my old friend the darkness to arrive. I've done my homework and know the boat show is on at Earl's Court Exhibition Centre. I have absolutely no interest in it, but it is nearby and doesn't close until eleven. It's a good place to hide myself. In a crowd, among the herd.

I mingle with them, my mask as secure as ever. It would be all too easy to lash out at them. Drag whoever into the stinking toilets and slaughter them there. But it is lack of control that more often than not undoes my kind. Control is the key. Control is everything.

How I admire the man with the rifle in Germany who features in the news reports every now and then. Every three months or so he blows the head off a nobody and disappears. He is a rare breed indeed. Most sniper killers take a rifle, find themselves a nice little vantage point, and kill until they are killed.

Why? Because they lack the control. Once they taste the power to kill, they just can't stop. To take one life and then calmly pack away the rifle and go home is too much for most. They get greedy, drunk on the killing, and before they realize what's happened, they're surrounded by police marksmen. Most make the decision to go down fighting, but not this one in Germany. He is to be admired. I shouldn't think he'll ever be stopped.

Me, I prefer a knife. Or my own hands. A rifle's not personal enough. I like to smell their last breath in my face.

I leave the show after eleven. I walk back to Shepherd's Bush. It's a fair walk, but I could use the exercise. It's a good warm-up and also means I avoid potential witnesses like bus or taxi drivers. Pedestrians in London rarely look at each other. I'm carrying a small knapsack slung over my shoulder. It contains all I need.

By the time I get back to Minford Gardens, it's close to midnight. Late enough for most people to be tucked up in bed, early enough for the sounds of the night not to be too alarming.

I move around to the side of the house. I checked the window here a few nights previously. It's a sash window, leading to the bathroom. The lock is a classic style. A simple spin-around metal latch. Any thin metal object will make short work of opening it. She should have added side deadlock bolts. She probably used to share the flat with a man. That made her feel safe when she slept. Now she's alone, but hasn't had time to see to the window. On these warm nights she sleeps with the windows closed. Clearly she's not totally unaware of the dangers that lurk in this city.

Most of the upstairs windows are virtually impossible to reach, but not the bathroom window. There's a solid metal drainpipe that runs past it. It's secured to the wall with large steel brackets riveted to the brickwork. It'll take my weight. I've already tried.

I begin to strip. I remove my shirt and tie. My trousers. Shoes, socks, underpants. I fold them all very neatly and place them in a pile beside the drainpipe. The alley by the side of the house is dark and quiet. No one would have cause to come down here at this hour. The feeling of standing naked in the warm dark night is beyond the imagination of most. The blood pumps through me, bringing me to life. I stay in the alley longer than I'd intended, but it is not a moment to be rushed. I wish I had a full-length mirror to watch myself in—and rain. Heavy warm drops of rain pounding against my skin, forming small, fast-flowing streams that would find the channels of my swelling, aching muscles, making my skin shine like steel in the moonlight, the water flowing over my body looking like liquid metal, like mercury. If only it was raining. Never mind.

I pull a pair of tracksuit bottoms from the bag and put them on. I bought them from JD Sports in Oxford Street about a month ago. I also pull on a tracksuit top, bought at the same time, from the same place. They're matching blue. I take a roll of wide gaffer's tape from the bag and meticulously tape the bottom of the trousers around my ankles and the tops of the shoes. I need to seal the gap. I take a pair of new leather gloves bought from Selfridges and put them on. Rubber ones would have torn on the drainpipe. I use the tape to seal the gap at my wrists. I pull a stocking over my head. It doesn't cover my face; there's no need for that so long as it covers my hair neatly.

Last but not least, I put on a pair of flat rubber-soled shoes, bought a week ago from Tesco. I've never worn any of the items before. I hid them in the tiny parking garage at work until I needed them, in one of the ventilation shafts.

The shoes have little grip so I use my upper-body strength alone to pull myself up the drainpipe. I'll let my legs dangle. If I start to use them to climb, I run the risk of making too many scuff marks on the wall. I'd rather keep the police guessing as to how I got in for a while, although ultimately I want them to work it out.

I make certain the knapsack is secure over my left shoulder, hanging so the bag is to my front. I begin to climb. I keep my legs crossed at the ankles, to help resist the temptation to use them to help. The leather gloves give me a good grip as I pull myself up. It's not too difficult and I keep enough control to make the climb fast and silent.

The ledge of the bathroom window is narrow and rotting, but I can rest a knee on it safely enough. I hold on to the drainpipe with my right hand and slip the other into the bag. I pull out a small metal ruler, the type favored by architects and surveyors. I work it into the gap between the upper and lower panes and begin to work the latch.

It takes a few minutes to do it quietly. Millimeter by millimeter I rotate the catch. My right arm is burning with the effort of holding on to the drainpipe and my knee is growing sore. It'll be bruised for sure. That's unfortunate.

Once the catch is open, I put my left hand flat against the

bottom pane and push the window in gently. I can feel it is a little loose in its fitting. It'll make a noise if I'm not extremely careful and patient.

I pinch the protruding wooden frame and carefully apply upward pressure. At first nothing happens. The window is stiff. I ease on more force. It slides upward too much and makes a noise. Damn it to hell. I freeze flat against the wall, clinging to the drainpipe like a lizard. I listen hard. I wait like that for at least a minute. It seems an hour. I'm glad I've been exercising as much as I have.

Nothing stirs. I slip my left hand under the window's base. I'll be able to apply more even upward pressure now. I'm past the worst, though I still take my time.

When the window's open fully I throw my left leg through, then my left arm. I have to contort to get my head and upper body through. My right leg and arm trail after me through the window like smoke seeping through a gap under a door.

As soon as I enter the flat, I can smell her. Every room will smell like her, I know it. The bedroom will be the strongest odor of all.

It's dark in the bathroom, but my eyes are already used to it. I can see I'm standing in her bath. The chrome taps are on my right, shining in the dark. I have little interest in the bathroom. Too many other smells that mask her scent. I can see that the door is closed. Unfortunate. More risk of noise. It's only midnight. She may not be asleep yet. Noise is my enemy now. Sometimes it is my ally.

I move stealthily across the small bathroom. I exaggerate my movements. I look like a ballet dancer performing an animalistic dance, my muscles tensing together. I wish I could be naked to feel her presence against my skin, but I can't take that risk. I remain sealed in my forensic cocoon. I turn the handle on the bathroom door. It's in good order and makes no noise. I inch the door open, patiently, controlled. As the door opens to the rest of the flat, the smell of her rushes through the gap. I inhale deeply, almost too deeply. I feel a little dizzy. My blood flows so quickly I can feel my temples thumping. A drop of sweat is cool in the cleft of my upper lip. I wipe it away. I won't leave any of me here. Not even a drop of sweat.

My erection is growing fast, but I won't rush. There are things to prepare. I move along the corridor, away from her bedroom. The entire flat is in darkness. No flickering of a TV screen. No noise at all.

I enter the living room. It's too dark to make out details, but it looks fairly cluttered. Too much furniture. Too many cheap prints on the walls. Too many ornaments. I stand in the middle of the room, away from the windows, relishing being here alone. What was hers is now mine. This will be the best yet. I've learned so much. I'll take my time, and when I'm finished her very being will be mine.

After almost half an hour I move to the kitchen and silently search through the cupboards and drawers until I find what I need. A knife. It's not very new or sharp, but it's a nice intimidating shape. Slightly curved blade and a metal handle. It'll do.

I go back to the corridor and begin to walk toward her bedroom. The corridor is much darker than the room ahead. The streetlights don't penetrate this far into the flat. The warm glowing yellow light of the bedroom draws me like a moth. I move so very slowly. This is perfection. Exactly how I've seen it. Each step is choreographed. How I wish I could be naked. My penis is so hard I fear I may reach orgasm before even getting to the bedroom, but I will not rush this.

I reach the open bedroom door. I begin to push it slowly open with my left arm. It swings gently aside. I can see her. Lying in her bed.

I cross the bedroom. She hasn't closed the blinds properly. The streetlights cast a long shadow of me as I walk toward her.

I reach her and stand by the bed. She hasn't sensed me yet. I watch her breathing. Her skin looks metallic in the dark. Like the black-gray metal of a gun. Her chest rises and falls gently, but I can tell she is not yet in a deep sleep. I am surprised she hasn't woken. I stand and wait.

She turns onto her back and stops. Her eyes begin to open. She sees me and blinks a couple of times. She seems to recognize me. Her mouth is open in surprise, but she doesn't scream or speak. The surprise is overwhelming her.

She becomes fully awake. I see the fear spread across her face. I smash my right fist into it. She begins to turn before the impact and the blow hits her full in her left cheek. I think I feel the bone break. She makes a funny little noise.

Before she regains her senses, I grab her around the throat with my left hand and lift her upward and backward with one arm. I crash the back of her head into the wall and let her fall, unconscious, back onto the bed. I watch her for a few seconds. She's still alive. Good.

Her mind woke a split second before the rest of her body. When the body caught up, her eyes fired open. *Jesus, God please help me.*

She desperately needed to fill her lungs with air, but couldn't. Something was across her mouth. She tried again to open her jaws. It was no use. She couldn't tell what it was, but it hurt.

Had she been raped? Why had he left her like this? For the first time since regaining consciousness, she felt the pain in her cheek. It was an excruciating dull, throbbing pain. Her left eye was already swollen shut. It was so painful it masked the pain at the back of her head completely.

She tried to get up off the bed. Simultaneously something

tightened around her throat and ankles. She tried to move her hands. Something tightened around her wrists. She felt around with her fingers as much as possible. She realized they were touching her own feet. She'd been tied like a dead animal. She became aware of her own nakedness. The panic that could so easily kill her began to rise to new levels as the horror of what could have happened while she was unconscious dawned.

She heard a lamp being switched on. The room was flooded with a soft red light. She didn't recognize it. She didn't have red lighting in the room. A gloved hand slipped under her jaw and twisted her head around toward him. She gripped her eyes as tightly closed as she could. She couldn't bear to look at him. She didn't want to see him.

He said nothing. Just held her head and waited. Her breathing was terribly fast and erratic, as if she was having an asthma attack. Slowly she began to open her eyes. There was enough light to see.

She looked into his face. It took a few seconds to recognize the man. He looked different and had something over his hair. It was him. The policeman. Sean. She stopped breathing, trying to comprehend what was happening. She almost began to feel relieved. She knew this man.

She saw a spark of red light reflect off the blade of his knife. He moved so quickly and surely. She was still lying on her stomach. He pointed the knife at her swollen eye. He brought his face close to hers. He spoke quietly into her ear.

"If you do as I say, you will live. If not, you die."

It was the most exquisite experience of my life. The others were wonderful, but this was so much better. To spend so much time with her before she died.

After I bound and gagged her, I tortured her for a while. Then I put on two extra-strength condoms and entered her.

I'd already shaved off all my pubic hair, so there was no chance of leaving them a hair sample. I told my wife I had a suspected hernia and the doctor had asked me to shave myself before he examined me. The stupid bitch will believe anything I tell her.

She looked shocked when I entered her. As if she just couldn't believe I could do this to her. If she knew me better, she wouldn't have been so surprised. When she was gone, she slumped to the floor on her side. Very carefully I removed the condoms, putting them in a self-sealing freezer bag and then into my knapsack. I took the tape off her mouth and put that into another self-sealing bag. I would have so liked to have been naked myself, but it was too dangerous. I must work out how to be naked next time, without leaving a treasure chest of evidence.

I pulled my tracksuit trousers up and grabbed the knapsack. I checked the room and saw the dressing gown was still over the lamp. It had given off a delicious light, making her pale skin appear blood red. No need to remove it. The drawer I had taken the tights from was open too. No need to close it. There was a slight blood smear on the wall behind the bed. No need to clean it.

I moved quietly across the flat to the bathroom, leaving the same way I came in. I want the police to find it, so considered leaving it open, but decided that might be too obvious. My muscles have grown somewhat tired by now, but I have enough strength to hold on to the drainpipe with one arm while I move the catch back to the locked position. I make sure I leave enough scratches on the latch so even the police can find them.

I climb down the drainpipe as quietly as a spider on a thread. I strip off the clothes worn in the flat and put them in large bin liners. These in turn I place inside the rucksack. My other clothes wait in their neat pile for me. I take my time to dress. No need to hurry. I enjoy the calm I feel spreading beautifully through my body and mind, feeling a hundred times more powerful than I did before my visit. The warm night air wraps around my body like smoke around a smoldering log. I put the bag over my shoulder and head toward Shepherd's Bush.

I will go visiting again soon and next time will be the greatest yet.

CHAPTER 20

Thursday

Sean, Sally, and Donnelly were back in Sean's office. They were assessing the feedback from Sally's appearance on *Crimewatch* and Sean's press conference. It wouldn't take long. The phone lines hadn't exactly been set on fire—a couple of teenage prank calls and a few rough descriptions of men seen in the area of Daniel's flat, possibly on the night of the murder, maybe not. Far from a deluge of information.

They'd expected as much: Hellier was too cautious to have allowed himself to be seen by witnesses at that time of night. But at least the dedicated surveillance team was back, so Hellier wouldn't slip away quite so easily again.

Donnelly was called to the phone. He crossed the office, took the receiver from a young detective constable.

"Dave Donnelly."

"DS Donnelly? How you doing?" Donnelly didn't recognize the voice. "I'm a friend of Raj Samra. He said you wanted a call if anything out of the ordinary came up. Said you wanted a call before anyone else."

"That was my request." Donnelly was naturally suspicious. He didn't know this man who was doing him a favor. He wasn't about to let himself be set up. "Sorry, I don't think I caught your name."

"DS John Simpson. SCG out west. Murder Investigation Team."

"Can I call you back in a minute?" Donnelly asked.

"Sure," Simpson replied. "I'm on a mobile. Want the number?"

Donnelly scribbled the number on a small notepad. He wasted no time in calling Raj Samra. He confirmed that DS John Simpson existed. He vouched for him too. That was good enough. Donnelly called him back.

"DS Simpson."

"Sorry about that. I was right in the middle of something," Donnelly lied. "So, what have you got that may interest me?"

There was a worrying pause before Simpson answered. "A body. But I think you'd better come and see for yourself."

Donnelly thought hard for a few seconds. Should he go? Was he sure enough yet? Probably not. "Okay," he answered. "I'll come and take a look. Unofficially for now."

"I understand," Simpson reassured him.

"Where are you?"

"It's a flat over in Shepherd's Bush. Seventy-three D, Minford Gardens."

DC Zukov saw Donnelly appear on the pavement outside the crime scene and head toward him, moving nimbly, looking naturally strong. He stamped his cigarette out as Donnelly got closer.

"You got one of them for me?"

Zukov pulled a squashed packet of Marlboro Lights from

his trouser pocket. Donnelly seemed paler than usual. "Well?" Zukov asked. "Did you do it?"

Donnelly lit up and took a deep drag. "No."

Zukov went quiet. He looked Donnelly up and down. Had the big man lost his nerve? "Why not?" he finally asked.

"Because I'm not sure, that's why."

"You're not sure it's linked?" Zukov asked.

"Oh, it's linked," Donnelly said. "I'm sure all three are linked."

"So what's the problem?" Zukov was pushing way more than he'd done before. He wanted this done. He wanted to be part of a successful murder inquiry and he didn't want to wait any longer.

"I'm not sure Hellier is our man." He tossed the cigarettes back to Zukov. "Do you live alone?" he asked.

"Why?" Zukov answered.

"Just answer the question."

"Yeah. I live alone."

"Good," Donnelly said. "Then you won't have to worry about somebody stumbling across this." He pulled the small sealed evidence bag containing Hellier's hairs from the cigarette case he'd been concealing it inside. "I'm sick of carrying it around. Take it home with you and remember to keep it in your fridge. That way they'll look fresh. I'll tell you when I need them again." Zukov took the bag without complaining. "Now piss off and find us some coffee," Donnelly told him. "I've got a phone call to make."

Sean moved to the rear of his car and pulled a full forensic suit from the boot. He struggled into the blue overalls before showing his identification to a severe-looking female uniformed officer guarding the cordon. He told her he was from the Murder Squad, he just didn't tell her which one. He could feel the forensics team and local detectives watching him—they'd probably guessed he was the reason they'd been kept out of the scene. Their important work was being delayed and it was his fault.

He walked along the driveway toward the front door of number 73 Minford Gardens, his focus intensifying on the half-open front door. He felt tunnel vision overtaking him, the usual surreal feeling that accompanied him when he approached a murder scene.

He gave the constable guarding the front door his name and rank. The constable didn't ask why Sean needed to enter the scene. He should have. Sean began to climb the communal stairway to the first-floor flat. He could already smell murder.

Love, hate, terror were tangible things. Real things, not simple emotions. They left overpowering traces of themselves wherever they called. The horror and fear of the previous night had seeped out from the flat and stained the surrounding area with its overpowering odor. It was in the wallpaper, the cheap worn-out carpet. Now it was all over Sean. In his clothes, his hair. The longer he stayed in this place, the deeper it would penetrate him, and before too long it would be in his blood. Then he would feel cold and displaced all day until he could get home and shower, be with Kate, be with his children. And even then he might not be able to find his way back to the comfortable world most lived in.

He climbed the stairs silently. He could hear quiet, muffled voices coming from inside flat number 73D. At least the detectives at the scene were showing respect for the dead. It wasn't always the case. He reached the front door. One last deep breath, and he knocked gently on the door frame. The two men standing in the narrow hallway turned to face him. They were both wearing full forensic suits. Sean was relieved.

"Hello, gentlemen." He was being as polite as he knew how. He had the rank, but he was the outsider. "DI Sean Corrigan.

SCG South. My sergeant tells me you have a scene that may be of interest to us."

"Guv'nor," DS Simpson said. He seemed affable enough. "Come in, please." He and the other detective offered Sean rubber-gloved palms. They all shook hands. The other detective introduced himself as DC Zak Watson. Even in his forensic suit Sean could tell he was built like a boxer. Scarring to both his eyebrows suggested he'd been no stranger to the ring.

"I read your circulation," DS Simpson said. "Said you were interested in anything out of the ordinary. Well, I've never come across a scene like this. I've been unfortunate enough to work dozens of murders, but this one's . . ." He struggled to find the appropriate words and gave up trying. "Anyway. Your circulation said contact you if we find anything out of the ordinary and this is certainly that."

Sean was looking around the hallway. Everything seemed normal. No signs of disturbance. No tipped-over furniture or ornaments. No blood smeared or sprayed on the walls. DS Simpson saw him checking it out.

"The whole place is like that. Nothing out of place. Nothing at all. Except the bedroom. It all seems to have happened in there." He looked along the corridor to the room at the end. Sean followed his gaze.

There was no metallic scent of blood. Clearly she hadn't been stabbed or cut. Something else. He could smell the faint odor of urine. He assumed from the victim. Had she fouled herself before or after she died? If it was before, then something, someone, had frightened her enough to make her lose control of her bladder.

Sean wouldn't rush his questioning of the two detectives. He wanted to jump to the end, but he wouldn't. Keeping it chronological was the key to not losing yourself. Follow the time line. It helped build up a clearer picture of how the horror had come and gone.

"How did he get in?" Sean asked. He meant the killer.

"Not sure," DS Simpson replied. "We haven't had a proper look around yet. We've been keeping everyone out, as you requested, so forensics hasn't had a chance to help us with that."

"Anything obvious?" Sean asked.

"Forced entry? Nothing we can see. The door was locked and all windows are secure."

"It was warm last night," Sean said. "But she kept the windows shut?"

DS Simpson shrugged. "We're only on the first floor here, but the windows are still pretty high above ground level. They'd be almost impossible to reach without ladders. Would I sleep with the windows open? Sure. But would my wife? I don't think so."

Sean nodded in agreement. "Who raised the alarm?"

"Her work," DS Simpson replied. "Apparently she was a real early bird. A bit of a workaholic. They expected her to turn up around eight, if not before. When she hadn't arrived by nine thirty they rang her. No answer, mobile or home. No problems reported on her tube line and she hadn't suggested she would be late or taking the day off, so they began to get a little concerned.

"She's popular enough at work, so I'm told. Anyway, her boss sends a male colleague around here to make sure she's okay. They guess she's in bed with the flu. There's a bit of a summer virus going around. The male colleague's a guy called Darryl Wilson . . ." DS Simpson paused.

"Is he all right?" Sean wasn't asking about Wilson's welfare, he wanted to know if he was under any suspicion.

"Yeah. He's fine. Anyway, he gets over here midmorning. No answer to the buzzer, so he goes round the side to see what he can see.

"Her blinds still look at least half shut and there's a faint red light on inside. He's not happy, so he borrows a ladder from a neighbor and puts it up to her bedroom window. He climbs the ladder and manages to peek through the blinds, sees her on the bed, shits himself, almost falls off the ladder, and does what he should have done in the first place and phones us."

"Did he enter the flat?"

"No way," Simpson replied. "He saw enough through the window to turn him into a quivering wreck. Wild horses wouldn't get him inside after that."

"Neighbors see her come home with anybody? Hear anybody calling at her flat?" Sean asked.

"Too early to say."

"Who's your DI?" Sean should have asked earlier.

"Vicky Townsend," Simpson told him.

That was good news. Sean knew her of old. He gave a slight nod.

Simpson saw it. "You know her then?"

"Yeah," Sean replied. "We used to work together."

"She's solid," Simpson said. It was a major compliment. She'd been solid when Sean knew her too. "She'll be here soon. Shall we?" Simpson pointed to the living room. The door was wide open.

Sean took the lead. He felt Simpson and Watson were about to follow him, but he needed to do this alone. "Listen," he said as pleasantly as he could. "You've already been through this place. Forensics won't be happy if you walk through again just to help me. I'd rather not cause you any more grief than I probably already have, so best you wait here, or outside if you fancy some fresh air. I'll find my own way around."

The two detectives nodded to each other and headed for the front door. "I'll send DI Townsend up when she arrives," Simpson told him.

"Thanks," Sean replied. He was already in the living room. Leaving the outside world behind. Entering the killer's world.

Hellier had arrived home sometime after 3 A.M. to find that his wife had been waiting for him. She had a lot of questions she wanted him to answer, but he'd insisted he needed to be alone, that the stress of the police investigation was getting to him. He'd told her he loved her, that she and the children were his life. She'd cried tears of both joy and fear.

But someone else had been waiting for him when he arrived home—the police. He could feel them easily enough. They must have been sitting out there all night waiting for him and now they didn't know where he'd been for over nine hours. Had Corrigan slept at all? He had more unpleasant surprises for DI Sean Corrigan.

It was almost midday and he still hadn't been to the office. He'd called them to say he'd be working from home in the morning. He'd be in this afternoon. He stood on Westminster Bridge and gazed northwest across the Thames at the Houses of Parliament. He never did buy himself a politician. A cabinet minister would have been handy. Not to worry. Maybe next time.

The midday sun sparkled on the surface of the Thames. It was quite beautiful. Parliament's reflection was as impressive as the real thing. Most of the architecture along the banks of the great river pleased him. Especially the north bank. Some unpleasant monstrosities had somehow been allowed to appear on the south bank, but it was still magnificent. A river to rival any in the world. He made a note to himself. Wherever he went next must have a river running through its heart, or at least a dominating harbor. Yes, he could make do with a harbor. Or even a lake, surrounded by mountains.

His mobile phone rang in his breast pocket. He considered

tossing the damn thing into the Thames. A symbolic gesture of leaving this city. Instead he answered it.

"Mr. Hellier? Mr. James Hellier?" It was the same nervous voice from the previous day. He recognized it immediately.

"I don't appreciate having my time wasted," Hellier snapped.

"I was being followed." The voice sounded strained. "I couldn't risk leading them to you."

"Who was following you?" Hellier demanded. "The police? The press?"

"I don't know, but I need to see you. I'll contact you soon."

"Wait. Why do you need to see me? Wait." The voice was gone. Hellier no longer felt tired. Who was this man, this man telling him he was a friend? James Hellier didn't have any friends. If the voice belonged to a journalist, then what was he waiting for—what was his angle? Hellier couldn't see it, and that bothered him. Maybe it was time to consider the possibility that his *friend* was something entirely different.

Sean didn't like being in the flat alone, but the quiet peace was a blessing. He could hear what the scene was telling him. He moved around the living room, keeping to the edges to avoid stepping on microscopic evidence. He touched as little as possible and made a permanent mental note of anything he did.

The room was comfortable, almost snug. Too much furniture. Too many colors. A real room. Years of impulse buying and fitting presents from family and friends into the space had produced an uncoordinated history of the occupier. Kate would have hated it. He quite liked it.

Did the killer come in here? If so, why? To be among her things? To spend a moment with the photographs of the victim that were scattered all over the room? Would he have put a light on to see better? Sean doubted it. Maybe he used a torch? If he did and if he was the same killer, it would have been the first time he used one. Again, Sean doubted it.

He'd been in here though. Sean was sure of it. He scanned the room over and over. Is this where the killer came to prepare himself? Not to put on his gloves and other protective clothing—he would have done that outside, before he entered. But to be among her possessions, the very heart of her life. To form a connection with her. The more he connected with her, the sweeter it would be when the moment came to move down the corridor to her bedroom.

Hellier had a connection with the second victim, Daniel Graydon, albeit a fleeting one. Did he have a connection with the first, Heather Freeman? Had the murder team in the east missed something? Sean resolved to go back and check. Was there a connection between the killer and this latest scene? Between Hellier and the third victim?

Did the killer touch anything in here? Take off a glove and touch anything? No. He was too controlled for that. Always in control. No mistakes. He would have confined himself to looking. So he'd stood and looked. Just as Sean was doing now.

Sean left the room and moved back into the hallway. He pushed a door open on his left. It was a small bedroom, being used for storage. Stuffed and tied bin liners littered the floor. The room wasn't in keeping with the rest of the flat. It was cold and impersonal. Whoever lived here didn't come in very often. What was in those bin liners? They appeared to be waiting for someone to come and take them away. Sean spotted the handle of a cricket bat protruding from one of the bags. A man had recently been living in the flat. Had he lived with the victim? Probably. Was he a jilted lover? Almost certainly. A suspect? He would have to be.

If the room held little for the victim, then it would hold less

for her killer. Sean couldn't feel him in this place. He left, pulling the door back as he found it, careful not to touch the handle.

He moved slowly down the hallway and pushed open the
next door on the left. The bathroom. It smelled like a woman's
bathroom. Dozens of bottles of brightly colored liquids could
be seen all over. Creams, makeup, cotton balls, lotions and
potions of all descriptions had found their way onto most of
the flat surfaces. Sean thought about how a single man's bathroom would look in comparison. A comb, razor, shaving foam,
maybe some hair and shower gel. Aftershave, if he really cared
about his appearance. The victim clearly liked to spend time
in this room. The room reminded him of Kate. He shook the
thought away. His wife had no place here.

The bathroom was very personal to the victim. Was it therefore personal to the killer? He would definitely have been in
here, but did he stay? What would have attracted him? What
was so personal to her that he may have had to touch it? Maybe
he held it up to his face, to his nose, to be as close to her scent
as he could. Maybe he had to taste her? Maybe he licked something? If he did, he would have left his DNA.

Sean looked hard at the items in the bathroom. Nothing particularly caught his attention. She kept it cluttered but
clean. There was nothing here the killer couldn't have resisted.
A hairbrush that still had some hair in the bristles was the most
likely, but Sean wasn't hopeful. Nevertheless, it might be worth
special attention. Send it to the lab for DNA and fingerprints
instead of dusting it on-site.

As he turned toward the door a sunray hit the catch on the
small sash window. The reflection was wrong. Uneven. There
should have been one starburst of light off the chrome catch,
but Sean could see dozens.

The window was directly above the bath. Sean didn't want

to have to climb into the bath to get closer. If the killer some-how came in or went out through this window he would almost certainly have had to put a foot in the bath. Sean wouldn't risk stepping on a print. He couldn't see one with the naked eye, but it didn't mean it wasn't there.

He examined the window frame from where he was. No deadlocks, only the catch. Easy to open. Horribly easy. A nov-ice burglar could do it in seconds. Sean couldn't help but think how a ten-pound deadlock might have saved her life. He felt sick at the thought.

He imagined the killer climbing in and out of the window. Where would he have been least likely to touch? He decided on the area of wall directly below and central to the window. He crouched down and reached across the bath with his left arm. He placed the side of his gloved palm against the wall and leaned forward so his face was only inches from the window catch.

Scratches. Dozens of small thin scratches. Fresh, without a doubt. Fresh cuts in metal were always screamingly obvi-ous. They glared like shiny new wounds, but within days they dulled, rusted, or stained. These were newborn.

There would be a drainpipe outside the window. This was the bathroom, so there had to be a drainpipe. He would check the outside, but he already knew what he'd find.

Another change of method, Sean thought. This man's al-ready thinking of court. A decent defense solicitor would have a field day with this one. The police trying to say three com-pletely different murders were all linked. Sean wiped sweat from his forehead with the back of his arm.

He knew more than ever that he needed something to hang Hellier with. Some piece of indisputable evidence. If he could at least prove Hellier had committed one murder, maybe he would confess to the others. Appeal to his ego. If he didn't confess, no one would ever know how clever he'd been. How he'd outfoxed the police. If Sean could prove one, he'd run with it. He wouldn't wait to be able to prove the others. But a sudden chill froze him, as he pictured the image of a man snaking in through the bathroom window—a man who *wasn't* James Hellier. The sudden unexpected doubt momentarily terrified him—was he derailing the investigation with his own prejudice against Hellier and all his perceived type stood for? No. He shook the doubt away, remembering how he felt every time he was in Hellier's presence, the animalistic scent of a survivor, a predator that he'd smelled on him the very moment they first met. He was right about Hellier—he had to be. He mustn't allow himself to be confused by Hellier's camouflaging tactics.

Memories of Hellier's lies and all-too-convenient alibis reassured him, his considerable efforts to avoid their surveillance, and the crucial fact that he knew at least one of the victims—Daniel Graydon. Sean had no doubts. Hellier was psychopathically bad to the core, so if Hellier hadn't killed Graydon then that would have to mean Graydon had randomly come into contact with not only one killer, but two. The chances of that were negligible. Satisfied, Sean breathed out a long sigh.

Carefully, he moved out of the bathroom and back into the corridor. The bedroom loomed before him. He had another room to see first. He crossed the hallway and entered the kitchen, again standing to the side to preserve any evidence on the floor. He was suddenly aware of a crushing thirst. But he wouldn't use a tap at the scene, fearful of destroying evidence that might be hiding in the drains of the sink, just waiting to be found. His thirst would have to wait.

The kitchen was small and a little dingy. The units were from the early eighties and badly needed a face-lift. The oven was old too, made of white metal and free-standing. The killer wouldn't have liked this room, Sean decided, but he would have come in here. Maybe he took a knife from a cupboard to threaten the victim with? Maybe he took a knife to kill her with, only to change his mind? If he was to be true to form, he'd want to change the way he killed as well as the way he entered. All the knives in the kitchen would be taken away for examination as a matter of routine.

Sean didn't stay in the kitchen long. Neither had the killer. He stepped backward into the hallway. The door to the bedroom was closed, but not shut altogether. Had it swung shut itself, on uneven hinges? Or had DS Simpson or DC Watson pushed it to in an attempt to show the victim some last respect?

Sean put the side of his left palm on the place the suspect was least likely to have touched, the very top center, between the two oblong panels. He pushed gently. The door swung silently open.

Donnelly and Sally stood next to their car, smoking. Sally had found a café nearby that sold good coffee. It didn't taste like the coffee sold in the cafés around Peckham. Her mobile rang. She flicked her cigarette away before answering. "Sally Jones speaking."

"Detective Sergeant Jones?"

"Who's asking?" She hadn't recognized the voice.

"You probably won't remember me. My name is Sebastian Gibran. We met at my office when you came to see an employee of mine—James Hellier."

She remembered now. It was the senior partner from Hellier's finance firm. "I remember," she told him. "But what I don't remember is giving you this mobile number."

"I'm terribly sorry, I phoned your office first, but you weren't there. Another detective was good enough to give me your number."

She wasn't impressed. Giving out a team member's mobile

number to unseen parties was a definite no-no. "What is it I can do for you, Mr. Gibran?"

"Not something I want to discuss over the phone, you understand? I feel it's better if we meet, somewhere private. It's a sensitive matter."

"Why don't you come to the police station?"

"I'd rather not be seen there, if it's all the same to you."

"Where then?" Sally asked.

"Can you meet me for lunch tomorrow? I know a place that'll fit me in at short notice. We'll be able to talk freely there."

Overconfident bastard, but what was there to lose? "Okay. Where and when?"

"Excellent," Gibran responded. "Che, just off Piccadilly, at one o'clock tomorrow."

"I'll be there," Sally told him.

"I look forward to it." She heard him hang up. Her expression was pensive.

"Problem?" Donnelly asked.

"No. At least I don't think so. That was Sebastian Gibran, Hellier's boss. He wants to meet for a chat."

"Well, well. Maybe Hellier's fancy friends are getting set to abandon him to his fate."

"The ritual washing of hands," she declared. "Not to mention a free lunch for yours truly."

"Do you want some company at this little get-together?"

"No. I get the feeling it'll go better if I meet him alone."

"Fair enough, but don't forget to run it past the boss before you go," Donnelly warned her.

"Naturally. Listen, I need to follow up on something over in Surbiton. The boss can do without me here for a while. I'll check back with you later, okay?"

"Suit yourself," Donnelly replied. "I'll let the guv'nor know you've commandeered his vehicle."

"No doubt that'll make him very happy," she said. "Almost as happy as when he finds out I still haven't eliminated Korsakov as a possible suspect."

"You will."

"I'm not so sure."

"What's that supposed to mean?"

"It means, the more I look into it, the more I don't like it. Something's not right—I don't know what it is yet, but I know it's something."

"Christ. You're getting as bad as the guv'nor."

"No, seriously," Sally argued. "It's like everything to do with Korsakov has disappeared, as if someone made him vanish."

"Why would anyone do that?"

"I don't know. Maybe, for some reason, they're hiding him, so he can commit further offenses without being identified. Or maybe . . ."

"Go on," Donnelly encouraged her. "You're among friends here."

"Or, maybe someone got rid of him—killed him."

"Like who?"

"One of his victims, or someone connected to one of his victims, someone looking for revenge."

"An eye for an eye," Donnelly suggested.

"Or," Sally continued, "someone got rid of him so they could commit crimes they knew we would eventually blame him for, because of the similarity of the method—have us chasing a dead man we'd never be able to find."

"Now you really do sound like the guv'nor," Donnelly told her. "Speaking of which, have you discussed this with him?"

"Sort of. But he's so fixated on Hellier, I don't think he took it seriously."

"I know what you mean," Donnelly agreed. "But don't let him stop you doing what you think you should be doing. Re-

member, it's our job to keep him on the straight and narrow—
anchor him a bit—you know?"

She knew. "I'll catch you later," she said, and headed for
the car.

The large bed was straight in front of Sean, the victim lying on
it, a pretty red light softly illuminating the room. Sean checked
for the source of the light. He found it in the far-right corner
of the room. A thin red silk dressing gown was draped over a
lampshade. At night the red illumination would have been far
stronger. Had the victim constructed the homemade light? Did
it stir a childhood memory? Had her nursery been lit with a red
light and now the color helped her sleep?

No. The killer had made the light. He was sure of it. But had
he made it after he'd killed her or before? And why? What did
the victim look like as she died, painted with red light? Had the
red been a replacement for her blood? But if blood is so important to him, why not cut her like the others? Method, Sean reminded himself. He's changing his method again. Disguising
his work.

The killer was showing his intelligence, his control, and
his imagination. It was extremely rare for killers to have the
ability to change methods so completely. They lack control.
Their killings are repetitions. Some try and disguise their
kills, but usually only after the murder. They'll burn the body,
place it in a car and push it off a cliff, sink it in deep water; but
to plan the disguise from the outset, to ensure that everything
from the victim selection to the murder weapon changes every time—that was incredibly rare. It made the killer all the
more dangerous.

Did this killer have enough control to simply stop? To walk
away and never kill again? That would be the ultimate show of
his strength. Had he killed enough now to live off his memories?

Sean thought of Hellier's public face. Absolutely calm, calculating, and clever. But he had seen glimpses of the creature that hid behind Hellier's public facade. The snarling, arrogant Hellier. Could that Hellier stop killing? No, he decided. Hellier liked the game too much. He would have to be stopped.

Staying as close to the walls as he could, he moved clockwise around the room toward Linda Kotler.

He passed a set of wooden drawers. They looked solid and expensive. One drawer was still open. He looked in without touching anything as he took one large step around them. He could see it was where the victim kept her tights and stockings. Had the killer or the victim opened the drawer? One glance at the body told him the killer had. He wouldn't risk buying or stealing his own. A man buying stockings could easily be remembered by a sales assistant. A wife might become suspicious if her stockings or tights went missing. She might read about this murder and begin to suspect a husband, a boyfriend, a son. The killer would have been relatively sure he'd find what he was looking for inside the victim's home. No need to risk bringing his own.

Sean kept moving around the room until he was no more than three feet away from the victim. He stopped. He wouldn't go closer for fear of disturbing any forensic evidence. The three-foot circumference around the body would be the golden zone.

He studied the body, slowly and deliberately scanning it from head to toe and back. He tried to remain dispassionate, removed, as if the body weren't real, as if this was only an exercise.

She was lying on her left side. Naked and pale now. Lifeless. She looked anything but peaceful. The dead never looked peaceful, at least not until a skilled undertaker did his work.

One eye was half open. The other was swollen shut. He tried to imagine her alive. She'd have been quite attractive, he thought, but it was hard to tell.

Her legs were bent painfully far back. The thin, tightly stretched tights bound her ankles. They had cut into the skin. They were connected to another pair that ran up her back to her neck. This was in turn connected to another pair of tights or perhaps stockings, tightly bound around the neck. The flesh of the throat bulged around the ligature, concealing most of the material. Her hands had been bound separately at the wrists with more of her own tights. The hands had become swollen by the tightness of the bindings. Why had the hands been tied separately? So elaborate. It reminded Sean of the rigging on a yacht. The knots used would have to be analyzed. What sort were they? Were they used in sailing or some other sport or hobby?

Why did he need the bindings to connect so precisely? Bondage? Hellier's favorite. Was he deliberately tormenting them?

She must have been in terrible pain. She would have tried to call out in pain, scream for help. Her killer wouldn't have let that happen. He would have gagged her. But her mouth wasn't covered. Sean leaned closer to her face. The area around the mouth was a little red. It looked sore. Had the killer used tape that he'd taken away with him? If so, he'd done that before. Heather Freeman had been taped across the mouth, but the tape had been removed and taken from the scene. The more he killed, the more similarities would start to appear. No matter how hard he worked at disguising his methods. The mouth area would need to be swabbed for traces of adhesive at the postmortem.

The left side of her face was badly bruised and swollen. Judging by the level of bruising, the injury had been caused at least an hour before she died. He guessed this was the first blow, used to incapacitate her. The killer hit her as she rose up from her sleep, knocking her senseless. There was no blood or cut around the injury. He probably used a gloved fist.

A small amount of blood on the floor, by the back of the victim's head, caught his attention. Nothing more than a slight smear. He carefully moved around the body to get a better look. He saw the telltale signs of a bleeding head injury. The sticky hair. Not much, but a definite injury.

He scanned the room for an obvious weapon. He saw something, on the wall behind the bed. He stood and bent toward it, careful not to step too close. There was blood on the wall. Not much, but he was sure it would later be confirmed as the victim's. The killer had slammed her head into the wall to make certain she was unconscious, because he needed time to find the bindings and secure her.

And then what? She wasn't killed quickly. The bruises to her face, ankles, wrists, neck: they all told the same tale of a slow, painful death. Was that what the elaborate bindings were for? To torture her before killing her? Spending time with them after the killing wasn't enough anymore? The killer had progressed to spending time with them before they died. Or was it merely another attempt to muddy the waters and confuse those who hunted him?

Unlike Heather Freeman, this victim was a grown woman. Fully developed. She'd been stripped naked and bound. Was she sexually abused? Raped while she was still alive? He was sure she had been. Forensic tests would no doubt confirm his hypothesis. Another progression, or another act of camouflage by the killer?

The longer he was alone in the room with Linda Kotler, the harder it was to treat the murder scene like an exercise. Her pain and sorrow had begun to penetrate his shield. The more he discovered, the closer, the more real the murder became. It began to run in his head like film footage. Now he had almost a full scene. The killer entering through the bathroom window, stalking through the flat. He finds her in bed and looms over her. She awakens and sees him standing there. A fist smashes into her face. Before she can recover, he lifts her and smashes her head into the wall. She falls unconscious. She awakens. She doesn't know how long she's been out. She can't move. She feels the pain of her bound limbs. Something around her neck stops her breathing properly. She desperately needs air. Something over her mouth stops her from calling out. Stops her from begging for her life. Then she feels him on her. He forces entry into her. It hurts like nothing before. She blanks it out of her mind. Staying alive is all that matters. But when he's finished, he doesn't leave. He spends time torturing her. And then, finally, he strangles her to death.

Sean could hear her voice in his head. Pleading with the killer to leave her alone. Pleading with him not to hurt her. Then pleading for her life. All wasted. The gag meant he wouldn't have heard her. He would have liked to listen to her begging, but he couldn't risk the noise.

A loud knocking on the bedroom door made him jump. Instinctively he reached for the telescopic metal truncheon clipped to his waist belt. Then he looked to the door and recognized DI Vicky Townsend standing there, grim faced.

"They told me it was a bad one," she said. "Seems they weren't exaggerating."

"Bad enough," Sean replied.

DI Townsend made to cross the threshold of the bedroom. Sean shot a hand up, palm outstretched toward her. "Not dressed like that you don't."

She looked herself up and down. She was wearing one of her favorite suits, dark blue and tailored, with two-inch heels to match. She feigned insult. "This is my best suit."

"Then you wouldn't want me to take it off you and stick it in a brown paper bag as evidence."

"You would too, wouldn't you?" she asked. "Well, you certainly haven't changed."

"You wouldn't want me to."

"No, probably not."

DI Vicky Townsend waited for Sean outside the flat in the street. She watched him pulling off the forensic suit and laughed a little as he carefully placed the suit and shoe covers into evidence bags and sealed them. Ever the professional, she thought. He'd always been the most meticulous detective she'd worked with. Back in his street clothes, he approached her.

"How've you been, Vicky?" he asked.

"Good, Sean. Good. Kids drive me mad, but you know."

"I've got two myself now," he told her. "Two girls."

"Still with Kate then?" She'd only met Kate a couple of times, briefly. Most police liked to keep work and home very separate.

"Yeah," Sean answered. "She's good, you know. A good mother."

"Good," Vicky replied. They were both avoiding the obvious question. This was Vicky's territory. It was up to her to challenge Sean, friend or foe.

"So what are you doing over here, Sean? Why's a DI from SCG South arriving at my murder scene before I know about it?"

Sean looked a little sheepishly at Vicky. She hadn't changed much either. She kept her auburn hair short and neat, for the practicalities of being a mother rather than those of being a police officer. Her plain face was improved by lots of laughter lines.

"I think this murder's linked to others," he told her.

"Linked in what way? A drug war? Gangland?"

"If only. This is something else. A possible repeat offender."
He hated using the term "serial killer." It seemed to somehow glamorize tragedy.

"As in Yorkshire Ripper–type repeat offender?" Vicky asked.

"I suppose so."

"And you've been authorized to run a task force on this?"

"My superintendent is happy for me to take on any suspected linked cases. He'll square it with yours in due course. In the meantime, I could do with all the help I can get."

"Such as?" Vicky asked.

"I need a few things to happen straightaway."

"Go on."

"Check the mouth area for tape residue. I think her mouth was taped and the killer took it away with him. Check the drainpipe at the side of the house, and the bathroom window needs special attention. That's how he got in and out. And I would like you to use my pathologist. He's the best in London and he's worked one of the other victims. I can make the call to him and get him to look at the body while it's still in the flat. After that he'll probably want it taken to his own mortuary at Guy's Hospital."

"All victims from West London should go to Charing Cross," said Vicky. "The postmortem should be performed by the pathologists for this area. There's a lot of red tape around things like that. People get pissed off pretty quick if you start to ignore protocols."

"I understand, but the man who did this is still out there and he doesn't give a shit about our red tape. He doesn't care if he kills in South London, East London, or West London. He just kills, and he'll do everything he can to not get caught. So why don't we stop helping the bastard and break a few rules ourselves? Because if we don't, I reckon we've got about one or maybe two weeks before I'll be standing outside some other flat in some other part of London having the same conversation with some other DI." He ended with a plea. "Let's not let that happen. Please."

Vicky studied him for a couple of seconds. "Okay," she said finally. "I have a pretty good relationship with the pathologist for this area. I'll explain that it's an unusual situation."

"Thanks. Now we need to get started. Time is not my friend here."

"It never is," she reminded him. "And it never will be."

Sally waited for the door to the Surbiton house to open. When it did she noted the look of surprise on Paul Jarratt's face.

"DS Jones," he said.

"Sorry to disturb you again," she apologized, "but would you believe it, I just happened to be in the area when I suddenly remembered something I needed to check with you."

"Such as?" Jarratt asked, before remembering his manners. "Please. Come in."

Sally stepped inside and followed him to the living room. "I spoke with an old colleague of yours, DC Graham Wright— only he's a DS now."

"Graham?"

"I was doing some digging into Korsakov's history and was hoping to compare his conviction fingerprints with marks found at our murder scene."

"And?"

"They've gone missing. Seems they got up and walked out of Scotland Yard all by themselves."

"I wouldn't have thought that was possible."

"No. Nor would I," Sally agreed. "DS Wright told me that he'd taken the prints from the Yard at your request. Do you recall why you pulled the prints?"

"I seem to remember the prison where Korsakov was doing his time wanted them, but I can't remember the details. Although I do remember giving the prints back to Graham so he could return them."

"And return them he did, at least according to Fingerprints' records."

"Then I don't see how I can help you find them."

"It's just that you requested them back in ninety-nine," said Sally. "Not long before Korsakov was released from prison. That seems a little unusual."

Jarratt laughed. "DS Jones, everything to do with Korsakov was a little unusual. However, I remember now. The prison needed the prints to copy onto their records. They liked to keep fingerprints of prisoners they deemed to be more dangerous than the norm. I suppose they consider it to be some sort of deterrent."

"Why would they wait until a few months before his release to decide that Korsakov needed such a deterrent?"

"That, I cannot answer," Jarratt told her. "You would have to speak to the prison."

Sally sighed. "Oh, I don't think there's any need for that," she lied. "At the end of the day it still wouldn't explain how the prints went missing. Probably just an administrative cock-up at Fingerprint Branch. I've wasted enough of your time."

"Not a problem," said Jarratt.

They said their good-byes and Sally made her way to her car. She drove a couple of blocks before pulling over and retrieving the Korsakov file from her bag. She flicked through it and found the number she was looking for. Then she paused momentarily, remembering that Sean knew nothing of her investigation's progress. Perhaps she should call him now, put him in the picture; but he had so many other things on his mind it would be better to speak to him later. She dialed and waited a long time before a military-sounding voice answered.

"Wandsworth Prison. What can I do you for?"

Sean and Vicky approached the Barnes police station. They'd been outside the scene for a while, briefing the forensics team and liaising with the coroner's office. Sean had arranged to meet Sally at Barnes and update her. The police building was as ugly as ever. They parked outside the four-story construction, bright red bricks in too-straight lines. It was hard to spot a window. When you did it was blacked out.

Vicky led the way to her office. It was three times the size of Sean's and ten times cleaner and more organized. Sally, having returned from Surbiton, was waiting for them outside the office. Sean introduced her to Vicky and vice versa. The two female detectives eyed each other with a little suspicion. Sean felt it.

Vicky lifted a note she found on her desk. She looked at Sean. "It's for you. Your pathologist has arrived at the scene, a Dr. Canning."

"Good."

"And we've traced a sister. The first detectives on the scene, Simpson and Watson, found it in her address book. She's already on the fast train up from Devon. Squad car will pick her up at the station and bring her straight here. Should be with us soon."

"Parents?" Sally asked.

Vicky scanned the note. "Yeah. They live in Spain. Retired. Apparently they'll be here when they can get a flight. That won't be easy at this time of year. Do you want to see the sister?"

Sean glanced across at Sally. "Yeah. Why not?"

"I'll arrange it now. Meanwhile, why don't you tell me about your suspect? What've you got on him so far?"

"James Hellier," Sean said. "A wealthy, polished act. Works for a fancy firm of financiers in Knightsbridge. Self-confessed sadomasochist. Last night he took our surveillance team on a runaround. He lost them about six P.M. He wasn't picked up again until he got home, sometime after three A.M."

Vicky raised her eyebrows. "The man knows he's under surveillance and still he travels to Shepherd's Bush and commits murder?"

"He can't stop himself," Sean told her. "The fact he knows he's under surveillance probably only adds to his pleasure."

"If you're so sure, let's arrest him, strip him, swab him, and have forensics do the rest," said Vicky.

"We've tried that," Sean explained. "With the first murder. We found samples matching him at the scene, but he had an answer for everything. Claimed to have been having a long-standing sexual relationship with the victim. It was a waste of time. We showed our hand too soon. Handed him the initiative.

"The second scene was different," he continued. "A young girl called Heather Freeman, a runaway teenager. She was abducted and killed on waste ground out near Dagenham. He cut her throat, but still the scene was left as clean as a whistle. Nothing but a plain footprint.

"So we wait. If we get alien samples from the scene, we'll move and arrest Hellier, but we wait until then." Sean saw Vicky moving in her chair. He knew what she was thinking. He held a hand up. "I know," he said. "But trust me. Hellier won't be contaminated with anything from the scene. Any clothing he used will be destroyed by now."

"You're absolutely certain of that?"

"No," he replied. "Not absolutely, but certain enough. I need something irrefutable. Whether it's from one of the scenes or whether it's something Hellier leads us to, I don't care. But I'm not going to have him dance circles around me in an interview again. I need something damning."

"It's your call, Sean, but don't forget the Stephen Lawrence inquiry. Those guys were slaughtered for not making early arrests and seizing clothing for forensics. If you go down, I go down with you."

"No you won't," Sean assured her. "Make an official note of your objections. I'll do the same, and then you're covered."

"Hold on," Vicky said. "That's not what I meant."

"I know it isn't," Sean replied. "But the branch I'm on is too thin for two people. You register those objections. They'll be entered into my decision log."

Vicky didn't argue further.

"I'd like to get a briefing out to the media today." Sean changed the subject. "You do it, Vicky. Keep my name out of it and don't mention the link to other murders. Make it an appeal for public assistance. I want to see it in the *Evening Standard* tonight."

"Not a problem," said Vicky. "Their crime editor owes me a couple of favors."

A knock at the door ended the conversation. Sean turned to see a detective he didn't recognize. "Sister's here, guv'nor" was all he said.

Sean's hand hesitated as it rested on the handle of the witness room. Linda Kotler's sister waited inside. Sally was with him, but he'd decided to do the talking this time.

Telling someone a loved one had died was one thing. As devastating as that news could be, it was nothing compared to telling them someone they loved had been murdered. That news would shatter lives. The living would be forever haunted, imagining the last moments of those now dead. The worst was telling parents a child had been murdered—few marriages survived that burden. The parents see their dead child every time they look at each other. Eventually they can take no more reminding, no more torture, and push each other away.

Sean gently nudged the door open. He wanted her to see him entering. Debbie Stryer looked up. She was younger than he'd expected, healthy, and slightly tanned. Her country complexion made Sean conscious of his own ghostly city skin. She'd been crying. Her eyes were pink and rimmed bright red. She wasn't crying now. It was a long trip from Devon. Had she run out of tears?

She began to stand before Sean or Sally could stop her. Her sore eyes darted between them. Sean had seen that look on the faces of other victims' loved ones. Fear, disbelief; desperate for information.

She spoke first. "Hello. I'm Debbie Stryer. Linda's sister. Stryer's my married name."

Sean nodded that he understood. Sally held out a hand. When Debbie Stryer took it, Sally gently pulled her hand forward and held it with both of hers.

"I'm Sally Jones. I'm a detective sergeant. I'll be helping to catch whoever did this to your sister. I'm so sorry for your loss. Everybody tells us Linda was such a good person." Sally waited for a reaction. The tears began to fall in heavy drops from Debbie's eyes. Real tears, like those of a child in pain. "You need to know we'll catch the person who did this to Linda," Sally promised her.

Sean looked on in admiration. His plan to take the lead just hadn't happened. If he tried to emulate Sally now, he would sound clumsy. He would introduce himself and help explain any procedural matters Debbie might wish to know, but little more.

He waited for Debbie Stryer to take her hand away from Sally. It was a long wait. She was struggling to speak clearly through her grief.

"Thank you," she told Sally. "Thank you." She turned to Sean. The awfulness of the day was beginning to break her. She seemed to be visibly shrinking.

He held out his hand. She accepted it. "I'm Detective Inspector Sean Corrigan," he said. "I'll be in charge of this investigation." He wanted to say more, but couldn't find the right words.

Debbie almost immediately stopped crying. She looked at him strangely. This was not what he had expected. He'd only introduced himself. Just said his name. He couldn't have said the wrong thing already.

"She told me about you," Debbie said. She couldn't help herself from checking Sean's left hand. She saw his wedding ring and almost smiled. "She didn't tell me you were married. That's typical of Linda."

Sean and Sally simultaneously turned to each other, confusion and surprise etched on their faces.

CHAPTER 21

Sean had briefed DI Townsend on the meeting with Debbie Stryer. She had listened almost without speaking. The only thing she said was that there must have been some mistake. Sean knew better. He was being played. Hellier was laughing at him.

But Hellier was taking an unnecessary risk in doing so. Showing off came with a price. Debbie Stryer was able to tell them he had approached her sister close to her home, sometime between eight and nine, maybe a little earlier. Christ, he'd even had a conversation with her in the middle of the street. He was beginning to think he was uncatchable. His sociopathic arrogance was matched only by his violence.

Sean and Sally donned forensic suits and entered Linda Kotler's flat. It looked very different from how Sean remembered it, forensic examiners going about their work making it seem full of life. They went directly to the living room, where Sean had seen the docking unit for Linda Kotler's home phone. He examined it without touching and saw traces of aluminum powder on both the phone and the base. "Has this phone been dusted yet?" he asked a middle-aged woman, shapeless in her paper suit. They all resembled workers in a nuclear power plant.

"Yes," she answered. "I did it."

"Have the messages been listened to?" Sean asked.

"No. We'll do that back at the audio lab, for continuity." But Sean had had enough of waiting. He pressed the message play-back button and hit the speaker on switch. "I don't think you should be doing that," the woman protested.

"DI Corrigan. I'm in charge of this investigation."

The machine beeped, long and shrill. A ringing tone could be heard. Linda Kotler's voice filled the room. Everyone stopped and listened to the woman who had been murdered only two plaster walls away.

They listened as the sisters chatted. This was it. Sean's heart was going faster and faster. He knew what was coming, but he didn't want to hear it.

"And does this man have a name?" Debbie asked.

He could see Sally watching him out the corner of her eye.

"Sean," Linda's voice said. *"Sean Corrigan."*

The middle-aged forensics officer was staring at him now. "Haven't you got work to do?" he snapped. She moved quickly away.

Sean stood and led Sally to the bedroom, where they found Donnelly wearing a forensic suit. Sean also recognized the slim figure of Dr. Canning, kneeling over Linda Kotler's life-less form. A number of labeled specimen jars and exhibit bags were spread across the floor close by, within easy reach of the pathologist. DC Zukov was doing his best to assist Canning.

"Anything interesting yet?" Sean asked.

Dr. Canning was stone-faced. "Inspector Corrigan. I shall assume you are responsible for dragging me halfway across London."

"Sorry, but I felt it was necessary."

"Because you believe you have two connected murders. Ser-geant Donnelly here filled me in on the details."

"Three murders," Sean corrected him. The pathologist frowned. "There was another. The first of the series occurred about two weeks ago. Postmortem's already been done, but I'd like you to cast an eye over it."

"Very well," Canning replied. He went back to work. He talked as he examined the body.

"So elaborate. Probably the most elaborate bindings and ligatures I've ever encountered."

"Why?" Sean asked. "What's the purpose?"

Canning pointed to the knot on the stocking that ran along the victim's spine. "That's a slip knot. My best guess at this time would be that it's a type of harness.

"He positions the victim facedown on the bed, then by pulling the slip knot up and down he can control the tightness of the bindings around her throat and legs simultaneously. Quite the instrument of torture."

"Anything else?" Sean asked.

Canning scanned the body, wondering where to begin. "You'll have to wait until the postmortem before it's confirmed, but I'm sure the cause of death will be strangulation." He pointed to the victim's neck. "You can see the ligature's sunk into the flesh quite deeply. Far more deeply than was necessary to kill her. Quite a surprise the skin didn't break. There's other severe bruising too. Probably all caused by the same ligature." Canning took a deep breath. "This is a strong man you're looking for, Inspector."

"What caused the other bruising around the neck?" Sean asked.

"I believe the killer repeatedly tightened the ligature around her neck, but released it before death."

"And before she passed out too," Sean added.

"I wouldn't be able to say."

"He wouldn't have let her pass out," Sean assured him. "He

wouldn't have let her escape into unconsciousness. Not even for a second."

Canning raised his eyebrows. "It would appear he had knowledge of autoerotic asphyxiation," he continued. "Popular with sadomasochists."

Hellier's face flashed in Sean's mind.

"She was sexually assaulted too. Raped both vaginally and anally by the look of things. No immediate signs of semen or a lubricant. I suspect he used a dry condom."

Canning spoke to DC Zukov. "Could you pass me that halogen lamp, please, Detective?" Zukov passed him a metal-cased lamp that was big enough to be a helicopter searchlight. Canning flicked the lamp on. It gave off a less bright light than expected, but that wasn't its purpose. Held at the right angle, it would allow the naked eye to observe otherwise near-invisible marks. Fingerprints, footprints, hairs, tiny fragments of metal . . .

Canning began to slowly sweep the light across the body. He started at the lowest point. In this case it was the knees. The legs were still bent and tied back so her feet almost touched her buttocks. The light moved to her back. "Hello there." Canning had found something. He froze the light on the victim's back. Sean moved two steps closer.

"Careful," Canning warned him. "We haven't examined the entire area around the body yet."

Sean stopped and crouched down. He craned his neck to get a better view of the victim's back. "What is it?"

"If I'm not very much mistaken," Canning said, "it's a foot-print." He moved the lamp to another angle. "Yes. There." The shoe-shaped bruise came more into focus. "Definitely a shoe mark. Pretty plain, though. No ridges or pattern."

"A plain-soled man's shoe, between size eight and ten."

"Yes," Canning agreed. "That would be my guess. I'll have

it photographed back at the mortuary. Should show up well enough."

"Why would he do that?" DC Zukov asked the question, the disgusted look clear on his face.

Sean knew why, but he wouldn't say. He knew Canning would work it out.

"He pressed down on her back with his foot while pulling the ligatures tighter. That's probably when the other marks around the neck were caused."

"Sick bastard," Zukov said. "Sick, evil bastard."

No one disagreed.

Needing a break from the scene, Sally stood outside in the street smoking. She doubted whether the male officers felt what she did for the victim. Did they ever feel vulnerable and scared like a woman could? Did they ever consider how intimidating a big man could be to a woman, just by standing a little too close in a bar, at a bus stop? Probably not.

What must it have been like for Linda Kotler? Those last minutes, God forbid hours, of her life. Totally overpowered by this man, this wild animal. Did the male officers have any real idea how hundreds of thousands of women across London would feel when details of the latest murder were released to the press?

Many would stop going out at night until he, the killer, was caught. Others would rush to buy rape alarms, some would start to carry offensive weapons. All would check the locks on their doors and windows. They would want their men home before dark.

Sally would be no different. When she thought of Linda Kotler, the way she had died, she couldn't help but see her own face on the body. She shivered repeatedly. The cigarette helped a little.

God, she wished she had a lover. Someone special to share her life with, good or bad. Her achievements and her failures. Her hopes and her fears. This wasn't an easy job to do alone.

Her thoughts turned to Sebastian Gibran. Was that what he wanted? To be her lover? When they'd first met, his eyes had definitely rested on her for longer than normal. She was pretty sure he would be married, but maybe that didn't matter to him. How did she feel about being a mistress to a wealthy benefactor? Was the whole "something sensitive to discuss" a ruse to get her to meet him for lunch? Wine and dine her? Seduce her? She couldn't deny she had found him attractive: power and presence in a man were strong aphrodisiacs. She would find out soon enough.

The cigarette grew hot between her fingers, snapping her back to the present. She tossed it away and headed back inside the scene, all thoughts of pleasanter things a distant memory.

Dr. Canning moved the halogen lamp to the victim's head. He held a fine-toothed comb in his other hand, the better to groom the victim's hair before the body was moved. A tiny, vital piece of evidence could easily be lost when moving a body. With the help of DC Zukov, he'd lifted the head very slightly and slipped a three-foot-by-three-foot white paper sheet under her head. He began to comb the hair slowly, from the scalp outward.

As he combed, a little of her hair fell onto the sheet. Then he saw it, floating the short distance to the sheet. It landed gently. He dared not breathe. He swapped the comb and lamp for a plastic evidence bag and a pair of delicate metal tweezers. He moved the tweezers stealthily closer to the hair. When he was no more than an inch or two away, he suddenly moved quickly, grabbing the hair in the small metal claw. He allowed himself to exhale.

Sean had been watching intently. As Canning held the hair

above his head, Sean could see it glistening. "The victim's?" Sean asked.

"Definitely not," Canning replied. "Too fair. And there's a root on it. Your lab shouldn't have too much trouble getting DNA off it."

Sean hid the excitement swelling in his chest, making it difficult to breathe. The root of that hair could solve this murder on its own.

"What are the chances it belongs to our killer?" he asked.

"Unless there was another person here with the victim last night, I'd say it's almost certainly the killer's," Canning answered. "This hair wasn't buried deep in among the victim's. It was virtually sitting on top of hers, waiting to be found."

Sean was still concerned. He wanted it to be absolute. In court it would have to be absolute. "How could that be?" he asked. "A hair, with a root, just lying there?"

"Most likely caused by the killer removing a head cover of some description," Canning surmised. "When you remove a hat or something similar, there is always a good chance you'll pull a hair out, and often the root will come with it."

"So you think he took his off?" Sean asked.

"Yes. Hairs like this, with roots attached, don't fall out naturally."

"Why the hell would he take his head cover off?" Sean wondered.

"That I can't answer," Canning said. "But if he did take a head cover off, then we've a good chance of finding more hair on the body or around it. That would further diminish the possibility of an accidental transfer of hair from body to body at some other point during the day at another location." Sean understood the importance of eliminating that possibility. Defense solicitors had become skilled in arguing their way around forensic evidence.

The pathologist handed the evidence bag containing the hair to DC Zukov. He handled it as if it were an unstable bomb. Canning picked up his lamp again and began to examine the area around the body. He bent so low his face was almost on the carpet. Sean hadn't blinked for minutes. He watched as Canning's eyes suddenly narrowed. He saw him stretch out with his tweezers and snare the thin fiber. Canning looked directly at him.

"It would seem the forensic gods are with us today, Inspector."

"The same?" he asked.

"I would say so," Canning answered. "This has a root too. DNA will no doubt confirm they come from the same person. If your killer's in the National DNA Database, then it'll be case closed for you."

"The man who did this isn't in the database," Sean told him. "But that doesn't matter, because I know where to find his DNA."

Canning looked a little confused. "And where would that be?"

Sean answered: "In his blood."

Hellier hadn't been asked to see any clients in over two days. He no longer cared. Only a few weeks before he would have taken steps to ensure that the firm wasn't trying to cut him out. Now it was irrelevant. The firm had served its purpose. He didn't need them anymore.

It was almost 6 P.M. Only he, Sebastian Gibran, and the perfect secretary remained in the office. It was a shame he couldn't be alone with the secretary. He would have liked to give the beautiful bitch a going-away present she wouldn't forget, but he couldn't risk it with Gibran lurking inside his office. Maybe sometime in the distant future their paths would cross again.

His mobile phone began to ring, the display telling him the number had been withheld. Something told him he should answer.

"James Hellier speaking."

"Mr. Hellier. You are in great danger." It was him again.

"Like I said earlier—you were supposed to meet me last night." Hellier sounded strong. He knew how to dominate. "I don't like being fucked around."

"I just want to help you," the voice said. "You must believe me."

"Why?" Hellier demanded. "Why do you want to help me? You don't know me."

"Are you sure of that?" the voice asked.

Hellier didn't answer. He was thinking. The caller sensed his doubt.

"Corrigan. I can give you something, show you something that'll keep him away from you. Keep them all away from you."

"I'm not worried about the police." Hellier sounded insulted. "They can't touch me."

"Yes, they can," the voice replied. "Corrigan. He's not intending to take you to court. He won't risk that."

"What are you talking about?" Hellier began to sound more concerned. "What do you mean?"

"Meet me tomorrow night if you value your neck as much as I think you do."

"Where?" Hellier asked.

"Somewhere in Central London. I'll call you again tomorrow. At about seven. And don't bring the police. They're still following you."

"Wait a minute." Hellier was too late. The line was dead.

The three unmarked cars drove down the middle of Bayswater Road. Traffic on both sides yielded to their sirens and madly spinning blue lights. They were heading toward Knightsbridge. Toward Hellier.

Sean had the forensic evidence he'd been praying for. The killer had made a serious mistake, but it was too early to say anything other than that the hairs appeared to be the same color as Hellier's. Sandy.

Sally drove while Sean sat in the passenger seat. She broke the silent tension. "Maybe we should process the hair first, guv'nor. Get its DNA profile and compare it to the DNA database?" She had to shout to be heard above the screaming sirens.

"Hellier's not on the DNA database, remember. He's got no previous," Sean argued.

"Maybe the hairs aren't Hellier's," Sally persisted. "We could process them first and have them compared to profiles on the database. It could show they belong to someone other than Hellier and then we'd have a cast-in-iron suspect. And if we don't get a hit on the database, then it'll point more strongly toward Hellier being our man."

"Believe me," he reassured her, "Hellier's our man."

"Then why don't we compare the samples to the ones we've already taken off Hellier?" She referred to those taken in the Belgravia police station at the beginning of the investigation into the murder of Daniel Graydon. "Then before we even arrest him we'd know he killed Linda Kotler."

"You know we can't use them," Sean shouted above the noise inside the car. "That was a different murder. We'd be slaughtered if we were ever found out." It was true. They couldn't use elimination samples taken from a suspect or witness for one crime to prove they were involved in another. The suspect would have to be told specifically what investigation their samples were being used in, or they would be deemed to have been taken illegally.

"Maybe we could do it so no one would know?" Sally continued. "Just do it so we would know for sure it was Hellier. Don't tell anyone. Don't mention it in his initial interview, keep it to ourselves, then do it legally. Take new samples, whatever we have to, but at least we would know it was him. Interview him and let him hang himself with lies."

"No." Sean shook his head. "I can't risk that. We do it properly. It's Hellier, I know it. There's no need to take shortcuts."

Sally gripped the steering wheel harder and said nothing.

Sean tapped the number of the surveillance team leader into his mobile.

"DS Handy." Sean could hear the radio chatter in the background.

"Don—Sean. Where's my man?"

"He's on the move," said DS Handy. "Just left his office on foot."

"Heading home?" Sean asked.

"Heading to the tube station."

"We're on our way to you," Sean told him. "We're gonna take him out."

"Wait a minute," DS Handy said, "he's hailing a cab." There was a pause. "Want us to take him out for you?"

"No," Sean said. "Can you follow the cab?"

"Shouldn't be too difficult. Given that it's lime green with a giant packet of Skittles on its side."

"Follow it," Sean said, making the decision. "But keep me up to date. You follow him and we'll follow you."

"No problem."

Sean could feel Sally looking between him and the road as she drove fast through the traffic.

"I hope you know what you're doing, sir," she said.

"There's more out there for us, Sally. This could be our last chance to let Hellier lead us to something."

"What more do we need? We have his hair. His DNA will match." She was nervous for both of them. Sean was taking a risk. Maybe one he didn't have to take.

"We have hairs," Sean pointed out. "Not necessarily Hellier's. And they bother me. Too easy. All of a sudden he drops two rooted hairs right where we can find them. Hellier's smart. Certainly smart enough to plant someone else's hair at the scene. Imagine what that would do to any case against him. His defense would have a fucking field day. We'd never even get it to court. If I think I can get more, I'll take the chance."

"Just because it was easy doesn't mean it's not right."

Sean didn't answer her. She tried again.

"The law says that when we have evidence to arrest, we should arrest," Sally said, quoting the Police and Criminal Evidence Act. She was right and Sean knew it.

"Only until he goes home," Sean said, seeking to assure her. "If he doesn't lead us to something before then, we arrest him."

Sally exhaled and tried to concentrate on the road ahead.

"Bryanston Street. Marble Arch," Hellier calmly told the cabdriver, who gave a nod and pulled away without speaking. Hellier tried to relax in the back, but he knew he was being followed again and there were more of them this time—he'd already counted fourteen. He could run around the tube system, but there was a chance they would have enough bodies to stay with him. He would try something else.

The cab drove into Bryanston Street. Hellier tapped on the glass screen designed to keep the drunks and psychotics at bay. "Here's fine," he said. The taxi pulled into the curb. Hellier poked a ten-pound note through the screen, got out, and walked away without waiting for change. He entered the Avis car rental shop. He knew they were still watching.

Sean's phone rang, startling him. He was walking a tightrope that left him feeling wired.

"DS Handy, guv. Looks like your boy's about to hire a car."

"Problem?" Sean asked.

"No. I'd rather he was in a car than running around on foot."

"Fine. We stay with him until I say otherwise." Sean hung up. Sally said nothing.

Hellier rented the largest and fastest car they had. He used the driver's license in the name of James Hellier and paid with an American Express Black card in the same name. He would miss James Hellier.

The black Vauxhall slipped into Bryanston Street. The three-liter V-6 engine gave a reassuring growl. Hellier began to relax a little as he listened to the engine's cylinders gently thudding above the low revs.

At the end of the road he turned left into Gloucester Place and joined the three lanes of traffic all heading north. He kept pace with the traffic, but no more. He stopped carefully at traffic lights and showed no hurry to pull away. He didn't need to check his mirrors. He knew they would be following, running parallels along the adjacent streets, leapfrogging to the junctions ahead, changing the cars immediately behind him as often as they could.

He turned left into the Marylebone Road and headed west. The traffic was lighter than he had expected. That was unfortunate. He drove carefully.

He headed up and onto the Marylebone Flyover and joined the Westway, a small motorway raised above the heart of West London and designed to speed commuters to the traffic jams of the M4 and M40 that inevitably awaited.

He began checking his mirrors constantly. They couldn't run parallels to him now. As he drove above Paddington and Notting Hill, they had only one way of staying with him: follow him along the Westway.

He began to make a mental note of all the cars ahead and

behind him. Any one of them could be the police: best to remember them all and assume the worst. Effective countersurveillance relied on the target assuming the worst.

He drove for about ten minutes before reaching his exit. The
sign read SHEPHERD'S BUSH AND HAMMERSMITH. He moved
into the exit lane. He glanced in his mirror. He saw several cars'
indicators blinking, signaling that they too would be leaving
the Westway. Any police cars that had been ahead of him were
already out of the chase. They would have to stay on the motorway until they could exit at Acton, another four miles along. By
the time they rejoined their colleagues, he would be gone.

He left the Westway and followed the large access road, the
West Cross Route, that took him to a major traffic circle. Only
at the traffic circle did he make the final decision as to where
he would go. He could turn left along Holland Park, back toward Central London. Or straight over toward Earl's Court,
along Holland Road. No. He needed traffic. He turned right at
the traffic circle and drove past Shepherd's Bush Green on his
right and then turned left into Shepherd's Bush Road, heading
toward Hammersmith.

The three cars of the arrest team waited in Hyde Park for an
update. Alone in the middle car, Sean and Sally listened to the
surveillance team's coded chatter on the radio. It made little
sense to them. They tried to work out where the team could be,
but it was no use. They relied on telephone updates alone.

Sean's phone rang again.

"Smart lad, your boy," DS Handy told him. "He took the one
route I didn't want him to take. Over the Westway. He dropped
off at Shepherd's. We've already lost our two lead cars. They're
trying to make their way back from Acton."

"Do you still have him?" Sean's tension was palpable.

"Yeah. We've got plenty of coverage." Handy sounded calm in comparison.

"Where is he now?"

"Approaching Hammersmith."

"We're on our way," said Sean. "Traveling time from Marble Arch. Don't lose him, Don. Whatever you do, don't lose him."

Hellier cruised toward the chaotic one-way system of Hammersmith that was little more than a giant traffic circle. Four lanes of traffic looped around a central shopping complex. The traffic was always a disaster.

The traffic lights immediately ahead were green, but he wasn't ready to enter the one-way system yet. He stopped at the green light and studied his rearview and side mirrors. The white van behind him beeped twice, politely. When he didn't move, it gave him a long angry blast of the horn. Still the lights were green. Still he wouldn't move.

He could see the van driver in his mirror, leaning out of his window now, shouting obscenities. Another blast on the van's horn. The van would be a useful barrier between him and his pursuers, but it alone would not be enough.

The lights changed to red just as the van driver was climbing from his cabin, malicious intent spread across his face. Hellier didn't wait for a break in the traffic speeding across in front of him. He floored the accelerator. The rear wheels of the big automatic gripped almost instantly and launched the car toward the passing vehicles.

"Move. Move. Move," DS Handy screamed at his driver. "Stay with him. For fuck's sake, stay with him. Shit." He could see Hellier had pulled farther ahead. "You're losing him."

"What's the fucking point?" the driver snapped back.

"We're burned. He's wasted us. We can't follow him driving like this and not show out."

"Don't worry about staying covert," Handy was shouting. "Take the fucker out. Take him out."

Hellier had already turned right into Hammersmith Road. He gunned the Vauxhall east, toward Kensington. Confused drivers jammed the road in front of the surveillance cars. They couldn't move, trapped in traffic. Hellier was gone.

Sean spoke into his phone. He didn't say much, just the occasional word. "How?" "Where?" He paled noticeably the more he listened. "Get back to Knightsbridge, and cover his home too."

He felt sick. Hellier was lost again. He'd made a bad decision, one he was going to have to live with. He rubbed his reddening eyes, hard. Exhaustion threatened to overtake him. He looked at Sally. "Dammit."

"We'll find him," Sally reassured him.

"Only if he wants us to," he said. "Only if he's still playing games with us. With me."

Hellier dumped the car and made absolutely sure he was alone before walking the short distance to the High Street Kensington underground station and descending calmly to the platforms. He caught the first District line train for two stops to South Kensington. Out of the station, he walked quickly along Exhibition Road, scanning the area for police. There were none. He turned right into Thurloe Place and walked along the row of shops. He knew exactly where he was going.

He looked through the window of Thurloe Arts, casting a knowledgeable eye over the paintings that adorned the interior. It was more of a mini-gallery than a shop, although he decided most of it was crap.

An old-fashioned bell rang above the door as he opened it.

Almost immediately the owner appeared from the back of the shop, breaking into a welcoming smile when he saw Hellier.

"Mr. McLennan. What a pleasant surprise. How are you?"

"I'm very well," Hellier replied. "How has life been treating you these past few years?"

"I mustn't complain. Business is a little unpredictable, but could be worse."

"Then I hope our arrangement has been of some financial assistance?"

"Indeed it has, sir," the shopkeeper answered. "Am I to take it that is the purpose of your visit?"

"You are."

"If you would be good enough to wait here a moment."

Hellier nodded. The owner went to the back of the shop, returning a couple of minutes later. He held the door to the rear area open.

"This way, please."

Hellier walked behind the counter and into the rear of the shop where he was led to a small windowless room lit by a single uncovered lightbulb. There was a table and one chair in the middle, surrounded by bare yellow walls. On the table was a metal box, one foot by nine inches, a heavy combination padlock hanging from its side. Hellier entered the room and found it just as he remembered it from his previous visit, three years ago. The shopkeeper made his excuses and left.

Taking a seat, Hellier examined the outside of the box. It seemed intact. He studied the lock closely. It was untainted. No telltale metal scratch marks. The dials remained at the settings he had left them on three years ago. He pulled a pair of thin leather gloves from his pocket and slipped his hands into the silk lining.

He turned the combination dials and pulled at the lock. Three years was a long time. With a little effort it popped open.

He wiggled it free from the box and placed it carefully on the table.

He lifted the lid up as if opening a precious jewelry box. He removed an object wrapped in a white cloth and placed it next to the lock. He would look at it later. He needed to check something else first.

He lifted a heavy parcel from the box. It was wrapped in several yellow cloths, which he patiently unfolded as if peeling back the petals of a tropical flower. The black-gray metal inside shone. He was pleased he'd taken the effort to oil the Browning 9-millimeter automatic pistol before locking it away. He'd made plenty of enemies over the years. He doubted they could find him, but just in case they did, he had insurance.

He checked the two magazines: each held a full load of thirteen 9-millimeter high-velocity bullets. They had been harder to obtain than the gun itself. Soldiers were happy to sell weapons stolen from poorly guarded armories, but for some reason they were reluctant to sell the bullets to go with them.

Hellier pulled at the back of the gun. The top slide glided backward and smoothly cocked the weapon. He squeezed the trigger. The hammer hit the firing pin with a reassuring metallic click. Satisfied, he pushed one of the magazines into the butt of the gun. The other he slid into his inside jacket pocket. He tucked the pistol into the small of his back, held in place by his belt.

He opened the other parcel. He laughed at the items inside. A dark brown wig with eyebrows to match. A mustache, no beard. A pair of prescription spectacles. He tried them on. They affected his eyesight, but he could see through them. He picked up the tube of theatrical makeup glue. He squeezed a drop onto his left index finger and rubbed his thumb and finger together. The glue was still good. He rolled the parcel back in the cloth and stuffed it into his trouser pocket as he stood.

He shut the box and replaced the padlock. He set the numbers as he had found them and left the room. The shopkeeper was waiting for him.

"Everything as it should be?" he asked.

"Yes. Everything was fine," Hellier replied. "Tell me, is there a sports shop near here?"

Sally and the others had decided to retreat to the one pub they ever used, close to the Peckham police station. The landlord was only too happy to be running a "police pub." It all but guaranteed that his premises remained free of trouble, except for the occasional bust-up between coppers. And that was always dealt with in-house so no black marks went against his license.

Sally's phone rang.

"Sally Jones speaking."

"DS Jones, I'm Prison Officer English, from Wandsworth Prison."

Sally hadn't expected the prison to call her outside of office hours. "You have something for me?"

"Your inquiry into a former prisoner: Korsakov, Stefan, released in 1999. You wanted to know why we requested his fingerprints?"

"Yes."

"We made no request for his fingerprints from Scotland Yard."

"Are you positive?"

"Absolutely. Our records are correct. There's no mistake."

"No," Sally said, more to herself than anyone else. "I'm sure there isn't. Thank you." She hung up.

Donnelly appeared next to her. "Problem?"

"Someone's been lying to me."

"About what?"

"Never mind," she said. "We'll talk about it tomorrow. Right now I need another drink."

Hellier found the small sports shop easily enough. He selected a dark blue Nike tracksuit, the plainest he could find. He added a white T-shirt, white Puma training shoes, and a pair of white socks to his basket. He asked for the items to be placed in separate plastic bags. He had been an easy customer who paid cash. The assistant was more than happy to lavish him with extra plastic bags.

He left the shop, headed back to the tube station, and caught a train to Farringdon. He didn't have to search long to find what he wanted. A bar where men and women in suits mixed easily enough with others wearing casual clothes, even tracksuits.

He ordered a stiff gin and tonic from the bar. Gin, lots of ice, lime not lemon. The barman was good. The long drink both refreshed him and gave his brain a nice alcoholic kick, without affecting his clarity of thought—his control.

Hellier sat and familiarized himself with the layout of the bar. Satisfied, he went to the men's toilet, entered a cubicle, and shut the door. It was fairly solid. That was good. He looked up at the window. It was quite high. If he tried to climb out of it, he would be seen. It was probably sealed shut anyway.

He checked the toilet cistern. It was low on the wall. That was good. He lifted the lid from the cistern. Then he emptied the contents of the plastic bags onto the toilet seat, taking the gun from his belt and the spare magazine from his jacket pocket. He placed them on the tracksuit. Next he took the training shoes out of the box and wrapped them, the T-shirt, and the socks in the tracksuit, making a tight parcel; the shoes flattened to little more than the width and thickness of the soles, the light material of the T-shirt and tracksuit folded to almost nothing. He placed them in one of the smaller plastic bags and tied a knot at the open end. He placed that bag inside another and fastened it with a tight knot.

At the last minute he recalled that the man who described himself as a friend would be calling on his mobile phone tomorrow at seven. He pulled the phone from a pocket and looked at it pensively. If the police were waiting for him, they would surely seize the phone. They always did. It was the only way he had of allowing the "friend" to contact him. He decided he couldn't take the risk, but no matter what, he would have to recover the phone before 7 P.M. the next day. Separating the phone from its battery, he undid the plastic bags and dropped both phone and battery in. Then he wrapped and knotted the bags again.

Hellier was about to place the plastic bag in the toilet cistern when he stopped short. The gun was too big a prize to risk. Maybe he should just check into a hotel for the night instead of going home; that way he could stay hidden until it was time to meet the man from the phone calls. He shook his doubts away. He would go home. The police would undoubtedly be waiting for him there, but it wasn't as if they were going to arrest him. What did they have? Nothing. If they had, they would have arrested him earlier instead of trying to follow him. And even if they did arrest him, so what? He would be out in time to make the meeting and he would know whatever the police were thinking too. It was an uneven match. Every time the police moved against him, they had to tell him what they knew. The laws of the land demanded it. This was a fair and just country. He, on the other hand, had to tell them nothing. And if they were stupid enough to try and follow him again after today, which he absolutely believed they were, then he had made plans for that too.

All doubt gone, he smiled to himself and tucked the plastic bag containing the clothes and pistol neatly into the toilet cistern, expertly packing it around the working parts as he'd practiced hundreds of times before, ensuring that enough water was allowed into the small tank. He flushed once to make certain it still worked and watched the cistern fill again. Satisfied, he replaced the lid and left the bar carrying the largest of the plastic bags containing only the empty shoe box. He would squash it flat and dump it in a bin on his way to the underground station and home.

It was almost 10 P.M. on Thursday. Sean sat alone in his office. The inquiry room was dark and quiet. The rest of the team had adjourned to a nearby pub, where they would be deep into analyzing what had gone wrong. They would argue that Hellier should have been arrested earlier, that it had been an unnecessary risk to try and follow him around London on the off chance he would lead them to some clinching evidence. Sean's absence from the pub would be noticed, but it would be welcome too. They could speak their minds better if he wasn't around.

He unlocked his bottom desk drawer and pulled out an unopened bottle of dark rum and a heavy, shallow glass. The rum had been in there for months. He only kept it out of a sense of tradition. He had rarely felt the need to use it, until now.

He poured an inch of rum into the glass and rolled it around. He put the glass tentatively to his lips and drank a quarter of it in one go. It was a lot for him. The back of his throat burned painfully, but he enjoyed the warmth of the liquid.

He reached forward for his desk phone. He needed to call Kate. His ringing mobile stopped him. He answered sounding tired and dispirited.

"Guv. It's Jean Colville." DS Jean Colville was running the relief surveillance team, brought in to cover while DS Handy's team regrouped and licked their collective wounds. "Thought you'd like to know your man just arrived home like nothing happened."

Sean sprang to his feet as if suddenly standing to attention. "What's he wearing?" he asked.

"Suit and tie," Jean answered.

"How's he look?"

"Fine. Normal, I guess." She sounded puzzled.

"Okay," Sean said. He checked his watch. Damn. Half his team would be semidrunk by now, the other half would have headed off toward whichever corner of London they lived in. Had there been time since he went missing for Hellier to find a victim, kill, and calmly return home? Sean doubted it. No, this evening he'd been up to something else. Better to let the team rest for a while. What more could he lose?

"I need you to keep him under obs tonight," he told DS Colville. "I'll be there in the morning to take him out. Hopefully he won't move again until then."

"No problem, guv," Jean answered. "If he moves, I'll let you know."

"Thanks." Sean hung up, waited a few seconds, and called Sally. When she answered he could hear she was in the pub.

"Sally. It's Sean."

"Please tell me you're not still at work." She sounded sober enough.

"Contact Donnelly and the rest of the team." He knew Donnelly at least would be close by. "Six A.M. briefing back here. We're taking Hellier out before he leaves for work."

"Before he leaves for work?" she asked. He could hear the confusion in her voice. "He's gone home?"

"Don't ask me why," Sean replied. "I don't know what he's up to, but we're going to finish this tomorrow."

The light shining through the front door's window was not a good sign. It was past eleven and he'd expected all to be quiet and dark inside. He turned the key as quietly as he could and carefully pushed the door open. The scent of the family who lived inside pleasantly assaulted his olfactory system. As he stepped inside he could hear the television quietly playing in the living room. He followed the sound. Kate lay on the sofa, and Louise lay across her chest, sleeping fitfully.

"What is she doing out of bed?" Sean asked his wife.

She shushed him before answering. "She has a temperature. Something going around at nursery."

"Is she all right?"

"She'll be fine. I've given her some ibuprofen. I just hope she doesn't give it to Mandy. I could do without having to look after two sick children." Louise stirred on Kate's chest.

"If it comes to that, I'll take some time off work and help out."

"Take some time off work?" she whispered. "How do you plan on doing that?"

"We've had a break in the case. Things should start happening pretty quickly now. With any luck we'll be able to charge our suspect and wrap things up within a few days."

"And then, no doubt, you'll inherit another case and we'll be back to the same old routine."

"It's late and I have an early start tomorrow," he said. "This is probably not a good time to discuss this. You're tired and stressed. Having this conversation won't help."

"Yes. You're right. I am tired and stressed, as you would be if you'd been at home alone with two young children, one of whom is sick." She managed to keep her voice down, despite her frustration.

"What do you want me to do, Kate? I get away from work as soon as I can, but sometimes it's not possible to walk away at five o'clock. I don't have that luxury. I don't do a normal job."

"It's this damn Murder Squad. It's too unpredictable. I never know when I'm going to see you. When the kids are going to see you. I can't plan anything like normal people do. When was the last time we did anything as a family? When was the last time we had a decent holiday? When was the last time you helped bathe the kids, Sean? You know, I work too. Sometimes I need you to be here to help out."

"I want to be here," he told her. "But I don't know how I can make things easier. I don't sell fucking shoes, Kate. I solve murders. I stop people who kill. I can't do this job with one hand tied behind my back."

There was a silence before Kate replied, "Is that what we are to you, Mandy, Louise, and I? Some kind of handicap you'd be better off without?"

"No. No," he insisted. "That's not what I meant. You know that's not what I meant, but I need my mind to be clear if I'm going to have any chance of catching these people quickly. If I'm constantly worrying about getting home for bathtime or dinner, I can't think properly. I can't think the way I need to think. You and the kids have no place in that world, believe me."

"But you're missing them, Sean. Before you know it, they'll be leaving home and you won't be able to get that time back. It'll be gone."

"Do you want me to leave the police? Is that what you're saying?"

"No," she assured him. "That's the last thing I want. Doing what you do makes you what you are. You need to be a cop. It's a calling for you, not a job. But maybe it's time to consider doing something else in the police. Something you can have more control over. Something more predictable. Get away from all this . . . death."

"But it's what I'm best at. Where I can do things no one else can."

"You've done your bit, Sean. You've given enough of your-self. No one is going to think less of you if you ask for a change."

Sean glanced at his watch and sighed. "Maybe you're right. I'll start asking around to see what's on offer, but it'll take a while. They won't let me go until they've found a replacement."

"I understand that," she said. "And I don't want you to rush into anything either. Just think about it. That's all I ask."

CHAPTER 22

None of it matters to me anymore. The police. My wife. My children. Staying here, in London. I always knew it would only be a matter of time before I had to move on, but it's not quite come to that yet. There's one more game to play.

My target has been selected. Nothing can save them now. It will happen exactly as I have pictured it. But don't feel sad for them; be sad I have not chosen you. Once my hand touches them, they'll be more in death than they had ever been in life.

The next will be the most difficult and therefore the best yet. It will be worth the risks. Besides, I've made allowances. The police are drinking from a mirage. I will let them fill their bellies with sand.

I wish I could reveal myself to you. Let you share my secrets. Unfortunately I cannot. For the moment, all I can give you is the gift of my nature.

I would like nothing better than to put my name to my work, but so few of you would be capable of understanding. You should sing my praises as a genius, but instead you would put me in a cage. How your psychiatrists and psychologists would like that. They could waste their time poking and prodding me. Would they tear up their textbooks when I tell them I had a happy childhood? That I never bit my classmates or tortured animals? Never killed the family cat and buried it in the woods?

I don't hear voices in my head. I won't claim God ordered me to kill. I'm not a disciple of Satan. I don't believe in either. I don't hate you. You are simply nothing to me.

I scored well in my exams. Took part in school plays. Played hockey and cricket for my county. Was the favorite brother to my sisters, son to my mother and father. I went to a famous university and obtained a degree in accountancy. I was admired by my peers and respected by my tutors. I had several girlfriends, some serious, some not. I got drunk on Fridays and felt sick most Saturdays. I took my washing home for my mother once a fortnight. I was popular.

None of it meant a thing.

I'm not sure how old I was when I first felt it. Maybe five, maybe younger. I constantly checked the mirror. How could I look the same when clearly I was so different? I was both scared and exhilarated. So young to be absolutely alone. So young to be freed from the mediocrity and pointlessness of a normal life.

Despite my age, I knew not to mention it to anyone. Not to talk to anyone about it. I had to bide my time. Fit in. Imitate those around me. I did very well in school, but was careful not to excel. Not to stand out.

The years passed painfully slowly. Still I resisted the temptation to explore my growing strength. I waited patiently. I didn't know when the time would come, only that it would.

As I grew older, I continued to gather the trinkets of normal life. A job. A wife. A house. Children. They were my sheep's clothing. My smiling mask. And all the while I was waiting.

Then, a few months ago, I awoke. I looked in the mirror and knew the moment had arrived. To everyone else I seemed the same, but not to myself. A new creation stared back upon itself. At last.

My first instinct was to slaughter my family, but I quickly realized I wasn't strong enough yet. I had only just been born. I was still covered in Nature's afterbirth. I still needed their protection. But with each visit I grow stronger and stronger. I become more complete, what I am meant to be: not a man, but a man above men. A different evolutionary strain of man. To you, almost a god.

CHAPTER 23

Friday

Sean had kept the briefing quick and simple. They would drive from Peckham to Hellier's house in Islington. Sean would arrest him. Sally would direct another search of the house. He knew the audience of bleary-eyed detectives wouldn't be able to absorb much information at 6 A.M.—most looked like they'd opted for one last drink instead of stocking up on the most precious commodity to a detective: sleep. If they felt tired now, it would be worse for them later.

Donnelly banged on the front door of Hellier's Georgian town house. The thick black paint shimmered like water with each knock. Sean and Sally were right behind him. The rest of the arrest team stood farther back. No one expected Hellier to fight.

James Hellier appeared in front of them. He was almost fully dressed and ready to leave for work. He looked good. Fit and strong. Immaculately groomed. He was casually threading a gold cuff link through his sleeve.

Sean stepped forward, and before he spoke he could smell

Hellier's expensive cologne. It seemed to take Hellier a second to recognize him. When he did, he began to smile.

Sean held his identification close to Hellier's face. He didn't back away.

"James Hellier. I'm Detective Inspector Sean Corrigan; these other officers are with me."

"Please, Inspector," Hellier cut in. "There's no need for introductions here. I think we all know each other."

Sean wanted to hit him. If Hellier didn't stop smiling, he thought he probably would. Instead he pushed him back into the house and spun him around to face the hallway wall. He could see Elizabeth Hellier coming down the stairs.

"Who is it, James?" she called out. "What's going on?" she asked, her panic growing.

"Nothing to worry about, darling," Hellier called up to her. "Just call Jonathon Templeman and tell him I've been arrested again." He turned to Sean. "I am being arrested, aren't I, Inspector?"

Sean pulled Hellier's arms behind his back and clipped a handcuff tightly round each of his wrists. "This time you're mine," Sean whispered into Hellier's ear. He stepped back and spoke so everyone could hear, especially Hellier's wife. "James Hellier, I'm arresting you for the murder of Linda Kotler."

Hellier was still smiling. "What?" He didn't attempt to hide his disdain. "This is pathetic. I've never heard of the woman."

"You do not have to say anything unless you wish to." Sean spoke over Hellier's protests. "But it may harm your defense if you do not mention when questioned something which you later rely on in court."

"Tell me, Inspector," Hellier was almost shouting, "are you going to arrest me for every crime you can't solve?"

"Anything you do say may be used as evidence," Sean continued.

Hellier craned his neck so he could see Sean over his right shoulder. "You're a damn fool. You've got nothing on me." His smiling face and sweet breath made Sean feel nauseous.

"Who are you?" Sean asked him. "What the fuck are you?"

Hellier's grin only broadened. He spat the words into Sean's face:

"Fuck you."

Sean peered through the peephole into Hellier's cell. The smug bastard was sitting bolt upright on his bed, as if in some kind of a trance. If only there were some way to find out what he was thinking. Sean moved away from the cell door and headed back to his office. He would interview Hellier when his solicitor arrived.

He sauntered into the inquiry office. The team sensed his mood. It transferred to them. Sean had the upper hand now.

"Any news from the lab, Stan?" Sean shouted across the office.

"Three days for a DNA match, guv," Stan called back. "Two, if we get lucky. They'll need our suspect's samples by midday if they're to have any chance of doing it that fast, but it'll only be an initial comparison, which won't give us a definitive match. A full comparison and definitive match will take a week. Minimum."

"Not good enough," Sean replied. "Call the lab back and tell them one in forty thousand isn't good enough. I need better odds than that and I need them by this time tomorrow at the latest."

The phone in Sean's office was ringing when he entered. He snatched it up. "DI Corrigan."

"Morning, sir. It's DC Kelsey, from SO11 telephone subscribers' checks. You left some coded numbers with me a while ago. I said I'd have a play with them."

"Go on."

"Well, I worked out the code," DC Kelsey said matter-of-factly. "It was relatively simple, but effective."

"Have you run the subscribers' checks too?"

"Yes. Some are overseas numbers, so we don't have them back yet. I'll e-mail what I have across to you. Be warned, there's a fair few to go through."

"Thanks. And good job," Sean said warmly. "Let me know when the overseas numbers come back."

"No problem."

"And thanks again."

Sally appeared at his office door. "Hellier's attorney's here," she announced. "They're in consultation."

"Good. When they're ready, you can help me interview." Sally made a show of checking her watch. "You need to be somewhere?" he asked.

"As a matter of fact, I have a lunch appointment today. I was hoping Dave could do the interview with you."

"Lunch appointment?" Sean sounded surprised.

"It's not what you think. I'm supposed to be meeting Hellier's boss, Sebastian Gibran. His idea. I can only assume he wants to discuss Hellier."

Sean studied her in silence for a while. "I'm not sure about this, Sally," he said. "These people look after their own. I doubt he wants to help us. Unless he has some other motivation for meeting you."

"Such as?"

"You know what I mean."

"I guess you never know your luck."

Again Sean studied her for a while. "Okay. Meet him. See what he has to say."

"There's something else too," Sally continued. "Remember the suspect Method Index turned up—Stefan Korsakov?"

Sean shrugged his shoulders. He thought that little problem had been dealt with. "Yes."

"I've been trying to put it to bed, but it hasn't been that easy."

"In what way?"

"His conviction prints should be at the Yard, only they're not."

"Borrowed?"

"The original investigating officer told me the prison holding Korsakov had requested the prints, only I checked with them and they didn't."

"So he's lying to you. Any idea why?"

"Not yet."

"Do you want to get Ethics and Standards involved?"

"Maybe," Sally answered. "But maybe we should start treating Korsakov as a viable suspect, until we know for sure he isn't?"

"Fine," Sean agreed. "But if he does start looking like a reality, you tell me straightaway. Don't go running off solo, trying to be Cagney without Lacey."

"I won't. I promise."

Sally turned on her heels and headed out of the office. "By the way," Sean called after her, "have a nice lunch."

Hellier and Templeman sat close together in the interview room that served as their private consultation room.

"I need to be out of this fucking dungeon by six at the latest," Hellier told him. "No excuses, Jonathon. You have to get me out."

"It's difficult to make that promise," Templeman answered nervously. "The police won't tell me much. Until I know what they've got, I can't be expected to judge our position."

"*Our* position?" Hellier asked. He put his hand on Templeman's thigh and squeezed hard. Templeman winced. "No matter what, you'll be walking out of here. It's me they want to nail to the wall. Keep that in mind."

Hellier released his grip and gently laid a hand on Templeman's shoulder. He knew the man was scared of him. "I know you'll do your best." He spoke softly. It only added to his menace.

Templeman swallowed his fear and spoke. "Before we can even think about bail, we have to prepare for the interview. If they've rearrested you, they must have something. If you know what that could be, you need to tell me now. They want to start the interview as soon as they can, but they're only telling me the minimum they're legally obliged to. You have to help me to help you. We don't want to walk into a trap. You should answer everything 'No comment.'"

Hellier could barely disguise his contempt. "Trap! You think they're clever enough to trap me? They've got nothing, and Corrigan knows it. He's trying to make me panic. Well, let him do his worst. You just keep your mouth shut and try to look professional. Let me do the talking and follow my lead. If Corrigan wants to play, fucking let him. Tell them we're ready to be interviewed."

Sean began the interview with the usual formalities, Hellier responding with a nod when asked if he understood the caution and his other legal rights. He nodded again when Sean repeated why he had been arrested for the suspected murder of Linda Kotler. His face was expressionless.

In an effort to gain credibility with Hellier, Templeman immediately went on the offensive: "I would like it recorded that it has been almost impossible for me to properly instruct my client, as the investigating officers have told me nothing about the allegation. Nothing about any evidence they may have that indicates my client could in any way be involved in this crime."

Sean had been expecting as much. "The allegation is one of suspected rape and murder. It occurred less than thirty-six hours ago. I'm sure your client will be able to answer my questions without being given prior knowledge." Sean waited for a protest. None came. "I'll keep the questions simple and direct." He and Hellier locked eyes across the table, then Sean launched into the interrogation: "Did you know Linda Kotler?"

"No," Hellier answered.

"Was that a no comment or a no?"

"That was a no. I don't know anyone by the name of Linda Kotler."

"Have you ever been to Minford Gardens in Shepherd's Bush?" Sean was trying to shut him in.

"I don't know. Maybe," Hellier answered.

"Maybe?"

"I've been to Shepherd's Bush, so maybe I've been there."

"Minford Gardens?" Sean repeated.

"Wherever."

"Have you ever been to number seventy-three Minford Gardens?"

"No."

"Sure?"

"Positive." Hellier sounded bored.

"Are you absolutely sure?" Sean had to be precise. Any ambiguity now would be exploited later by the defense. Hellier didn't answer. "I'll take that as confirmation. But you're lying. You have been there," Sean continued.

Hellier gave no reaction other than raising one eyebrow slightly. Sean noticed it.

"You met Linda Kotler. You met her the same night you killed her."

"Really, Inspector," Templeman jumped in. "If you have evidence to support your allegation that my client was involved, then why don't you just say so and tell us what it is. Otherwise this interview is over." Sean ignored him. Throughout the interruption he maintained eye contact with Hellier.

"Where were you the night before last?" Sean asked.

"You mean you don't know?" Hellier tormented him. "All those policemen following me and you have to ask me where I was. How galling that must be for you."

"No games." Sean was trying to keep the pace going. "Where were you?"

"That's my business," Hellier snapped.

Good. His calm was breaking.

"And now it's mine," said Sean. "Who were you with?"

"No comment."

The questions and answers came quickly. Templeman kept on the lookout for a break, a chance to object, but he knew neither Sean nor Hellier would listen to him. This was between the two of them. Personal.

"If you've got an alibi, you'd better give it now," Sean told him.

"I don't have to prove a damn thing," Hellier retorted.

"You weren't at home."

"Your point?"

"And you weren't at work."

"So?"

"So between seven P.M. and three A.M. the next morning, where were you? During the time Linda Kotler was murdered, where were you?" Sean's voice was rising.

Hellier fought back. "Where were you, Inspector? That's what people will really want to know. Would she be alive now if you'd done your job properly? You're desperate and it shows. You stink of fear. It's blinded you. What have you got? Nothing but theories.

"So you don't know where I was the night this woman was killed. That proves nothing." Hellier leaned back, satisfied.

"How long did you watch her for?" Sean suddenly asked. "For a week, like you did with Daniel Graydon, or was it longer?

Did you spend days and days fantasizing about killing her, the images in your mind growing ever more vivid, until you could no longer wait? You followed her home, didn't you, James? Then you watched her windows, waiting for the lights to go out. And when they did, you waited until you were certain she was asleep before you scrambled up the drainpipe and climbed through her bathroom window. Then you knocked her unconscious, tied her in your favorite bondage position, and raped and sodomized her. And when you were finished, you strangled her—didn't you?"

Hellier made as if to answer, but Sean held up his hand to stop him as the images in his mind revealed further details. "No, wait, I'm wrong—you didn't strangle her *after* you'd raped her. You killed her while you were still inside her, didn't you? That's how it had to be for you, wasn't it?"

Hellier's eyes raged inside his stony face, the muscles in his cheeks visibly flexing as he fought to keep control. Finally he spoke. "That's a nice little story you've cooked up, Inspector. But it proves nothing—nothing whatsoever."

"You're right." Sean sounded humble. "It doesn't prove a thing. But these will." He slid a copy of a form across the table. "Item number four," Sean said. "Item number four should be of particular interest to you."

Hellier scanned the list of items submitted to the forensics laboratory. He saw that item number four was two hairs. He shook his head as if he failed to realize their importance. "This concerns me how?"

"We need samples of your hair and blood, for DNA comparison," Sean informed him.

"You've already taken samples."

"I can't use those. This is a different case. I need fresh samples."

Hellier looked across at Templeman, who nodded confirmation that Sean was telling the truth.

"Fine," said Hellier. "Take your samples and get me out of here."

"I'm sorry," Sean said. "Get you out of here? No, that won't be possible. You're staying in custody until the DNA comparison's complete."

"Fuck you," Hellier exploded. He was standing now. "You can't keep me locked in this fucking cage." Templeman pulled him back into his seat.

Sean spoke for the benefit of the tape recorder. "Interview terminated at twelve twenty-three P.M." He clicked the machine off. "I'll arrange for someone to take your samples." Then he walked out of the interview room, leaving Donnelly to deal with Templeman's protests. He smiled as he closed the door behind him, listening to the raised voices fading in the background.

Featherstone sipped a coffee as he waited outside the custody suite. He knew Sean would head that way eventually. Much as he liked the guy, even believed in him, he was aware that, so far as the top brass were concerned, Sean had a tendency to sail way too close to the wind.

"Sean," Featherstone said, surprising him as he clattered through the door. "You got a minute?" He gestured toward an unoccupied room.

"Can this wait?"

"Best not. We won't be long."

Reluctantly, Sean followed Featherstone into the room.

"It seems some influential people are beginning to stick their noses into your investigation," Featherstone warned him. "Calls have been put in to the Yard and the brass are getting nervous. I'll keep the hounds at bay, but you'd better make sure you've got some evidence to back up any move you make."

"We found hairs at the latest scene," Sean told him. "We can get DNA off them. We match them to Hellier and then it's all over."

"That's a start," Featherstone said. "But we can't hold a suspect in custody while we wait for a DNA comparison. So what's the plan?"

"I need to keep him rattled. Keep him off balance. Let me keep him locked up for a few hours." Sean spoke quietly, suppressing his anger. "Then I'll bail him, once he's nice and wound up, not thinking straight. The surveillance team can pick him up the second he leaves the station."

Featherstone inhaled deeply. "Okay. We'll play it your way, but be careful with this one, Sean. Hellier has some very powerful friends."

"Thanks for the warning."

"One other thing," Featherstone said as Sean turned to leave. "What's this I hear about the victim in Shepherd's Bush saying she'd met you the night she was killed?"

"You heard?"

"There's not much I don't get to hear about."

"Hellier likes to play games."

"You need to be careful," Featherstone warned him again. "Be very careful. People are watching this case. People are watching you. My advice—make sure you can prove where you were and who you were with the night Linda Kotler was killed."

"You can't be serious?" Sean asked, incredulous. "You don't actually think . . . ?"

"Not me," Featherstone assured him. "But this investigation is turning out to be more complex than anyone expected. It's making the powers that be very nervous, Sean."

Sean felt a huge weight pressing down on him, as if Featherstone's words and inferred suspicion were slowly crushing the life out of him. "I'll bear that in mind," he said curtly, turning his back on the superintendent and walking out of the room.

He made his way along the corridor and into the communal toilet. After checking to make sure he was alone, he filled a sink with cold water and bent low over it, scooping up handfuls and burying his face in it before straightening to meet his own reflection staring back. His eyes were sunken with tiredness and dehydration, Featherstone's words still ringing around inside his head. He reached out for the reflection, but the image looking back at him kept distorting to someone else: to the disfigured image of Daniel Graydon, the horrified face of Heather Freeman, and finally Linda Kotler's face, contorted with agony and fear. He rubbed the mirror, smearing it with water then waiting for it to clear. When it did, it was his own face again, staring back and asking the question: could he have killed Linda Kotler? He swallowed drily, remembering the images he'd seen in his head at the murder scenes and other murder scenes in the past. Not for the first time he found himself asking another question: were these images from his projected imagination, or were they memories—memories of crimes he had committed?

"You were at home with Kate the night Linda Kotler died, and the same when Daniel Graydon was killed—you were at home." Desperately he tried to remember where he'd been the evening Heather Freeman was killed, but he couldn't. He felt the panic seeping through his very soul. "You were with your wife," he hissed into the mirror, but he couldn't chase away the doubt, the possibility he was no different from half the inmates of Broadmoor. Could it be that his home life was a fantasy, his wife a figment of his imagination, his entire family nothing more than a mirage—a projection of what he wanted most but could never have?

"No," he banged the mirror with the underside of his fist. "For Christ's sake, get a grip. You're tired, that's all. You solved those other murders. The people who did them are locked up for life because of you." He took a deep breath. "Hellier killed these people. I'm real. My life is real. It's real."

Suddenly the door was thrown open by a uniformed officer desperate for the toilet. He stalled for a second at the sight of Sean standing in front of the mirror, face dripping wet, hands gripping the basin. With a brief nod at Sean, he disappeared into a cubicle. When the door closed behind him, Sean quickly dried his hands on a bunch of paper towels and made for the exit.

Sally entered Che shortly after 1 P.M. and immediately spotted Gibran seated at a table, sipping a glass of amber-colored wine. He stood when he saw her. A waiter pulled a chair out for her as Gibran indicated for her to sit with a wave of his hand and a smile.

"DS Jones. I'm very grateful you were able to see me."

"Please," she said. "Call me Sally."

"Sally, of course. And you must call me Sebastian—deal?"

"Deal," Sally agreed.

"Can I get you a drink? Or is that against the rules? I wouldn't want to get you in trouble." He gave Sally a boyish grin, full of mischief. She already felt relaxed in his company.

"Why not? Whatever you're having will be fine."

Gibran nodded once at the nearby waiter, who scuttled away immediately. "The venison here is excellent," he informed her, "but a little fussy for my taste. You'll find I'm a simple man with simple tastes, except when it comes to people, of course."

It seemed to Sally that he was trying to impress her with his modesty and down-to-earth attitude, despite his obvious wealth and influence. She was duly impressed, but she wasn't about to let it show. Not yet.

"So, what is it I can do for you, Sebastian?"

"Straight to the point." He stalled while the waiter served Sally's wine. "I hope you like it. Dominico here tells me it's a very fine Sancerre and as I am nowhere near as well informed in these matters, I'm completely in his hands." Gibran waited for the wine waiter to leave before speaking again. "You must tell me if the wine's any good, then I'll know whether Dominico's been ripping me off the last few years."

She took a sip and smiled at him, holding his gaze for a little too long. She concentrated on sounding businesslike. "It's very nice, thank you. Now, why am I here?"

"I wish I could say it was purely for pleasure, but I'm guessing you've already assumed that's not the case."

"I'm a detective. I try not to make assumptions."

"Of course. Sorry," Gibran said with natural charm. "We're here because we have a mutual interest in a certain party."

"James Hellier?"

"Yes," he confirmed, his expression suddenly serious, the flirtatious, boyish personality evaporating in an instant.

"Mr. Gibran—Sebastian. If you're here to try and somehow influence my opinion of Hellier's involvement in this case, then I should warn you—"

"That's not my intention," Gibran insisted, tapping his glass while speaking. "I wouldn't insult your intelligence. I thought you should know my feelings on the subject, that's all."

"Your feelings on the subject would only be of interest to me if they were somehow relevant to our investigation. So, are they?"

"To be honest, I'm not sure if it's relevant or not. I just thought someone connected to the investigation should know, which is why I called you."

"Why didn't you contact DI Corrigan?"

"I get the feeling he's not my biggest fan."

"Well, I'm here," Sally said with an air of resignation. "So what is it you think I should know about?"

"How can I put this?" Gibran began. "When James first came to us, he was a model employee. He served the firm above and beyond all expectations for several years." He paused. "However..."

"However what?" Sally encouraged.

"I'm sorry." Gibran shook his head. "It's not in my nature to talk out of school. I would imagine it's the same in your job, rule number one being to look out for each other."

"Well, you haven't broken any rules yet, because so far you haven't told me anything."

"And under normal circumstances I wouldn't tell you." Gibran's blue eyes drilled deeply into Sally's, showing her a flash of his true power and status. She found him no less attractive for it. "It's just that, lately, well, I've found his behavior to be somewhat... erratic. Unpredictable. Troubling, even. Half the time I don't know where he is, or who he's with. He's missed several high-profile meetings the last few weeks, all of which is out of character." Gibran appeared genuinely concerned.

"When did you first become aware of this change in personality?" Sally asked.

"I suppose it started a couple of months ago. And now this latest episode, the police raiding our office, dragging James away like a common criminal. Not exactly the image we're hoping to portray at Butler and Mason."

"No. I don't suppose it is."

Gibran leaned across the table, and spoke quietly. "Do you really believe he killed that man? Is James capable of such a thing?"

"What do you think?" Sally asked.

Gibran leaned away again before replying. "I'm not sure, to be honest. Not now. My head's spinning a little at the moment.

I'm coming under some fairly intense pressure from above to resolve this situation."

"Has something happened to make you feel that way?"

Gibran sipped his wine before answering. "The other day, I went to James's office to speak to him, to see what I could find out."

"I hope you haven't been playing amateur detective," Sally warned him. "That could cause us procedural difficulties, especially if you've questioned him at all."

"No," Gibran replied hastily. "Nothing like that. But you should understand that I am responsible for a great many things at Butler and Mason and a great many employees. I am, if you like, Butler and Mason's own internal police force. I will do whatever I have to do to protect the firm and the people within it. If James is putting either at risk, then . . ." Gibran let his statement linger.

"You do what you have to do. But make sure you don't cross over into our criminal investigation. That would leave us both in a compromised position."

"I understand," Gibran assured her. "You've made yourself clear. I have no wish to fall out with the police, especially you."

"Good," Sally said, ending the debate. "So what did Hellier have to say for himself during this little chat you and he had?"

"Nothing specific. He seemed very distracted."

"Not surprising," Sally said dismissively.

"Indeed. But it was more a feeling I had," Gibran explained. "I've known James for several years and this was the first time I've ever felt . . . well, uncomfortable in his presence, even a little intimidated."

"Go on."

"I almost felt as if for the first time I was meeting the real James Hellier, and that the person I'd known up till now didn't really exist.

"Tell me, Sally," Gibran asked, his tone suddenly light-hearted, "are you familiar with the work of Friedrich Nietzsche?"

"I can't say that I am," Sally admitted.

"Not many people are." Gibran dismissed Sally's lack of knowledge before it could make her uncomfortable. "He was a philosopher who believed in men being ruled over by a select group of benevolent supermen. Nonsense, of course. I was talking to James about it, trying to relax him, make him feel less like he was being interviewed, but I almost felt as if James believed in it. I mean, *really* believed it. He started talking about living his life beyond good and evil, as Nietzsche had decreed. Normally I would have dismissed it, but given all that's happened, suddenly it sounded . . . sinister."

"Is that it?"

"Like I said," Gibran replied, leaning back into his comfortable chair, "it was just a feeling."

"Well," Sally said after a long pause. "If you find or feel anything else, you know how to get hold of me."

"Of course." Gibran looked around him uncomfortably. "You take someone under your wing. You trust them, think you know them. Then all this happens." He sipped his wine. "He's not the man I used to know. He may seem the same, but he's different. To answer your original question: do I think James could be involved in killing those people? The truth is, I simply don't know anymore. The fact that I can't dismiss it out of hand is bad enough, I dread to think . . ."

"One way or another, we'll all know the answer soon enough."

"Excuse me?" he asked.

"Nothing," she said quickly, recovering herself. "Nothing at all."

"Good," he declared. "Now that's out of the way, we can enjoy our lunch. I do hope you don't have to run off anywhere. It'll make a change to have a civilized lunch with someone who isn't boring me out of my mind with their latest get-rich-quick idea."

"No," she said. "I'm due a break. Besides, I don't think I could stand the sight of another sandwich."

"Then here's to you," he said, raising his glass slightly. "Here's to us."

Sally returned the toast with a cautious smile. "To us."

"It must be difficult," said Gibran, suddenly cryptic.

"What must?"

"Learning how to use all that power you have without abusing it. I mean, I meet a lot of people who truly believe they're powerful, but power through money and influence has its limits. Being a police officer, to have the power to literally take someone's human rights away from them, to take their freedom from them—now that's real power."

"We don't remove people's human rights; we can only temporarily remove their civil rights," Sally explained.

"All the same," Gibran continued, "it must be very difficult."

"Maybe, at first. But you get used to it, and before long you don't even think about it."

"I'm guessing it can make relationships with men very difficult. So many are intimidated by powerful women. We like to think the power is always with us, so to be involved with a cop would be, I guess, challenging."

"And are you?" Sally asked. "Intimidated?"

"No," Gibran answered, his face as serious as Sally had ever seen him. "But then again, I'm not like most men."

Sally looked at him for as long as she could without speaking, trying to read his thoughts. Gibran broke the silence.

"One thing that's always fascinated me," he continued, "is how people who seem to have been born to kill somehow find each other, as if they can recognize their own kind when they meet them: Hindley and Brady, Venables and Thompson, Fred and Rosemary West, and God knows how many others. How do they find each other?"

"I wouldn't know," Sally answered. "That's my boss's field of expertise. He's a bit more instinctive than most."

"DI Corrigan? Interesting," Gibran said. "When you say he's instinctive, what do you mean?"

"Just that he seems to know things. He sees things that no one else can see." Sally suddenly felt uncomfortable discussing Sean with an outsider, as if she was somehow betraying him. Gibran sensed her mood.

"An interesting man, your DI Corrigan. Do you think perhaps it's his dark side that makes him so good?"

Sally was impressed. It struck her that many of the same qualities she saw in Sean were present in Gibran. She decided that if Sean could ever get beyond his preconceived ideas of Gibran, he would probably like him.

"DI Corrigan's a lot of things, but I've never seen anything you would call a dark side. It's more a question of him being willing and able to search for answers in those dark places the rest of us are too afraid to go, in case we see something about ourselves we don't like."

Gibran nodded his understanding and approval. "It's because he's prepared to accept his responsibilities," he said. "And it sounds as if we have more in common than either of us understood. Perhaps when this is all over and he sees me for what I am and not what he thinks I am, we'll have a chance to speak on friendly terms."

"Don't hold your breath," Sally warned him.

"No," Gibran answered, "I don't suppose I will." Again they took a moment to look at each other silently before Gibran spoke again. "But there's one thing I must make clear to you—I cannot and will not let anything or anybody put the reputation of Butler and Mason at risk. Of course, I respect the fact that your police investigation must take priority, but other than that I will do what must be done to finish this matter with James one way or another, for better or for worse for him."

Sally glanced away for a second as if considering his words. Then she looked him in the eye. "I understand," she said. "You do that. Provided you tell us everything we need to know about Hellier, you have my word we won't interfere in any internal decisions your company makes about him. But tread carefully, Sebastian, for both our sakes."

Hellier glanced at his watch. Almost 5:30 P.M. The police had been deliberately slow in bailing him. DI Corrigan had been conspicuous by his absence. No matter. He had enough time. Just.

He wore the clean clothes that Templeman had arranged. The police had seized the ones he'd been wearing and once again they'd emptied the wardrobe and drawers back at his house. They didn't have much to take this time around. He was still in the process of refilling them after the first raid when they'd seized every item of clothing he possessed. Corrigan was costing him a fortune.

There was no time to go home first. Never mind. He had done well to plan in advance. He had a change of clothes, his phone, and the weapon waiting for him. Not that he was expecting a fight. He was the master of gaining instant control. Years of practice ensured that his strength was seldom matched. He feared nothing and nobody, but the gun was nice insurance all the same.

He stood on the front steps of the Peckham police station. He'd already exchanged farewells with Templeman, who had no idea how final Hellier had meant it to be. One more thing to take care of and then he would be gone. He didn't anticipate needing Templeman's services again.

He scanned up and down the street. They were back. Did Corrigan never learn his lesson? Fine. If they wanted him to make fools of them again, he was happy to oblige. He looked for a black cab. This was Peckham. There were none. Realizing that he stood out far more than he wanted to, he began walking toward what passed for the center of this southeast London suburb.

Hellier entered the first mini-cab office he came across. A group of elderly, cheerful West Indian men sat around smoking and laughing loudly at some joke Hellier had just missed. One of the men spoke. He spoke slowly and thoughtfully, curbing his accent enough for Hellier to understand.

"Yes, sir. What can I be doing for you today?" he asked.

"I need to get to London Bridge."

"No problem, sir. I'll take you myself," the cabbie replied. Seconds later the car pulled away, and as it did so, six other cars and four motorbikes began to move with it. The driver was unaware he had become the focus of so much police attention, but Hellier knew they were there. Occasionally he stole a glance in the near-side mirror. He spotted one of the motorbikes, nothing else; but he didn't have to see them to know they were there.

"Lovely day," Hellier said to the driver.

"Yeah, man," the driver beamed. "Just like being back in Jamaica." They both laughed.

Sean was back at his desk, weighing up the options. So far he'd come up with a dozen what-ifs, but none of them helped the investigation. None of them helped him. He'd had no choice but to let Hellier walk away on police bail. Taking a deep breath, he reminded himself to be patient. When the DNA results came back, he could bury Hellier. He was certain of it.

He rubbed his tired eyes with the sides of both fists. For a second he couldn't see properly. When they cleared, he found himself focused on his computer screen, reminding him he needed to check his e-mail. It was the first chance he'd had to check his in-box. Among the dozens of e-mails there was one from SO11. The details of the telephone numbers from Hellier's address book. He wasn't in the mood to start plowing through names and numbers; his quota of patience had been used up hours ago. He peered out into the main office, looking for anyone he could delegate it to, but everyone appeared busy. His conscience got the better of him and he started to read through the list himself.

Most appeared to be the numbers of banks, both in the UK and abroad. Other numbers were of accountants, diamond dealers, gold merchants, platinum traders. Hundreds of names, but only a handful of personal numbers. He paid particular attention to these. He read through the names slowly and deliberately. Daniel Graydon's number was there, as he'd expected: both his home and mobile numbers. So what? It meant nothing, now that Hellier admitted knowing him. He checked for the names of the two other victims, Heather Freeman and Linda Kotler. He didn't expect to find the runaway's name, but perhaps Kotler's. It wasn't there. He was disappointed, but not surprised.

The mini-cab dropped Hellier off on the outside concourse at London Bridge. He was delighted to see thousands joining the great commute home and even considered waving along the street at the police following him. He couldn't see them, but he knew they would be able to see him. A little wave would get them thinking, but he resisted the temptation—this was no time to show off. Soon he'd be gone, but first he had some business to take care of. Top of the list being his mysterious friend.

He'd considered leaving, not even bothering to meet the man, but he wasn't a gambler. He only played when he could manage the risks, and that meant finding out what this man knew, if anything. Could he damage him? Hurt him? Hellier had to find out. No loose ends, he reminded himself. Leave things nice and tidy, just how he liked it. That didn't mean there wasn't time for one last thrill. One last indulgence.

Hellier walked fast into the train station, ducking into WH-Smith, watching the main entrance through the magazine shelf, waiting for the surveillance team to enter. They were good, only one standing out as she scanned the crowds for him. Commuters never looked around. They were on autopilot. She stood out like an amateur, but the others were invisible.

He took the other exit from the shop and walked back across the inside concourse and out the same exit he'd entered, all the while trying to remember the faces he passed. If he saw them again, he would assume they were police. He crossed the short distance to the underground station, stopping suddenly at the top of the stairs and spinning around. No one reacted. A smile spread across his lips. They were very good indeed.

Once again he descended into the underground that had served him so well in the past. He followed his normal anti-surveillance pattern, tactics designed to lose even the best: traveling short distances on trains and then stepping off at the last moment, walking swiftly through tunnels, past zombified commuters, onto another train and away again. Over and over he repeated the procedure, but they stayed with him, leaving him both annoyed and impressed. No matter. As always, James Hellier was one step ahead.

Finally he arrived in Farringdon and made his way to the bar he had chosen the day before. It was busy enough but not heaving. Ideal. He headed straight to the toilet unnoticed. The cubicle he wanted was unoccupied. Two customers stood at the urinals, not noticing him as he shut the door. He didn't have time to wait for them to leave—in fact, it was better they were there. Soon the police would be here, inside the bar looking for him. He began to undress.

Sean's mobile vibrated on the desk in front of him. He kept reading the e-mail as he answered absentmindedly. "Hello."

"Guv. It's Jean Colville." Sean recognized the surveillance team's DS. "Your man certainly knows his countersurveillance tactics."

"I noticed," said Sean ironically. "Where are you?"

"Farringdon. Trying to keep up with your target. He's in a bar in Farringdon Road. He gave us the right runaround, but we're still on him. Bit thin on the ground, but the others are doing their best to catch up."

"Is the bar covered?" Sean asked, concerned.

"Just. I've got one unit around the back—there's only one exit there. Three in the bar and two more out the front. Apparently your man's in the toilet. There's no other way out of there other than the door leading to the bar. So as long as he stays in there, we're solid."

"Good." Sean breathed easier. "Don't give this one an inch. If you can't see what he's doing, assume he's doing something we'd rather he wasn't."

"Understood. I'll call you if the situation changes."

"It'll change," Sean warned her. "Just be ready when it does." He hung up.

"Problem?" Donnelly asked, appearing at Sean's open door.

"Not yet," Sean replied. "They've followed Hellier to Farringdon."

"Well, so long as they don't lose him this time. By the way, you should know Jonnie Dempsey has turned up. Handed himself in at Walworth. The locals are holding him for us. Apparently he's telling them that he'd been helping himself to a portion of the night's takings from his till on a regular basis. He thought the management was onto him, so he took off. When he heard the place was crawling with Old Bill, he decided to lay low. But eventually he realized things were getting a bit too serious to ignore and thought it best to hand himself in."

"Scratch one suspect," Sean said.

He saw Sally enter the main office. He hadn't spoken with her since that morning. He caught her eye and beckoned her over. "How did your meeting with Gibran go?" he asked.

Sally took a seat without being invited. "It was interesting enough. He certainly didn't give me any reason to suspect Hellier less. Said he'd been acting out of character lately, missing appointments and so on, and that he felt he was only now seeing the real James Hellier. That the other Hellier, before this all started happening, was the fake. He also said Hellier had been rambling on about living his life beyond good and evil."

"Nietzsche." Sean spoke involuntary.

"Pardon?" Donnelly asked.

"Nothing," said Sean. "It's not important. Anything else?" he asked Sally.

"Not really," she replied. "He was probably just trying to find out what we knew."

"So long as he paid for lunch," Donnelly said.

"As a matter of fact, he did," Sally told him. "Which is more than you've ever done," she added.

"Harsh, but fair," said Donnelly.

"What did you do with the rest of the afternoon?" Sean asked, not meaning to sound as though he was checking on her.

"Lunch took longer than I'd expected." She blushed, recalling her time with Gibran and how she'd been in no rush to end their meeting. "After that I chased down some inquiries at the

Public Records Office, but they didn't have my results yet. I hear Hellier's been bailed."

"We can't hold him until the DNA results are confirmed," Sean explained. "Takes too long."

"And if the DNA isn't Hellier's?" she asked.

"Then I'll be in the shit," Sean said bluntly. "So don't be standing too close."

Hellier had been in the toilet for less than a minute. He could hear people coming and going outside the cubicle. He moved quickly now. Unconcerned about noise. He stood in only his underpants and socks.

He lifted the lid of the toilet cistern and placed it on the toilet seat. He pulled the plastic bag from the cistern and untied it. Carefully, he undid the parcel and laid out the gun and spare magazine. He checked his watch. Six forty-five. Fifteen minutes to spare. He clicked the battery back into the mobile phone. He would turn it on once he'd left the bar.

He dressed in the tracksuit, T-shirt, and trainers. He stuffed the gun in the back of his waistband and tied the trouser cord tight. He put the phone in one of the top's pockets and the spare magazine in the other.

Finally he unwrapped the remaining cloth. He twisted the lid off the tube of theatrical glue and rubbed a little on the back of the fake mustache. He stuck it above his lip, using touch to ensure it was placed perfectly. Next he did the same with the matching eyebrows. The wig he donned last. He didn't need a mirror to know his appearance had been transformed. He smiled to himself.

He neatly folded his discarded clothes and placed them along with his shoes into the plastic bag. He replaced it in the cistern. He might need it later. You could never tell. He delicately replaced the cistern's lid. One last deep breath to compose himself and he left the cubicle. He caught a glimpse of himself in the mirror as he left. He smiled. He walked out of the toilet and then he walked out of the bar.

DS Colville checked her watch. Ten minutes had passed and still the only updates she was hearing on her team's covert body-set radios were "No change." Sean's words rang loudly in her head. She spoke into the radio.

"I don't like this. Tango Four, check inside the toilet."

Her radio made a double-click sound. The officer code named Tango Four had received and understood her transmission. She waited for an update. Two minutes passed. They seemed like two hours. Her radio hissed into life.

"Control. Control. Tango Four."

"Go. Go," she instructed.

"We have a problem, Control."

DS Colville gritted her teeth. "Expand, over."

"Target One isn't in the toilet, over."

"Does any unit have eyeball on Target One?" she called into her radio. Silence was her only answer. "Look for him, people. Does anyone have eyeball on Target One?" Silence.

She turned to the detective driving their unmarked car. "I don't believe this," she muttered. "Okay. Target is a loss. Repeat, target is a loss. All units bomb burst. Foot units search the bar. Everyone else swamp the surrounding area. Find him."

Throwing the radio onto the dashboard in disgust, she reached for her mobile phone. She searched the phone's menu for Sean's number.

Sean listened as DS Colville told him what he most dreaded hearing. Hellier was on the loose once more. "How?" he said into the phone.

"We don't know," DS Colville replied. "We had him cornered in the toilet one minute, then he disappears. No one sees him leave. We didn't miss anything. He just disappeared. We'll keep searching the area until we pick him up."

"Save yourselves the bother," Sean said wearily. "You won't find him until he wants to be found. Cover his house and office. Call me when he turns up." He hung up.

"Please tell me that wasn't what I think it was?" Sally said.

"I wish I could."

"How?" Sally asked.

"It doesn't matter how."

"What now?" Donnelly asked.

"We keep our heads," Sean told them. "Hope he resurfaces. In the meantime, contact Special Branch and get a photograph of Hellier to them. Make sure they circulate it to all ports of exit, planes, trains, everywhere."

"You think he'll try and skip the country?" Sally asked.

"DNA evidence is difficult to argue against. Hellier knows that. Perhaps he's decided he has no choice but to run."

"Is that his style, to run?" Sally didn't look convinced.

"He's a survivor," said Sean. "He'll do whatever it takes to survive. If that means running, then he'll run."

Hellier sat on a bench in Regent's Park waiting for the friend to call. He had said he would call at seven. It was now almost half past.

What was this damn game? Hellier had no friends. No real friends. Most likely it was a journalist, trying to set him up. He stared at the phone in the palm of his hand, willing it to ring. He had to know who the friend was. His overpowering need to control everything meant he simply had to know. Once he knew, once he decided whether they were a threat or not, he would deal with them accordingly. After that, home. The children he would leave alone, but his wife, she would be his parting gift to DI Corrigan.

The police would be watching his home though. He would have to be careful. He would let his wife take the children to school in the morning. He would fake illness. When she returned, he would be waiting for her. After he'd finished with her, he'd spend the rest of the day running the police around town. He would lead them a merry song and dance for hours. They could never stay with him for that long. Not him. He knew their tactics too well. And once he was certain he had lost them, he would disappear.

By the time they became suspicious and broke into his house, it would be too late. He would be thirty thousand feet above their heads. A false passport was already waiting for him in a Hampstead fine china shop. Once he collected the tickets, he would catch a train to Birmingham. His flight for Rome left at 8 P.M. After a two-hour wait at the Rome airport he would board a connecting flight to Singapore. Two flights later he would arrive in his new home.

His phone began to vibrate. He answered it calmly. "James Hellier."

"It's me," said the friend's voice. "Sorry I'm late."

"I don't like being kept waiting." Hellier wanted to dominate. "This is your last chance to impress me."

"Oh. You'll be impressed. I can guarantee that." Hellier sensed a change in the friend's voice. He thought he could detect an arrogance that hadn't been there previously. There was a hint of danger too. He didn't like it.

"I'm going to ask you a question," Hellier responded, determined to take charge, show his strength. "You will answer yes or no. You have three seconds exactly to answer. If you answer no or fail to answer in the time allowed, I will hang up and we will never contact each other again. Understood?"

"I understand." The voice didn't argue. Hellier had expected he would.

"Will you meet me?" Hellier asked. "Tonight?"

"Yes," the friend answered on the count of two. "As long as you promise you'll do one thing."

"I don't make promises to people I don't know," Hellier answered.

"Stay away from other people until we meet," the voice asked regardless. "No bars or restaurants, and don't go home or to your office. The police will be waiting there. Stay alone. Stay hidden."

Now Hellier understood. In that second it had become all too clear to him. It all made sense. His eyes opened wide as he realized who he was speaking with. Who else could it be?

"Fine," he said. "I'll do as you say until we meet."

"I will call you, later tonight, and let you know when and where. Agreed?"

"Agreed." Hellier hung up.

What did his friend expect? That he would hide in a bush in the park, like a frightened, wounded animal? Not him. This was London, one of his favorite playgrounds. And he had so little time left to play.

No. He had better things to do than cower and wait.

"I know who you are, my friend." He spoke to himself. "And when we meet, you'll tell me a thing or two. Then I'll feed you your own testicles, before I gut you like a pig."

CHAPTER 24

Sean arrived home late, again. He'd hoped Kate would be in bed, but as he quietly opened the front door he could sense her presence. He followed the glow coming from the kitchen and found her tapping at her laptop, hair tied back, heavy glasses adorning her fine-boned face. "You're up late" was all he could think of to say.

"You're not the only one who has to work late. I work too, remember?" This was not how Sean wanted the conversation to begin. He'd had enough conflict for one day. "I need to get this plan for restructuring the A and E department finished or I might not be part of the new structure myself." Again Sean didn't answer. "You're not really interested, are you?"

"Sorry?" Sean asked over his shoulder.

"Never mind," she snapped, shaking her head with disapproval. "We've been invited to dinner at Joe and Tim's next weekend, so make sure you book the night off, all right?"

"Err . . . ," escaped from Sean's lips.

"Well, I'm overwhelmed by your enthusiasm at the thought of spending an evening with me," Kate said sarcastically.

"It's not you," Sean tried to assure her.

"I thought you liked Tim, and there'll be other people there too," Kate encouraged.

"I don't know Tim. I've met him, but I don't know him."

"Come on, Sean," Kate appealed. "Just book the time off."

"It's not that easy, is it?"

"Why?" Kate asked. "Can't you bear being away from your police friends even for one night?"

"They're not my friends," Sean answered too quickly.

"Whatever, Sean, but you know and I know that you can't stand to be with 'nonpolice' people"—Kate simulated quotation marks with her fingers—"because you're all so fucking important that the rest of us mere mortals might as well not exist. True?"

Sean waited a long time before answering. "Don't swear. I don't like it when you swear."

"Well, stop giving me so fucking much to swear about." Sean turned his back. "Come on, Sean," Kate softened. "I don't sell insurance for a living, I'm a doctor in Guy's A and E. Whatever awful things you've seen, I've seen them too, but I manage to lower myself to speak to people who live normal lives—so why can't you?"

"Because they're . . ." Sean managed to stop himself answering truthfully, but it was too late.

"Because they're what?" Kate pursued him. "Because they're boring, because they bore you?"

"Jesus, Kate," he protested. "Give it a rest, will you?"

"So you're never going to speak to anyone again who isn't a cop?"

"That's ridiculous."

"No, it's not. It's the truth."

Sean grabbed a bottle of bourbon from one of the kitchen cupboards, a glass from another, and poured himself a generous measure. He took a sip before speaking again. "Christ, you know what it's like. As soon as people find out what I do, all they want to talk to me about is the job, fishing for the gory details. They haven't got a bloody clue. If they did, they wouldn't ask."

"Maybe it's us who haven't got a clue, Sean," Kate said quietly. "Maybe we're the ones who've got it all wrong, wasting our lives knee deep in life's crap."

"Why, because we know the truth? Because we know life isn't really a shiny advert?" Sean argued. "I'd rather be awake and live in isolation than be like all those mugs out there, walking around without a fucking clue."

Kate breathed in deeply and cleared her head. She'd dealt with this before and knew she'd have to deal with it again. "Is this about your childhood or about being a detective?"

"Oh, come on, Kate. Let's not get into that, not now," Sean answered.

"Okay," Kate agreed. "But if you ever need to talk about it, I'm here."

"I'm tired, that's all. I'm fine," Sean insisted. "I'm just very tired."

"Of course you're tired," Kate agreed. "You haven't slept more than three hours a night since this new one started. Look, I'm going to bed. Why don't you come with me?"

"I need a minute or two to unwind," Sean told her. "I'll be there soon."

"Come now," Kate pleaded. "I'll rub your shoulders while you fall asleep."

"I'll be there in a few minutes—promise," he lied. The thought of tossing and turning, fighting the ever-present demons was unbearable.

"Don't be long," she said, turning from him.

He watched her move from the kitchen table and glide toward the stairs, once looking over her shoulder to smile at him, the harsh words of seconds ago forgotten, at least by her. Once she was out of sight, Sean reached for the bottle of bourbon and poured another generous measure.

Sally parked her car close to her flat. Sean had sent them all home. They might as well get a few hours of sleep before Hellier turned up again, if he ever did. She searched for her front door keys, buried deep in the bottom of her handbag. Breaking one of her own rules—never stand at the front door fumbling for house keys.

"For God's sake," she grumbled, losing her grip on her handbag and spilling the contents onto the ground. She stared at the disaster. "Fucking great."

Sally knelt down and began to collect the debris. At least she'd found her keys. Something made her spin around. Still kneeling, she surveyed the area around her. Suddenly she couldn't remember what had startled her. She gave a nervous laugh and gathered the rest of her belongings.

She stood and looked along the street. It was almost unnaturally quiet. The way only city streets could be in the night. Somewhere streets away a dog barked. The sound somehow made her feel better. She unlocked the communal front door, entered, and closed it behind her. She pressed the light timer switch in the hallway, giving her thirty seconds of light before the darkness returned.

Hurriedly she climbed the stairs to her first-floor flat, again fumbling for her keys and cursing herself. Why was she nervous? Slow down. Put the key in the lock and turn it. The door opened. She almost fell into the flat. She hadn't realized she'd been leaning on the door so hard. Closing the door behind her, she threw the bolts across the bottom and top.

She disliked the harsher overhead lights, choosing instead to walk across the dark room she knew so well to the lamp in the far corner. She reached for the lamp switch, but something touched her hand. Material. Silk or nylon. She didn't understand. She recoiled as if she'd touched a spider's web, but curiosity overcame her fear. She moved her hand through the darkness to the lamp. Again, the material. She pushed her hand through it, finding the switch and turning the lamp on. Light shone through the red silk neck scarf that was now draped over it. It had been a present to herself for Christmas. The room glowed red. This wasn't right. A cool breeze brushed against her face. It came from the kitchen. That shouldn't be. The window shouldn't be open.

She felt him behind her. Close enough to hear him breathing. She almost fainted. Then she almost vomited. He was waiting for her to make her move. Like a snake lying within striking distance, but she was frozen. Fear controlled her.

Finally she forced her body to move, turning toward him, inching herself around, desperately trying to recall her self-defense training. Aim a knee for his groin. God help her if she missed. A knee in the groin and then run.

She forced herself to speak. "Please." Her voice was almost inaudible. "Please. You know what I am. Leave now and this won't go any further. I promise." She was face-to-face with him. She almost fainted again. He stood above her. He was only about five foot ten, but he looked like a giant.

He wore a dark tracksuit and rubber gloves. A tight-knit woolen hat covered his hair. She could see that every muscle in his body was tense, his arms rigid by his sides. The red lighting made his teeth shine like rubies.

Sally studied his face. It was distorted by the light and his contorted muscles, but she could see him clearly. He was letting her see his face. She knew who he was. Knew he wasn't going to let her live. She was going to die and nobody else in the world knew. She had so many things she wanted to do, wanted to say to people, but now she was going to die.

He moved so quickly she hardly saw him. She had no time to react. A hand gripped around her neck, slowly crushing her throat. He was so strong. Was this how he would do it? Crush her throat. The other hand flashed a blade in front of her face. She thought she recognized it from her own kitchen. He pulled her so close she could see the fine wrinkles in his skin.

"Make a sound, you die. Struggle, you die. Do as I say and you live."

It was a lie. She wasn't like the others. Clinging to the hope that he could be telling the truth, they'd have done anything for the chance to live. But she had seen his face. She knew he would never let her live. She nodded her head anyway.

"Do you know how lucky you are to have been chosen?" He spoke slowly through clenched teeth. He held the knife to her throat and released his grip.

"I'll do as you say. I promise," she pleaded.

He smiled and licked his lips. She felt the knife drop away from her throat slightly. Only a few millimeters. It would have to be enough.

Without warning she smashed her right fist as hard as she could into the underside of his jaw. The knife flashed across her throat, but she'd already leaned back. It slashed through the air. She brought her knee up into his groin. He began to bend double. She sprang for her front door. She would live.

The top of her head suddenly burned with pain. Her run jarred to a stop as her legs fell from under her. He gripped her by the hair, twisting it around his fist as he pulled her back. She could feel the tears stinging the backs of her eyes. She had to scream.

She filled her lungs as he spun her in his grip to face him.

She saw him make a quick move, his free arm jabbed toward her. The air in her lungs deserted her, yet she hadn't screamed. She hadn't been able to.

It felt like a punch, like having the wind knocked out of her. Nothing more than a dull ache in her chest. Her head was forcefully bent forward. He wanted her to see the knife buried to the hilt in the right side of her chest. He tugged the knife free. It didn't come easily. Her chest muscles had gripped the foreign body, trying to stem the breach. She wheezed horribly. She could physically feel the air from her lung rushing out through the wound.

He pulled her closer. "Fucking bitch. Slut, bitch. It wasn't supposed to be like this. This is not as I saw it. This is not how it was supposed to be."

Pushing her away, he held her at arm's length. Another flash of his hand. She felt the same dull pain, but something else too. The knife had hit a rib. He pulled to free it, but it wouldn't move. It was jammed in her rib.

The pain and shock were too much. She fell unconscious. The only thing stopping her falling to the floor was his grip on her hair and the knife wedged in her chest. Finally he let her slip to the floor. He placed a foot on the left side of her chest and pulled on the knife. It wouldn't move.

"Fucking pig whore," he hissed. He wanted to spit on her, but wouldn't risk leaving his DNA in the saliva at the scene.

He stood over her, watching the crimson spreading across her white blouse. Her breathing was shallow, but she was alive. Suddenly he was hypnotized by her. He cocked his head to one side like a bird of prey watching its kill, writhing, trapped under its talons.

But it was spoiled. This was not how he had foreseen it. No matter. He calmed himself. He would finish her quickly and leave. All great men suffered frustration, he reassured himself. He would learn from his mistakes.

He pulled at the knife protruding from her chest. Still it wouldn't move. She was all but finished, but he wouldn't take the chance and leave her like this. He peered through the living room to the kitchen. His mind tried to recall what other knives he had seen in the drawer when he had selected the one now embedded in Sally's chest. Most had felt blunt. He recalled running a finger carefully along their cutting edges, blunt. She hadn't taken care of them. So be it. He would cut her throat with a blunt knife. It would take longer. It wouldn't be clean and neat. She had only herself to blame.

He studied her once more. Air leaking from her chest puncture made the blood around the entry wound bubble and hiss. It reminded him of when he was a boy, fixing punctures on his bicycle. Should he drag her to the kitchen, keep her close? No. Quicker to leave her there.

Decision made, he turned and strode to the kitchen. Despite the disappointment, he still felt magnificent. Powerful. Untouchable. Like a god. He knew which drawer to open. The knives weren't organized. He shifted the knives around with a gloved hand, ignoring the large carving ones. Trying to find something with a four-inch blade. Smooth or serrated edge, it didn't matter, but it had to be rigid. Thick and strong from hilt to tip. A chopping knife would be best. He'd already used the best one, but he found a substitute. A black-handled vegetable knife. He held the knife up to his face, slightly above his eye line. It would do.

He turned back toward the living room, expecting to see Sally's head and upper body lying on the floor, the rest of her obscured by the sofa. Instead he saw her open the front door and stagger into the communal hallway. Somehow she had gotten to her feet. He saw the blood smear around the top door bolt. He had underestimated her strength. Her will to live. To survive. It had been a mistake.

Should he flee? He glanced over his shoulder at the open window in the kitchen. He looked back at Sally. Could he reach her before she started pounding on the neighbor's front door? Would she reach their door? It was less than ten feet away, but it would feel like a marathon to her. He willed her to collapse.

He couldn't let this happen. She had seen him. His grip tightened around the knife. He watched her stagger sideways, but remain on her feet. He began to walk toward her, long confident steps propelling him forward.

She fell, crashing into her neighbor's door, and banged her fist twice, as hard as she could, on the door. Still he strode toward her, cutting through the dim red light that now spilled into the hallway. She had to die. She could destroy him. He couldn't allow that to happen.

It was past 11 P.M. when George Fuller, inside flat 4, heard something crash into his front door. The surprise made him jump and spill some of his beer. The cold drops fell onto his wife's face as she slept in his lap on the sofa. He had been watching a bad sci-fi film. She woke with a moan.

"George," Susie Fuller complained, "you've spilled beer on me."

He was annoyed his wife had been woken. Now she would want to watch the other channel. "It'll be that bloody woman from across the hall again." He was already up and heading toward the front door. He was a big man. His two favorite places were the gym and the pub. The results were intimidating. "She must be a prostitute or something, the hours she keeps."

He was only steps away from the front door when he heard

the two thumps. They came from lower down on the door. As if someone was sitting on the other side. Someone in trouble maybe? Someone drunk? Drunk, he decided.

"George," he heard his wife inquiring. "Who is it? What's going on?"

"Stay there," he told her. She could hear the anger in his voice. He reached the door and yanked it open. His chest was full, ready to power a verbal onslaught at whoever he found. The door opened wide in one sweep. Sally's still body slumped heavily onto the floor, at his feet. He could see she was bleeding, but didn't see the knife.

He sensed danger. Five years as an officer in the Parachute Regiment had honed his instincts. He didn't think. Didn't hesitate. He bent over fast and grabbed Sally's arm. He began to drag her back into his flat. A movement caught his eye. Something in Sally's flat opposite. He looked up into the dim red light. Something moving fast. Too fast. Was that a man? The dark shape slithered through the small kitchen window and was gone.

He snapped himself back into action, dragging Sally into his flat and slamming the door shut. He bent to examine her then turned his attention to the front door. He secured every lock he could see. His wife appeared in the hallway.

"George?" she asked. The worry was loud in her tone.

"Call the police," he shouted, loudly enough to make Susie hug herself. "And get a fucking ambulance." He was back in Afghanistan, shouting orders at teenage soldiers.

His wife was staring at Sally, lying on her floor. She started to cry with fear. "What's happening, George? What was it?"

George looked at his own bloody hands. "I don't know. I don't know." His voice grew calmer. "I saw something out there. A dog, or a fucking big cat or something. It escaped through her window."

He examined Sally more closely. His battlefield medical trauma training came back to him as he rolled her onto her side and checked for the wounds. He saw the knife, making him recoil. It had been a man he saw.

"Jesus Christ," he whispered quietly. "Get me some tape and plastic bags." He was shouting again. "Come on. Come on," he spoke to Sally. "Hold on, girl. Help's on the way. Just a little longer. Just a little longer."

The mobile rang loudly. Kate woke first. Sean slept deeply, sedated by alcohol. He'd hit the bourbon pretty hard after Kate had left him. It was the only way he could chase their argument and Hellier from his mind long enough to get to sleep. She turned the bedside lamp on and looked at her husband sleeping. She wished she could leave him be, but a phone call at 2 A.M. would have to be important. She shook him as gently as she could while still waking him.

"Sean." She spoke softly. She wanted to wake him, not the children. "Sean."

He moaned and rolled over to look at her, his eyes vacant, wandering between the real and dream worlds. He didn't hear the phone yet.

"Your phone," Kate whispered.

"What time is it?" he asked.

"About two. And keep your voice down."

Sean moaned again then grabbed the phone. "Hello."

"Sorry to call at this hour." He didn't recognize the voice. "I'm Inspector Deiry, the night duty inspector for Chelsea and Fulham. I'm trying to trace a Detective Inspector Sean Corrigan."

"You've found him," Sean said. His head thumped mercilessly. The nausea spread from his stomach to his throat. He remembered why he rarely drank more than a glass or two of beer.

"I'm sorry to be the one to have to tell you this . . ." The inspector sounded grim. "Do you work with a DS Sally Jones?"

Sean's mouth was as dry as his heart was frantic. He managed to answer. "Yes. She's on my team. What's happened to her?"

"She was attacked, earlier tonight. In her flat. She's very badly hurt."

The blood rushed from his head, then just as quickly flooded back. He'd never felt so cold. "But she's alive?"

"Yes."

"Jesus Christ," Sean said. "Where is she?"

"Charing Cross Hospital. She's still in surgery."

Sean checked his watch. "I'll be there in less than an hour."

He hung up and swung his legs over the side of the bed, staggering a little as he stood. Kate noticed it.

"What's happened?" she asked.

"Sally's been attacked. In her own flat. She sounds bad. I've got to get to Charing Cross Hospital."

"Oh my God. Who would want to hurt Sally?" Sean looked at her without speaking. "Not the man you're after?" Kate asked. "You told me they never came after police."

"This one's different."

"Different how?"

"In every way imaginable," Sean said. "I've got to go."

"Get a shower," she insisted. "Then I'll drive you."

"No. I'm fine."

Kate was already out of bed. "I'm phoning Kirsty. She can watch the kids till morning."

"Don't bother," he argued. "I can drive myself."

She grabbed the sides of his face in her hands and locked eyes with him. "The last thing Sally needs is for you to drive under a bus drunk. I'll drive you. After you've had a shower to sort yourself out."

Sean knew she would have her way. He headed for the

shower, reeling under the effects of the shock. He had to call Donnelly. The team needed to know what had happened. Any one of them could be next.

By the time Kate had driven them to Charing Cross Hospital, the last effects of the alcohol had almost faded. Kate and he met the uniformed inspector in the Casualty Department waiting room. He was with a female uniformed sergeant. Sean introduced himself to the inspector. He didn't introduce Kate and the inspector didn't introduce the sergeant.

"Where is she?" Sean sounded harsh. "Can I see her?"

"No. She's still in surgery," the inspector told him. "It'll be a few hours before anyone can see her."

"What happened to her?"

"She hasn't spoken since the neighbor found her. All we know is she was attacked in her own flat. And she has two very serious stab wounds to her chest, both on the right side. It's a life-threatening situation, but she's holding on."

"Who's the neighbor?"

The sergeant referred to her notebook: "George Fuller. Ex-paratrooper captain. Now works for the local council. Found her at about eleven, slumped in the communal area against his door. Two chest wounds. The knife was still in her." She glanced up from her notes in time to see Sean wince. "Mr. Fuller was a medic in his army days. He used cellophane tape and plastic shopping bags to seal the wounds and keep her chest cavity airtight. The admitting casualty doctor said he had undoubtedly saved her life."

"Where is he now?" Sean wanted to see the man who had saved Sally.

"He went home," the inspector answered. "He insisted on coming with DS Jones in the ambulance, but I sent him home a little while ago."

"What's happened to her flat?" Sean asked.

"Nothing," said the inspector. "We've sealed it off for the time being."

"Good. Post a guard on the flat. No one is allowed in without my say-so."

The inspector looked quizzical. "I'm sorry, but this is a local matter. Our CID will be in charge of the investigation. The scene's secure. There's no need to guard it."

"Wrong." Sean was feeling angry and tired. He didn't want his instructions to be questioned. "I'm the officer in charge of this investigation. Any problems with that, phone Detective Superintendent Featherstone, Serious Crime Group South." He gambled the inspector wouldn't. Not at this hour. "I'll liaise with your CID and put them in the picture."

Sean could see the inspector needed more. "This attack is linked to a series of murders I'm investigating. DS Jones was part of that inquiry team. Whoever committed those murders is the same man who attacked her. So get me the guard on the flat," Sean demanded. "What security have you put in place here?"

"I've posted a uniformed officer to stay with her," the inspector explained.

"I want at least two officers watching her," Sean insisted.

"I'll do what I can." The inspector looked shaken.

Sean spied Donnelly thundering along the corridor. He charged up to them.

"That bastard's dead" were his first words. "I'll tell you that for nothing. He's going straight out the fifth-floor window. Aye, I fucking promise you that." His Scots accent had suddenly grown stronger.

Sean held a hand up and was on the verge of telling him to calm down when he was distracted by his mobile ringing.

"Sean Corrigan."

"It's DS Colville, sir. Sorry about the time, but I thought you'd want to know, Hellier's just arrived home."

Sean and Donnelly approached Hellier's house. The local night-duty CID had arrived to assist them. That made four of them in total. They met in the street, fifty meters short of the house. They swapped names and shook hands.

"Is this it?" Sean asked. He had hoped the local station, Islington, would have provided more assistance.

"We've already got a couple of uniform lads hiding round the back," one of the DCs informed him.

Donnelly looked at Sean. "Your call, boss. We could wait for backup. We could have a firearms team within an hour."

Sean would have preferred to take Hellier by himself, have some time alone with him. Clearly Hellier didn't have the guts to come after him or Donnelly, so he went for Sally. Well, now they'd come after him.

"Let's do it," Sean said. "No more waiting."

The younger Islington detective opened the boot of their car and pulled out a heavy metal battering ram. It was known as an Enforcer. "We brought this," he announced. "Just in case."

"Shame to waste it," Sean said grimly. "Listen, he may not look like much, but he's killed at least three people already. And now he's gone after one of ours. Don't drop your guard."

They all nodded their understanding and walked silently but rapidly toward the house. Carefully they opened the black wrought-iron gate and moved to the front door. There were three stone steps. The older detective spoke to the officers at the rear of the house on the radio, his voice just above a whisper.

"Units at the rear. Units at the rear. We're going in through the front."

The radio crackled but they all heard the reply. "Understood and standing by, over."

The young detective holding the Enforcer nodded to Sean. Sean counted him down with his fingers. Three. Two. One. The detective smashed the Enforcer into the center door lock. It exploded, but the door held. It had top and bottom dead bolts. He stood and hit the top lock hard. The door began to flap open. He crouched and took out the final lock. The door imploded.

They poured in through the door holding extendible metal truncheons and screaming, *"Police! Police! Police!"*

Sean and Donnelly ran to the staircase. The Islington detectives ran through the ground floor. As Sean neared the top of the stairs, Hellier appeared. Sean saw him just in time. He partially avoided the kick aimed at his head. It stung his cheekbone as it made impact. He slumped against the staircase wall for a second, shaking off the effects of the kick, but was after Hellier before Donnelly could overtake him.

Hellier climbed the next flight of stairs and disappeared. Sean followed, but slowed as he approached the top. He wouldn't be caught again. He warned Donnelly to slow down. From below came the sound of the Islington detectives beginning to climb the steps.

Sean moved on to the second-floor landing. Hellier was there somewhere. He found the light switch on the wall and flicked it on. There were five rooms.

Someone appeared at the door closest to him. Instinctively he almost lashed out, but realized in time it was Hellier's wife. He leaned forward and grabbed her, dragging her to the floor where he pinned her before she could speak.

"Stay there and don't move," he shouted. She was too scared to move or argue. Too scared to speak.

He moved carefully along the landing, his back pressed

against the wall. Donnelly and the other detectives followed. The element of surprise was lost. Now they needed stealth.

He flicked the light on in the room Hellier's wife had come from, pushing the door wide open so that he could peer inside before entering. A glance over his shoulder told him Donnelly was close. The Islington detectives had begun to search the rooms across the landing. They moved cautiously.

He slipped into the room, back to the wall. Donnelly followed. Sean dropped into a push-up position and checked under the bed. Nothing. He moved across to the closet, stretching to grasp the handle without exposing himself to a full-frontal attack. He yanked the doors open. Clothes still wrapped in plastic dry-cleaning bags swooshed into the room. Nothing.

He'd had enough. His heart needed a rest. He nodded for Donnelly to check behind the curtains. Donnelly did so. Nothing. He nodded toward the door and led the way out. They moved to the next room.

A child's voice called from the landing below. It sounded stressed. The mother looked at him, appealing. He put his finger to his lips. The last thing he wanted was a crying child walking into the middle of this.

The distraction had been enough. Hellier seized the opportunity. Sean felt an incredible pressure close around his right wrist. He tried to hold on to the telescopic truncheon, but the grip forced his fingers open. His weapon fell to the floor. He was pulled into the room and spun around by one powerful jolt. He felt his right arm twist up his back. Cold metal pressed into his throat. Some instinct told him not to move. Told him he was teetering on the edge of a cliff.

He felt Hellier's bristles rub against his ear. He could smell his sweet breath. It made him want to vomit, to pull away. Hellier pressed the blade harder into his throat.

"Ah, ah, Inspector." He recognized Hellier's voice.

Someone flicked the light on in the room. It was Donnelly, who froze when he saw them. Hellier smiled. Donnelly regathered himself. "Put the knife down, man."

It sounded like a request, not a demand. Hellier gave a shallow laugh. He turned his face to Sean, but kept his eyes on Donnelly. His tongue curled from his mouth. Slowly, deliberately, he licked the side of Sean's face, his body quivering with the thrill of tasting Sean's fear. He gripped the earlobe in his teeth and closed his eyes in ecstasy. He released his grip and stopped smiling. He looked deadly serious. He whispered in Sean's ear.

"Remember who let you live."

Hellier threw the knife on the floor and stepped away, placing his hands behind his head. Sean spun around and caught him full in the mouth with a left hook. His amateur boxing days made the move effortless.

Hellier fell backward into a dressing cabinet. He fell hard. Framed pictures smashed under his weight. The mirror shattered. He rolled onto the floor, landing on all fours, and looked at Sean, smiling through bloody teeth. Sean stared back, only he didn't see Hellier's face, he saw his father's. His torturer's.

Sean delivered a powerful kick to the rib cage that lifted Hellier off the floor. He landed on his back, but still he smiled. Sean knelt next to him and began to pile punches into Hellier's face. He didn't know how many he landed before Donnelly pulled him off, or that he had been screaming *Bastard!* as each punch found its target. Nor had he realized he'd broken a bone in his right hand and that his knuckles had been sliced open on Hellier's teeth.

It took him a while to come back to the world. When he did, he shrugged himself loose from Donnelly's hold and stared at the bloody mess that was Hellier's face. Hellier was lying on his back, only partly conscious, spitting blood from his mouth. His nose was broken.

The two Islington detectives ran into the room. They saw Hellier lying in his own blood. The knife on the floor. Sean breathing like a madman. His hands bloody and swollen. They didn't ask questions.

CHAPTER 25

Saturday, 10 A.M., and news had spread of the night's events. The office buzzed. Hellier had come after one of them.

Sean pressed an ice pack wrapped in an old T-shirt to the swelling Hellier's kick had left on the side of his face. The other hand was badly swollen. His little and ring fingers were taped together, as were his index and middle fingers. He refused to go to a hospital and have it put in a cast. The police surgeon had done her best. He used the broken hand to press the phone to his ear. The hospital updated him on Sally's condition.

She had survived her operation, the first of several. Still in Intensive Care. She hadn't regained consciousness. Drugs would ensure she didn't. For the time being at least.

A familiar silhouette appeared at his door. Featherstone had come to see and be seen. He entered Sean's office without ceremony.

"You look like shit." He sounded unconcerned.

"Thanks," Sean replied.

Featherstone's expression turned serious. "How is she?"

"Too early to say. She's in Intensive Care."

"Well, if there's anything I can do . . ." He let the offer hang. Sean said nothing. "And you—should you be at work?"

"I'm fine."

"If you want someone to steer the ship for a couple of hours while you get some rest, let me know."

"I'll be fine," Sean repeated.

"Of course you will." He paused before continuing. "Do we have enough evidence to charge Hellier?"

"I have a team searching Sally's flat and another going over Hellier's."

"What about his office?" Featherstone asked.

"No need." Sean was blunt. "Surveillance confirms he didn't return to his office. We're concentrating on his house and Sally's."

They were interrupted by Donnelly banging on the door. "Lab's on the phone, guv'nor." Sean could tell Donnelly was excited, an excitement that leaped across the office and into Sean's chest. His heart rate accelerated, becoming irregular. "They've got a match to the hairs found in Linda Kotler's flat." Donnelly paused, enjoying the drama. "They're Hellier's."

Sean slumped back into his chair. Featherstone slapped his thighs and smiled. It was over. Sean had his critical evidence. The few seconds of pulse-racing excitement were replaced by an overwhelming relief. Finally it was over. He'd been proved right. Hellier was finished.

A female detective appeared in the doorway: "Someone on the phone for DS Jones, guv."

"Transfer them to my phone," he instructed. She nodded and left. He waited for the ringing and answered. "DI Corrigan speaking. I'm afraid DS Jones isn't available. Is there something I can help you with?"

"This is the Public Records Office at Richmond calling," the male voice explained. "DS Jones had me run a couple of inquiries. I have the results for her."

"I'll take them," said Sean. He grabbed a pen. "I'll see DS Jones gets them."

"She wanted birth and death certificates for two individuals: a Stefan Korsakov and a James Hellier." Sean felt his heart miss a beat. "I have a birth certificate for Korsakov, but no death certificate, so if he's still in the country, he's alive."

"And Hellier?" Sean asked.

"Both birth and death certificates for him. Poor little chap never got past his first birthday."

"Excuse me?"

"He died in childhood." The possibilities rushed into Sean's mind.

"What year was Korsakov born?"

"Nineteen sixty-seven," came the answer.

"When did Hellier die?"

"Interesting," the clerk said. "Also nineteen sixty-seven."

It had to be. Somehow Sean knew it. It had to be. "Thank you," he managed to say. "I'll have someone collect them." He hung up and turned to Donnelly. "Remember the suspect Sally was working on?"

"The one from Method Index?" Donnelly asked.

"Yes, Stefan Korsakov. Do you know where she kept the inquiry file?"

"In her desk, I presume."

Sean moved quickly across the office to Sally's desk. Donnelly followed, intrigued. Sean tugged at the locked drawers. "Have you got a skeleton key for these damn things?" Most good detective sergeants did, although they would rarely admit it. Donnelly didn't look too happy about it, but produced the key anyway. Sean hurriedly unlocked the top drawer. A brown file with the name "Korsakov" written across the front lay inside. He flicked it open and began to read.

"Do you want to tell me what's going on?" Donnelly asked.

"Did Sally discuss this inquiry with you?"

"Not really."

"Anything at all?" Sean persisted.

"Only thing she told me was that someone was lying to her."

"When did she tell you that?"

"I think it was Thursday."

Sean continued to search through the file, forward and backward, almost oblivious to Donnelly's presence. Finally he looked up. "Bastard has been getting help."

"Sorry?"

"Sally told me his fingerprints had gone missing from the Yard. His photograph from his intelligence file. She told you she was being lied to—but by whom?"

"Guv'nor," Donnelly kept his voice down, "what are you talking about?"

"Don't you understand?" Sean asked unfairly. "Hellier is Korsakov, the man Sally identified through Method Index as being a possible suspect for our murder. Stefan Korsakov is Hellier, but everything she needed to make that connection disappeared. In spite of that, she was getting closer, closer to finding out the truth, even if she didn't know it herself."

"Wait a minute," Donnelly pleaded. "Hellier is Stefan Korsakov?"

"I'd bet my fucking life on it," Sean answered. "When Korsakov got out of prison, he needed to reinvent himself or he was finished in this country. He'd have to take his money and run. That's not his style. All it took was a new identity and someone in the police to make his past as good as disappear. The new identity is easy enough. He goes to a graveyard and picks someone who was born in the same year he was, but who died in childhood, the younger the better. Less history."

"And he gets a bent copper to make his photos and fingerprints disappear," Donnelly finished for him. "That's why Hellier attacked Sally, because she was getting too close to finding out his secret."

"Hellier wouldn't be the only one who would want to stop Sally. Whoever was helping him had as much to lose as Hellier."

"Our bent police friend," Donnelly surmised.

"It has to be a possibility," Sean admitted.

"Then perhaps the attack on Sally isn't connected to the other attacks?"

"It is," Sean assured him. "They're all connected somehow. We just need to complete the circle of events. Once we do that, we'll know how this all fits in."

"Where do we start?"

"We find this bent copper."

"How?"

Sean scanned the file. He found what he was looking for: the name of the original officer in the case. Detective Sergeant Paul Jarratt. "I know that name."

"Come again?" Donnelly asked.

"Paul Jarratt, the original investigating officer, I know that name."

"Maybe you used to work with him?"

"No," Sean muttered. "Something recent. Something I've seen."

Sean studied the man who opened the door of the neat Surbiton home. He and Donnelly showed their identification and introduced themselves. Jarratt seemed nervous, but composed.

"I believe you know a colleague of mine," Sean said. "DS Sally Jones?"

"Yes," Jarratt answered. "She called around here a couple of times, asking about an old case of mine."

"I know," Sean told him. "Unfortunately I have some bad news concerning DS Jones."

"Bad news?"

"I'm afraid she was attacked and seriously injured last night. She's stable, but critical. I thought as you'd been helping her you should know."

"Yes," Jarratt stuttered. "Thank you. Thank you for thinking of me. Can I ask how it happened?"

"You can," Donnelly said, nodding his head toward the inside.

"Yes, of course," Jarratt answered. "Please, come in." He led them to the kitchen and sat. Sean and Donnelly remained standing.

"I don't know a lot of details," Sean explained. "We know she was attacked with a knife in her own flat and received two serious injuries. She managed to escape and make it to her neighbor's. She's lucky to be alive."

"My God," Jarratt said. "Who would attack a copper in her own home?"

"Maybe you can help us with that?" Sean asked. Jarratt's jaw dropped slightly. Sean noticed it.

"Of course," Jarratt answered. "I'll help in any way I can, only I'm not sure how."

"DS Jones was trying to trace a suspect—Stefan Korsakov, a man you'd had dealings with some years ago."

"Yes."

"Only she was having trouble locating his fingerprints."

"Yes, I remember her mentioning it."

"Her inquiries led her to discover that you had requested the fingerprints be removed from Fingerprint Branch. Apparently Wandsworth Prison needed them to make copies for their records."

"Yes, I told DS Jones all this."

"And you're positive the prison requested them?" Sean asked.

"Yes. My colleague at the time, Graham Wright, collected the prints for me and returned them. Perhaps he could help you."

"Do you know a man called James Hellier?" Sean asked without warning.

Jarratt was silent for a while. He appeared to be struggling to recall the name. "No, I don't think I know anyone by that name."

"You're sure?"

"It's not a name that means anything to me," Jarratt answered.

Sean pulled an envelope from his jacket pocket. "Will you do me a favor?" he asked. "Take a look at these photographs. Tell me if you recognize the man in them." Sean emptied the surveillance photographs of Hellier onto the table in front of Jarratt.

Jarratt leaned forward and shuffled the photographs around, apparently uninterested. "No," he said. "I don't recognize this man. I've already told DS Jones I don't know this man, when she showed me a photograph of the same man when she first came to see me."

"Are you sure?" Sean asked. "Are you absolutely sure the man in these photographs isn't Stefan Korsakov?"

"Stefan Korsakov?" Jarratt asked, disbelief in his voice. "This isn't Stefan Korsakov."

"If not Korsakov, then what about James Hellier? Is the man in this photograph James Hellier?" Sean persisted.

"I don't know anyone called James Hellier, so I wouldn't know if this was or wasn't him," Jarratt answered, the increasing anxiety in his voice palpable.

Sean said nothing, instead tossing a piece of paper in front of Jarratt. "What's this?" Jarratt asked.

"Take a look," Sean told him.

Jarratt lifted it from the table and began to read through the list of names and telephone numbers on the printout of the e-mail from SO11. "I don't understand," he said, shaking his head.

"What's the matter?" Sean asked. "Don't you recognize your own name, your own telephone number?" He leaned over Jarratt and stabbed his finger into the printout. "Right there: Jarratt, Paul. And here: your address and your number."

"What is this?" Jarratt asked.

"This is a list of telephone numbers taken from a notebook belonging to one James Hellier, who is currently under investigation for murder. What is your telephone number doing in his notebook, Mr. Jarratt?"

"I have no idea," Jarratt pleaded. "So he has my telephone number, what does that mean? There could be any number of reasons why he has my number."

Sean fell silent. He sat next to Jarratt. "If it was only the telephone number in his book, I might believe you," he said. "But you've already hung yourself. You see, I found out that DS Jones checked with the prison and they told her they never requested Korsakov's prints. You lied." Jarratt didn't respond. "And then there are these," Sean continued, tapping the photographs of Hellier. "On our way to see you, we called in on an old colleague of yours, DS Graham Wright, and I showed him these very same photographs. And you know what he told me, without any hesitation whatsoever? He told me that the man in these photographs is Stefan Korsakov. The same Stefan Korsakov who now goes by the name of James Hellier. But you already know that, don't you, Mr. Jarratt?"

"I . . . I . . ." Jarratt struggled, trapped.

"It's over," said Sean. "You were a detective once. You know when the show is over. It's time to save yourself. Talk to us. Did Hellier attack Sally? You warned him she was digging around his past and he got worried she was getting too close, so he tried to stop her the only way he could—by killing her."

"No," Jarratt insisted. "He didn't attack her."

"So you admit to knowing him?" Donnelly asked.

"Yes . . . I mean no."

"What's that supposed to mean?" Donnelly demanded.

"All right, for Christ's sake. Yes, I've been in contact with him," Jarratt admitted. "But I've got nothing to do with DS Jones being attacked."

"But you made Korsakov's photographs and fingerprints disappear, yes?" Sean asked.

Jarratt's body slumped. "If I talk, you'll look after me, agreed? You guarantee me no prison time and I'll talk."

"I can't make that sort of promise, but I'll do what I can. Now talk."

"Shortly before Korsakov was due to be released from prison I decided to visit him."

"Why?" Sean asked.

"Because we'd never recovered the money from his frauds. Millions of pounds outstanding."

"And you fancied helping yourself to an early retirement present, eh?" Donnelly accused.

"No," Jarratt claimed. "It wasn't like that. Or at least, not at first. It's often worth visiting people shortly ahead of their release to remind them that you're watching them. Make it clear to them that as soon as they start spending their ill-gotten gains you'll be there to seize everything they have." Sean was aware of the practice. "Sometimes you can cut a deal, get them to surrender most of the money, in return for allowing them to keep a proportion as a reward for playing the game. All very unofficial, but everybody wins. We get to show moneys recovered, the victims get some compensation, and the thief gets a little sweetener.

"But that's not the way Korsakov wanted to play it. He wasn't about to hand over a penny. However, he could see the point in making sure the police weren't on his back."

"Go on," Sean encouraged.

"He offered me a cut. All I had to do was make a few things disappear."

"Like fingerprints and photographs?"

Jarratt shrugged.

"How much did he pay you?" Donnelly asked.

"Initially, ten thousand, with further installments to follow, but . . ." He paused. "The next time we meet, he shows me photographs. Some were of the two of us together, with me counting the cash."

"He set you up?" said Donnelly.

"Yes, but there was more. He had other photographs—of my kids, for God's sake, at school, in the park, in my own garden."

"He threatened them?" Sean questioned.

"He didn't have to," Jarratt replied. "I knew what he was capable of. I wasn't going to spend the rest of my life watching over my shoulder, waiting for the inevitable."

"As soon as he did that, you should have stopped it, cut your losses and stopped it," said Sean.

"And end up in prison? Old Bill don't have it good inside. I decided to bide my time and hope that eventually Korsakov would move on and forget about me. Then all of a sudden your DS comes sniffing around, asking all the wrong questions. As if that wasn't bad enough, Korsakov contacts me, asks me to get you off his back. It was like a nightmare coming true."

"You warned him about DS Jones?" Sean accused. "Let him know she was asking about Korsakov?"

"No," said Jarratt. "Why would I do that? If I'd told him, he would have asked me to do something about it. Things were bad enough without me making matters worse."

"Are you saying Hellier didn't know Sally was looking for Korsakov?" Sean asked.

"He had no idea, as far as I know. He was convinced I'd all but made his past disappear. I thought the same, until your DS came to see me and I realized I'd missed something. His file held at Method Index. I didn't even know his details had been sent to them. Graham must have decided Korsakov would be of interest to them and sent them the details of his crime, but he never told me he had, so I never knew, until now."

"He did," said Sean. "I guessed you couldn't have known about it, otherwise it wouldn't still exist. So I asked Wright and he confirmed he was the one who sent the file to Method Index."

"And the fingerprints?" Donnelly asked. "How did you make them disappear?"

Jarratt smiled for the first time since they'd met him. "Korsakov's idea. I had Graham pull the prints for me, but we knew Fingerprints would want them back, so Korsakov had me destroy his real prints and replace them with another set, all correctly filled out on the proper forms, everything kosher. Only we used a novelty ink Korsakov bought at a joke shop. Within two days the ink disappears and you're left with a blank piece of paper, or in this case a blank fingerprint form. When Graham returned them, they looked fine and no doubt got filed. Then they simply faded away to nothing. Korsakov thought it was hysterical."

Sean and Donnelly stared at each other in disbelief.

"You are joking?" Donnelly asked.

"You know Korsakov?" Jarratt asked. "Or I suppose I should say Hellier. He's as intelligent as he is vicious. Imaginative and dangerous, but he didn't attack DS Jones and I doubt he killed the other people you think he did."

"Why?" Sean asked.

"Because he would have told me."

"Why would he want to do that?"

"To remind me of what I had become. To remind me that I belonged to him."

Sean and Donnelly looked at each other in silence. Finally Sean spoke.

"Mr. Jarratt, it's time you met a friend of mine." A short, stocky figure dressed in a scruffy dark suit walked into the kitchen. "This is Detective Inspector Reger, Professional Standards and Ethics, or as you may remember it, Complaints Investigation."

Reger casually showed Jarratt his identification. "Paul Jarratt, you're under arrest for theft and assisting an offender. Get what you need—you're coming with me."

The two tape cassettes in the recorder turned simultaneously. Hellier had said nothing. He sat silently. Face badly bruised, his broken nose taped open to let him breathe. He refused to confirm his name. Let Templeman do the talking until he felt it necessary to speak himself. First he would wait and see if the police were wasting his time again.

DC Fiona Cahill sat at Sean's side. He wanted to have a woman police officer in the interview, so he could see how Hellier reacted to the allegation that he'd attacked Sally. If his eyes darted to DC Cahill, it would be a good indication he felt some guilt. Could Hellier ever feel guilt?

Sean was looking forward to this interview. Until now, he'd been at a disadvantage, but the discovery that Hellier was Korsakov had tipped the balance in his favor. He completed the preinterview procedure, eager to get under way.

"Mr. Hellier, James, it's time for you to talk to us," Sean began. "It's over." Hellier said nothing. "It will go much better for you if you talk to us," Sean continued. "Help me understand why you did these things."

Nothing.

"Why did you kill Daniel Graydon?" Sean asked. "Why did you kill Heather Freeman? Why did you kill Linda Kotler? Why did you try to kill Detective Sergeant Sally Jones?"

Sean knew he had to keep going. He knew Hellier wouldn't be able to remain silent much longer. His ego wouldn't allow it.

"What did these people mean to you?" he persisted. "Did you know them? Had they done something to make you angry? Did they deserve to die?"

"You know nothing," Hellier snapped.

"Why did you kill these people?" Sean demanded, his voice raised now.

Hellier regained his stoicism. "No comment."

"She's still alive, you know. DS Jones is alive—and she's tough. She'll pull through. She'll confirm it was you who attacked her."

"Really," Hellier said.

"Yes. Really."

"Ha," Hellier said, laughing. "You're a damn fool."

"You're just damned," Sean countered.

"Probably." Hellier seemed pleased at the prospect. "But right now I'm just bored."

"Maybe I can get your interest? At your last interview, you gave us samples of blood and hair. Remember?"

"No comment."

"You can answer that question," Templeman advised. Hellier turned his head slowly to him. He stared at him, eyes slit.

"No comment."

"For the benefit of the tape," Sean explained, "Mr. Hellier was arrested yesterday on suspicion of having raped and murdered Linda Kotler. On that occasion he provided samples of hair and blood for forensic comparison to hair samples found in Linda Kotler's flat. Does that refresh your memory?" Hellier feigned disinterest. "Those samples have since been analyzed at our forensic laboratory. It has been confirmed that the samples taken from the scene are a DNA match to samples provided by you."

At this, Hellier focused on Sean, eyes narrowed, head turned slightly to one side. Sean noted the reaction.

"It's over," he said. "No more games. You can't argue with DNA evidence. Like I said, it would be better for you if you start talking."

Hellier said nothing. Sean spoke almost sympathetically: "Tell us about the things you've done," he encouraged. "I want to hear about the . . . *exceptional* things you've done."

"No comment."

"What was the point in doing the things you did if you don't tell the world?" Sean tried to appeal to his ego.

"You and I both know you're lying, Inspector. You couldn't have matched my DNA to this woman because I've never set eyes on her."

Hellier's response surprised Sean. He hadn't expected that. Hadn't expected such a definitive denial. He'd assumed Hellier would try and talk his way around the DNA evidence, as he had with Daniel Graydon. In spite of everything, the man was capable of knocking him back, souring what should have been his moment of triumph. No matter, the DNA evidence alone would hang Hellier.

Hellier studied Sean. His eyes twitched with the concentration.

"You think I'm lying?" Sean asked. "Mr. Templeman will confirm I'm not allowed to lie about evidence. Only suspects are allowed to lie."

"I think we're at the stage where you should be specific about the DNA evidence you have," Templeman said.

"Two hairs," Sean answered confidently. "Both recovered from the crime scene at Linda Kotler's flat. One on the body. One next to the body. We could tell by their positions that they had very recently been deposited, and both those hairs belong to you, Mr. Hellier."

Hellier was without emotion. "No comment."

"Can you explain how your hair came to be in Linda Kotler's flat?" Sean asked.

Hellier glared at him contemptuously. "No comment."

"This is physical evidence from the scene. I want to remind you that if you fail or refuse to explain here and now how your hair came to be in Linda Kotler's flat, then a jury can draw a negative inference from your failure or refusal to do so. Do you understand, Mr. Hellier?"

"No comment."

Sean leaned across the table, closer to Hellier. "I don't blame you for not answering. And I know why you won't, because there is only one explanation, isn't there? That you went to her flat and you killed her."

"No comment," Hellier answered quickly.

"You raped her and killed her."

"No comment."

"You raped her. You tortured her. And you killed her." Sean's anger was rising.

"No comment," Hellier raised his voice to match Sean's.

"Do one decent thing in your life," Sean snapped. "If you can find one shred of humanity in your body, then use it to help the people whose lives you've shattered. Give the victims' families some closure. Admit to these crimes."

"If you have the evidence, then you give them closure," Hellier taunted. "Charge me. Tell them you've put the man who killed their darling daughter or son behind bars. Why do you need me to confess? Do you lack belief, Inspector?"

"Belief's got nothing to do with it, James—or should I start calling you by your real name, Mr. Korsakov? Mr. Stefan Korsakov?"

Sean waited for Hellier's reaction. A slight smile, nothing more.

"Like I said, it's not about what I believe. It's about what I can prove, and I can prove who you really are and that ex–detective sergeant Jarratt has been helping you cover your crimes for years."

"So the pig finally squealed," Hellier spat. "How appropriate."

"And that's why you tried to kill DS Jones. You had to. You knew she was getting close to the truth. Jarratt warned you, so you had no choice. She was going to bring your whole house of cards crashing down, so you broke into her flat and you tried to kill her."

"You're delusional. You think I'd kill to protect Jarratt?"

"No. To protect yourself."

Hellier leaned forward as close to Sean as the table they sat across would allow. "I don't care if you think you know who I am, or even if you do know who I am. I can be anyone I want to be. I can go anywhere I want to go. Do anything I want to do. Jarratt, a corruptible cop—ten a penny, Inspector. Not reason enough to kill your little pet."

Sean swallowed his mounting anger as best he could. "Nice touch, by the way," he told Hellier.

"What are you talking about now?" Hellier asked. "More delusions, Inspector?"

"Using my name when you approached Linda Kotler. Telling her you were me. Did you have a false identification with you? Or did Jarratt provide you with a real one, in my name? Did you show her the card when you were telling her you were me?"

"I don't know what you're talking about. You're insane, man."

"No," said Sean, icy calm. "Not me. It's you who is insane. You have to be." The room fell silent, Sean and Hellier locked in combat while Templeman and DC Cahill looked on uncomfortably, aware they were little more than intruders in a private duel.

"I think this interview's gone on long enough," Templeman interrupted, his head spinning with new revelations, even if Hellier's was not. "Given the injuries Mr. Hellier suffered while being arrested, I feel this interview should be stopped until such time as my client has received further medical treatment."

Sean's broken hand was throbbing to distraction. The double dose of painkillers he'd swallowed two hours ago was wearing off. He was in no hurry. They would take a break. He checked his watch.

"The time is now one thirty-six and I'm suspending this interview so that Mr. Hellier can have his injuries examined by a doctor. We'll continue the interview later." Sean moved to press the off button. Hellier stopped him.

"Wait," he insisted. "Just wait a second."

What now? What the hell was Hellier up to? Was he finally ready to end the charade?

"I don't care what your laboratory says or doesn't say. I didn't kill these people and I didn't attack your precious Sergeant Jones."

"We're not getting anywhere," Sean interrupted. "This interview is over."

"We're both being used, Inspector," Hellier snapped back. "Last night, the night your sergeant was attacked, I received a call from a man. I received the call at about seven thirty. It was the same man who called me the night the Kotler woman was killed, at about seven P.M. He always called me on my mobile, except the first time. That was earlier in the afternoon, also on the day the Kotler woman was killed. On that occasion he telephoned my office. The secretary can confirm it.

"Whoever made those calls was ensuring I had no alibi. He always arranged to meet me in places where there was nobody about who would remember me, but he never turned up. He made sure I went to great pains to lose the police surveillance. He always insisted I lose the surveillance—and now I know why."

"And I suppose this same mystery man planted your hair at the murder scene of Linda Kotler?" Hellier shrugged his shoulders. "I haven't got time to listen to this crap," Sean snapped.

"I'm afraid you have no choice," Hellier reminded him. "It is your duty to investigate my defense statement, as I'm sure Mr. Templeman was about to point out. You have no choice but to try to discover who it was that called me on those days at those times, whether you think it's a waste of your precious time or not. If you don't, then there's not a judge in the land who wouldn't throw the case against me out of court."

Sean knew Hellier was right. As ludicrous as the alibi was, he had to investigate it. He had to prove it false.

"Fine," Sean said. "I'll need the number of the caller."

"I don't have it."

"You said he called you on your mobile, so the number would have been displayed on the screen."

"Whenever he called, the number was blocked. The display said nothing."

"Did you try dialing 1471?"

"Same result. The number was withheld."

"Then there's not much I can do."

"Come, come, Inspector," Hellier said. "You and I both know that with the right tools the caller's number can be obtained. You already have my mobile phone. I suggest you have your lab rats examine it."

"It'll be done," Sean said. "But it'll take more than that to save you. This interview is concluded." Sean reached for the off switch, but stopped when he heard a sudden urgency in Hellier's voice.

"I sense your doubt," said Hellier. "Behind your determination to prove me guilty of crimes I didn't commit, I know that really you're not sure, are you? Something grinding away inside you, pulling you in a direction you don't want to go, pulling you toward the belief that maybe, just maybe, you've got the wrong man. And although you wouldn't give a fuck if I rotted in prison, that thought would always be with you, wouldn't it? The thought that someone out there got away with murder."

Sean shook his head and gave a slight laugh. "You know, in a strange way I thought there would be more to you than this. I don't know what exactly, but something. But it turns out you're just another loser trying to save his worthless neck. There's nothing special about you. You thought you couldn't be caught, that you never made mistakes, but you did—not only the hair at Linda Kotler's murder scene, but the fingerprint in Daniel Graydon's flat."

"I don't think so," Hellier said coldly. "Like I told you, I knew Graydon, I'd been to his flat. Anything belonging to me you found there means nothing."

"That's true," Sean agreed. "But one thing's been eating away at me about that ever since we found your fingerprint in the flat, and it's exactly that: the fact that we found only one print, on the underside of the bathroom door handle."

"What's your point?" Hellier asked.

"*One* print? That makes no sense," Sean explained. "If you had no reason to conceal the fact you'd been there, then why didn't we find more of your prints? We should have found dozens. You know what this says to me? It says you cleaned up the scene, wiped down everything you touched, but you missed one thing: the door handle."

"Daniel was very house proud," Hellier argued. "My other prints must have been wiped away when he cleaned."

"No," Sean snapped. "He couldn't have, because we found multiple prints belonging to other people who had been in that flat after the date when you said you'd been in there. Daniel didn't wipe your prints—you did. And why would you do that if you hadn't killed him? Why, James?"

"Because that's the way I have to live my life," Hellier answered. "I look after myself. I've always had to. No one has ever done anything for me, ever."

It was the first chink in Hellier that Sean had seen. The first crack in his persona, allowing a second's glimpse into his soul. And in that second he could see that Hellier was made the way he was by some terrible circumstances in his past. What those circumstances were, Sean would probably never know, but now he knew that Hellier wasn't born bad; someone had made him that way. He felt a pang of empathy for the man, but this was no time to wonder about the boy Hellier had once been. A boy whose childhood may very well have mirrored his own.

"I like to stay paranoid," Hellier continued, bringing Sean back to the present. "It keeps me ahead of the game. I touched little in his flat, and that which I did touch I wiped clean. People like Graydon are not to be trusted. He could have caused me problems."

"So you killed him before he had a chance to. Why not? You'd already killed Heather Freeman, but you were going to kill him anyway. You selected him as your next victim and a week later you killed him."

"No," Hellier shouted. "I didn't kill any of them. You're wrong. Completely wrong."

"We're getting nowhere," Sean said, the frustration in his voice obvious. He was so tired he doubted he could properly structure a sentence let alone any intelligent questions. "We'll take an hour's break and try again." He reached for the off switch, but once more Hellier stopped him.

"Does she have a guard?" Hellier hurriedly asked. "At the hospital, your DS Jones. Does she have a guard?"

"That's not something I would ever be prepared to discuss with you," Sean answered.

"Of course she does," Hellier continued. "Are they armed as well, these guards? I think so. I am right, aren't I, Inspector? Which rather begs the question: why would you have her guarded by men with guns if you truly believe I am the one who would have her dead, when I'm safely locked up here with you? I just can't work that one out. Can you?"

"Standard procedure," Sean answered without commitment.

"Oh, I don't think so," Hellier argued. "I really don't think so. You have her guarded because you know I'm not the one. Her would-be destroyer is still out there, and you know it, don't you? Don't you, Inspector?"

"I haven't got time for this." Sean tried to push the fog of doubt from his mind.

"I know who it is, Inspector. I know who killed these people and tried to kill DS Jones. The realization washed over me like a revelation. A moment of absolute clarity. It could only be him. Only he could know so much about me. Only he could watch me so closely."

"Who?" Sean asked, voice rising. "Let's play your little game. Tell me who."

"You already know." Hellier's voice rose to match Sean's.

"Tell me, dammit," Sean demanded. "You need to tell me and you need to do it now, or this interview will be over and you'll end up rotting in Broadmoor for someone else's crimes."

"You already know," Hellier repeated. "If I know, you know. Use your imagination. Think as he thinks. Think as we think."

Sean leaned forward to answer, but suddenly stopped, scene

after scene suddenly playing in his mind, no longer under his control: the first time he entered Daniel Graydon's flat, the body on the floor in a pool of blood; the autopsy; walking into Hellier's office, the stench of his malevolence; Sebastian Gibran watching them. The photographs of Heather Freeman, her throat cut, green staring lifeless eyes; Hellier's snarling face when he arrested him at his office; Sebastian Gibran watching. Linda Kotler's twisted and tortured body; Hellier admitting he practiced sadomasochistic sex; Sebastian Gibran watching. Sebastian Gibran contacting Sally, meeting her, watching her. Sally attacked in her own home. The phone calls Hellier claimed to have received, the instructions he was given that denied him alibis; Sebastian Gibran watching, watching them all, playing them all—him against Hellier and Hellier against him, led by the nose like two lambs to the slaughter. But Hellier had worked it out, his hunger to survive driving him to the answer. And now the revelation washed over Sean too— *Sebastian Gibran. Sebastian Gibran. Sebastian Gibran.*

His eyes fell away to the ground as the pieces of the puzzle fell into place in his damaged mind. "Jesus Christ," he finally declared as the face formed behind his eyes. "I need to get to the hospital. I need to go now."

Sean jumped to his feet, knocking his chair over, the sound of Hellier's growing laughter tearing at his ears.

"Run to her, Inspector," Hellier tormented. "Run to her before he beats you to the prize."

Sean ran from the interview room, almost knocking Donnelly over as he headed for the exit to the holding cell and the car park.

"Problem?" Donnelly asked, bewildered.

"I've got to get to the hospital. I've got to get to Sally," Sean said, continuing to move.

"Why?" Donnelly tried to keep pace. "And what about Hellier?"

"Let him go."

"After what he tried to do to you?"

Sean glanced down at his swollen hand; the image of Hellier's bloodied face flashed in his mind. "I'd say we're even. Just get rid of him and tell him I never want to see him again." On reaching the exit, he turned to face Donnelly. "And then get to the hospital as fast as you can." He backed out of the exit and was gone.

Only the closing door heard Donnelly's reply: "Will somebody please tell me what the fuck is going on?"

CHAPTER 26

Saturday afternoon

I sit on a bench in a pretty little garden in the hospital grounds. It's where people recovering from amputations caused by cancer come to smoke. No one pays me much attention, dressed as I am in a dark blue male nurse's uniform. A wig, mustache, and spectacles conceal my true features, and the handles of the coiled cheese-wire dig uncomfortably into my hip as they hide in my pocket. A crude weapon, but quiet and effective in the right hands.

I begin to walk to Charing Cross Hospital's main entrance, feeling the syringe taped to my chest pulling my shaved skin as I stride forward. The sheathed knife tucked into the small of my back feels uncomfortable, but reassuringly so.

I like to plan meticulously, but there's been no time for that. I must be pragmatic, play things by ear. It will be dangerous for me, and even more so for anyone who gets in my way, but there is no choice, not now. If the pig bitch survives, she will tell the world I was the one who visited her last night. My beautiful charade would be over. I would have to run . . . But if I am able to correct my mistake, I will remain anonymous.

It was easy enough to find out where she had been taken. Everybody in this area either gets taken to the Chelsea and Westminster Hospital or, as she had, to Charing Cross. A few phone calls were all it took to find out which, and that she was in the ICU. They were also kind enough to tell me it was expected that she would recover from her injuries. People really ought to be more careful with information they give out. You never know who you're talking to.

I make my way confidently through the never-ending, winding corridors to the laundry room. Medical staff and porters wander in and out of here endlessly, nobody paying anybody else much attention. These giant hospitals are about as personal as a rush-hour train station. Their security is a joke.

I help myself to several clean and neatly folded sheets, all wrapped in transparent plastic wrap, and make my way to the lift that will carry me straight to the Intensive Care Unit and her. As the lift rises my heart begins to race. The power surges through my veins. I feel giddy with excitement. It makes me want to lash out at the other people in the lift, pull the knife from the small of my back and cut them all to pieces, but I won't. I keep control. I have other business to take care of today.

As the lift doors slide open I see the Intensive Care Unit stretch out before me. It's different from the rest of the hospital: darker, warmer, and quieter. It feels safe. I step into its peace and allow the lift to fall away to rejoin the chaos. Immediately, I know which room she must be in, dutifully advertised by the armed police officer standing outside. I have anticipated it. Good. I'll make excellent use of his uniform. Once I have that, I'll be spending a few farewell moments with the little bitch.

Then I'll use the syringe I've brought to inject a bubble of air into her already fragile body and send her quietly to meet her maker. After all, who's going to question a cop with a gun?

A nurse steps from a room into the corridor and looks me up and down dismissively, my uniform marking its wearer as a lower creature in the hospital hierarchy. I look down at the sheets I carry.

"Laundry said you were running low," I say in the most effeminate voice I can muster.

"News to me" is all the self-important slut can say for herself. "Laundry cupboard's around the corner, outside the toilet."

No *please,* no *thank you.* How I would like to teach her some manners. Another time maybe.

I follow her directions, acknowledging the armed pig with a nod of the head as I pass. I place the laundry in the cupboard then walk to the communal toilet and open the door. But I do not enter. Instead I contort my face to falsify an expression of concern and walk quickly and quietly toward the pig. I speak with the voice of a homosexual, keeping it low so the nurses can't hear.

"Excuse me. I think there's something in the toilet you should see."

He casts an eye over me, barely able to disguise the disgust on his face, as if he wants to swat me away like an annoying fly. Eventually he walks toward the toilet fearlessly, as all pigs with guns would, safe in the false knowledge they are untouchable. I hold the door open for him as he enters.

"What's the problem?" he asks. It's the last thing he'll ever say. I pop the cheese wire around his throat and pull it nice and tight. He manages to get several fingers under the wire, a futile attempt to save himself. If need be I'll cut through his fingers. I drag him silently into the middle of the room, where he tries to reach for anything that will make a noise, anything that will raise the alarm. He realizes he can't. He gasps for air, his rubber-soled shoes kicking quietly on the hard floor tiles. Eventually he falls still. There's blood on his shirt and body armor, but nothing I can't conceal. Should I kill the nurses? No. It would take too long. If they notice the pig's change in appearance, they'll just assume a change of guard.

Now it's time to right a wrong.

CHAPTER 27

Sean's siren screamed at the ever-present choking traffic in the streets of Hammersmith as he drew closer and closer to Charing Cross Hospital and Sally. The blue light magnetically attached to the roof of his unmarked car gave other drivers little and often too late warning of his scarcely controlled approach. If he crashed now, he had no backup, no one to continue the race toward Sally. Even in his fear and panic he knew he should have contacted the local police and had them cover the hospital, but how long would it take to explain his fears? How long would it take to get authority to deploy more armed guards? And what if he was wrong? What if this was Hellier's last hurrah, to make him look a fool? To discredit him as a detective? No, he had to do this himself. Donnelly would organize backup, do the sensible thing, but Sean had to come alone. Right or wrong, he had to come alone. Somehow he knew everything would end soon. Everything.

As he swung into the hospital parking lot he killed the siren and lights, suddenly feeling the need for stealth. Ignoring the signs for the main entrance, he made straight for the Accident and Emergency Department. He parked the car in an ambulance bay and abandoned it, keys in the ignition and door open.

Sean ran as quickly as he dared through the swing doors. He didn't know this hospital as well as he did the ones in southeast London and the East End, but he remembered where he'd seen the lifts last night when Sally was first brought here.

He jabbed the arrow button to summon the lift and waited, beyond impatient, for the metal boxed carriage to arrive, while studying the hospital floor guide for Intensive Care. He found it just as the lift arrived. Without waiting for the doors to open fully, he leaped in and punched the floor he needed with the side of his fist. Thank God there was no one else in the lift, no one to slow his ascent to Sally. Two floors short of his destination the lift suddenly stopped and doors slid open painfully slowly. A gaggle of chatting nurses stepped toward the entrance. Sean flashed the identification he already held in his hand.

"Sorry," he almost shouted. "Police business. Use another lift." He jabbed the lift's button and the doors closed on a mix of protests and disbelieving giggles.

Finally the lift drew to a smooth halt at the ICU floor. The doors silently opened, the warmth and silence of the unit wrapping around Sean, mechanical whirs and beeps that appeared so reassuring.

As Sean stepped from the lift he saw the armed uniformed officer standing outside what he assumed would be Sally's room. The officer had his back to the wall; Sean presumed this was so he could see in both directions along the corridor. His eyes were immediately drawn to the automatic pistol on the officer's thigh, as any policeman's eyes would have been. The officer's flat hat was pulled low over his forehead, military style, almost totally hiding his upper facial features. Sean guessed he would have been an ex-soldier, a guess made all the more likely to be true by the macho mustache the officer proudly wore. Sean's eyes darted around the unit, checking for other signs of life. Two ICU nurses busied themselves quietly with another ravaged soul in a room two doors away from Sally's.

Sean held his identification aloft. "DI Corrigan. I need to see DS Jones." The uniform nodded his permission as Sean entered through the already open door. He walked slowly toward Sally, already fearing the worst, his heart pounding out of control, making it difficult to breathe; his stomach felt painful and knotted. But as he drew closer he became aware of the comforting, rhythmic sounds emanating from the machines that surrounded Sally. Heart-rate monitors, pulse monitors, blood-pressure monitors all reassuring him that she was alive. Even the ugly, impossibly big tube that snaked into Sally's throat, feeding her oxygen, somehow made Sean feel at ease. He finally inhaled a long breath and blew it out through pursed lips.

He placed a hand on Sally's forehead and gently stroked her hair back. He was struggling for something to say when he suddenly felt a presence behind him, some change in the atmosphere of the room. He spun on his heels, heart rate soaring, adrenaline already beginning to prepare his body for combat.

"Bloody hell," Sean said as he saw Donnelly step into the room. "You got here fast."

"Aye. I hitched a ride with the uniform lads in a response car, blues-and-twos all the way. No expense spared." Donnelly's tone changed. "Is she okay?"

"I think so," Sean replied.

"Care to tell me what's going on? Why we're here? Why we let Hellier walk away a free man again?"

Sean opened his mouth to explain, but no explanation came forth, only a question. "Where's the guard? The armed guard? Did you see him?"

"I didn't see a guard," Donnelly answered. "Just you."

"No. You got here right after I did." The fear was back again, the knot in his stomach worse than ever. "There was a guard outside this room."

"Okay," Donnelly said calmly. "I believe you, guv'nor. Christ, he's probably gone for a piss."

"The toilet," said Sean. "I have to check the toilet."

"Why?" Donnelly asked. "What's the problem?"

"I know who the killer is," Sean answered, already racing along the corridor, searching for the toilet, shouting now. "He's here. I know he's here."

"Hellier's the killer," Donnelly argued. "But you let him go."

Donnelly's words would have stung Sean, but he wasn't listening, he was frantically searching for the toilet and the uniformed officer. At last he found the communal toilet and threw the door open. Three sinks lined one side and three toilet cubicles the other. Only one of the cubicle doors was shut. Sean walked slowly into the room.

"Hello," he called to no one. "I'm Detective Inspector Corrigan. I need to know if anyone is in here . . . Is anyone in here?" Silence. He moved to the closed cubicle and placed his palm on the door. The small square of green told Sean the door wasn't locked. Gently he pushed and the door swung open.

Sean couldn't help taking two steps backward, repelled by the sight of the nearly naked man slumped on the toilet, eyes bulging grotesquely, his swollen purple tongue protruding from his mouth, rolled to one side. The burgundy color of his face contrasting pitifully against the pale, now waxlike skin of the rest of his body. Sean stared at the scene, his mind processing the information. He saw one of the man's arms fallen across his lap, while the other was still raised, the fingers desperately grasping at the thin metal wire that was buried in his neck and throat. Drying blood stained the dead man's hands and chest, blood that had run from the virtually severed fingers.

Donnelly appeared at Sean's shoulder, ready to continue the argument until he saw the body.

"Jesus Christ," Donnelly said. "What in God's name is going on?"

"It's Gibran," Sean told him. "Sebastian Gibran killed him and all the others."

"But who is this poor bastard?"

"Our armed police guard. Gibran must have taken his uniform. I walked straight past him, bastard." Sean turned and began to run toward the lifts, drawing concerned glances from two nurses who'd come out to see what the commotion was about.

"Where you going?" Donnelly called after him.

"Stay here and watch over Sally," Sean commanded, punching the lift button. "I'm going after him. He can't have taken the lift, else you'd have seen him, so he must have used the stairs. I can make up the ground."

"That's not a good idea, guv," Donnelly shouted. "If he took the uniform, then he took the gun too. Let an armed unit—"

The lift doors closed, cutting off the rest of the sentence. As it began to descend, Sean left Donnelly's world and entered one that few people would ever truly understand and even fewer could ever survive.

Sean ran frantically through the crowded lobby of the hospital, straining, searching in all directions for any sign of Gibran, any sign of a uniform striding through the crowds. Increasingly desperate, he approached passersby, thrusting his identification into their faces.

"A uniformed officer," he demanded. "Has anyone seen a uniformed officer?"

Most recoiled from him in fright, but finally he came upon a startled hospital porter who nodded in response to his question.

"How long ago?" The porter just gawped at him. Sean grabbed the man by the collar. "How long ago?"

"A couple of minutes," the man stuttered.

"Which way?"

"Out the main exit, toward the car park."

Sean released the porter and made for the exit, sprinting now, not caring who saw him, who he knocked out of the way, oblivious to the panic he might be causing. He kept running toward the parking lot, in blind hope more than belief.

He'd been running hard for over a minute and his lungs and thighs were on fire, but there was still no sign of Gibran. Sean bent over, resting with his hands on his hips, desperately trying to draw new oxygen into his exhausted blood. After a few seconds he straightened and began to scan the vast lot. His mobile vibrated in his pocket. Donnelly's name came up on the screen. Somehow he managed to speak.

"I've lost him" was all he said.

"Where the hell are you?" Donnelly asked.

"In the main car park," he answered breathlessly. Then, about a hundred meters ahead of him, bobbing his way through the legions of parked cars, he saw a figure clad in a police uniform, the peaked cap prominent. "He's here, in the car park. I can see him." He hung up without waiting for Donnelly's response.

The excitement electrified Sean's body. The pain in his chest and legs was soon forgotten as he sprinted faster than he knew he could toward the walking figure, so fast that he knew he would catch up with the man—but if it was Gibran, why wasn't he running? What was he waiting for?

As Sean closed the last few meters, the man turned to face him with the speed of a snake. Sean saw nothing but the knife in the man's hand. The shinning, gleaming knife that Sean was about to run onto. Sean tried to stop, but knew he would be too late. He braced himself for the unbearable pain that he knew was about to cut into his stomach or his liver or his chest.

The last thing Sean saw before he closed his eyes were Gibran's white teeth, his lips curled back in a grin as he prepared to impale Sean on his short, sharp blade. But no cutting pain ripped into Sean's body. Instead he was hit in the chest by an incredibly powerful force, like being struck by a medicine ball fired from a cannon. It lifted him off his feet and threw him backward. He landed on a car bonnet and rolled onto the ground, immediately springing back to his feet, instinctively checking his chest for blood. There was none.

Sean quickly regained his bearings, his eyes searching for Gibran, his mind trying to work out what it was that had hit him. Even as the scene in front of him became clear, his mind struggled to make sense of what he was seeing.

James Hellier was holding Gibran in a grip not even he could escape from. The knife that had been in Gibran's hand was now in Hellier's. He pressed it hard into Gibran's throat, breaking the skin, allowing a trickle of blood to escape. Hellier's other hand pushed the pistol he'd already slipped from the holster on Gibran's thigh into his kidney. Swiftly tucking the pistol into his waistband, Hellier used this free hand to enhance his physical dominance over Gibran, who squirmed in protest.

"Ah, ah," Hellier warned him and pushed the blade a little deeper into his throat. Sean watched as Hellier suddenly pulled one of Gibran's arms behind his back. Sean heard a click and knew what was happening. Gibran visibly winced. With practiced ease Hellier pulled the other arm backward and another clicking sound. Again Gibran winced as the handcuffs were tightened around his wrists. All the while, Hellier kept the knife pressed to his throat.

Hellier spoke to Gibran, Sean a mere observer. "If you cross me, you have to pay the price. You have to pay the ferryman."

"Don't do it, James," Sean said calmly, trying to somehow wrest control of the situation. "Can you hear that?" Above the sounds of the city, the wail of approaching sirens announced that reinforcements were closing in. "I know you didn't kill anyone, James," Sean continued. "But if you kill him, you'll rot in prison all the same."

"I can't let him live," Hellier explained. "He tried to make a fool of me. He used me." Gibran wriggled in protest. Hellier jerked him into obedience.

Sean tried to find the words that would get through to Hellier. Normal threats or promises he knew would have little effect.

"I took my kids to the zoo," Sean told him. "A couple of weeks ago, you know, I'd promised my wife, so . . ." Hellier stared, but remained silent. "They had a tiger there, this beautiful tiger in this cage, you know, but all it did was walk up and down, head bowed, like it had given up. Like all it wanted was for someone to put it out of its misery. It was all I could think about for days after. It was . . . it was one of the saddest things I've ever seen and I've seen some sad things. You couldn't survive in a cage, not after the last time, James. And you know it. Let him go."

Hellier's eyes narrowed but immediately became animated and wide again, a smile spreading across his face. "Don't worry, Inspector. I'm not going to kill him. Not yet, anyway. I want him to live in fear for a while. I want him to taste fear every day until the day comes when I decide he's lived long enough, then I'll do for him what someone should have done for your tiger." Hellier pushed Gibran the short distance toward Sean, who grappled to hold on to him, hindered by his broken, throbbing hand, surprised and somewhat intimidated by Gibran's strength. How had Hellier overpowered him so easily?

"Consider this my going-away present," Hellier said, beaming. "Not quite what I had in mind, but he'll have to do, for now.

Oh, and by the way, be careful, Inspector: he's as dangerous as he thinks he is, and I should know."

"I'll see you in hell," Gibran spat toward Hellier.

"I'll be waiting for you there," Hellier answered, matter-of-factly.

The sirens had shifted from the background to the foreground. Sean glanced over his shoulder and saw the marked police cars pulling up at the perimeter of the parking lot, officers climbing from the vehicles.

"Give me the gun, James. We'll need a statement from you. You help us, we can make a deal on the Jarratt thing."

"I don't think so, Sean." It was the first time Hellier had used his Christian name. "Not all of your kind will be so understanding. Besides, it's time for me to move on. You've already killed James Hellier, Sean."

Hellier began to walk away, ready to melt into the city that had been his playground for so long.

"James," Sean called after him. "James, you can't just walk away."

"Remember what I told you: I can be anyone I like and I can go anywhere I want. Good-bye, Sean."

"James," Sean called, the distance between them growing ever greater.

Hellier turned toward him one last time. "I'll hold on to the gun, if you don't mind, just in case anyone foolishly decides to follow me. Good-bye, Sean. Take care now." Hellier turned his back on Sean, waved once without looking, and disappeared behind a parked van.

"James!" Sean shouted. "Stefan! Stefan!" But Hellier was gone.

The sight of the uniformed officers closing in precipitated Gibran making one last effort to break free. Sean pushed him over a car bonnet and lay across him. Despite the handcuffs, it took all his strength to control him.

"You can't prove a fucking thing," Gibran challenged.

"You're wearing a dead police officer's uniform, you piece of shit. You're finished, Gibran. I'll fucking make sure of it."

Sean stepped out of the lift and moved fast toward Sally's room. The ICU was quiet. The maelstrom hadn't broken over the crime scene yet, but it soon would. Sean entered Sally's room. Donnelly was standing over her.

"Bloody hell, guv'nor. I didn't expect to see you back here. I heard on the radio you got your man."

"Plenty of time to deal with him later," said Sean. "I take it I have you to thank for the cavalry turning up?" Donnelly waved his mobile by way of an answer, but Sean was already searching through the cabinet next to Sally's bed.

"Looking for something?" Donnelly asked.

"Sally's personal stuff," Sean answered.

"Why?"

"I need it. I need to make sure."

"Of what?" Donnelly inquired.

"That Gibran goes down for what he did to her." Sean nodded toward Sally.

"Her personal stuff's probably locked up and logged."

"Not necessarily. She came in through A and E, remember. They had better things to do than worry about bagging and tagging property."

He pulled the bottom door open and saw what he'd been praying for: a plastic bag containing Sally's personal items. Her simple watch, some jewelry, even an elastic headband, and the thing Sean sought most—her identification.

"Is the bag sealed?" Donnelly asked in hushed tones.

"No." Sean almost whispered the answer. "Her ID's in its own bag, but it's not sealed." Sean held the bloodstained police identification gently in his uninjured hand. He knew what he had to do.

"This needs to be found in Gibran's home when it's searched," he told Donnelly.

"I understand," Donnelly assured him.

"It's best if you don't find it yourself. Leave it for one of the other searching officers to find. Understand?"

"Perfectly, guv. Leave it to me."

"You're a good man, Dave."

"I know" was Donnelly's only reply.

Gibran sat, impassive, his hands resting unnaturally on the table in front of him. Sean and Donnelly sat opposite. There was no one else in the interview room. Sean hadn't been surprised when Gibran waived his right to have an attorney present. He was far too arrogant to believe anyone could protect him better than he could himself.

Sean completed the introductions and reminded Gibran of his rights. Gibran politely acknowledged everything Sean asked him.

"Mr. Gibran, do you know why you're here?" Sean asked.

Gibran ignored the question. "I've never been inside a police station before," he said. "It's not quite how I imagined it. Lighter, more sterile, not as threatening as I thought it would be."

"Do you know why you're here?" Sean repeated.

"Yes, I understand perfectly, thank you." Gibran smiled gently, untroubled, at peace with himself.

"Then you know you're accused of several murders, including the murder of one police officer and the attempted murder of another?"

"I am aware of my situation, Inspector."

"Yes," Sean continued. "Why don't we talk about your situation, Mr. Gibran?"

"Please, call me Sebastian."

"Okay, Sebastian. Do you want to talk about the things you've done?"

"You mean the things I'm accused of doing."

"Are you denying that you killed Daniel Graydon? Heather Freeman? Linda Kotler? Police Constable Kevin O'Connor? Are you denying you tried to kill Detective Sergeant Jones?"

"What is it you want, Inspector?" Gibran asked. "A confession? For me to tell you where, how, and why?"

"Ideally," admitted Sean.

"Why?"

"So I can understand why those people died. So I can understand why you killed them."

"And why is it you want to understand those things?"

"It's my job."

"No," Gibran said, still smiling slightly. "That's too simple a reason."

"Then why do I want to know?" Sean risked asking for Gibran's opinion.

"Fear," Gibran answered. "Because we fear what we do not understand. So we label everything: a nice, neat explanation hanging around a murderer's neck. He killed because he loved. He killed because he hated. He killed because he's schizophrenic. The labels take away the fear."

"Then what should we put on your label?" Sean asked.

Gibran's smile grew wider as he leaned back from the table. "Why don't we just leave it blank," he answered. "It would be so much more interesting, don't you agree?"

"It won't help you in court," Sean reminded him. "Life imprisonment doesn't have to mean life."

"I understand you're trying to help me, Inspector, but from

what I can tell, you're a long way from convicting me of anything."

"You will be convicted," Sean assured him. "Be in no doubt of that."

"You sound very sure of an unsure thing," Gibran said. "But I'll make you a deal. If I'm convicted of these crimes, then we'll talk again, maybe in more detail. If your evidence fails you and I walk away a free man, then we shall never discuss the matter again."

"Confessions after conviction are worth nothing," Sean told him.

"Maybe not to the court, but to you it would be worth a great deal, I believe."

Sean sensed Gibran was trying to end the interview. Was he tiring? The effort of attempting to appear sane and polite exhausting him? Sean had to keep going.

"Tell me about yourself," he said. "Tell me about Sebastian Gibran."

"The short, abridged history of Sebastian Gibran? Very well. I was born forty-one years ago in Oxfordshire. I am the second oldest of four children, two boys and two girls. My father was something big in agriculture, while my mother was left to raise us. We were quite wealthy, although not rich. I was privately educated at a very good local school, where I did well enough to gain a place at the London School of Economics.

"Armed with a degree in business finance I made my way into the big bad world and became a valued employee of Butler and Mason International Finance. I rose through the ranks to become one of the senior partners. I am married with two adorable children, one of each. Quite an unremarkable life, I'm afraid."

"Until recently," Sean said, studying Gibran intensely. "Until something that is indeed remarkable happened to you. You changed. Something inside of you couldn't be restrained any longer."

"I'm not mentally ill, Inspector. I don't hear voices in my head telling me to kill. There is nothing in me that cannot be restrained. Nothing I do not control. I am no human monster created by my background. My childhood was a happy one. My parents loving, my siblings supportive, and my friends numerous. I didn't pull the legs off spiders when I was a boy. I didn't bite my classmates at nursery or torture and kill the family pets."

"Then why?"

"Why what?"

Sean swallowed his growing frustration. "Why did you kill those people? Daniel Graydon. Heather Freeman. Linda Kotler. Why was it so important to you that they died?"

"And you want me to tell you so you can understand me?" Gibran asked. "You want me to take away your fear."

"Yes," Sean responded.

"There's really no point," Gibran said dismissively. "I have no answer that could satisfy your need to know why. There is nothing I could tell you that could possibly help you understand. In some ways I wish there were, but there really isn't."

"Try me," Sean insisted.

More silence, then Gibran spoke. "Tell me, Inspector, are you familiar with the fable of the frog and the scorpion?"

"No," Sean answered.

"One day," Gibran began, "a frog was basking on the banks of a river when suddenly his slumber was disturbed by an anxious voice. When the frog opened his eyes, he saw a scorpion standing only inches away. Understandably nervous, the frog hopped away, then a pleading voice stopped him. 'Please, Mr. Frog,' the scorpion said. 'I simply must get to the other side of this river, but I can't swim. Could I please crawl onto your back while you carry me to the other side?'

"'I can't do that,' answered the frog, 'because you are a scorpion and you will sting me.'

"'No,' said the scorpion. 'I won't sting you. I promise.'

"'How can I take the word of a scorpion?' the frog asked.

"'Because if I sting you while we are crossing the river,' the scorpion explained, 'we will both drown.'

"The frog thinks about what the scorpion has said. Won over by his logic, he agrees to take the scorpion to the other side. But as they are crossing the river, the scorpion does indeed sting the frog.

"With his dying breath the frog asks, 'Why did you do that, for surely now we both will die?'

"'I couldn't help myself,' the scorpion tells him. 'It's my nature.'

"I always feel sorry for the scorpion," Gibran continued, "but never for the frog."

Sean let a few minutes elapse before he spoke. "Are you telling me you killed four people for no reason other than you believe it's in your nature to?"

"It's just a story," Gibran answered. "One that I thought might appeal to you in particular."

"Let me tell you why I think you killed these people," Sean said. "You killed them because it made you feel special. Made you feel important. Without it, your life felt pointless. Making money for other people: pointless. You felt pointless. And you couldn't stand that empty feeling, every day having to admit to yourself that you were just another nobody, living a nobody's life. Every single day, the same feeling of emptiness, of nothingness. It drove you insane.

"You could have been anything you wanted to be. Life gave you all the privileges and opportunities, but you didn't have the courage to do anything truly special, to do anything that would set you apart from other men. You believe we should all bow down to you merely because of who you are. But nobody did and it made you angry, angry at the world.

"So you decided to teach us a lesson, didn't you? You decided to show us how special you are by doing the only thing your feeble mind could conceive of. Your twisted sense of self-importance convinced you it was your right, your destiny, to kill. It excused your crimes—and crimes are all they are, no matter what you may think.

"But committing murder doesn't make you special. It doesn't make you anything other than one more sick loser, no better than all the other sick losers locked up in Broadmoor. You can talk about scorpions and your nature and any other bullshit you like, but we both know that, deep down, underneath this polished act, this mock menace, you are nothing. Nothing at all."

"If believing that makes you comfortable," Gibran responded, "if it takes away your fear, then you should cling to that belief."

Sean knew then that Gibran wasn't going to talk, wasn't going to confess and explain all. He had to come to terms with the fact that they might never know why. He felt Gibran studying him, expressionless.

"What about Hellier?" he asked, making one last-ditch effort to bring him back. "What was his part in all of this? Were you working together?"

"James could never be anything other than my employee," Gibran answered. "I would never dirty my hands working with him as an equal. That could never happen. He was a tool to be used by me to achieve what I needed to achieve. He was nothing more than an illusion. James was made by circumstance, a cheap man-made replica. Pathetic, really. I was born to achieve all that I have achieved. The path I was ordained to follow formed while I was still in my mother's womb."

"You used him as a decoy," Sean accused. "You crafted the murders so it looked like Hellier had committed them."

"Murders?" Gibran feigned surprise. "I'm sorry. I thought you were talking about corporate finance."

"Of course." Suddenly it was starting to make sense. Eager to explore the unexplained revelation before it could slip back into the dark recesses of his mind, Sean continued: "I understand now. You gave Hellier his job at Butler and Mason in the first place, didn't you? As soon as you met him, when and wherever that was, you knew, didn't you? You knew he was the one you'd been waiting for, the one you could hide behind. And you made sure you had sole responsibility for checking his background, because you couldn't risk anyone else discovering Hellier was a fraud. Did you even check his references, his employment history, or was it so irrelevant that you didn't even bother? It wasn't his financial skills you wanted—you wanted him. You needed to have him where you could watch him, learn everything about him, manipulate him, didn't you?"

"Hellier was a subordinate, in every way a subordinate, put on this planet by powers you could never understand to be manipulated by people like me," Gibran answered. "It's the law of Nature."

"Really?" Sean replied. "So Hellier is inferior to you? Not as smart as you?"

Gibran answered with a shrug of his shoulders and a smile.

"But if that's so, how come he outsmarted you in the end? He's probably already setting himself up with a new life of privilege and luxury, while you're sitting here with us, preparing to spend the rest of your life rotting in some prison hellhole. So tell me, Sebastian, who's the smart one now?"

Sean studied Gibran's reaction, watching as his smile fell away, his lips narrowing and growing pale, his once relaxed fingers beginning to curl into claws. At last Sean had found a way to peel Gibran's facade away.

"I mean, Hellier practically handed me your head on a plate. He read you like a cheap novel, predicted your every move, and when the time was right he served you to me on a platter."

Sean watched Gibran's breathing grow shallow and then accelerate. *Keep pushing him. Push him until he explodes and fills the room with shrapnel fragments of undeniable truth.*

"He made a fool out of you," Sean stabbed at him. "He's made you look like a damn fool. A predictable idiot, and there's nothing you can do about it. He's won."

Sean waited for the eruption, certain he had done enough to provoke the truth out of him. But no arrogant rant of self-importance came; no declaration of the genius of his crimes spilled forth. Instead, to Sean's horror, the smile returned to Gibran's face.

"That's very presumptuous of you, Inspector, to declare the winner before the game's even over," Gibran replied, calm now.

"This is no game," Sean answered, "but it is over. For you, everything is over."

Sean knew he was wasting his time. All he was doing was providing Gibran with a stage to perform on. Tired of listening to him talking in riddles, he decided to end the interview.

"Mr. Gibran, is there anything you want to tell me? Anything at all?"

"I know what you are," Gibran said without warning.

"Excuse me?" Sean asked.

"I smell it on you the way I smelled it on James. You can hide it from others, but not me. You were made what you are by circumstance, just like James. Only you're not like him. He controlled his nature, his unacceptable instincts, but you suppress yours. You live in fear of your true nature, never embracing it. Such a waste."

"I don't know what you're talking about."

"They trained you like a wild animal in captivity," Gibran continued, his voice aggressive now, assertive but still controlled. "Taught you to conform, beat you into submission with endless counseling and behavior-suppressing drugs. You could have been so much more than you are."

"You know nothing about me," Sean snarled.

"I know that every time you look at your children, you think of your own childhood. It was your father, wasn't it? Your abuser. It was your father who touched you in those special places, who told you it was a special secret only you and he shared. And as you grew older and didn't want to be touched, it was your father who forced himself on you, who beat you when you said no."

Sean could feel the blood draining from his face. How did Gibran know? How did he know?

"You're finished." He spat the words at Gibran.

"I was born the way I am," Gibran snapped back. "You were made by circumstances, but made you were. How long can you deny your nature? How long before your own hands reach out toward your children? How long before you and they share a special secret they must never tell Mummy? That's why you were able to see James for what he was, because every time you look in the mirror you see James Hellier, and all the other so-called killers you've locked away, staring back at you. But you never saw me, did you? You and he are mere reflections of each other, whereas I am something you could never begin to comprehend."

Sean tried to jump to his feet, his hand already clenched into a fist. He felt a heavy arm across his chest. Donnelly eased him back into his chair.

"Play your games, if you like," Sean said, back in control of himself. "But it'll take more than games to stop you from going away for a very long time."

"I don't think so."

"Your arrogance is your undoing," Sean told him. "You didn't think you could make mistakes, but you have. DS Jones is alive and she will recover. And when she does, she'll confirm it was you who attacked her. Why? Because she saw your face. You wanted her to see it was you. You wanted her to see her killer. You wanted them all to see your face. Wanted it to be the last thing they ever saw. You were too proud of yourself to hide behind a mask. The moment you allowed DS Jones to escape, it was over for you."

"I doubt DS Jones had more than a fleeting glimpse of her attacker," Gibran argued. "And I understand the attack was at night, probably in poor light. How could she be sure of anything? Her identification would be useless."

"And there'll be security tapes from the underground," Sean continued. "Tapes that will show you following Linda Kotler. Now that we know who to look for, it'll be only a matter of time before we find you on those tapes."

"So maybe you can prove I was in the area. Hardly enough to convict a man of murder."

"There'll be tapes from the club Daniel Graydon was in the night he died. And what about the bouncers there? What if they can pick you out of an identification parade?"

"What if they can, Inspector?" Gibran smirked. "You have nothing."

"You're forgetting about the visit you paid DS Jones in Intensive Care. The police constable you killed there. You were still wearing his uniform when you were arrested. Mistakes, Sebastian. Too many mistakes. Too much evidence to explain away. Not to mention the syringe taped to your chest."

"A harmless, empty syringe," Gibran explained.

"We've already spoken to the medical staff. If you'd injected air into Sally's bloodstream it would almost certainly have caused a heart attack or stroke. She would have died and nobody would have known it was murder. With DS Jones dead, you could have melted into the background, leaving Hellier to take the fall."

"Theories and hopes, Inspector. That's all you have."

"And the uniform you were wearing?"

"Then charge me with impersonating a police officer."

"You killed a man and took his uniform."

"Prove that, can you? That I killed him? Do you really have indisputable evidence of that? My fingerprints on the murder weapon? My DNA on his body? Maybe CCTV of me in the act, so to speak? But you don't, do you?"

Sean sat silently considering how best to play his final trump card, trying to guess how Gibran would react. Would he grow angry and reveal his true self? Would he be humbled and confess? Would he continue his calm ambiguous denials? Slowly, deliberately, he pulled a transparent evidence bag from the pocket of his jacket, hanging over the back of his chair. He casually tossed the bag containing Sally's bloodied identification across the table.

Sean saw Gibran glance down at the bag. For the first time he thought he saw a hint of confusion in his face.

"DS Jones's identification," he said. "Found hidden under the lining of a desk drawer in your home. How did her ID find its way into your house?"

Gibran lifted the evidence bag and studied the contents. "It appears I've underestimated your determination," he said.

"How did it get there?" Sean repeated the question he knew Gibran couldn't answer.

"We both know that's not important," Gibran answered. "You will try and convince a court that I took it as a trophy. That I took it because of a need to maintain a connection to my victim. That I used it to help relive the night when she should have died. They may believe you. They may not."

"And what will you tell the court?" Sean asked. "What will you tell them to convince them you're not what I say you are?"

Gibran leaned forward, smiling confidently. Sean thought he could begin to smell the same animal musk leaking from Gibran he'd smelled on Hellier.

"For that, Inspector," Gibran said smugly, "we'll all have to wait and see. Won't we?"

Donnelly joined Sean in his office, where the pair of them sat listening to the recording of Gibran's interview. When it concluded, Donnelly was first to speak.

"He told us fuck all."

"He was never going to talk," Sean said. "But I needed to be near him for a while. To watch him. Listen to him."

"And?" Donnelly asked.

"He's our man. No doubts this time. Hellier was nothing more than his pawn."

"Jesus," Donnelly said. "He must have spent years planning this. What sort of man spends years planning to kill strangers?"

"One who never wants to stop," Sean answered. "He knew we would catch him eventually, unless we weren't looking for him, and we'd only stop looking for him once we had someone locked up. Someone we were convinced was guilty of the murders. It nearly worked too. I took the bait like a fool. Let my feelings toward Hellier blind my judgment. I almost sent the wrong man to prison."

"No one would have cried too much for Hellier," said Donnelly.

Sean shook his head. "That's not what bothers me," he said. "The only safe place for Hellier is behind bars, but I almost missed Gibran, almost handed him the whole game. If Sally hadn't survived, who knows? Maybe we would never have caught him."

"But we did catch him," Donnelly reminded him. "*You* caught him."

"I know, but how many people would still be alive if I hadn't wasted so much time chasing Hellier?"

"None of them," Donnelly answered unwaveringly. "Gibran was a bolt of lightning. He came from nowhere. We couldn't have caught him any sooner. It wasn't possible. We did what we always do. We followed the evidence, concentrated on the most likely suspect. We shook trees and waited to see what would fall out. And eventually the right man did.

"If it had been anyone else in charge of the case, Gibran would still be out there and Sally would be dead. You need to know that."

"All the same, this doesn't feel like a success."

"Does it ever?" Donnelly asked.

"No. I suppose not."

"By the way, Steven Paramore turned up."

"Who?" Sean asked, the name wiped from his memory.

"Remember, the guy recently released after serving eight for the attempted murder of a gay bloke?"

"Yes. Sorry. I remember now."

"Immigration nicked him coming back into the country on a false passport. He'd been enjoying the pleasures of Bangkok for a couple of weeks. Another suspect eliminated—not that you ever thought he was, right?" Sean didn't answer. "How did you know, by the way? How did you know Gibran went after Sally?"

"Something Hellier said, that it could only be one man. Only one man knew so much about him. Then I remembered Sally telling me about her meeting with Gibran, the things he'd said about Hellier, deliberately feeding our suspicions. It suddenly became so clear to me. Clear who the killer was and even clearer that he would have to get to Sally, even if it meant revealing that Hellier wasn't the real killer. At least he'd have stopped us discovering it was him. You know, if Sally hadn't survived the night she was attacked, Gibran would still be out there and we wouldn't have a bloody clue. Sally getting out alive collapsed the foundations of everything Gibran had built."

"Why do you think he chose Hellier?" Donnelly asked.

"Somehow he knew what Hellier was. The moment he met Hellier, he knew. There was no way he could have pinned his crimes on some clean-living man on the street. He needed someone we would believe in. Hellier was perfect. Maybe he even found out about Hellier's real past. Who knows? But once he found him, he showed his patience, his control. He spent years watching him, learning all he could about him. Even made sure he was employed by Butler and Mason so he could keep him close. And Hellier never suspected a thing, not until right at the end.

"I can't prove it yet, but I'm pretty damn sure Hellier's solicitor will turn out to be a company man too. Butler and Mason would have been picking up his tab, not Hellier. No doubt he was all too happy to keep Gibran informed of the investigation's progress."

"That would have been useful," Donnelly said.

"Very," Sean agreed. "All we have to do is try to prove it, somehow." He shook the doubts away, for now at least.

"The hairs from Linda Kotler's flat?" he asked. "I'm still waiting for someone to explain how Hellier's hairs found their way into the crime scene."

"Aye," Donnelly said sheepishly. "I was meaning to tell you about that. Remember when we met Hellier at Belgravia?"

"Of course."

"We took his body samples . . ."

"I'm listening."

"Including some head hair . . ."

"Oh dear," Sean said with a wry smile. "Whose idea was that?"

"Mine. I figured it wouldn't hurt to keep a couple of hairs for ourselves, leave them at an appropriate scene if things started getting desperate."

"So you planted them at the Kotler scene for Dr. Canning to find? Very nice."

"No," Donnelly said, "not me. To tell you the truth, I wasn't convinced about Hellier, so I held them back, but . . ."

"But what?"

"I gave them to Paulo to look after, just until we needed them . . ."

"And Paulo was convinced about Hellier and decided not to wait?"

"That's about the size of it."

"He told you all this?"

"Aye. Once you nailed Gibran, Paulo 'fessed up. No need to panic, though—I've already made it look like an administrative balls-up. As far as anyone will ever know, Paulo accidentally sent the wrong samples to the lab. He mistook the samples taken from Hellier for hairs gathered from the Kotler scene, so no surprise they found a match. But it's covered. Trust me."

"I take it he understands he'll have to explain this administrative balls-up in court at the trial?"

"Aye," Donnelly answered. "He doesn't really have much choice."

"Has he learned his lesson?"

Donnelly knew what he meant. "He was trying to do the right thing, but he won't do it again, not without checking first."

"Fine," Sean said. "I'll deal with it myself, before anyone has a chance to make more of it. I'll make sure he knows when to and when not to give an investigation a helping hand."

"I owe you one," said Donnelly.

"No, you don't" was Sean's reply.

"And what do we do about Gibran?"

"Run it past the CPS. Tell them we think we've got enough to charge him with two counts. The attempted murder of Sally and the murder of PC O'Connor." Sean leaned back in his chair. "At least we've got a decent chance of getting a conviction there. While he's banged up on remand, we'll keep digging on the other murders. Maybe we'll get lucky."

"And if we don't?" Donnelly asked.

"Pray we get a friendly judge with the brains to read between the lines. If we do, then Gibran will spend the rest of his natural behind bars.

"Changing subjects, is PC O'Connor's family being looked after?"

"As best we can," Donnelly said. "Family liaison's with them already, for what it's worth."

"Any kids?"

"Three."

"Christ's sake." Sean couldn't help but imagine his own family sitting, holding each other, crying in disbelief as they were told he'd never walk through the front door again. He felt sad to the pit of his stomach. "Having a dead hero for a father isn't going to be much use to them, is it?"

Donnelly shrugged an answer.

"Last but not least," said Donnelly, "what do we do about Hellier? Or rather, Korsakov?"

"Leave him to DI Reger at Complaints. He can have Hellier and Jarratt as a package, assuming he can find him. And good luck to him there."

"That's the thing I don't get about Hellier," said Donnelly.

"He had the money and the means to disappear whenever he wanted. Why didn't he run when we first came sniffing around him? Why didn't he just fuck off to the tropics then? Come to think of it, why was he working for Butler and bloody Mason in the first place? He didn't need the money, he already had a small fortune stashed where the sun don't shine. He could have put his feet up on a beach someplace where the sex is cheap and the booze is cold, and stayed there happily for all eternity. Why fuck around in London, pretending to be a financier? He may have been a fraud, but he was still working for a living. It doesn't make sense."

But it did to Sean. The more he knew about Hellier, the more he understood him.

"It wasn't about the money with Hellier. For him it's the game, always the game: proving he's smarter than everyone else."

"Proving it to who?" Donnelly asked.

"To himself," Sean answered. "Always to himself. Proving to himself that everything they said about him was wrong."

" 'They'?" Donnelly asked. "Who are they?"

Sean had said enough. "It doesn't matter. It's not important."

"Whatever," Donnelly said, dismissing it. "Anyway, speaking of Hellier, Korsakov, whoever the bloody hell he really is, how do you suppose he got to the hospital so soon after we did?"

"Nothing surprises me when it comes to Hellier. Maybe we should check to see if any of our fast-response cars are missing." Sean managed a slight grin.

"Indeed," Donnelly replied and stood to leave, but stopped in the doorway. "What was all that about, by the way?" he asked. "In the interview, when Gibran started saying all that shit about your childhood and how you and Hellier were the same?"

"It was nothing," Sean told him, his voice a little too loud. "It meant nothing. Just rantings. Gibran's last chance to try and do some harm."

"Aye," Donnelly responded. "That's what I thought." As he turned to leave Sean's office, he almost walked into Featherstone. "Guv'nor," he acknowledged.

Featherstone nodded his appreciation and watched Donnelly leave before turning to Sean. Without speaking, he closed the door and took a seat. Sean had no idea whether he was about to be praised or pilloried.

Finally Featherstone spoke. "Ordinarily, I'd say congratulations—but I'm betting that would feel rather hollow right now."

"It would," Sean agreed.

"No one could have done a better job," Featherstone reassured him. "You displayed some, shall we say, unusual insights. Had you not, Gibran would still be out there. I think you've saved some lives today, Sean." He didn't answer. "Anyway," Featherstone continued, "the real hard work starts now, yes? So I'll leave you to get on with it, but don't kill yourself. This would be a good point to practice the art of delegation. Your team's capable. You need to get that hand seen to and to get some rest. Spend a little time at home. You'll feel better for it."

"I'll see what I can do," Sean promised.

Featherstone rose to leave, then sank back into his uncomfortable chair. "One more thing you should know." His words made Sean lean away from him. "Your . . . shall we say, special talents have been noticed. Certain people have begun to take an interest in you." Featherstone wasn't smiling.

"Such as who?" Sean asked.

"People within the service, mainly. Our seniors, sitting in their ivory towers at the Yard."

"Mainly?" Sean asked.

"Sorry?" Featherstone replied.

"You said people *mainly* in the service. Who outside would be taking an interest?"

"Nobody who wants to do you any harm," Featherstone answered. "We all work together these days. Partnership approach, remember? My advice—if you want it—is to play the game when you have to and don't be surprised if a few high-profile, *interesting* cases start finding their way to your door. Well, I'll let you get on, but don't forget what I said about getting some rest."

Sean watched silently as Featherstone rose and left, his eyes following him until he could see him no more.

He knew what Featherstone was telling him—he was about to become a tool, a commodity not to be wasted on tick-the-box murder investigations, where husband kills wife, drug dealer kills drug dealer. They would use him. A freak to catch freaks.

EPILOGUE

Strong turbulence shook the twin-engine jet and woke Hellier from a light sleep. He could hear the concerned voices of his fellow passengers, unaccustomed to the shaking passenger planes received as they approached Queenstown Airport on New Zealand's South Island. He peered out of the window and saw the Remarkables mountain range stretching as far as he could see to the south. From peak to base the mountains were reflected in the still, clear waters of Lake Wakatipu. He had left behind a Northern Hemisphere summer and arrived in the middle of the Southern Hemisphere winter. The mountains were covered in snow, which was what most of his fellow passengers had come for. But not Hellier. The plane's PA system advised the passengers to prepare for landing in five minutes. Reluctantly he fastened his seat belt and stared out of the window, a slight smile on his face, oblivious to the stomach-churning buffeting as the winter winds gripped the jet. Finally they bumped to ground, the engines roaring in reverse to halt the plane on the short, perilous runway. His fellow passengers breathed a collective sigh of relief.

Thirty-six hours ago Hellier had been on the other side of

the world. Soon he would be safe in his long-ago-established retreat. He had flown from London to Singapore using a British passport, but instead of catching a connecting transfer flight to his destination, he had taken his carry-on suitcase containing a change of clothing and toiletries, and passed through Customs and Immigration. Outside the airport he had hailed a cab that took him through the shining skyscraper metropolis Singapore had become, a soulless, generic, New Age Eastern business center.

Finally he arrived in Old Chinatown, with its mix of Chinese, Malay, and Indian architecture. Bustling brown-skinned people filled the streets, trading, talking, eating, living. These streets suited him far better than the glass valleys that filled the rest of the island. He'd made his way to a nondescript ornament and souvenir shop in Temple Street. The owner recognized him immediately and fetched a safety-deposit box that he handed to Hellier. He'd placed his British passport in the box and taken out an Australian one in the name of Scott Thurston. Then he made his way back to the airport. Two hours later he was flying Air New Zealand business class to Auckland.

After an eleven-hour flight he touched down at Auckland Airport feeling refreshed and alive, having slept most of the way. Once again, rather than take a direct transfer flight, he'd cleared Immigration and exited the airport. A cab driven by an overtalkative Samoan took him to Mount Eden, an area popular with young, successful Aucklanders. The owner of the antiques shop almost froze with fear when he saw Hellier enter. He needn't have been afraid; within minutes, Hellier was heading back to the airport to catch his flight to Queenstown. This time he traveled under a New Zealand passport bearing his photograph and the name Phillip Johnston.

Now he walked through the domestic arrivals exit at

Queenstown Airport without attracting a second glance from the security services casually floating around the terminal. People came here for a good time; summer or winter, it didn't matter. Nobody expected trouble. Nobody suspected who or what he was.

A short cab ride took him to the offices of a property letting and management agency in the center of town. Hellier entered Otago Properties Ltd. and scanned the premises for familiar faces. The middle-aged man recognized him at the same time that Hellier spotted him. Both men smiled, the manager getting to his feet and striding across the office, hand outstretched in friendship. Hellier accepted it.

"Bloody hell, Phillip Johnston, where the hell have you been?" the manager said in his nasal South Island accent. "I thought you must be dead!"

"Not yet," Hellier answered. "Not yet."

Twenty minutes later, he used the key he'd collected from Otago Properties to open the heavy wooden door of the house built into the side of a mountain. He stepped inside and spent several minutes surveying his surroundings, mentally noting every item he saw. After a while he was satisfied that everything was as it should be. He dropped his suitcase and closed the front door, walking straight through the house to the living room, with its panoramic view from the huge sliding glass doors. A long wooden coffee table, surrounded by antique leather armchairs, was positioned in front of the windows. A brand-new laptop computer sat in the middle of the table, just as Hellier had arranged, its standby light blinking green, drawing him toward it.

He stood over the computer and opened its lid, the screen immediately filling with the site he'd programmed it to display from the other side of the world: bank account details for

Butler and Mason International Finance. The message on the screen questioned him: *Are you sure you want to continue with fund transfers?* He paused for a while, not wanting to rush this sweet moment. After a minute or so he finally pressed the enter button and watched, only his eyes showing any emotion as they excitedly darted around the screen following the rows and columns of numbers as they gradually fell away to zero. Tens of millions of pounds had flowed out of Butler and Mason's primary bank account into accounts all around the world set up by Hellier. Not a penny of it entered his own accounts; he already had more money than he could spend. It flowed into the accounts of people he might need in the future: people of influence, people who could get him things that would otherwise be difficult to obtain. And millions more poured into the bank accounts of charities he cared nothing about, under the guise of anonymous benefactors. And it was all absolutely untraceable. When the transactions were complete, he turned the computer off and unplugged it. He would throw it in the lake after nightfall. His face showed no flicker of emotion, no happiness. Only a satisfied sigh betrayed his pleasure.

He walked to the giant windows and undid the latches. Throwing the doors open, he stepped out onto a balcony the size of a tennis court. The lake and the mountains stretched out before him as far as he could see. Seemingly miles below, the TSS *Earnslaw*, a hundred-year-old steamship, left a shallow wake that spread from shore to shore. He walked to the edge of the balcony and held the rail. Closing his eyes, he allowed the freezing mountain air to hammer against his body, sweeping away the stale air of long-haul travel.

Standing there on the balcony of his long-standing hideaway, his life in London as James Hellier fast-forwarded through his mind, from its very beginning to its very end. The time had come to kill James Hellier, to bury him where he would never be found, just as he had done to Stefan Korsakov. James Hellier was gone forever, and all that went with him. All, that was, but for two names: Detective Inspector Sean Corrigan and Sebastian Gibran. Those two he would never forget.

Hellier opened his eyes, stretched his arms into a crucifix position, and began to laugh.

Two weeks later

Sean sat alone in his office. He waded through a mountain of requests from the Crown Prosecution Service, most totally unreasonable, nothing more than an evidential wish list. It was clear they weren't entirely happy with the evidence against Sebastian Gibran. Neither was he.

He thought of Sally. He missed having her around the place. Everyone did. He wondered if he would ever see her barreling around the office again, filling it with life. She remained in Intensive Care, but she had phases of consciousness and was expected to live. During one of those phases she had confirmed that Gibran was her attacker.

A knock at his open door made Sean look up. A uniformed constable he didn't recognize stood waiting to be acknowledged.

"Yes?"

The constable entered and held a large brown envelope out for Sean to take.

"This arrived in the front office," he said. "It's addressed to you."

Sean half stood and leaned over his desk. More CPS requests, no doubt. Thanking the constable, he took the envelope.

The exotic stamps told Sean this envelope didn't contain memos from the CPS, or anything of that nature. It had been sent from Singapore. Placing the envelope carefully on his desk, he patted it gingerly, feeling for small hard objects: the telltale signs of a letter bomb. It was something he had never done before Korsakov and Gibran came into his life.

There were no suspicious lumps. All the same, Sean opened it carefully, cutting a fine edge away from the side of the envelope with a pair of scissors. He avoided the folded areas where he was meant to tear it open. Just in case.

He remembered himself almost too late. Dropping the envelope, he pulled open his bottom drawer and reached for the box of latex gloves kept there. He pulled a pair on, his hands feeling instantly hot and sweaty. Then he picked the envelope up and spilled the contents onto his desk.

The first items to emerge were photographs. Excellent quality. Color. They appeared to have been taken by a professional. He recognized both of the two men in the shots: Paul Jarratt and Stefan Korsakov. The pictures formed a sequence covering about thirty seconds. Korsakov handing Jarratt a plain brown envelope. Jarratt opening it. Half-pulling fifty-pound notes from inside. Pushing them back in. A handshake. Jarratt walking away. DI Reger would be very interested in the pictures.

As he shuffled through the photographs, a folded piece of paper fell out. A letter. He opened it. It had been folded only once. He saw the blue handwriting, neat, but not ornate. Clear, but not printed. There was no sender's name or address. It could only have been from one person. He began to read.

Thought these might come in useful. I used them to en-sure his loyalty for a time, but I have no use for him now. He failed me. He shouldn't have done that. I only regret I won't be able to give evidence at his trial.

Sorry about skipping off. I'm sure you understand. I had no intention of becoming a corpse for the media vultures to pick over. Your fault entirely. I haven't for-gotten.

Imagine Gibran thinking he could outwit me. I look forward to seeing him again. I'll have a nice little sur-prise waiting for that jumped-up fucker.

How are my wife and children? Crying for my re-turn, no doubt. They don't know what they pray for. If they did, they wouldn't.

I'm sure we'll meet again. I feel I still owe you some-thing.

Sean held the letter for a long time. He had hoped he'd heard the last of Stefan Korsakov, but in his heart he knew he hadn't. Korsakov liked games too much.

His desk phone rang, making him jump. He tossed the letter aside and answered. It was Kate.

"How are you doing today?" she asked. She had called him a lot more often these last two weeks. He used to seem so invulnerable. Now there was something tenuous about him. As if he might easily be snatched away.

"I'm doing all right," he said, before she could continue. "Listen, I was thinking. Maybe we should get out of London."

"And move where?" Kate asked.

"Well," Sean answered, "I got an e-mail the other day. The police in New Zealand are looking to recruit British cops. I can even do a direct transfer as a DI. We'd get full residency. The kids would love it."

"And me?" Kate asked.

"Come on, Kate," he reassured her. "You're a doctor. There isn't a country in the world that doesn't want more doctors."

"What brought this on?" Kate asked cheerfully.

Sean looked at the letter on his desk. "Nothing," he lied, remembering how close he'd been to falling off the edge— remembering being alone in the toilet, staring into the mirror and seeing the swirling darkness of his nature. "I guess I'm just sick of the traffic."

Free, I was a thing of nightmares. Now, in my cage, I have become the object of morbid fascination. You lock me away to lock your fears away. You view me from a safe distance. The newspapers and television your window into my cage. The gaps between the bars through which you peer.

And what is it that scares you most? Is it that there's a little bit of me in all of you? That little bit of madness waiting to be let loose? When that person standing too close on the underground stamps on your foot, they apologize and you tell them it's all right, it doesn't matter, but really you want to stamp on their head until blood and brains cover your feet. Instead you swallow the violence down. Keep the madness deep inside.

As for me, I'm not finished yet. The British legal system will give me a chance. Anything is possible. The judge will call my arrest and prosecution a travesty. The police will be lambasted. The media will rally to my cause. I'll walk free from the court. Will there be cheering crowds? So many other killers have been greeted by cheering crowds, why not me? I'll raise my arms in victory as I walk toward the waiting photographers. I'll call to them, "Innocent. Proven innocent."

DI Sean Corrigan's dark past has given him the ability to step into a crime scene and see it through the eyes of the offender. He understands what drives evil—but sometimes his gift seems more like a burden . . .

THE KEEPER

BY LUKE DELANEY

When a woman is kidnapped from her home, Corrigan and his homicide team are surprised to be pulled onto the case— they have no reason to believe she's dead . . . yet. Then a body turns up in the woods. It's not the woman they're searching for, but someone who looks just like her.

Sean knows that it won't be long before someone else goes missing, or until another body surfaces.

This killer is looking for the perfect woman—and when he finds her, he's going to keep her.

Coming in January 2014